STARK

September

By C.D. Bradley

Brandy,
I hope you
enjoy the journey

C.D. Bradley

1

Acknowledgements

I would like to take a moment to thank those who inspired and encouraged this project:

My best Friend Abby

Aunt Jackie and Daddy Don I love you with all my heart.

My ER girls who helped start this whole thing.

My UC Ladies who encouraged and at times demanded the next chapter.

The band Qiet for your inspiration, talent, and friendship.

The Men and Women of our Armed forces, the sacrifices you and your families make every day are more than we could ever repay.

Carissa and George thank you for your inspiration, fact checking, and dedication to this country.

Editor: Marla Esposito

Finally I would like to thank my husband, truly my better half. You my darling are my inspiration every day. I love you beyond words.

Chapter 1

Kira looked at herself in the mirror. *What the hell have I gotten myself into?* she thought, frustrated and a little panicked. The reflection staring back dressed in full fatigues was a soldier who bore an eerie resemblance to the girl of her youth. Hastily she attempted to get her unruly wet hair into some form of a ponytail. *Seriously, on the first solo day of clinic I am going to be late. Why on earth did I run so long this morning?* Running was her way of coping: she ran for exercise, ran for stress relief, ran away from crazy ex-boyfriends and joined the army. Kira scurried around the cramped bathroom making sure she hadn't missed anything important like—*Oh shit! Deodorant!*

She had always been a bit of a tomboy, preferring climbing trees and playing in the creek, but the *army?* she thought back through the years of hard work and perfect grades, struggling to pay for her undergrad tuition. Despite all the scholarships, she still had to work. She manned the night desk at campus security for four years. She remembered the elation she'd felt at her excellent MCAT score and at being accepted into medical school, then the harsh reality hitting that there would be no way to pay for it. The army had seemed like such a logical choice. They pay for school, then she would serve during her residency. Perfect plan, right? Well, now it was time to pay the piper. Here she was, waiting to report for duty for her first day in an actual clinic. She tucked the last dark brown strand of hair up into her ponytail and dashed out the door. She had to get to the CO's office to drop off the last of her paperwork before the clinic opened. *How am I ever going to get used to all this paperwork?* For a brief moment she considered driving, then the image of her last battle with the aging Honda Prelude flashed in her mind. She was sure a cloud of profanity still hung in the air above it. In silent frustration she hustled across the base.

Fort Carson was bustling that crisp autumn morning. The lawn was sprinkled with wet leaves despite the efforts of young privates who seemed to work tirelessly to contain them. She was careful to stay out of the way of groups of soldiers running and marching. Their voices blended in unison as their feet hit the ground to the beat of the cadence. The rhythmic sound was nearly drowned out by the howling of chilly gusts sweeping down from the surrounding mountains. The cool wet wind chilled her and she was thankful for the jacket with her army combat uniform, or ACU. As she ran, she pulled it more tightly around her. The heavy canvas was warm and reminded her of her dad. Briefly she wondered what he would have thought of her joining the service.

The base was surrounded by peaks dotted with evergreens. The mountains in the distance reminded her of home

4

in West Virginia. Kira longed for the beautiful palette of reds, golds, and oranges that signaled the end of September and the beginning of fall. How long had it been since she had sat on her aunt's porch peeling apples? The crisp autumn wind carried scents of cobbler, even if only in her imagination, and made her ache for her childhood.

She climbed the steps to the CO's office two at a time, lost in her daydream. She reached the top just as the door was flung open. What happened next was a blur. The door slammed into her and a tall dark-haired man burst through the doorway, cursing vehemently to his companion. She briefly glimpsed the sky, the stairs, and sky again as she tumbled down the steps, coming to rest on the concrete.

"Oh shit . . . I'm sorry. Ma'am, are you ok?" The man who had knocked her down asked with genuine concern in his husky voice. "I'm really sorry. Can you talk? Hello . . . ?" Slowly his face came into focus. Kira struggled. *Wow, those are some eyes.* As she stared, Kira realized she was in the arms of the most beautiful, rugged Adonis of a man she had ever seen. He was built like a god, with deep blue-green eyes that you could sail away in.

"I'm . . . uh, fine. Good . . . and fine." She struggled to remember how to talk. "Wow, guess you really sweep a girl off her feet, huh?" She quavered as her voice and her sense of humor came back to her. He set her upright again and helped to

5

gather her papers. Once she stood up, he held onto her, steadying her for a moment. His hands on her back and shoulders were powerful yet felt so warm, so tender. He kept holding her, looking into her eyes as if he was waiting for her to say something. She felt her cheeks flush hot. *Oh, he smells so very good.* Even more embarrassed with that thought, she pulled away. "I'm fine, really. I'm ok." And she rushed back up the stairs and into the building.

What the hell was that? I'm just shaken from the fall. Once safely inside and out of view, she leaned against the wall, taking several deep breaths. She wasn't sure what was more unnerving—her tumble or those eyes. *Oh that voice . . . deep and rough, yet he spoke so softly to me. Put him out of your mind this second!* She remembered she was here to get a job done. Finish her residency and get the hell out of here. Seeing all these soldiers dedicating their lives to their country broke her heart. She saw her father's face in theirs. From birth she had grown up in a military home. Despite her deep reverence for the army, she also feared what it could do to her, what it had done to him. While she felt so honored now to be a part of it, her father's death made being here so much harder. She hadn't thought it would be this difficult until she was actually back in this life. No, she just had to stay focused and on track, get her work done. Under no circumstances was she going to get involved with any man on this base.

With new resolve, she finished her paperwork and headed over to the clinic. Of course, the clinic was in another area of the base and required a fifteen-minute jog to get there. She was thankful for the opportunity to run off some of the adrenaline from the encounter with the sex-god soldier. She giggled but kept an eye on her surroundings, hoping she wouldn't have to face him again. As she reached the clinic, she felt a mix of relief and disappointment. He was gone. No sight of him as she crossed the base.

Head still spinning from her earlier run-in with the soldier, Kira was thankful to settle into her morning in the clinic. The office was bustling. A whole new group of NUGs were in for their initial physicals. *NUGs: New Useless Guys. Yeah, that about sums it up*, she thought, looking at the group of loud, freshly crew cut kids filing into her waiting area. *Well, it beats death by PowerPoint*, she thought, painfully remembering her first month on base. The NUGs filed into the room one by one. Each one had the same nervous, guarded face and loud cocky attitude to cover his anxiety, brown shirt, ACU, and boots. She was assigned to a pod in the clinic where she would perform physicals on new, deploying, and returning soldiers. The duty was bottom of the barrel for assignments but it was good to be in the clinic. She was new and this was her first actual assignment. She wanted to do a good job in everything they gave her, not just to pay back her tuition, but for her dad's

7

sake. Kira briefly wondered if he would be proud of what she was trying to do.

She went through her morning processing one soldier after another. Her mind kept returning to the sexy soldier from this morning. Getting lost in those eyes was like drifting away in the Aegean Sea. There was an intensity and fierceness in his face but a gentleness in his strong hands. Oh and that voice, so soft and husky.

Get a hold of yourself! She snapped back to reality, realizing she had just poured coffee all over the counter.

"Are you ok?" Abbey, her head nurse, asked. Abbey was a stout woman of about forty. She was the head nurse of that part of the clinic and she ran a tight command. "You've been a little off all morning." Thankfully Abbey had taken her under her wing when Kira had first arrived on base. Abbey had proven to be not only a valuable guide but also a friend.

"I'm fine. I took a little tumble this morning. Not a big deal," Kira said, smiling. She rubbed her still aching head and tried to look confident.

"Sounds like you should see a doctor," Abbey joked and added, "Dr. Riley, they added a last minute physical to your schedule this morning. They called from Personnel and wanted it done today. He's just back in country, something about the medical officer being out . . ." Abbey was still talking but she suddenly sounded miles away. A semi-hush fell over the waiting area. The NUGs appeared almost reverent as a man walked in.

Their eyes met. Kira felt at once nauseous and excited. An unfamiliar burning inside her caused her breath to catch in her lungs. He casually walked to the reception desk, never taking his viridian eyes off her. "Sergeant Stark reporting for a post-mission physical," he said to the clerk. That voice again. She could feel it all over her. Her skin tingled where he had touched her.

Kira was confused. She hadn't noticed it this morning but he didn't look like a regular soldier. All the men she had taken care of today looked exactly alike. Sergeant Stark was strikingly different. His dark hair was longer and unruly. He had unkempt stubble on his tanned face, which made him look more like a swarthy Middle Eastern hit man rather than a U.S. soldier. A flush of embarrassment flooded her cheeks. Quickly she looked away to escape his trance. She noted how his jeans hung from his narrow hips and perfectly taught ass, barely encasing his massive granite thighs and how his T-shirt was stretched perfectly over his incredibly muscular chest.

The shattering of her coffee cup on the tile floor brought her back to her senses. "Shit," she muttered, feeling the flush in her cheeks turn into an inferno. She avoided his gaze and grabbed a towel and began to mop up the mess.

"Are you all right, ma'am?" He was at her side in a second, his baritone voice tender with concern.

"She had a bit of a bump on the head this morning," Abbey said, walking up behind her.

"Oh, I am so sorry about that, ma'am. I was upset and in a hurry. You're so small I really sent you flying. You should have let me help you. I could have brought you to the doctor. Here, let me clean this up." He bent to help her, but Kira had gathered the sopping towel and stood. "I'm fine. I've got this." Kira turned and headed for the break room, leaving Stark standing empty handed in the waiting area.

"Now I see," Abbey laughed, following her into the break room. "You really did take a tumble this morning. One might say you were swept right off your feet. Sergeant Sexy out there seems to have fried your brain."

"Stop it," Kira pleaded. "It's nothing. He is just another soldier and I have a job to do. I've told you I have no interest in getting involved with a soldier. Ever. Just put him in room three." Kira took a moment to compose herself. With a trembling hand she pushed a loose strand of hair back into her ponytail.

She could hear Abbey, in a fake singsong voice, say, "Right this way, Sergeant. Room three. Go ahead and undress. The doctor will be right in." Abbey flashed her a grin as she walked back up front. "Maybe this will turn out to be an interesting day after all."

Kira collected herself and walked in to exam room three. As she opened the door her senses were alive with the smell of him: his body wash, his cologne. The smell was intoxicating. Her heart stopped. There, on the exam table in his underwear, was this god of a man, staring at her with those eyes. She could feel herself being pulled into them. A small brown fleck stood out like a cliff in the crystal waters. What she wouldn't give to . . .

Oh, Jesus. I am a professional, I am a professional. I can do this. She crossed the room to her desk, looking anywhere but at him. She did her best to appear calm and in control, although she felt like a befuddled mess on the inside. *How is it possible for him to look that good?* The room felt much warmer.

"So you've just returned from a mission?" she began. *That's it—calm, collected.*

"Something like that," he said calmly, a slight grin on his face. He seemed to be enjoying her obvious abashment.

"Were you out of the country long?"

"I'm not at liberty to say," he replied coolly.

11

"What sort of environment were you in?" she asked, trying to get an understanding of disease processes about which she should be concerned.

Smiling, he replied, "Captain, you don't have clearance for that kind of information."

"Ok, then. Have you been exposed to malaria, dengue fever, sand fleas, gonorrhea, chlamydia, or HIV?" she snapped, frustrated by the game he seemed to be playing.

Chuckling, he replied "Yes, yes, no, hope not, hope not, and no. You haven't been in the military very long, have you?" His eyes sparkled with mischievousness. He was enjoying the game.

"No," she answered, somewhat contritely. She tried another line of questioning. "Any new injuries or physical complaints?" Getting back into routine, she slowly regained her professionalism.

"Not really. Just a small scratch on my left shoulder. Just a flesh wound, really," he joked in his best English accent.

Kira looked up, surprised by his dry humor. He didn't seem like the joking type. She examined his shoulder. The wound was moderately healed and looked as though he had been burned, cut, or both a few days ago, as it had partially begun to heal. She noted how massive his strong shoulders seemed in comparison to her small hands. The definition of his shoulders and back was unnerving. "How did it happen? Or are you allowed to say?" she asked with genuine concern.

"Could have been a lug nut, a piece of bumper, who knows. These things tend to happen when a vehicle explodes in front of you. One minute it's there, then a single flash of light and it's gone. Happens all the time." His voice was very nonchalant, but there was a trace of something there . . . pain . . . sadness—she couldn't put her finger on it.

"You mean an entire Jeep exploded?" She gasped. "What happened to the driver? Or the other people in it?" She made a failed attempt to hide the horror in her voice.

"Again, for that, Captain, you don't have clearance, but you're a smart girl. You can figure that part out. And for the record we haven't used JEEP in the army for some time. They're called Humvees. You really *are* quite new, aren't you, ma'am?" His voice was grave now, a little reserved. She recognized his attempt to change the subject and decided not to press any further.

She gently began to clean the wound. It was starting to show redness and signs of early infection. While she cleaned, she struggled to think of something to say. His eyes were upon her the entire time, burning into her. After dressing the wound with ointment and sterile gauze, she examined the rest of his back. He had a large tattoo across most of his upper back written in Chinese characters. She noticed several scars across his broad shoulders and lower back. Her fingers gently palpated a jagged scar on the other shoulder. Standing so close to him, feeling the heat off his body, inhaling the intoxicating scent of him, her mind began to wander to dark and sultry places, and she struggled to maintain her professionalism.

"Your tattoo, what does it mean?" she asked as she studied the large markings.

"Relentless," he said, turning to meet her gaze. His voice was so low it reverberated each syllable into her.

"Is that you? Is that what you are? Relentless?" she whispered, almost afraid of the answer. His quiet intensity both frightened and excited her. She shuddered to think of him angry. She feared for anyone who was his enemy. *Yet what could this quiet, gentle man do with that intensity . . . that relentless spirit?* The thought warmed her, kindling a fire she had forgotten she could have.

"Yes, ma'am, I guess so. When I'm after something, by myself or with my team, nothing stands in the way. We move as a team and with unforgiving force to obtain our objective." His eyes flashed dark steel. His cool tone chilled her. But his eyes were burning fire, staring deep into her. He leaned in closer and said, "Once I set my sights on something no force in heaven or hell will stand in my way."

"That's your work. That's your job. How does that affect your family?" she asked, and considered the post-traumatic stress disorder, or PTSD, questioning she would have to cover. The staggering numbers of service men and women suffering from these effects had been a large part of her training since arriving on base. She felt she had a grasp on what this would entail but according to Abbey she hadn't seen anything yet.

"This is my life, ma'am. My team is all the family I need." His quiet response was difficult to read. Kira was caught off guard by the sudden change in him. The flirtatious young man had disappeared into this career soldier. Somehow, she sensed an air of sadness under his confidence.

Kira continued her exam. She listened to his lungs and then to his heart. Standing this close, their bodies almost touching, one hand on his back and the other holding the stethoscope on his heart, she could feel his pulse quicken. The room was definitely getting warmer. She could barely hear his heartbeat over her own. The spectacular ripple of muscles down his incredibly well-sculpted chest and abdomen was breathtaking. She realized she had been holding her breath. And those legs—shit, he was so built; the sheer power of his perfectly toned body had her picturing all sorts of wicked things. She did her very best to avoid looking at the massive bulge in his

15

underwear. They remained in place for what seemed like an eternity, bodies and faces so close. Her chest tightened as her breathing struggled. *Oh, to be taken by this Adonis, this relentless warrior!* Snapping out of her daydream she backed up hastily, almost bumping into the desk.

"Well, that about does it. You're cleared. I'm writing an antibiotic for your arm. Re-check with your group doc in about five days. If you have any problems, let us know," she blurted quickly as she turned to leave. *I have to get out of this room. I cannot spend any more time with this man.* She slipped out the door before he had a chance to say another word.

Kira braced herself against the wall in the hallway. She had to catch her breath before making her way down to her office. *What the hell am I doing?* Almost sprinting, she raced for the solitude of her office. She closed the door, exasperated, excited, and half-hoping to never see him again.

***

Owen Stark sat speechless on the examining table as she rushed out of the room. *Wait! What the hell was that?* But she was gone before he had a chance to say anything.

He realized his heart was racing. Who was this crazy, beautiful girl? He looked around the modest examining room. The cold steel and clinical air of the room chilled him. His clothes sat on the plastic chair in the corner. Her seat had rolled aimlessly into the corner when she hit it as she exited hastily. *What am I thinking? Fuck, she's an officer! Fraternization is strictly forbidden. But damn, she is beautiful.* His heart and groin ached mercilessly at the thought of her. The impact made him realize how long it had been.

The past few months in the hills of Afghanistan did not present an opportunity to indulge in such fantasies. While back on leave for a little R & R, he had thought to hook up with Lila or Paige, but that seemed empty and pointless now. Now all he could think of were those tiny gentle hands and that perfect pouty mouth.

He recalled seeing her for the first time that morning, sprawled at the bottom of the steps, amidst a sea of dark hair. The bewildered look on her soft beautiful face had moved him. Her eyes were such an incredibly bright blue they reminded him of cobalt. *How did I not see her?*

He had been in a fierce debate with his team member Sergeant Colin over the recent explosion that took the life of Sergeant Jackson in Afghanistan. The army's lack of action where this was concerned made him see red. He had been mad as hell as he burst out of the CO's office. Then seeing her on the ground, realizing he had caused her to fall, his heart almost stopped. He had rushed to help her but felt suddenly helpless, looking into those innocent eyes.

When he picked her up, for the first time he could remember, he had been at a loss for words. She was a complete stranger, a sexy-as-hell stranger, but the warmth and strange familiarity of her touch made him feel alive. *Really* alive, when so much of him had been dead for so long. The rush he felt with her in his arms shook him to his core. Her voice was soft and sweet; it flowed from her full lips like a melody, exciting him. He had instantly wanted to claim that sweet mouth. And then she was gone.

He had waited around for a while, hoping she would come back out but he had to get ready for his post-deployment physical. Of all the fucking luck—she turned out to be the doctor who did his physical. *That makes her a captain and off-limits,* he reminded himself.

But he knew she felt something too. He had sensed it when she was close to him. Seeing her blush while she worked with him was so disarming. He groaned, thinking of the way her eyes sparkled as if some deliciously wicked thought was playing out in her head. *Oh, I can show you wicked thoughts, baby.* His cock throbbed at the memory of her standing so close, touching his skin, examining his shoulder. Her cheeks had flushed so pink . . . how he would like to see her pink all over. The thought of bending her over the exam table and warming that perfect ass with the sting of his hand almost sent him over the edge. Remembering he was still in the office, he quickly dressed and went out toward the reception area. There was no sign of her. He stood in the hall for a moment, listening for her voice.

"Whew! Bet that was some exam!" A nasally singsong voice mocked. He whirled around to see the middle-aged nurse behind him. She was bossy and outspoken as hell but there was a twinkle in her eye that let him know she was on his side—an ally in his new pursuit. The crafty nurse smiled as she continued, "Sounds like you're going to need to do some running to wear off all that energy. Don't see how you kids do it, running morning and night up there on the new trails." She turned as if to make sure he was still listening, then added, before sauntering into the next patient's room, "Why, with all that running and working, it's no wonder the doc doesn't have time to date . . . "

Sergeant Stark made his way into the waiting area. He stopped at the clerk's desk to get his script and check out. *Christ, this can't be it. I have to find a reason to stay.* "Will I need a follow-up exam for my arm?" he asked in an attempt to schedule more of his sexy doctor's time.

The clerk stared up at him dreamily. "Oh, you can follow up with your team doc or we'd be happy to see you back here," she replied, gushing at him as most women did. He was surprised at his near annoyance to her reaction to him. Nevertheless, he thanked her and took the appointment before he turned to leave. The sight of the NUGs reminded him that they too would be getting physicals. The thought made him flush with jealousy. *What the hell! Who cares, it's her job.* He realized his feelings were childish but the thought of her touching those punks or worse, the little pukes enjoying it, pissed him off. *Best damn turn and cough of their lives. Fuck! Hey, I didn't get a hernia check . . . shit, I should have complained about something below the belt. Why couldn't I have had shrapnel in my upper thigh?*

Stopping in front of the NUGs as he left, he leaned into the group. "On your best behavior in there you little shits, or you will pay for it for months." His voice was cold and menacing. The NUGs nodded wide-eyed and confused.

Stark walked out the door. He knew it was crazy. He knew it went against all the rules, both professional and personal. He knew it would probably be the biggest mistake of his life. But he didn't care—he knew that some way, somehow, he had to see her again.

Chapter 2

Kira sat in her office thankful her workday was over. She had processed thirty-six intake physicals. After a while they had all started to run together. She was beginning to realize why this was an assignment for the low person on the totem pole. Strangely, all her afternoon patients had been exceptionally well-behaved, their cocky attitudes replaced by something else. Fear, maybe? She couldn't be sure, but they'd all seemed like children called into the principal's office. Though she did her best to fight it, her mind continued to drift back to *him*. Sergeant First Class Owen Stark. *Oh holy hell, he is a beautiful man.* She pulled up his file. He had been deployed several times. The medical tab was extensive: physicals from deployment returns, with notes on various minor injuries during deployments among other information. She was perturbed and impressed that he hadn't been joking; she *didn't* have clearance for information about his deployments. Most details in his file were left out or marked classified.

Stop lusting after him! She scolded herself. *Do you really want to end up like your mother, heartbroken and alone? Or your children to end up like you, having to take care of themselves since their mother is too distraught to function? No, getting involved with anyone in the military was strictly off-limits.*

Finally with all her charts caught up, Kira was anticipating a nice long run. She was going to hit the hills and run until she forgot Sergeant Stark, his husky voice, that scent . . . What was that cologne? It was mysterious, earthy, with a hint of lemon and bergamot. It enticed her into a dark, deep place with angelica, something bitter like green galbanum, and possibly cedar. When Kira closed her eyes she could almost smell him. All she could see were those blue-green eyes sparkling like the sun on a thousand tiny waves in a perfect tropical sea. Lacing up her running shoes, she willed herself to toss the fantasy out of her mind. She set off on the trail, determined.

The sweat ran down her back and breasts. She had been running for about three miles. *Now I'm starting to feel good.* She remembered her dad and the rhythmic exchange of his worn shoes on the pavement as she ran along behind him when she was little. Kira was always in awe of his even breathing and relaxed stride while she struggled to keep up. She had definitely gotten her love for running from him. It had been their time. Her mother, while small-framed and beautiful, was not an athlete in any way. Her father, Kendall James Riley, had been a wonderful man: strong, quiet, a skilled soldier, and the fastest runner she had ever seen. Aside from running, the times she remembered

22

most was when he'd read to her. *The Flight of the Zephyr* was her favorite book. Oh, she'd loved the sound of his voice as he made the pages come alive. He had taken her to meet the author once. He bought her a copy of the book and they had it signed. It was one of the best—and one of the last—memories she had of her father.

Kira kept running. Her heart ached at the memories. She remembered her mother that day the men in uniform pulled up to the curb while her father was away. The somber look on their faces spoke volumes. Her mother tried to back away and block out what they were trying to say. She could still hear her mother's screams, her crying. The crying became uncontrollable sobs and ultimately, her mother withdrew. She just stopped. She stopped being there. She stopped functioning as an adult, as a parent. Kira's childhood had ended. At age ten she effectively became the parent in her home.

She ran harder, pushing herself up yet another hill. She struggled on, aware that the stinging in her eyes was from the tears running down her face. Running was her solace. She put all her hurt, anger, and resentment into the run as she fought for one more mile, pressing on as if she were fighting all her demons with each step. As she crested mile eight, her legs gave way. She hadn't eaten much at all and fatigue overpowered her. She stumbled and, panting, came to rest beside the dusty trail. Looking around, she was overwhelmed by the beauty of her surroundings. She had crested a small knob on the mountain and had an astounding view of the expanse before her. The scene was so majestic it practically took away what little breath she had left. The vibrant colors of the distant mountains were fiery displays of orange and red, so bold they almost didn't look real. The vast valley below was still green, reluctant to relinquish the last of summer. The hillside between was dotted with rocks and cliffs. She sat basking in the immense beauty, watching the sun descend, ending the day in an array of pinks and blues. The horizon transformed into a composite of colors that lifted her soul. She sighed, finally feeling at peace with the day and the memories.

That brief peace promptly departed, when—*holy fuck!*—jogging toward her at a ridiculously fast pace was a *very* fit Sergeant Stark. *Shit! How am I going to get out of here before he sees me?* He was getting closer. *It's too late; he's looking right at me.* His relaxed face and body did not betray the stress of running eight miles. He looked as calm and non-effected as if he was walking into the mess hall.

"Captain Riley, you seem to spend an awful lot of time on the ground," he chided as he approached her.

He's making fun of me! Before her cheeks could flush, she retorted, "Sergeant, I seem to recall you like to push little girls around. I thought I'd save you the trouble this time." Her eyes flashed and a smirk formed her lips into a half smile.

"Well, in that case, my work here is done. Care if I sit?" His amused smile was charming and infuriating at the same time. Kira knew that he could see she had been crying. She winced for a moment imagining how smudged she must look. She put on a brave face and determined to laugh through anything.

If he felt pity for her, he didn't show it. "So, you're pretty new to the army. If you don't mind my saying, ma'am, you don't seem like the military type."

"You don't know anything about me," she snapped, unsure why his words stung so sharply, "and you don't exactly look like a regular soldier yourself. "

He laughed. "That's sort of the idea. The type of work I do, I have to blend in. I can't stick out like a 'regular soldier,'" he repeated her words.

I think you'd stick out anywhere. Damn your eyes are beautiful. And built like that, you belong in an underwear ad instead of a battlefield. Kira let her eyes trace over his immaculately sculpted body. A fine sheen of sweat glistened over his perfect muscles. There didn't seem to be a trace of fat on him. Seeing him again this close made her burn inside, and she could feel her desire building. Then his words hit her. "Oh, I see. So you're a special ops guy." Her disappointment as she made this realization was palpable. *This is like some freakish ironic tragedy. Special ops. Seriously? Surely the gods are rolling with laughter. Why hadn't she seen this in his file?*

"Yeah," he answered hesitantly. "What do you have against special operations?" He watched her pensively as she pressed her pouty lips together.

"Nothing against the teams. I have a lot of respect for the entire military but I know you guys have an especially difficult job. It's just . . ." Her voice trailed off and she looked out over the mountains. She just couldn't tell him about her dad. She stood to leave. "Look, I'd better go. Enjoy your run. Remember to take care of your shoulder." Her voice was suddenly flat and void.

"Wait! Hey, sorry. I didn't mean to upset you. Let me start over. I was trying to say, since you're new here, I could show you around. And you like to run—I can show you some trails through the mountains. What else do you like to do?" Owen's words came fast and almost clumsy like a rambling kid looking for something to say.

"I love running. This is the only trail I've found so far." Kira relaxed somewhat. She needed to make some friends and it would be incredible to hang out with such a hottie while she learned about the area. *Can I handle this? I shouldn't be spending any time with him.* Kira seriously doubted her ability to maintain self-control when it came to him.

Taking the opening, he continued, "The trail system here can be really tricky until you get to know it. But the views are spectacular." He sat, looking up at her silhouette against the backdrop of the mountains. The setting sun danced over her dark hair. "It can be very dangerous too. You shouldn't be out here by yourself. It's not safe. There are big cats and bears."

"And dark, dangerous soldiers, oh my!" she taunted, laughing. "I believe I'd be better off with the cats and bears." *They can only kill me.*

"I'm serious. You shouldn't be out here alone. I'll meet you and run with you." His voice was suddenly stern. Stark struggled to control his frustration.

"Wow, ok. I didn't realize this was such a hostile environment," she mocked as she consented, surprising even herself. Her instinct was to say, "Thanks for the advice, but hell no!" but the insistence in his voice, the intensity in his eyes . . . she felt powerless to resist. "Ok, you've got me. I won't come out here alone. It *would* be great to run together until I get to know more people. But I don't want to suck up all of your time. I imagine you're very busy."

Stark stood up, looking into her eyes as he stepped closer, "It's no trouble, ma'am. It would be my pleasure."

Hearing the word "pleasure" roll off his tongue in that rough, deep voice made her tingle deep inside. Before she could say anything he continued, "We better get going. It's getting dark. Do you have enough water?" He looked around for her supplies. He was acutely aware of the approaching darkness and the dangers that would bring. "Where's your light? Do you have a headlamp? Where's your pack?"

His questions made her feel suddenly inadequate. "I was just going for a short run," she replied hesitantly. "I didn't mean to be out so long." She started to slowly realize her shortcomings when interacting with this new environment. "Do you always run with a pack and carry that much gear along?" Her question was mocking but she was also slightly in awe.

"It's sort of what I do. It's part of the job. You wouldn't go to work without your stethoscope, would you?" he asked, seemingly annoyed and infuriated that she had put herself into such danger. He was more aggravated that he couldn't do anything about it, other than make sure she got home safely. "Here, let me help you put this headlamp on." He stood with his arms around her, securing the headlamp so that she could see well. Once again, they were standing so close, his lips just inches from her forehead. Her proximity was nearly overpowering.

"Let's head back," he said as he finished suiting her up for their return. They ran through the loop to get back to base. The run started as a moderately fast jog, but their competitive spirits wouldn't let that be it. Instead of running together, they jockeyed back and forth, escalating the electricity and tension between them. The last quarter mile was a full-on sprint, Kira giving it everything she had to outrun him. While she was fast, Stark used just enough power to stay two steps ahead of her the entire way back. As they reached the edge of the base and her apartment, she was amazed at his seemingly unscathed appearance. She had given all she had to fight through the miles, but he looked relaxed and at ease.

"So tomorrow then?" he asked, as they came to the top of her steps. He stopped and took her hands in his. "Thanks . . . for a very interesting day . . . ma'am."

Kira felt her heart almost leap out of her chest. She ached for more. Despite everything in her screaming, this is a bad, *bad* idea, the thought of seeing him in the morning was exhilarating. Before she could say anything he was heading down the stairs.

"See you tomorrow," he called over his shoulder, "oh six hundred." And with that he was gone into the darkness.

~~~

How can I be so stupid? Kira thought as she slipped into the shower. The hot water relieved her aching muscles. *But, God, he is so enticing. It's been so long . . . I just want to touch him.* Kira stood in the shower, breathless, thinking of the sensual man who had held her hands in his just a few minutes before. She leaned back against the shower wall, letting the day's events play over in her mind. She felt a shiver travel all the way down to her sex as she recalled standing close during his exam, touching him, smelling him. Fervently she wished for him, imagining his hands on her, holding her, those lips on hers. After her shower she slipped into an old T-shirt and slid into bed. As she wrestled with sleep, she was tormented with dreams of past losses, new fascinations, and dark new possibilities.

Kira's alarm blared to life at 0530. *Ugh! I'm not ready to get up.* Suddenly she remembered Stark would be there in thirty minutes and she was up like a shot. Donning her workout clothes and brushing her teeth, she was almost ready. The last minute battle of getting all her long brown hair into a ponytail was still underway when the doorbell rang. Even though she was expecting him, the sound at the door sent a jolt through her. Opening the door, her breath caught at the sight of him. *Damn, how does he look this amazing at six in the freaking morning?* He was leaning in the aged doorway of her bare-bones apartment, somehow looking like a Calvin Klein ad in the faded T-shirt and gray running shorts he wore.

Yes, please, she thought. *I'll buy whatever you're selling!*

"Hey there. You still have that headlamp?" he asked. "If we hurry, I have something to show you."

"Oh. Yeah, it's right here." She had set it out to return to him, but the sight of his magnificent frame in her doorway had sent her mind to other places.

"Let's get it on you. You can keep this one and I brought you a CamelBak. When you run or hike, you should carry water and basic supplies, *Captain.*"

"Thanks, *Sergeant,*" she snapped, stressing his rank, feeling a mix of inadequacy and gratitude.

They started off into the darkness. *I Will Follow You Into The Dark.* She smiled at the thought of one of her favorite Death Cab for Cutie songs. He led the way up a different route than they had taken before, which was a mix of trail running and climbing. Their pace was fast as they scrambled and raced up the mountain. "Stay behind me up here," he commanded. "It can be treacherous in some places."

Kira was careful to stay in his tracks. *Oh, this takes me back.* Kira thought fondly of her dad. A strange joy welled up inside her. She was taken back to memories of running behind her dad, excited that he was taking her with him, a feeling that bold new adventures lay ahead, waiting for her to explore.

Suddenly Stark stopped, bringing her back to the present as she collided with his warm back. He reached and took her hand. "Come with me. We've just made it. I want you to see this." He pulled her up onto the rock, never letting go of her hand. They were standing on the edge of a cliff in a small clearing that opened up over the vast expanse of the valley below. The first hint of light was beginning to peek out from the far rim of the mountains. The clouds were below them, giving the impression that they could just walk off into heaven. The light became brighter, spreading across the sky in a bright array of pink, gold, and blue. The bright sun became more apparent, splashing everything in gold. The clouds slowly dissipated, revealing the valley below and welcoming it to a new day.

Kira's heart melted. It was the most beautiful thing she had ever witnessed. She realized Stark was still there beside her, still holding her hand. "It's so lovely," she said softly, turning to look at him. The golden light across his strong features made him look more like a Greek god than a man.

"Yes, very lovely." He wasn't staring at the sunrise. He was staring at her.

Overwhelmed by the beauty of the moment and the intensity of his eyes upon her, she started to pull away and stumbled. At once his arms were around her as he caught her to keep her from falling. "Careful there, ma'am. We *are* on the edge of a cliff." His husky voice, so close, caused a shiver all the way through her. His arms were so strong and she felt warmed all over, overtaken by the uncontrollable desire to be kissed by this Adonis. *I want to feel those lips. All over me.*

"Owen," she whispered breathlessly as she gazed up at him, her eyes saying more than she dared. He was so close, bending near her face and a rush of anticipation flooded her. She could feel the warmth of his skin and eagerly breathed him in.

Then he stopped. With a pained expression on his face, he gently brushed against the top of her head and pulled away. "Come on. We'd better get you back."

What. The. Hell? What was that? she thought. They ran back toward base. She was confused, angry, and disappointed. He had built up to the most amazing moment, then—nothing. All the way back she fumed silently, fighting tears. As they approached her apartment he turned to say good-bye. "So I'll see you this evening," he paused, "for our run?" he asked awkwardly.

"No," she blurted. "I won't be running tonight, or tomorrow either. I have the confidence course in the morning so I'll get my workout there."

"You'll be doing the confidence course?" he asked with a sly grin, his eyes lighting up in amusement. "Well, in that case you probably won't feel like running on Thursday. We'll see about Friday then." And with that he was gone, heading down the street before she could respond.

Kira went inside, slamming the door harder than she meant. She was frustrated, turned on, and hurt. Cursing, she jumped into the shower to get ready for work. *Why doesn't he like me? Why the hell do I even care? I don't want to get involved with him anyway. This is exactly why I have to stay away!* The memories of that exquisite sunrise, and the golden light on his face was all too overwhelming. She chastised herself for being so easily charmed. *No, this has to stop. I can't spend any more time with him. Period. Friday I'll just tell him I've found someone else to run with.*

Hustling to work, Kira busied herself with patients, hoping to not think of him anymore.

"So how was your run this morning?" Abbey prodded, the look of anticipation in her eager eyes telling Kira she must have had something to do with him finding her on that trail.

"It was ok." She said it flatly, hoping to avoid an inquisition.

"Encounter any savage sex gods out there in the wilderness?" Abbey asked. "Sure would be a shame to lose one's sour mood to such a glorious beast," she teased as she walked to get another patient.

Kira was left standing there, mouth open, holding her coffee cup. "I'm not in a sour mood!" she hissed.

The rest of the day dragged. Kira saw patient after patient, trying desperately not to think of Owen, but wondering what had gone wrong that morning. That afternoon, just before heading home, Abbey popped into her office. "You heading out for another run after work?" Abbey's eyes looked hopeful.

"No, "Kira said softly. "I have the confidence course tomorrow."

"You've been quiet all day. Did something happen this morning?" Abbey asked, looking concerned.

Perhaps because it had been weighing on her all day or because she really had no one else to talk to, Kira opened up to Abbey about her encounters with Stark: the run, the beautiful sunrise, and the almost-kiss. "I just don't think he likes me that way," Kira finally said. Saying it out loud, she realized how much it hurt. "I know I shouldn't care because it's more trouble than it's worth but . . ."

"But you can't help it. I think he likes you more than you realize. But, honey, he's Special Forces. He's been places, seen things, and done things you'll never be able to understand." With a look of guilt on her kind face, she continued, "Maybe he would be better just as a friend." The look of pity on Abbey's face told Kira she knew it was already too late for that.

Kira made her way home and crawled into bed. Pulling the covers around her she closed her eyes, thinking of the breathtaking colors of the sunrise. The pinks, blues, and gold splashed across his glorious face.

Chapter 3

0600 came early. Kira jumped out of bed, excited and nervous for the confidence course. She knew there would be several obstacles and running intervals. The running she was sure she could handle but the obstacles could be anything. She had heard horror stories of frigid water and high ropes, but the course was an unknown. Kira hated cold water. *Hated* it. She buttoned up her ACUs, scowling as she looked in the mirror. She knew that they were necessary in a theater of war, but severely dreaded the idea of running fifteen miles in heavy wet canvas and sloshing in wet boots. *Suck it up, Captain! You knew this was part of the deal.*

She would be going through the course with other officers. Several of the other medical officers were previous military; others, like her, were fresh from school. Kira reported for duty and loaded on a bus with about twenty of them. She looked around, recognizing a few of the faces. The major at the front of the bus was going through a list of rules and precautions, as well as a talk about leadership and teamwork. He stressed the importance of staying on the course, as there were live fire ranges off to the right and a controlled burn area to the left. The course stretched over fifteen miles of rugged terrain. There would be significant elevation changes over the course. He explained that this would be a timed course and was an individual race rather than a team building experience. Helping one another was allowed, but they would be judged by their individual times.

Kira felt a twinge of anticipation as her competitive spirit came alive. From the time she started school Kira had been the smallest of the army brats but one the toughest. Throughout school she had raced and usually placed with the boys. Kira loved races and the adrenaline release as every fight-or-flight neuron came alive. While she wasn't as strong and probably wasn't as fast as most of the guys, she knew she was light, agile, and was eager to see what she could do on the course. She wasn't going to worry where she placed since there were only six other women in the group. She got off the bus, the nervous energy that she'd always got right before a race coursing through her.

With the shot of a gun, the course began. Kira raced forward. The first two miles were a narrow single-track trail up and down rolling hills with one final steep climb. She was in the middle of the group. The other female captains were farther back. She set her sights on one of her male counterparts up ahead. This had always been her game plan in high school track— chasing the man in front of her. Kira set her pace just a little faster than his so that she gained ground on him with each stride. They approached the first obstacle group, the red group. The first was called Belly Buster. *Lovely name*, Kira thought.

ok, I can do this one. Belly Buster was comprised of a series of logs suspended at chest height. The idea was to run and push up onto the log, and roll or flip over it.

Kira was thankful for her background in gymnastics and all the cross-fit classes she had done in college and medical school. She knew she was at a height disadvantage for this one, but she ran hard and jumped with every bit of strength in her legs to be able to push up onto each log, propel herself up, and drop over the other side. Up and over one after another she didn't look back. She finished with surprising speed for someone so small. Her size had been viewed as a disadvantage by every coach she ever had except in gymnastics. Kira made up for her lack of physical strength with sheer determination. She could hear her aunt's words, "There will always be someone faster, someone stronger, but on race day it comes down to who wants it more." Kira pushed on through the series. *I want it more!*

Next up was the reverse climb, which involved climbing up the underside of an inclined ladder, flipping over the top, and climbing back down. Kira felt a moment's hesitation as she neared the obstacle. She clenched her fist and reached inside for strength. Her aunt's weathered voice rang clearly in her mind. "Love it, Kira. Don't be afraid." Her aunt had been an inspiration and always encouraged Kira to keep fighting. She scrambled up, hanging on with all her might, and flipped over carefully at the top. She quickly climbed down the other side. The Weave looked like a monkey bar created by sadists. She hung suspended from it, going over, then under each of the beams. Despite her limited reach and modest upper-body strength, she managed to complete these without losing much time. In fact, she thought she was doing quite well as she progressed through the course.

Then she came to Hip Hip. This was significantly more difficult as it required high stepping or climbing over rungs of logs set at a man's hip height, but without any distance between each rung to run. *I can do this. Love it. Love my fate.* For some reason Kira remembered getting her brothers ready for school each day to get them on the bus and then sprinting through the woods to get herself to school since she had been kicked off the bus. She laughed recalling the reason for her exile. The stunned boy's face and broken glasses when she had decked him square in the face for grabbing her butt as she exited the bus one afternoon was still etched in her mind. That was the last time that year she had been allowed to ride. The race through the woods each morning had made her stronger and faster. She remembered having to climb and jump over logs and fallen trees in the thick undergrowth. *Love it.* Kira's heart was racing as she completed the obstacle bursting out of the other side and sprinting on.

The incline balance logs and island hopper were no problem. She sped through those, thankful for her excellent balance. This was one obstacle where she had the advantage.

Like a gymnast on the beam she navigated logs on delicate and carefully placed toes. As she hopped off the last log of that group, she caught sight of Stark. *What's he doing here?* She started off on her next running portion, another three miles of steep terrain. She pushed hard, hoping to make up time during the running portions. This, she had been training for all her life. But her mind was reeling. *Was that really him? It had to be— that dark hair.* There was no mistaking him, with those rugged good looks she found so unnerving. She fought to keep from thinking of being in his arms and how badly she wanted those lips on her skin. The adrenaline of the run combined with her wicked thoughts of being ravaged by those strong hands brought her to a new level of runner's high. She pushed forward, running with all she had toward the next obstacle. Kira wondered if she was running away from something or toward it. Knowing the dangers that lie ahead she pressed on. Surely this was insanity. Would Owen Stark turn out to be her greatest victory or her ultimate defeat?

As she climbed the last hill she was shaken from her delicious thoughts by the sounds of splashing and the yells of soldiers. Her heart sank. She knew the sound was coming from soldiers as they plunged into a frigid obstacle ahead. *Oh, fuck! Why, why, why cold water? Seriously!* As she crested the hill she could see it. At the bottom of the embankment was a large body of water with some sort of floating barricade out in the middle. She saw soldiers ahead of her swimming like mad, scrambling to climb onto the barricade and over the other side, back into the frigid water, and swimming to the bank. As she started down the hill toward the icy water she knew that if she simply splashed in, she'd lose her nerve and wouldn't be able to go in at all. Kira hated cold water. She could hear her cousin Byron taunting her for not wanting to play in the pond with him and her brothers. She could already feel the icy chill on her skin. Not wanting to look like some scared little girl, she took off running full-force down the hill and jumped out at the last minute so that her first contact with the glacial water would be as she plunged into its depths. *No going back.* Kira held her breath as the icy water engulfed her. She surfaced and began to swim for all she was worth. The frigid water stung her entire body. Involuntarily, she gasped as she fought to swim, her body trying to acclimate to the extreme change of temperature. Finally she reached the barricade and attempted to haul herself onto it. She struggled, since there was nothing to hold onto and her arms were fatigued. She couldn't touch the bottom; the water was just too deep. In an attempt to propel herself onto the barricade, she lowered herself as far under the water as she could reach while still touching the barricade and kicked her legs, pulling up at the same time. As she did, she felt two very strong hands grabbing the shoulders of her ACUs and pulling her up onto the barricade. Their combined efforts brought her up right on top of her helper and they toppled back. Kira looked down to see the face of the soldier who had come to her aid. His blond hair was soaked and stuck to his face. His bright blue eyes were wide with surprise. Kira rolled off him. "Sorry." She smiled. "But thanks."

"Trust me, it was my pleasure." He grinned, still looking up at her. He jumped up to finish the race. "I'm Captain Holt. You're doing great! Keep it up." And with that, he jumped off the other side and began to swim.

***

Stark had been sitting on a bank watching the race. Earlier he had been to the red course and was surprised at how well she was doing. He cut through the woods and now was watching the water obstacle when he saw Kira crest the hill. The look of horror on her face when she saw the water obstacle was amusing and rousing. *What is she doing?* He'd watched in astonishment as she barreled down the embankment and jumped into the water. *Man, she is really going all out.* He admired her courage as he watched her struggle to swim to the barricade. When he saw her attempt to get onto the barricade, then go under the water, he jumped to his feet. *God, she went under.* Before he could move, he saw another soldier grab her as she crested the water and pull her up. His relief was short-lived as he saw she'd been pulled onto the other soldier as they fell back onto the barricade. The soldier was holding Kira on top of him. Stark's blood boiled, a blistering vengeance brewing as he watched the soldier staring up at her. *Get your fucking hands off her, you piece of shit!* He watched Kira roll off. He couldn't hear what they were saying, but he could read the other soldier's face well enough to know what he was thinking. Jealousy had never been an issue for him before. Lila, Paige, hell even Zoe could do what they wanted and he never thought twice about it. He watched Kira jump back into the murky water. He had to resist the urge to go down there and escort her through the rest of the course. *This is crazy!* he thought. Everything in his life was calculated and controlled. She was a liability, an unknown variable. He should just walk away, but he couldn't dream of it.

***

Kira continued her swim and composed herself as she reached the bank on the other side of the pond. She jumped to her feet and ran full-speed to the next obstacle called Tough One. It looked somewhat like a medieval fort with a two-story cargo net at one end, followed by an angled pie-shaped ladder leading down to a "walkway" of precariously placed log beams, ending with *another* smaller cargo net to the ground.

Oh, shit! Kira took a breath. This one would be easier if she wasn't soaking wet and covered by mud from the pond. Gathering all of her courage, she began climbing the cargo net, slowly at first but then faster as she got the hang of it. At the top of the net Kira looked down. Realizing she was about thirty-

44

three feet off the ground, sweat broke out on her palms. She felt slightly nauseous as she made her way across to the center of the moving net. She swung over onto the top point of the inverted pie-shaped ladder. The rungs were three inches in diameter and slick as shit. *Fuck me!* She carefully lowered herself down, one rung at a time. Her heart was racing since the distance between each beam was nearly three-fourths of her body length. Finally she dropped onto the log walkway. Balancing carefully, she began to cross, beam by beam. Right beside her, another soldier misstepped and fell down between the logs onto the net below. *Fuck, that had to hurt!* she thought. She made it safe to the other side and scurried down the cargo net.

Kira could feel someone watching her as she dropped to the ground to start the next run. Looking up, she saw Stark. The realization that he was definitely there watching her was exhilarating. A sense of arousal swept over her as she realized she liked the idea. She wanted him to watch her. She set out on her run with her wicked thoughts keeping her company. She was tired, but thinking of him set her on fire. She ran hard and fast, definitely running toward something rather than away.

As she approached the clearing, the blond soldier reappeared. "You've made good time." He smiled brightly at her, looking a little surprised. He had the confidence of someone for whom things always go well. "You can do this. You're almost done." Holt's message was encouraging but his tone was patronizing as if he thought she was a sweet little thing.

Kira ran on and hoisted herself onto the lower log. This last major obstacle was actually called Dirty Name. *I can think of a dirty name or two for this!* The contraption appeared to be a series of three beams, each one higher than the next and about three feet apart. *Shit, shit, shit!* It was like a twisted, psychotic version of the uneven bars. She leapt into the air, grabbing the second bar. Dangling off the ground, she struggled to pull her body weight up onto the second bar. Her tired arms ached. She felt weak and wanted to give up.

"Don't give up, Kira," Stark's voice growled at her. *That voice!* Her body obeyed his command despite her fatigue. She pulled herself up onto the beam. "You *can* do this!" With all the strength she had left, Kira lunged for the last beam and hung on tight. Her fingers went white as they struggled to hold, her face twisted with pain and sheer determination. She pulled with her shaky arms. "Do it, Captain!" his loud voice commanded. She obeyed, pulling her body the last few inches up and onto the beam. *I did it!* Kira felt a flood of excitement . . . then the weightless sense of falling, a searing pain, then darkness.

***

Stark jumped up and ran to her as she lay motionless beneath the wooden contraption. He bent to help her. She looked so beautiful lying there amidst a sea of chestnut hair.

"What the fuck are you doing? Don't touch her!" a young voice yelled in an attempt to sound authoritative.

Stark looked up to see the little blond shit who had helped her earlier.

"Stand back," he continued. "I'm Captain Holt. I'm a doctor. Stand back so I can help her." The man knelt beside her and started to do an assessment. Stark did not budge. *Who the hell does he think he is?* Seeing the little shit putting his hands on her made him see red.

The other medical officers and field medics rushed over and began to check her out. A sudden panic rose in Stark. He desperately wanted her to be ok. He wanted the blond-haired punk to back the fuck up, but just then, Kira opened her eyes.

"Damn, I guess I blew that," Kira said shakily. She blinked and looked around as if she was trying to get the world to come into focus.

"You did great," Captain Holt said softly. "We're going to take you back to the ER. You've had enough for one day."

"No, no, I'm ok," she began slowly. "I want to finish the course. I'm not really hurt . . . well, other than my pride maybe." Kira's voice gained confidence as she spoke.

"Are you crazy? You could have been killed!" Holt scolded. "If this meddling e-dog wasn't trying to get you to do things you're clearly not ready for, you would have been fine."

Despite her bewilderment, Kira got up quickly to show them all she was ok.

Stark stepped forward to steady her. He reached out and braced her gently when Holt reached up and grabbed his arm. "This isn't your place," Holt squawked at Stark.

While still steadying Kira, Stark grabbed Holt's arm with his other hand and pulled him in close so fast and forcefully that Holt froze. In a deadly calm voice, Stark said, "Listen to me you, little piece of shit. You've been a captain for about a minute. And a doctor for about a day. You don't have the balls . . ." Stark pulled Holt in closer and looking down into his widening eyes, Stark's face darkened as he continued, ". . . to survive one day in a theater of war. You insignificant little fuck."

Seeing this side of Stark scared Kira. She pulled away, breaking the tension between the two. Stark turned to her and froze instantly,. Slowly at first, she began to run. The men stopped and watched her disbelievingly as she made her way toward the finish line.

She knew he was Special Forces but hadn't realized what he was really capable of. She saw the restraint he exercised and knew that he could break Holt, kill him in a second with those powerful hands. Hands that had held her so tenderly. She ran the last one hundred meters, with shaky legs, her heart racing and breaking at the same time. She realized that she and Stark could truly never be together. Hot tears stung her eyes as she flopped down for the final belly crawl. Under the barrier of the barbed wire, she fought her total dismay and aching heart to finish the course . . . and tell Stark good-bye. When she crossed the finish line she looked back across the field. Captain Holt stood there open-mouthed, staring at her. Stark was nowhere to be seen. He had gone.

Chapter 4

Kira poured herself into work after that embarrassing debacle at the confidence course, which ironically had done very little for her confidence. Regarding Stark, she was more confused than ever. He had been so, well, present after her fall— first attentive, then ferocious. And now she hadn't seen or heard anything from him since. Captain Liam Holt, however, was becoming an ever-present intrusion in her life. In the weeks since the course, he had found his way to her clinic at least once a day for various reasons.

"Twelve thirty, right on schedule," Abbey scoffed disapprovingly as Captain Holt strode into the office. Dressed in scrubs and a white lab coat, Holt was very attractive. He was tall and well-built. Even so, his blond hair and blue eyes reminded her more of a preppy Ralph Lauren model than of an Army doctor. He brushed past Abbey and into Captain Riley's office.

"Are you ready for lunch?" he asked Kira hopefully. "There's really nothing worth eating here on base. We can take my car and be back before your afternoon appointments." He worked his car into any discussion. The bright red BMW M6 convertible was hard to miss with its candy apple love-me paint. Kira was not impressed. To her the red convertible was too pretentious and insulting to those enlisted men like her father.

They worked and gave their whole lives to this country and would never be able to afford a car like that. Lately he had managed to park beside her almost every morning. His gleaming red paint made the duct tape holding the passenger side taillight on her rusting Honda stand out like a sore thumb.

Kira evasively stepped into the lab area where Abbey was finishing a urine specimen.

"A car like that says something about a man," Abbey sneered. "Or at least about what he is lacking. How much compensation can he really need?" Abbey's dislike for Holt grew daily.

Captain Holt followed Kira into the lab. "Let's go, Kira, I'm really hungry. You can't possibly want to stay on base."

Kira didn't really want to go but Holt was persistent. Silently she wondered what Stark was up to and where he had gone. Putting those thoughts away, Kira grabbed her jacket and agreed to lunch. Walking to the car, Holt placed his hand possessively at the small of her back. The sudden roar of a motorcycle caught her attention. A completely blacked-out Harley-Davidson drove by slowly, pausing at the stop sign. Every bit of chrome on the bike had been replaced by flat black including the spokes. The bike was dark and menacing but understated. No flash needed. Other people on the street paused to watch him roll by. They were all staring at him but the driver was looking directly at her. Her heart raced. Time slowed and stood still. Though the helmet was full-faced she knew it was him. The roar of her own heartbeat drowned out the sounds of the motor. Excitement coursed through her as she watched him drive away. She even stopped walking.

"Are you ok?" Holt asked.

"No," Kira said suddenly. She felt at once dizzy. *How can I be this affected by that man? This is crazy!* "You know what, I'm not feeling so well. I think I'll go back in. Maybe we can catch lunch another day." Kira turned on shaky legs and headed back into the clinic before he could say anything.

"What, no lunch at the Waldorf today?" Abbey grumbled. Kira was too unnerved by seeing Stark again to be irritated at Abbey's words.

"Abbey," Kira began cautiously, due to the other soldiers and officers in the office. "I took care of a patient a few weeks ago, for a post-deployment physical."

Abbey's face lit up and she was immediately paying attention. Playing along, she responded, "Oh? Yes, ma'am, Sergeant Stark. I think he had a wound on his arm."

"Yes, that's the one. Did we schedule a follow-up for him? I don't remember seeing it." Kira finished in a transparent attempt to sound professional.

Abbey got her the contact information to do a follow-up call. "Would you like me to call, Captain?"

"No, I think I should check up on him myself." Kira took the info and went back into her office. She sat for some time staring at the number. *Just call*, she told herself. Kira felt as if she was standing on the edge of a vast ravine. The chasm was deep and deadly; one wrong move and she would surely fall to her death. Fraternization is a serious offense. If her fellow officers like Holt found out they could end her career and Stark's too. *I can't do this.* She picked up the phone and held it in midair. Then she hung it up again. *I shouldn't do this! God! I know better.* A vision of the motorcycle rider staring at her flashed, and along with it, the dizzy feeling. *That was him.* Against her better judgment, she picked the phone back up and dialed.

"Hello." A sultry female voice answered the phone. "Hello? Can I help you?"

Kira froze and her heart sank. *He has a girlfriend . . . or a wife!* Panic set in. Her first instinct was to hang up, but curiosity and blind jealousy took over. "This is Captain Riley from the TMC clinic. May I speak with Sergeant Stark?" Kira mumbled weakly. *No wonder he didn't want to kiss me. God, I have made such a fool of myself. What a mess!* A wave of nausea hit her like a brick.

"Hmm, he must have made *some* kind of an impression. He's in the shower, but trust me, he's doing *just* fine." The lascivious voice purred into the phone, reminding Kira of a late night ad for phone sex.

Kira's blood ran cold, and felt as if all the air had been sucked out of the room. "Ok. Um . . . t-t-thanks," she stammered as she hung up the phone. Maybe that wasn't him on the bike. Maybe she was going crazy. Kira sat there, tears stinging her eyes. She fought to keep them contained. Sadly, she pushed the folder aside.

Abbey appeared at the door. "Everything ok?" When Kira didn't answer, Abbey changed tactics. "You know, this is a four-day weekend. You should get off-base for a bit. Head up to the mountains and do some skiing. You've been talking about that since you got here."

"That's a good idea," Kira said, putting on a brave face. Putting her full emotion into skiing and then getting shitty drunk at a mountain pub would be perfect. "Actually, Abbey, that's a great idea." Between afternoon patients, she started making plans. Kira was rather proud of herself that by the last patient she had all the details worked out. After giving Abbey a brief itinerary, Kira took off to get ready. She threw what she needed in her beat-up Honda and set off toward the mountains. If the weather held, she would be there by nine, maybe ten at the latest. She yearned for a sense of freedom. Driving the winding roads,

54

she rolled the window down to feel the crisp air. She embraced the beauty of her surroundings and willed herself not to think of Stark.

***

Stark opened his front door. He was still seething with rage. The sight of the little shit's hand on the sexy curve of Kira's back right above that perfect ass sent him into a rage. Feelings he had tried to block, came flooding back with a vengeance. *Why do I even care? I barely know this girl.* He had gone for a ride on his motorcycle to try to forget her. To let go. The last few weeks had been hell. He hadn't been able to stop thinking about her during his entire training mission. He kept seeing her, that vision of her sprawled on the ground looking up at him. There was something about her. He knew what he wanted was wrong but he couldn't remember wanting anything more. The rules were clear, no relationships of any kind between officers and enlisted soldiers. The idea was to prevent favoritism and breaking the rules could end both of their careers or worse. He didn't know how he had ended up at her clinic, but there it was. Driving up, he'd seen her and he'd wanted to go to her. As he got closer he saw Holt too, coming up behind her, touching her as they walked to that fucking candy-ass car. He could barely breathe. *So she was with him.* But the look in her eyes as she had returned his stare had seemed to beg him to come to her. He'd felt her stare holding him. He had wanted to jump off that bike and take her. Feel her. But he couldn't. Painfully, he remembered the look on her face when he'd lost his temper at the confidence course. He'd seen fear in her eyes when he'd shown the rage he felt. He knew that if she really knew him, she would leave anyway.

Mags came running, jumping into his arms and breaking the spell. "Hey there, little girl, I missed you too," he said, laughing. Mags planted kisses all over his face as he knelt down, ruffling her fur. The sight of Maggie always brought him back from whatever was haunting him. She had been his rock, his saving grace for the last ten years. Without her, he knew he would have died. Her bright eyes and speckled fur always made him smile.

"So you *are* back." A sultry voice called from the living room. Paige sat on the couch with a glass of wine, reading a magazine.

"Hey, Paige. Thanks for looking after Mags for me," Stark said, walking into the kitchen to get a beer.

"You ok? You look like you've had a rough day," Paige began, careful not to ask too many questions. She had learned long ago that after some missions it was best to leave him alone. "I hadn't heard from you, so I didn't know you were back till that captain called from the TMC."

"I was on a training . . . What? Who called? When?" Stark asked, surprised.

"Today, about an hour ago. She sounded all nervous, like a schoolgirl, not a captain. You always do leave them flustered." She laughed. "I think her name was Riley."

Stark almost dropped his beer. *She called! What could she want?* His mind was racing. "What did she say?" he blurted out, with no attempt to hide his desperation.

"Whoa there, tiger! You actually like this girl?" Paige asked, alarm bells going off. "You haven't been serious about a girl in . . . well, ever. Have you fucked her yet?" she snapped.

"Not now, Paige." He began searching for the TMC number. "Did she leave a number?"

"No, but don't worry I told her you were doing *just fine*," she retorted, hurt and accentuating the last words, stressing the implication.

"Damn it, Paige!" Stark yelled, now frantically searching for the number. Finding it, he dialed, praying someone would still be there. His hand tugged hard at his hair in exasperation.

***

Abbey had just finished the rest of her paperwork and was looking forward to a long weekend with her husband. She started to leave but went back for her purse. As she paused for a moment, glancing in the captain's office, the phone rang. *Leave it,* she thought. *It's time to go.* She turned to leave, but something drew her back.

"Hello, TMC Office, Clinic Four, Abbey Pistole speaking."

"This is Sergeant Stark, ma'am. I'm returning a call from Captain Riley." He sounded calm and cool but Abbey sensed the quiet desperation in his voice. Although uncertain about what the future would hold for those two, she could see the spark between them. That kind of chemistry you only find once in your life.

After a pause that seemed like an eternity, she spoke. "She went to the mountains, to Aspen, to get away from everything for a while. She's confused and upset."

"She's going over the mountains in that death trap of a car?" he asked in sudden panic. "There is supposed to be a storm and that thing has the ground clearance of a hamster. Is she crazy?"

Stark's alarm shook Abbey; she hadn't thought of the danger Kira was putting herself in. Quickly she gave Stark Kira's itinerary and cell number, as well as her own. "Call me if you run into problems. And Stark, with all due respect, if you hurt her, I will make your life a living hell," Abbey finished quietly.

Abbey walked out the door silently praying for Stark and Kira. She was so lost in her thoughts that she almost ran into Captain Holt. "Where's Captain Riley?" he demanded. His demeaning tone ruffled her as usual. But she smiled sweetly and replied, "Oh, Captain, you just missed her. She had to fly home to see her family. She'll be back in town on Tuesday."

"Did she leave a number or anything?" he asked, looking annoyed and dejected.

"The captain wouldn't give me that kind of information." Abbey smiled innocently, knowing his superiority complex would buy that. Her distaste for Holt was as strong as her growing affection for Stark. Abbey was a civilian. A damn good nurse, and the wife of Sergeant Major Joshua Pistole. She had been an army wife for well over twenty-three years. She saw a lot of her husband in Stark and could see how he felt about Kira. Holt, on the other hand, had come into the military as a captain. His arrogance oozed from every pore and sickened her. "See you Tuesday, Captain. Have a lovely weekend." Abby made her way to her car with a very satisfied smile on her lips.

***

Kira stopped for gas at the base of Mt. Elbert. She had been on the road for a few hours. She shivered as she got out of the car. The air felt much colder, and the wind bit as she pumped gas. As she started back on the road the first snowflakes began to fall. *How pretty,* she thought, oblivious to the danger. In her haste Kira had failed to check the weather before leaving. When she had quickly made her reservations the hotel clerk had warned of a possible storm coming in. She silently cursed herself for not being more careful. *What has gotten into me? I can't be this idiotic over a man!*

As she continued up the mountain, the wispy flakes became more abundant. After a few miles, they looked like a blanket covering everything. The road was completely white. As darkness approached, Kira realized it was taking a lot longer to get to her destination than she had planned. The snowfall had increased to near whiteout conditions and she struggled to see past the front of the car. The wind had blown snow into drifts along the road and obscured the edges, making it difficult to tell what was road and what was not.

Darkness surrounded her and headlights glared off the snow and ice. The road was icy in places, and her car began to slip this way and that. She struggled to maintain control. She thought of pulling over but couldn't tell where the edge of the road actually was. She continued on at a snail's pace, her knuckles white from gripping the steering wheel. A string of curse words escaped her lips as she realized the situation she had gotten herself into. As she crested the next hill, she was gripped with fear. At the bottom of the hill lay a sharp curve to the left. *Shit, shit, shit!* The car picked up speed as it began descending down the steep hill. Kira tried carefully tapping the brakes, attempting not to slide. *Please don't let me go over the edge,* she prayed as her car began to slide and spin. Thoughts of her family flashed through her mind as the snowy edge raced toward her. Panic set in when Kira realized she no longer had control of the car. For a fleeting moment time stood still. The image of Stark slowly going by on his bike filled her mind. Kira held on tightly as her car slammed into a snow embankment.

***

Stark had packed quickly and set out on the road. He knew she had at least an hour lead on him. He ran into the storm well before reaching the mountains. The roads were nearly impassable. He pressed on, knowing she was out there somewhere and he had to get to her. Mile after mile of worsening conditions filled him with dread. He pictured her driving that crap car in this weather. He wanted to find her, hold her, and then spank her damn stubborn ass for driving in this snowstorm.

His heart almost stopped as he saw the crumpled rear bumper of her Honda sticking out of a snow bank. He reached the car and began frantically digging the car out, fear gripping him, images of what he might find flooding his mind. He stopped suddenly, looking in disbelief at the empty car. She was gone. He knew at once she had set out on foot. He jumped back in his truck and took off in a desperate search. After a painful fear-drenched mile he came to a bar. He stopped, hoping she would be there or that someone had heard from her. He parked next to a line of rigs that must have pulled off to weather the storm.

He reached the door, his heart racing. As he opened it he heard a loud cheer. Entering the room, his eyes found the source of the trucker's delight. There, at the other end of the bar, dressed in the sexiest jeans he had ever seen, was Kira. Surrounded by an adoring but defeated crowd of truckers, she was gleefully saying, "Ok, best three out of five?" Her long chestnut hair whirled as she turned to get more darts for another game. She looked up and their eyes met. It was as if everyone else in the room disappeared. She stood frozen. He crossed the room in two long strides and pulled her to him.

"Sergeant Stark, what are you doing here?" she asked quietly, looking up into his eyes.

"I thought you were . . . I mean, I saw your car and I thought . . ." His voice broke. He couldn't even say it out loud. Unable to control his emotions any longer, he picked her up, kissing her deeply, all the need and restraint exploding in this one kiss. Holding her up in his powerful arms, pulling her tightly against him, he continued kissing her passionately.

Kira felt her entire body melt. His expert lips and tongue claiming her mouth, she reached up, holding onto his dark hair. He growled at her touch. She stepped back, stunned from the exquisite kiss. As her senses came back to her, she became aware of the room full of people once again. Kira looked around, then back at Stark, the blush creeping up her face, betraying the composite of emotions swirling within her. She was at once angry and eager for more. She had wanted this man desperately from the first time she had seen him. She had practically begged for this that morning on the mountain. But this was not on her terms. She had resolved to put Stark far out of her mind. She could see that she was heading down a dark and dangerous road.

"Kira, let's go. Let's get you out of here," Stark began, his voice tense with wanton need.

"I can't. What about my car? We can't just leave it in the snow," she protested.

Stark started over to the counter to make arrangements about her car with the owner of the bar. The burly trucker, who had been playing darts with Kira, stood from his ragged stool beside the bar.

"It seems to me she said she don't want to go with you. Maybe she wants to stay here with me," he bellowed, looking down at Stark. The trucker's semi-toothless grin and wild eyes startled Kira. Though slightly inebriated and a little grabby he had seemed harmless before Stark walked in. Now he stood ready to stake his claim. He was enormous, but Stark was unaffected. Despite standing nose-to-chin with the large fellow, Stark replied, completely in control, "I wouldn't ever make her do anything she didn't already want to do."

Kira couldn't help but be stirred by the double meaning in his words. She was sure her need was palpable. Despite her eagerness for Stark, she panicked, remembering his fury at the course. The trucker was so much bigger than Stark and she feared his temper would get the better of him this time.

Stark continued to the counter without further acknowledging the hefty trucker. The large man reached out to grab Stark. "I'm talking to you," he sneered. Before the trucker could touch him, Stark grabbed his hand and bent it . . . hard. Quietly, he said, "I have no problem with you, friend, but let me be clear. This doesn't concern you and if you insist on being involved, then that's your right. But you have that right because I have fought to give it to you. As for Kira, I just drove a hundred miles through blinding snow to be with her. So if you're still insistent in being a roadblock, then let's take this outside . . . but I guarantee you won't come back with the same conviction." Stark's voice was icily calm. A bead of sweat slid down the trucker's forehead and dripped off his nose. The wrinkled expression on his face betrayed the pain he was trying to conceal.

Kira didn't give him time to answer. Instinctively, she placed a very gentle hand on Stark's shoulder. To the trucker she said, "Thank you, but this is my friend Sergeant Stark. He's here to pick me up. I was just worried about my car, that's all." Her calm demeanor hid the anxiety inside. She was awed by Stark. He had maintained complete control. *Who is this man?* Kira felt excited and so alive. The fear, the need, his incredible strength, that kiss all raced through her head. She felt dizzy.

Stark made arrangements for her car. He grabbed her bags and repeated the command, "Let's go, Kira." The primal need in his husky voice screamed sex. Kira obeyed without question. Her body ached for more of his embrace. "Buckle up," he instructed as they climbed into the truck. "I know a place fairly close where we can stay tonight."

Coming to her senses as they drove into the darkness, Kira asked, "So what does your girlfriend think of you coming out in the wilderness to rescue me?" Her voice was hot with jealousy.

With a throaty laugh, Stark replied, "She's not my girlfriend."

"Wife then?" Kira asked, horrified.

"No, she's not my wife and not my girlfriend anymore. She was, a very long time ago," he said, as if that would suffice.

"Then why did she answer your phone? Does she live with you? She made it sound like you were more than friends." Briefly, Kira recounted her conversation with the sultry phone-sex goddess.

"*Damn* Paige!" Stark said. He sighed. "Her name is Paige. She was just playing with you. She doesn't live with me. Kira, I travel a lot. Sometimes I'm gone for months at a time. She comes and stays with Maggie while I'm gone. They have gotten really close. She's good to my Mags."

Oh God, he has a child! I am such a shit! "You have a child?" Kira asked hesitantly.

"NO! No." He was laughing harder now. "Mags is my dog. She's an Australian Shepherd."

"I love those dogs," Kira said, relieved. "How did you come up with Mags?"

"Maggie," he corrected. "I call her Mags for short just like I did my sister."

"Did?" Kira asked, contrite.

"It was a long time ago. I don't want to talk about it tonight." He turned and looked at her his eyes burning deep into her core. Kira had never been this affected by a man in her life. She could feel her breath hitch. The heat radiating off him warmed her side of the truck, awakening a need in her she had never felt before. Kira bit her lower lip as she watched him drive like a man on a mission. She was torn by her desperate need for his touch and the consequences she knew would follow.

"We're here, Kira." Stark's voice pulled her out of her lusty daze.

Holy fuck! Kira gasped as they pulled up to the house. When he said he knew a place close by where they could stay, she had envisioned a small cabin. Even in the darkness she could see the cedar and stone bastion rising out of the mountain. *How does he know about this place? Are we even allowed to be here?* Kira had never seen such a house up close. She looked at him hesitantly as he parked the car. "Are we allowed to be here?" she asked tentatively.

"Yeah, I know the owner and he definitely won't mind. He's very much in favor of it. Come." His husky voice sounded intent. Kira couldn't wait to be kissed again. Her anticipation building, she grabbed her things and followed him in. Once inside, Stark turned up the heat and started turning on lights. "I'm sorry it's cold. No one has been here in a while. We can sleep by the fire tonight." He gathered thick blankets from a massive closet in the hall and led her to the great room.

The room was bigger than her apartment, she noted in awe. Along a central wall stood an immense fireplace, the opening at least six feet across. The stone chimney stretched all the way to the dark wood ceiling. Stark began lighting the fire, and instructed her to make a pallet of blankets and to grab the large pillows from the aged leather couches. The leather of the couches was incredibly soft. Kira wandered about the vast room, wondering if the rest of the house was like this. She brushed her fingers over a collection of photos on a bookshelf. She thought the man and woman looked vaguely familiar but couldn't place them. There were several pictures of a boy and a girl. The reflection of the moonlight off the mountain caught her eye and Kira moved to the window.

Once the fire was built, Stark poured a glass of Jameson on ice. "Can I get you anything?"

"Not at the moment, thank you. I can't get over how the moon looks," she said in amazement looking out the thirty-foot windows still staring at the moonlight illuminating the mountains. "It looks like they're glowing," she noted in awe. Stark came up behind her, wrapping his arms around her, holding her for a moment. Bending her head forward, he gently brushed the hair away from her neck. She shivered at the touch of his powerful hands so delicately moving across her skin as if a cascade of electricity bolted down her body.

Kira struggled to find her breath. She could feel him so close to her. Slowly he began kissing the back of her neck. She moaned softly, relishing the sensation. *Oh God, those lips!* Kira knew this was crazy but could not resist. She wanted him badly. *How can I be so weak?* All thoughts of resistance were fleeing from her with each delicate touch. The hot breath from his lips on her neck and in her hair was mesmerizing. She felt herself losing control to all her fantasies, the longing, the waiting. She struggled to fight the overwhelming desire.

As if sensing her resistance, Stark whispered, "I know this is wrong, Kira. Tell me to stop and I will. I would do anything you say. But I can't stop on my own. I want you, need you." He paused, inhaling. Breathing her in. "I want to feel you, taste you." His hand tightened on her breast as he spoke. His other hand slid around her hip, holding tightly to her sex. The pressure and heat of his hands set her on fire. Her breath quickened. She could no longer resist. It had been so long without any contact at all other than her fantasies. Now here he was, wanting her, needing her. She burned for the sensation of his touch, the promise of his mouth. She felt the last of her self-control flee as he rubbed her long-ignored clit through her jeans. The friction driving her crazy, she could feel his hardness growing, pushing against her back He pulled her tightly against him, kissing her sensually on her neck and shoulders, grinding against her on either side with his strong hands and his cock.

Kira reached back and held his thighs, pressing her hips against him. He groaned loudly.

"Kira," he breathed, his breath short and raspy. "I've wanted you since the first moment I saw you. I've tried to stay away. God knows I've tried but I can't. I just can't." He spun her around, and began kissing her, slowly and tenderly at first, then more fiercely as his need began to take over.

Oh God, yes! His hands tightened over her ass and he pulled her head back by her hair as his lips and tongue took hers. She tasted the lingering whiskey on his lips and whimpered, feeling herself lose control of her body, wanting only to feel him inside her. Stark picked her up and she wrapped her legs around his waist tightly as he carried her across the room. His smell, the mix of smoke from the fire, and his cologne, were intoxicating. He lay her down gently on the blankets by the fire. The light dancing on his face, he kissed Kira tenderly on her face, her lips, her neck. The tension in the room was rising, her body at high alert, every fiber of her being alive with need. *I need him to touch me.* At once he is pulling her shirt over her head. His eyes blaze wildly as he stares at the soft skin of her breasts.

"You were going skiing in that?" he asked, amused, looking at the sight of the black lace bra barely restraining her ample breasts.

Kira nearly jumped out of her skin as he took her hands and pinned them high above her head. With the other hand he raked his nails gently over her breasts and down her abdomen to the top of her jeans. The sensation sent electrical currents coursing through her. She moaned, unable to contain her desire. He smiled wickedly and began kissing above the waistband. Then, with deft fingers, he undid her jeans, and she shivered, not from the cold on her bare skin, but from the anticipation of what was to come. A sudden panic set in as she realized he was moments away from revealing the mass of unkempt curls hiding just beneath her jeans. *Damn it! Why didn't I wax or shave or anything? FUCK!* Being ravaged in an immaculate ski chalet by a sex god had not crossed her mind of things that would actually happen to her. She felt the jeans slipping away and struggled in resistance. Fear creeping in, she looked up suddenly shy and embarrassed.

Stark looked at her with a puzzled expression. "I wasn't exactly expecting this," she stammered apologetically. "I mean, I'm not exactly prepared."

As if finally understanding, a smile crept across his face, and with a voice that could melt butter, he said, "In case you haven't noticed, Captain, I'm not a timid man. I'm not afraid to brave the jungle. In fact I like things a little wild." He traced his fingers over the lace of her now exposed panties as he spoke. "If

71

it bothers you, I can take care of this later. You will have to trust me completely."

Kira felt his lips on her again, breathing hot air over her skin and through her lace panties. She could feel herself growing wetter. *I want him so very badly.* Her hands were free now that he was holding her hips, arching her upward to his waiting mouth, and she reached out, grabbing his hair, holding on. He inched her wet panties down, kissing as he went. The stubble of his rough beard tickled her skin. She shuddered as his tongue found her clit, flicking it, and she struggled not to come as he began sucking, pulling the electric nub. One of those powerful hands found its way into her soaking slit, working the exquisitely sensitive spot. Her legs shuddered and she fought to stay still. The electrical current coursing inside her grew, driving her into a frenzy. She moaned louder, unable to control the waves breaking over her. Her groin tightened and ached with sweet, riveting pressure building until she could not breathe.

"Mmm, come for me, Kira," he ordered.

His command sent her over the edge as she ground fervently into his hand and mouth, pussy throbbing around his fingers, flooding them with her release. All the ache and tension of her long-delayed orgasm was so deftly delivered by his touch. He looked up at her, wild with need. He slipped her panties the rest of the way off and stood before her. *I can't believe this is real. Watching him undress is the culmination of every fantasy I have ever had,* she thought fuzzily. His muscular chest. Those abs, the perfect V cutting directly into his jeans, those thighs. Kira couldn't take any more waiting. Sitting up onto her knees, she ripped off his boxer briefs, freeing his massive cock. *Oh, dear God! I hope this is real. If not, I don't want to wake up till it's over.*

He stood there for a moment, gloriously naked. The sight of his perfectly sculpted body, so tall and rugged, revived Kira, instantly making her want more. Since seeing that bulge in her office, she had dreamed of this moment. Tenderly she stroked her hands down the expansive length, licking her lips, desperately wanting to put it in her mouth. She kissed him gently on the end, feeling a bead of sweet sticky cum form, and licked it off, looking up at him.

Stark stood, barely able to breathe, shocked . . . and driven crazy by her taking control. He looked down at her sweet face, now delightfully wicked, as if she had found a long-awaited prize. The gleam in her eyes as she looked up at him while slowly licking the tip of his cock took him made him lose control. "Fuck, Kira," he growled. "I want that mouth around my cock."

***

She obeyed. At that moment she would do anything he asked. Slowly at first, she began sucking at the tip, working the base with her hands, his deep moans letting her know she had him. Then starting at the foundation, she licked up the veiny throbbing shaft, taking him suddenly in her mouth when she reached the end. He gasped sharply, grabbing her hair. She loved having this effect on him. It made her hungry for more. She began working up and down, finding her rhythm, ravenously sucking and working with her hands. His hips thrust to meet her mouth. He became bolder, holding her head in his hands, fucking her mouth. His growing moans fueled her to take him as deeply as she could. He picked up the pace. Kira sucked hungrily each time he pulled out of her mouth and she allowed him entrance again. She held on to the back of his muscular thighs, allowing him deeper access and control over the rhythm. His body stiffened, and he threw his head back.

"God, Kira!" Stark cried out and with one final thrust filled her mouth with hot cum.

The sweet, salty caramel cream shot out of him in his final moment of ecstasy. She sucked it all down greedily, licking the tip for every last drop. *Mmm.* She sighed, pleased and satisfied with her prize.

"You are one wicked little girl," he said, smiling. Spent, he collapsed on top of her. "Don't think for a moment that this is over. I am going to make you scream."

Stark took a moment to put another log on the fire. He turned, and saw Kira wrapped in the blankets, the firelight dancing across her face and breasts. "Of all the places I have been, all the wonders I have seen pale in comparison to this moment with you." He came back to her, taking her in his arms and began kissing her intensely.

The feeling of his soft, sensual lips on hers, his tongue probing her mouth, gaining access and taking control was too much to resist. She surrendered completely. He pushed her leg aside with his and lay between her legs. She felt his massive cock fully hardened, pressing against her. He rubbed back and forth, the friction on her swollen and very sensitive clit sending her reeling. He put her hands far above her head once more and began to suck gently on her nipple, biting slightly. The combined effect was overwhelming. She was soaring, flying, her body weightless. She no longer felt the floor. His fingers worked their way into her tight slit, moving relentlessly in and out. The pulling and stretching made her even wetter. *I'm on fire.* She could feel another orgasm building. *So close.*

"You know I'm clean, I hope you are and are on birth control," he said. She nodded her head and then she felt the power, the pressure of that huge cock enter her, filling her to capacity. The intense fullness threw her into a frenzied state, wanton and desperate to come again.

Stark groaned deeply as he finally worked his entire length in her. "You're so tight." For a moment all the world stood still and then he started to move, slowly at first, then gliding in and out. She felt her body holding him, tightening around him as he pulled out, then filled her again. His pace quickened and she was fully flying now. He glided back and forth faster . . . faster . . . He lifted her hips, and the change of angle caused his thick cock to grind deliciously, stretching her in new ways. She struggled to breathe as her breathing came faster. Kira held on desperately to his muscular back. Her fingers traced the tattoo. *He truly is relentless*. Her head fell back, and, giving in completely to the moment, she felt his power. He seemed to know her body better than any lover she'd ever known, better even than she did, meeting each desire with newfound pleasure. His groans became louder, more fervent, his thrusts more forceful, and his grip on her arm and hip tightened. A sheen of sweat glistened on both their bodies. As he continued his skillful exploitation of her sex, her elation was building to an uncontrollable explosion. Suddenly his body stiffened, his arms holding her to him tightly. The intense pressure caused her to cry out as she came, unable to control the shattering of her ravaged body and she laid there a quivering mess, so very happy to be in his arms.

***

Stark lay there for hours, watching her sleep. She was so beautiful and she was his. For the first time in a decade he felt a sense of belonging.

Chapter 5

Sunlight streamed through the large windows as Kira finally awoke. She looked around slowly, getting her bearings. She wasn't quite sure if last night had really happened or if she had dreamed it. She pulled the blankets up around her and looked at the freshly tended fire. She took a moment to process that she was no longer in the great room but was in an exquisitely soft bed. The thick comforters enveloped her, tempting her back into sleep. The headboard was deep brown leather, a remarkable contrast to the white linens. On the opposite wall was a small stone fireplace much more intricate than the one in the great room. On either side of it was a mahogany lattice holding small round logs, all cut the exact right size to fit in the lattice and the fireplace. She thought the effect was beautiful, like a piece of art. To her right was an expanse of large windows, allowing a clear view of the freshly fallen snow. The beautiful blanket of white appeared innocent and new this morning. She thought of how menacing it had seemed last night.

Last night! Oh what the hell did I do? How could I have let this happen! Kira looked around for her clothes. She had slept in one of his soft T-shirts. *Mmm, this smells like him.* Without realizing it, she hugged the shirt to her and inhaled. In the corner sat an oversized upholstered chair. Her bag had been placed neatly on it. Kira jumped up and grabbed it. Mercifully, the bathroom door had been left open so she didn't have to go on a scavenger hunt. The bathroom was magnificent, all creams and whites, with heavy dark wood. She stepped cautiously on the marble floor, expecting it to be freezing but was pleasantly surprised to find it heated. As she started across the room, she gasped, catching sight of the unkempt tramp in the mirror. Her tousled hair and sleepless eyes told the tale of last night's endeavors. *Look at you with your just-been-fucked hair. What the hell, Kira! How did you let this happen?* But not only had she let it happen, she had *wanted* it to happen. She took the shirt off and let it drop to the floor. She stepped into the large glass shower practically the size of her bedroom, with multiple heads and nozzles. She stood in the hot water, willing the steam to wash away her transgressions. The heat of the water on her skin only reminded her of his touch. Despite her best efforts, she couldn't deny that he had moved her, touched her in ways no other man had. She had given over to him completely and he had taken her body places she had never imagined it could go.

After her shower she dressed quickly, the smell of breakfast and coffee reviving her senses. She walked down the beautiful stairs to the large rustic kitchen. The wood floors and ceiling gave a warm feel to the space. Stark had lit a fire in the kitchen fireplace as well. He stood in sweats, shirtless, making eggs and bacon. Kira realized she was starving. She settled on a seat at the large bar to watch him work.

"Good morning there, sleeping beauty," he chuckled. "I was beginning to wonder if you were going to get up. Would you like some coffee?"

"Yes, thank you," Kira said appreciatively. The coffee smelled wonderful. She was shy, unsure what to say to this man she barely knew but who had been inside her. Seeing him there in the kitchen without his shirt brought memories of last night flooding back. She blushed, looking up at him.

He returned her stare with a kind and knowing smile. "That look is very disarming, Captain," he said, his expression changing.

"Now, Sergeant, I imagine it's quite difficult to disarm you. You *are* the weapons expert, after all," she said playfully, referring to his position as 18 Bravo.

"It's all about having the right tools for the job, ma'am," he answered, grinning wickedly. "Now eat your breakfast so we can go skiing, unless you would rather see my arsenal—which can definitely be arranged."

Yes, please! But there's only one tool I'm interested in. Kira reined in her wayward thoughts. "I would love to go skiing. And, Stark, about last night, I . . . " Kira stopped. She struggled to find the words but her pained expression spoke volumes.

"Kira, don't. Last night was amazing. I know we can't do this. It's crazy and it's wrong, but can we have fun, just this weekend? I want to know you. Please." His voice was tender and sincere, and she heard a trace of vulnerability that she couldn't ignore.

"You do realize that if we get caught our careers, everything we have worked for are over. Dishonorable discharge, Owen, that's nothing to scoff at," she said, shaking her head.

"No one from base is going to see us here. Just for this weekend. Please." His eyes were shining like a child.

Kira couldn't believe her own foolishness. "Ok, just this weekend. Let's go have fun. I have been dying to ski since I got to Colorado. But when we get back this is all over."

Stark nodded in agreement but Kira suspected he was just patronizing her.   They bundled up in their gear and Stark fit her into a pair of skis and boots from the ski room. Kira couldn't help but notice the skis seemed brand-new, though the design was a bit dated. "These are great. Do they belong to the people who live here?"

Stark's face fell. "They did. They were my sister's . . . " His voice trailed off as he fastened her lift ticket to her jacket. Quickly he changed the subject. "I had these lift tickets sent over this morning. We're right on the slope so we can ski from here."

Kira could tell this wasn't a subject he wanted to talk about but she couldn't help saying, "I would love to hear about her someday."

"I don't want to talk about it now. Come on, let's go ski before you melt in all that gear." He started out the door as he spoke. Kira followed him out and onto the snow. The crisp air felt glorious on her face and nose, and she felt a rush of adrenaline as they prepared their skis to head down the first run. Looking back at the house she was able to appreciate its full glory. The sun reflected off the massive windows. Twenty-eight inches of snow had fallen overnight and the thick blanket of powder gave a soft, billowy effect to the architecture. The wall facing them was mostly glass with a large stone chimney rising up out of the snow and climbing thirty feet into the air.

Kira loved to ski. She had done a lot of skiing with her father when she was younger and had worked as an instructor for children at a small resort during college. She laughed out loud thinking of how small that mountain seemed in comparison with the majesty of this one.

"What's so funny?" Stark asked.

"I was just thinking of how tiny the mountains I've skied on seem in comparison with all this. They have always seemed so big to me." She started onto the trail. Stark took the lead as they started down Cascade run. The powder was thick, but fast in places. She felt so alive. Watching him ski was incredible. Stark had obviously been skiing these mountains since he was a little boy. He was so graceful and fast he appeared to be flying. Kira did her best to keep up. She felt the rush of the wind, the weightless feeling of finding her rhythm, gliding effortlessly down the slope. The world was so quiet as she glided over the powder, everything silenced by the blanket of white. The bright bluebird sky provided a stunning contrast to the white world. Tall pines whipped by in a blur of green. Her senses went into overdrive. The adrenaline, the weightless feeling of flying, watching Stark glide down the mountain . . . she thought of him gliding over her. She pictured him handling her with such skill and control. She was truly in awe of him and wanted him more than ever. He whipped his skis sideways, causing a large spray of powder as they neared the bottom of the mountain. "Are you doing ok?" he asked, smiling. She could see he was truly enjoying himself. She hadn't seen such a carefree, boyish smile on his face since they had met. He looked so much younger and happy. Really happy. Kira couldn't help but smile back.

"I'm great!" she managed between breaths. It had been a long time since she had skied this hard and it was work. Amazing, exhilarating work. "This is incredible! The powder is perfect! What a kickass bluebird day!" She couldn't get over the perfection of the weather and conditions. The storm had isolated them. Out here it was like they were the only two people in the world. No need to worry about rules and past hurts. The only thing that mattered was each other.

"Let's head over to the Two Creeks lift so we can start on the way to the top of the mountain. I want you to see the top of the world." He grinned again.

"You lead, I'll follow." *I would follow you anywhere,* she thought, but this time the thought didn't scare her as it did before. And they were off into the snow, gliding in and out of each other's tracks like a high-speed but effortlessly graceful ballet. They found a rhythm together, forming a flawless pattern in the snow. When they reached the lift Stark was beaming. As they sat on the cold seat of the lift he turned to her. "Give me your poles. I have something to help warm you up." He took her poles and placed them carefully under his leg. She loved how cool his brown ski pants looked. *Damn, even in ski gear you are so fucking hot!* She grinned, thinking he looked like a Burton ad. She imagined lusting over him in a magazine. *But he's here with me. Tonight, you are mine.*

Stark took a small silver flask out of his Burton jacket. "Some fine Kentucky bourbon to warm you up." He smiled, took a swig, and passed her the flask. She was careful not to drop it with her gloved hands. Kira put the cold flask to her lips and took a long swallow. The strong liquid warmed first her mouth, then spread to her body. Like his touch, the whiskey ignited her. She took a second drink before handing it back.

"Is that Maker's Mark?"

"Yeah, I'm impressed. I wouldn't have taken you for a whiskey girl," he mused.

"Just what kind of girl were you expecting?" She wasn't sure if she should be insulted or flattered.

"I don't know, exactly. Girly, I suppose. I don't mean anything bad—just not many girls drink whiskey or ski like bats out of hell."

***

Stark struggled to find the right words. He was so impressed and surprised by her. How could he tell her she was blowing him away? Stark sat staring at her soft face, so tiny and pure, but tenacious. Her fiery spirit and drive excited him. His mind drifted to last night, the sight of that beautiful innocent face looking up at him as she took his cock in her hands. Licked the tip. He felt himself growing hard at the memory of those eyes looking up at him. When she'd taken him in her mouth, he had been so shocked he couldn't breathe. Indescribable pleasure had coursed through him. He knew he would take that memory, that fantasy, with him forever. No matter where in the world he was sent, that one moment would be with him always. Stark had been with many diverse women, some very experienced in many things, like Paige. But never had he encountered someone like Kira. He throbbed suddenly, needing her. *Get a hold of yourself, you idiot!* Stark came back to reality, took another swig of the whiskey, and passed it back to Kira. He watched her luscious lips fit around the flask longingly.

***

Stark put the flask away and handed Kira her poles as they approached the end of the lift. "When you get off, head to the right so we can take Adams to the Alpine Springs lift." Kira exited as told and followed Stark down another blue run, her confidence building as she followed him. The Alpine Springs lift was faster and shorter. Once on the lift, she had a chance to see the mountain and the valley below. As they rose higher and higher, she sat, astounded, by her surroundings.

"This is so gorgeous." She happily basked in the beauty of the landscape. From the lift she could see out over all of Aspen and Snowmass, the distant mountains surrounding the valley below. "This is truly amazing . . . " Her voice trailed off. She was at a loss for words to describe the incredible landscape below: the snow-covered Rocky Mountains, the green of the valley far below, the perfect bluebird sky, and the crisp white of the slope below. She turned to Stark, who was staring at her.

"Incredible, isn't it?" he said, smiling. "Are you ready? We're going to get off in a minute. Go to your left. There's one more lift to the top. Trust me, it's worth it." Kira did trust him. She couldn't explain why. She had spent so long not trusting anyone and had built these perfect walls to keep others out. Yet he seemed to break through without any effort at all. It was as if he alone knew the door and had a key.

The last lift proved very steep and frightening. Kira was typically quite brave, but this lift went straight freaking up. Stark sensed her anxiety and put his arm around her, pulling her close. Through the layers of clothing she could feel his warmth. Sitting this close, with his powerful arm around her, she felt safe, as if she belonged right here. Now the lift lost its threat; in fact, now it was too short. All too soon, they were at the top and he let go. "Time to get off. This is the top of the Cirque lift. Top of the world here at Snowmass," he instructed. They exited and veered to the left toward the Cirque Headwall. Kira's heart raced when she saw the Double Black Diamond marking the sign.

"Let's go over here and stop for a second." Stark skied out of the way of the lift and stopped at the edge of the mountain. He sat and Kira followed suit. "Sit beside me," he urged softly. "I want to keep this." He pulled a small red camera out of his jacket, a rugged little Pentax. Stark lay back and put his legs with their skis out in front of him. Kira followed. Leaning back Stark took a picture of their boots and skis, with the incredible backdrop of the valley and mountains beyond. "There, now we'll know where we've been." Turning toward her, he took several pictures of her there in the snow and, then putting his arm around her, took one final pic of their faces. "You ready for this?" he asked as he stood and put the camera away.

"Yes," Kira lied. *Ready as I'll ever be,* she thought, looking over the edge. Here it was. She was on both a literal cliff's edge, and perched on the edge of her hypothetical abyss. Now she was actually preparing to go right over the edge, in more ways than one. She watched Stark disappear over the steep cliff. The powder was so deep the only tracks she could see were his disappearing in the distance. *I am going to follow him,* she thought, aware she was not thinking just about skiing. She said a silent prayer and pushed herself over the edge before she had a chance to get scared.

Gravity overtook her and she began a mildly controlled descent. Letting the mountain guide her, she rode fluidly on her skis, trying to keep her legs parallel. The intensity of this run dwarfed anything she had ever skied. She was at once exhilarated and scared shitless. She fought through the fear and powered down the mountain. Stark was in sight again. Her confidence had risen to new heights when she hit the moguls. Kira was an experienced skier, but the powder had covered the moguls so much that they caught her by surprise. She hit the first one. "Ditch!" she yelled, surprised. Then another. "Ditch!" The third was much larger, sending her airborne. "Son of a bitch!" she yelled as she sailed through the air. The ground came up at her quickly. Kira hit the snow and began to roll. A cloud of powder surrounded her. Snow, sky, snow—she rolled a moderate distance before she finally came to a stop. She looked back up the mountain and had to laugh at the yard sale of equipment she'd left in her wake. Stark had stopped some distance below her and watched anxiously to see if she was all right. She made her way back up the steep slope and gathered her equipment. Thanks to the deep powder, the only thing hurt was her pride, and perhaps confidence. Embarrassed, she reassembled herself and skied down to Stark. "Are you ok?" he asked worriedly. "We can stop if you need to take a break."

"Stop treating me like a little girl" she yelled at him. "I'm a lot stronger that you think."

She took off down the mountain, taking the lead. Stark followed. He was a far superior skier but he lagged behind. The smile on his face told her he enjoyed the view.

They reached the bottom of the mountain without further incident. He watched her as if in awe. "Are you hungry?" He tried a new tactic to get her to rest for a moment. It had been a few hours since they had breakfast. "We could get a bite to eat for lunch, and maybe a beer while we are down here," he added hopefully.

Thankful for the time to catch her breath, Kira agreed. She followed Stark to an eclectic little place called The Stew Pot. "You're going to love this place he said. I've been coming here since I was little." He smiled brightly as he spoke.

Kira enjoyed seeing him so carefree, his usual quiet intensity replaced for a while by this happy young man. They put their skis up and he led her into the restaurant, taking her hand. Once inside, they found a table and he helped her out of her jacket. A blond man with a beard came bounding over to them. "Stark! Hell, brother, it's been a while. Good to see you!" the blond man said, as he hugged Stark and shook his hand.

"Fletch! It's good to see you. It *has* been a while," Stark responded warmly. "Fletcher, this is Kira Riley. Kira, this is my good friend Fletcher Duke. He and his wife Sol own the place. These are the best soups and sandwiches in all of Snowmass and Aspen combined." Stark patted Fletcher hard on the back.

"You won't find a better man than Owen Stark," Fletcher said to Kira. Kira smiled. She was beginning to believe that.

She and Stark sat in the comfortable little restaurant, chatting over the best beef stew and sandwiches she had ever tasted. "So the house is yours?" she asked cautiously when they were alone, trying to gauge his reaction.

"Yeah, my parents built it when I was little. We spent so much time here. It's a great place to be all year-round. My parents were friends with the original owners of this restaurant . . ." He trailed off, apparently thinking to some happier place and time.

"Why didn't you just say it was your house?" she asked carefully, not wanting to sound accusing.

"I didn't want to get into a lengthy explanation. The house is mine. It belonged to my family. End of story."

"Hey, ok," she said, resolving to ask him later. "So what are our plans for this afternoon?" Kira desperately wanted to know more about him. However, it seemed each answer only led to more questions.

They skied hard that afternoon and into the early evening. He led her back to the house, where they stripped their gear in the ski room. Stark hung their boots and gloves over the warmer.

Kira noted the lockers against the wall. The beautiful wooden structures had names engraved into each one. Dad, Mom, Owen, Maggie. Kira's heart broke for him. This house appeared to hold such wonderful memories for him, but they only seemed to hurt him now. She wondered about his parents: where were they? Why weren't they here for their son? What had happened to the happy family from the pictures in the great room?

Stark broke her train of thought. "There's enough time to get a shower and get cleaned up before dinner," he said, invitingly. He reached up and brushed a lock of hair out of her face. His fingers traced to the tip of her chin, lifting it to meet his lips. He started kissing her slowly and as she melted into him, she felt her desire grow with his forcefulness. His other hand reached up behind her head and neck, holding her to him. The passion in his kiss overtook her. "Come take a shower with me," he breathed into her ear. Kira followed him up the stairs obediently . . . eagerly.

Once in the bathroom, Stark flipped a switch to warm the marble floor and set the steam going in the shower. Kira tried not to glance in the mirror at the wretched-looking woman who had been skiing all day. She worked her matted hair out of its ponytail. Stark smiled at her. "You are so beautiful, Kira," he said softly. "I can't take my eyes off you." There she stood in his bathroom, wild chestnut hair spilling around her face. Her insecurity almost palpable, yet he made her feel she had nothing to be insecure about.

"I will never be able to resist you." He reached out to touch her. His strong hands stroked her delicate face and then down her neck. "You can't take a shower in this," he said, tugging on her Patagonia base layers.

"You're one to talk," she mocked playfully, indicating his remaining layers.

"That's an easy fix." He quickly pulled his shirt over his head, revealing his bare chest. Kira gasped. It had been dark last night. Here, in the bright lights of the bathroom, the details of his muscular chest were breathtaking. *Oh, how can you possibly look this hot after skiing all day? I want you more than I can even say. I want to feel your hands on me.*

Stark smiled. He always seemed to know exactly what she was thinking. He came to her. "Can I help you with this?" he asked, as he started to pull her shirt off over her head. Casting it aside, he traced his fingers down her arms to her chest and down the sides of her breasts. He trailed to the edge of her waistband. Kira was breathing harder.

He turned her so she faced the mirror, forcing her to watch him touch her and to see her own uncontrollable response. He paused at her waistband, holding tightly. She felt the hot breath of his lips on her neck and shoulder. His eyes looked up and met hers in the mirror. A wicked smile played across his lips as he instructed her to be still. She watched helplessly as he began kissing her neck again, feeling those soft, hot lips and dreaming of them in other places. His strong hands expertly undid her bra, freeing her breasts. Kira watched him trace his fingers down to her nipple, tweaking it hard. He cupped his hands around her breasts, holding her to him, and she could feel the power of his hardness pressing against her soft ass. She reached back to touch him, to feel that cock. But he stopped her.

"No, Kira." He grabbed her hands and placed them palms down on the counter. "Be still."

The forcefulness of his words subdued her; she was unable—unwilling—to move or disobey. Kira stood helpless as he slowly peeled off her pants and panties. She was completely naked now, standing fully exposed before the mirror. He growled approvingly, sliding his large rough hand over her ass. She felt the sting of his hand as he smacked it, hard. She let out a soft moan, feeling moisture between her legs. He spanked her again, but this time held tightly to her ass with one hand and clasped her breast with the other. He started kissing her neck intensely. The hand on her ass slid around, gaining moisture from her now soaking slit, and found her aching clit buried in a mass of brown curls. He began working it slowly, keeping his eyes locked on hers in the mirror. The steam from the shower filled the bathroom, surrounding them in a warm cloud. He continued caressing her breast, squeezing her nipple. She panted harder, losing herself in his touch, in his eyes. She no longer felt exposed, but rather, enveloped in him. She could barely hear the water over the pounding of her own heart. She was desperate to come. *I need it.* The hand on her clit picked up the pace. The other hand glided down and into her wanton pussy. He worked those immense fingers in and out of her, building her to the point

94

of no return. Her breath came in short gasps as the intensity built her into a frenzied state and she struggled to remain still. Her senses were overwhelmed by the heat of his body against hers. And he stopped. *No!*

"All right, dirty girl, let's get you in the shower and get you clean." He was in complete control and he knew it. "If I remember correctly, you have a little problem that I promised to help with." The playful look on his face was irresistible. He took off his pants, freeing that massive cock.

Kira was at a loss for words as he guided her into the steaming shower. Her body was rigid with the ache of her abandoned orgasm. The water felt incredible to her sore, ski-beaten body. She stood for a moment, closing her eyes, letting the hot water envelop her. At once, he was standing behind her, the heat from his hard body pressed into her. She exhaled slowly, reaching back to touch him. He held her with one arm and reached for body wash with the other. She was suddenly surrounded with the scents of honey and jasmine. The aroma was exquisite, and she relaxed fully as he massaged the cream into a lather on her skin. His strong hands caressed and kneaded her shoulders and back, and he worked seductively down to her ass and legs. He paused at her thighs, paying delicate attention to each one, his strong fingers gently stroking the edge of her sex with each pass. He stood to get more body wash.

"I wouldn't have taken you for the honey and jasmine kind of guy," Kira said jokingly, hoping that this wasn't left over from Paige, the phone-sex whore.

Stark laughed out loud. "Hey, it brings out my sensitive side. No, I bought this for you today while we were in Snowmass village. While you were milling around the market, I ran into an old friend who manages the Hotel Jerome. This is Perlier, Honey and White Jasmine. It came highly recommended. Do you like it?" he asked hopefully. His tone was playful, but breathy with need. She could tell he was restraining himself, savoring this time.

"Mmm, I love it. It smells wonderful!" she answered, inhaling the intoxicating aroma. "Thank you."

Stark began to lather her neck, slowly massaging, sensually working his way down her arms. His hands held hers for just a moment, tenderly. Kira laid her head back against his chest, savoring the moment. Then he let go of her hands, rubbing his fingers firmly back up her arms to her breasts. She arched as the rush of excitement coursed through her.

His hands encircled her breasts now, gently manipulating them with his strong hands. He found her nipples and the friction of his rough skin on her sensitive flesh was exhilarating. She gasped sharply, and ran her hands down his sides to his muscular thighs. His hands lingered on her breasts, working them more intently. Using the lather that covered them both by now, she grabbed his thick shaft and began to work him with her hands. He moaned deeply at her touch, his massaging becoming more intent. She slid her hands up and down his length, his legs and hips working with her rhythm, as she stroked his now-throbbing cock. He held her tightly in one arm now, the other sliding effortlessly across her skin to find the prize between her legs. Deft fingers manipulated into her waiting slit, exposing and massaging her clit. Small, slow circles of movement at first, then they became faster, and Kira gasped. *How am I so close already?* As her dormant orgasm came racing back to the surface, her breaths were short and rapid, her heart racing. His hardness pushed against her thighs, and his hips began to thrust, sliding easily through her thighs and buttocks. He didn't enter her, but the friction was driving her insane. She was desperate to feel him inside her now.

"Not yet," he said quietly as if feeling her need. "We have a little problem to take care of remember." He took out a sliver-plated razor from a stand on the ledge. Kira stood almost trembling, watching his hands rinse the shiny blade under the steaming water. "I'll need you to be very still," he commanded quietly.

Kira was afraid to move. She had never trusted anyone this much. How could she let someone she barely knew take a razor blade to her delicate regions? She watched the blade coming closer and then delicately touch her skin. She realized one false move and she could wind up sans clitoris. *Holy hell what have I gotten myself into!*

"Trust me Kira, I will never hurt you." His voice soothed and transfixed her. She realized she had been holding her breath as the first pass of the razor crossed her skin. ok, no pain, no bleeding. "Relax Kira, I will take good care of you if you will let me. Let me worship every sweet curve." His voice deep, commanding yet strangely hypnotic permeated her every pore. Kira felt her muscles slowly soften and relax as if even her tension followed his commands. Her body seemed to obey before her mind could follow. Each delicate pass of the razor uncovered fresh new skin, she felt as if he was opening her up to him. Parts of her no one else had seen were now exposed and open. Yet her fear and hesitation melted away and flowed effortlessly down the drain with the remnants of hair. She had never dreamed shaving could be so sensual. The warm caress of his hands and the cold steel of the blade tortured her body with conflicting emotions.

"Let's get rid of this soap, shall we?" Stark grinned as he took one of the removable showerheads and began gently rinsing her from top to bottom. As he approached her sex, a wicked smile slid across his face.

Oh, my! The stream of warm water directly on her most sensitive flesh was overwhelming. She panted, barely able to catch her breath. He changed the water stream to pulse, holding the showerhead firmly in place. He pinned her legs apart with his, holding her there, vulnerable to the effects of the spray. The warm caress of the water on her newly exposed skin, coupled with the pulsing sensation of the spray, sent her into a frenzied state. He dropped to his knees before her; holding her hips in his hands, and began a slow, sensual assault with his mouth. His hot breath, that tongue, found its way into her. The coarseness of his tongue glided slowly over her swollen clit, sending an electrifying wave through her entire body. Barely able to stand, she struggled to breathe. Looking down, she was in awe at the sight of his thick muscular back and arms, those powerful arms wrapped around her legs. He held her in place, sucking, licking, fucking her with his tongue. Her hands went instinctively to his thick hair and she held on tightly, throwing her head back. Unable to stand any more, her body went rigid and she cried out loudly, coming hard and falling into his waiting arms.

***

Stark smiled at the vision he held close to him. "You're so responsive, Kira! I love making you come like that." His voice was content and triumphant. He stood, holding her steady for a moment. Kira rested against his firm body. Stark could feel the softness of her skin. She seemed so fragile in his large arms. She tilted her head up, looking at him with those eyes. He knew he was powerless to her. He wanted her, needed her, in a way he never had with any woman before. He let his hand trail gently from her neck down her shoulder, then her arm. He throbbed and ached to be inside her. He had waited, had wanted, to hear her, to feel her come. Now he needed to be inside her.

He reached down, finding her soaking slit and worked his fingers inside. Her soft moan encouraged him to further his entrance. "I'm going to fuck you from behind. Hold onto the ledge." Kira obeyed. Using his feet, he spread her legs wide once more. He worked her with his fingers in small circular motions, around and around, penetrating farther until she was ready. He smacked her ass. His eyes flashed wild, ardent desire overtaking him like an animal. He worked his thick expanse into her tight opening and, holding tight to her hips, he began moving in and out with purpose.

Kira struggled to hold the ledge. He was entirely in her now, stretching her, filling her completely. Then he withdrew and the void was unbearable. With each penetration, he claimed her fully. The power and momentum built and she was taken to a new place as the entire world fell away. The driving force between her legs consumed her. His power pushed her to a frenzied state once more. She gripped the wet ledge more tightly; he lifted her off the ground with each thrust. Water cascaded down around them. His moaning was deep and guttural now. She felt him tighten his grip. *He's so close.* His ragged state fueled her. She was overtaken by his relentless assault and surrendered into a shattering orgasm. Her release sent spasms around his thick cock, and instantly his body went rigid as his fervent need was satisfied. He contracted and shuddered, coming apart inside her. Leaning back against the wall, he held her to him.

"I guess we'd better get moving before we miss dinner entirely," Stark said., willing himself to move. He felt complete in this moment and hated to break away from it. "Of course, I *have* already eaten," he added playfully as he finished washing and stepped out of the shower.

"Mmm, I guess you have," she responded, smiling. Her eyes were bright. The whole world was alive and seemed to be spinning slightly. Kira hurried to finish her shower and get ready. When she stepped into the bedroom Stark had already gone downstairs. *ok, what do I have to wear?* Kira cursed herself for not taking time to pack more sexy clothing, but how could she have known how this weekend would turn out. Frantically, she dug through her bag. She finally decided on her new slate-gray Prada sweater. It had been her treat to herself for actually having a paying job in medicine. She loved the way it felt and hoped Stark would like it, too. She found her favorite Ralph Lauren jeans. She'd had these for several years, but they had that timeless worn look that was cool and sexy without trying. Kira loved these jeans. She had found them in a thrift shop while she was an undergrad. While to everyone else, they looked like designer jeans, to her they were as comfortable as her favorite sweats. As she sat on the bed to fasten her tall boots, her mind wandered to the colossal mistake that she and Stark were making. *What am I doing? By the time we go back I have to find the strength to end this. There's a reason he doesn't have a steady girlfriend. There is a reason I can't get involved with* anyone *here.* Kira's heart ached at the thought, which made her even more determined to end this nonsense before it went any further. She took the time to dry her hair and put on the slightest bit of makeup. *Who are you kidding?* She laughed at herself, as she stood looking in the mirror. Her cheeks heated at the memory of him taking her in this very spot. *How will I ever walk away?*

***

Stark went downstairs to let Kira finish getting ready. He knew staying up there would not end with going out to dinner. Sitting and watching her would prove much too tempting for him to resist. He shook his head to clear his wicked thoughts and reached for the phone.

"Rob McCormick, please. Tell him it's Owen Stark." Stark waited patiently for the reluctant maître d' to find his old friend.

"Owen Stark, is that really you?" the familiar voice asked. "How the hell have you been?"

"Really well, the last few days anyway," Stark answered, smiling. "How have you been? I heard you're the big chef in town now."

"Where are you? Are you in town?" his friend asked hopefully.

"Yeah, we got in last night. Did some skiing today. We were thinking of stopping in to see you for dinner."

"Looking forward to it. I'll have a table ready. It's not like you to call just for dinner. This a special occasion or what?" Rob asked.

"Or what. I've got someone I'd like you to meet. We'll be there around eight thirty. See you then, man." Stark hung up before his old friend could press for more information and looked up in time to see Kira coming down the steps. His breath caught for a moment. He could hardly believe the vision before him was actually real and his. He smiled up at her like a kid who had just gotten everything he wished for on Christmas, and Kira beamed back at him.

**

Holy shit! she thought as she descended the stairs, looking at the striking specimen of a man waiting for her.

He was wearing dark jeans that accentuated his muscular thighs. He had on an olive Henley that hugged his chest, just enough to remind her of what lay beneath, and a blazer. He looked rugged and sexy as hell. *Soldier sex god for sure!* Kira giggled and bit her lip, trying to keep her wicked thoughts in check long enough to have dinner.

"You look good enough to eat," Stark said playfully, smacking her on the ass as she walked past him.

"I thought you got enough of that earlier," she said, feigning disapproval.

"I'll never get enough of you," he growled wickedly, "but we do have a reservation for dinner if you're ready. I'll get your coat." Stark helped Kira with her coat and led her out to the warming truck. He walked close to her, resting his hand at the small of her back. When they reached the truck, he stepped ahead quickly to open her door.

"Aren't you the gentleman," she mocked, grinning as she stepped up. Stark cupped her ass in his hand giving her a boost into the truck.

"Just making sure you don't fall," he said innocently.

Before they pulled out he started his iPod. She instantly liked the music, but wasn't sure she was familiar with the group. "Who is this?" The sound was a mix of folk or bluegrass, but the group sounded possibly English.

"Mumford and Sons. I had the chance to see them in New Zealand. They're great."

Kira sat back, watching the snowdrifts and distant mountains out the window. She let the sweet melody take her, the soft guitar and mandolin, a man singing of past ghosts being driven away by a new hope. She stared out at the snow and wondered if there could be hope for them.

"Hey, we're here. This is The Little Nell. You're going to love Montagna." He had that eager boyish grin on his face again and Kira couldn't help but smile.

The Little Nell was a breathtaking village. There were homes and a hotel, but all the structures were reminiscent of an eclectic German village. It was exactly what she had pictured when she thought of Aspen. The Montagna was busy, a definite hot spot for tourists and locals alike. They were greeted immediately. Stark gave his name and the maître d' lit up.

"Right this way, sir. Mr. McCormick has a special table reserved for you," he gushed as he led them through the study, past a roaring fire in the main dining area. They arrived at an intimate corner table by a large window. He pulled out a chair for Kira by the window with a perfect view of the mountains and the fireplace. Stark chose to sit in the corner beside Kira, rather than across from her. Like her father, Stark had to sit where he could see the perimeter fully. *Always on alert*, she thought sadly. She remembered being in awe of that trait when she was younger. But in the end, it hadn't mattered. He had died anyway.

Stark ordered a bottle of wine. "The wine list here is extensive," he said, turning to her after the waiter had left them. "The food is incredible. Rob does an exquisite job. I think you will really like this place." They were just starting to look at the menu when a man wearing chef's attire came bounding over to the table. He was tall and very handsome. Stark stood to greet his friend, shaking hands and slapping each other hard on the back.

"Good to see you!" Rob said emphatically. "How long has it been?"

"Too long. Rob, I would like you to meet my girlfriend, Kira. Kira this is Rob McCormick, the best chef in Aspen. Hell, he's the best chef in Colorado."

Girlfriend! Kira's heart raced. She blushed and managed a polite hello. *Girlfriend.* Her stomach was suddenly in knots. Yes, they had just spent the last day and a half fucking each other silly, but they couldn't officially date. *He's lost his mind.* But Kira liked the way it sounded. *Owen Stark's girlfriend. Oh yes, I like that.* Suddenly she realized just how much she wanted it to be true.

Chapter 6

Kira sat glued to her seat, speechless as the truck drove noiselessly over the snow. The silence in the truck was deafening. *How could I have been so insensitive? Why did I have to push him for information there? Dinner was going so perfectly. Damn it!* Kira's mind raced back to the exquisite dinner and the perfect evening it had started out to be. Stark had called her his girlfriend. She had been elated. The two men, obviously enjoying their reunion, sauntered down memory lane. They talked about growing up, old flames, their parents, and then Maggie. Kira's interest had been piqued immediately, as she was dying to know more about his sister and what had happened to the beautiful family from the pictures. The appetizers had arrived, a seafood ceviche that was a composite of bright colors and smelled so fresh and tangy that Kira had been, for an instant, distracted from her quest. The beet, fennel, and citrus salad was fresh as well, the cilantro awakening but not overpowering. As they savored the delicious flavors, Kira had plotted how to move forward.

"Tell me about her, your sister. What was she like?" Kira started cautiously.

At first, Stark had been reluctant, again not wanting to talk about his past, but Kira was persistent. "I can tell you loved her very much . . . What was she like?" Kira followed. She was ready to find out. "Please, tell me about her."

Stark had looked away for a long time into the darkness at the falling snow. He had stopped eating and seemed to be a million miles away. "She was beautiful," he began softly. "Not just on the outside, although she brightened up a room the moment she entered it. She was so bubbly and joyful. She was like that from a tiny baby." Stark put his hand up to his chin and closed his eyes for a moment. "I was seven when she was born. I remember when they first brought her home. I wasn't jealous of her. No, I loved her. I knew I would do anything to protect her always. She was the shining light in our house."

They had been interrupted by waitstaff clearing the appetizers, which Stark had ceased to eat. Kira briefly had the clarity of mind to let it go so they could enjoy their meal and time together. However, Stark's next words were her undoing and she had to know more. The staff retreated, leaving a new course of a rich and satisfying gnocchi with a silky mushroom and ham sauce, and bay scallops with microgreens, possibly the highlight of the meal.

"She was just thirteen when it happened. So happy, so vibrant; my Maggie was amazing. I was so proud of her. It had started as one of the happiest days of my life, and then they were gone." Stark's voice was hollow now.

Gone? Who is gone? Maggie, but who else?
Questions raced through Kira's mind. She longed to know more about Stark. He already meant more to her than she could grasp, but he was so distant at times. It was as if there was this great chasm between them, a vast space of past hurt that they both held on to.

Stark looked up from his untouched plate. His eyes betrayed the severity of emotion he struggled to contain. At once Kira was afraid she had pried too far. Perhaps this was not the time or the place, but it was too late. Stark had gone to some horrible place and there was no taking it back now.

"I was in college at the time. A sophomore," he began slowly. "Mom and Maggie had come to visit me at school. It was to celebrate her thirteenth birthday. She and Mom flew out for the week. Mags and I had been so close when I lived at home. Even though she was seven years younger, we spent a lot of time together. She came to all my games, I went to all her meets, I picked her up from practice. I was the guy she looked up to. I kept her safe. Being home with my family that last summer was the happiest time of my life." Stark's voice faded but he was still deep in thought.

He picked at his food and continued. "That week we had gone to the Fine Arts Museum, the Contemporary Arts Museum, and the Boston Symphony Orchestra. She could play piano like an angel. I took her to their open rehearsals so they could hear her play. Mom and Dad hoped that she would go to Juilliard when she was older and her tutors had high hopes that she would make it."

He stopped talking for a moment. The anguish in his face broke Kira's heart. She knew that some things were just too painful to relive. She was so sorry for pushing him to talk, and longed to wrap him up in her arms and tell him all would be ok, but she knew it wouldn't. His sister was gone. Something terrible had happened to the happy family from the pictures, something irretrievable, something that had left this beautiful man broken. Kira sat in dread as he continued talking.

"The last day of their visit was sunny, a perfect afternoon. We went to Boston Common, which was very close to my apartment. We walked along with the warm September sun on our faces, and I listened while she talked about her school and her friends. She giggled as she told me about the boy she was crushing on. I can't remember his name; it's been so long. The soft melody of her voice ebbed and flowed with her excitement. She was so full of life . . .

"We were making our way around the water's edge when suddenly she was toppled by a pile of speckled fur. I remember her on the ground, looking up at me, smiling as this dog licked her face. She was laughing. The owner of the dog ran over and apologized, and told us the dog's name was Teddy. Mags wasn't hurt. She ruffled his fur and spoke to him. Her laugh showed how much she liked the dog. She wanted one badly but Mom and Dad weren't pet people, and she looked up at me with that face, the face I could never say no to. I asked the owner what kind of dog it was. He told me an Australian Shepherd. Seeing Mags' face, I called that very moment, and found a breeder back home in San Francisco, and ordered one for her birthday present. She squealed and cried, hugging me."

Stark paused for a long drink of his wine. "We went back after that to pick up Mom and spent that evening together watching movies. Mom told stories about when we were little and we took turns blaming each other for the mischief we had gotten into. Early the next morning, I took my girls to the airport. It had been a perfect week. I stayed with them through Logan airport to the checkpoints for security. I held them tightly and told them good-bye, told them to be safe. Maggie had a gleam in her eye as she stood there in her pink pea coat and jeans. I don't know why that image is so burned into my head. Her dark brown hair spilled under this silly gray beret she insisted on wearing because it matched the gray boots Mom bought her. It was way too warm for September. But she didn't care. That's just how she was." He gave a weak chuckle.

"She had three weeks to break the news of the puppy to Mom and Dad. She had her work cut out for her, but I had her back. I always had her back." Stark stopped talking. He was suffering, as if he was living it all over again. When he spoke again, this time his voice was so broken Kira could feel his torment. "I watched their plane take off. I just watched them go. The plane never made it to San Francisco. That was the last time I saw my mother or my Mags. They were gone . . . they were all gone." His voice trailed off into an excruciating silence that lasted the rest of dinner.

Kira struggled to say something. *How can I say I am sorry? I am sorry you lost everything and everyone important in your life.* Her curiosity seemed so petty and shallow now. She rode along beside him, the great chasm of darkness and silence all encompassing. She understood his reluctance to speak of it now. Her heart ached for that lost and broken young man. After what seemed like an eternity they arrived back at the house. Stark was still so quiet and she wanted to give him some space.

"I'm going to go change," she said hesitantly.

Stark nodded his acknowledgment but didn't answer. She watched him walk through the empty house. The empty house that had once held his blissful family. As he walked away, she could almost hear Maggie bounding down the stairs after him, saying, "Owen, wait for me!" But now there was only silence. She didn't know where his father was, or what had happened to the rest of Stark's once-perfect life. But she knew for certain that part of him had died. He was lost, too. As he had said, they were *all* gone.

Kira shut the bathroom door and let the tears fall. She cried for Stark and for his family. She hated that she had pushed him to talk about all this. She had wanted to know so badly and now she did, but at what cost? This house had to be painful for him and yet it held the only remaining sense of family he had left. Kira had an overwhelming desire to go to him, hold him. She finished in the bathroom and ran down the stairs, but the house was empty. She looked all over the first floor but he wasn't there. The flicker of light from the large deck and patio caught her eye. She looked out the large window. By the light of the fire, she could see Stark's wrecked expression. He looked so alone, truly and utterly alone.

She shrugged on one of his large parkas and her boots. She made her way through the snow to where he stood staring into the fire. Though she didn't have words to say, she stood beside him, wrapped her small arms around his large one and held on tightly. After a moment he wrapped his arms around her and held her to him.

"You're not alone anymore," she whispered. "I'm here. I'm not going anywhere."

His eyes met hers. She could see his tear-stained face in the firelight. He pulled her closer and began to kiss her tenderly. The softness became more forceful as the intensity of his pent up emotions poured through him. All the hurt and fear and anger and loss that had been with him for such a long time seemed to pour out of him in that kiss. Stark held on to her like a lifeline. He held her small face in his hands as he kissed her deeply, and picked her up, oversized coat and all, carrying her back toward the house.

Kira felt him peel off her coat with one hand while holding her with the other arm. His strength was a little unnerving. He left the coat in a heap on the floor as they crossed the great room, still kissing her hard, his lips salty with tears. She had her arms around his neck, her hands in his thick hair. As they mounted the stairs, deft fingers discarded her sweater and bra. They crossed the landing with broad steps, his lips fully claiming hers. At once they were in his room.

He dropped her onto the bed and attacked her jeans with purpose. Her need for him, to be filled with him was primal; she was wrecked with the raw emotion of his loss, and her need to heal it for him. Freeing her of her jeans, he stood over her. She surrendered willingly as he grabbed her ankles and pulled her toward the end of the bed, toward him. He pushed her legs apart and fell against her. The rough sensation of his jeans stung as they were pressed into her flesh by his immense cock. She winced at the mix of pleasure and pain. He took her wrists and held them at her sides, buried his face in her ample breasts. She gasped, feeling hot lips clasped around her nipple, sucking it in harshly. He was grinding into her, his jeans barely restraining his desire now. She needed him to be inside her.

He let go of her hands as he slid his hand behind her head, tilting it to his kiss. Once more his ardent mouth was on hers. With her hands free, she found his jeans and went to work. Kira was so distraught, she struggled with the buttons. Suddenly she felt the hot sensation of his thickness fall into her hand, heavy and hard, finally free. *I want it inside me.* She began stroking him, pulling hard, hearing him growl loudly. He slid his strong hand between her legs. Whether he read her desire or if his own took control, Kira will never know. His face changed as his hands found her wetness. He took his cock from her grasp and buried it in her at once.

Kira screamed his name, as he began a relentless onslaught on her aching pussy. He was not tender or gentle this time. No, he was fucking her hard, fucking the pain away. She was lying on her back at the edge of the bed. He stood between her legs, holding tightly to her right thigh, as her leg wrapped around him. His right hand held leverage on her left hip, pulling her hard to him with each forceful thrust. She wasn't hurt, but surrendered completely to his might. She heard her own voice as if it were far away, calling, crying out his name. She arched her back and hips to meet him, and her body spasmed hard as she began to come. But he didn't stop. He held her there, his rhythm enduring, stretching her orgasm, forcing her willingly into a shameless abandon. He slammed into her, holding her there as they exploded together. His entire body tensed, his grip tightened, and then he released—his body, his hurt, his past. He fell onto her, spent. Still shuddering from the intensity, Kira wrapped her arms around him and held him to her.

"I'm here," she whispered. "I promise, Owen. I'm not going anywhere." As she spoke the words Kira knew it was true. No matter how much she had told herself she would not get involved, that she wouldn't fall for a soldier, there was no turning back. As she drifted off to sleep she knew there was no place she would rather be.

***

"Owen, you silly goose!" Maggie's voice called to him from down the hall. Happily, she bounced into the kitchen where he was making coffee. How she was able to be this chipper at six in the morning he would never know. "Do you like it?" she asked, twirling to show off her new matching beret and boots. "Mom got them for me

yesterday! I just love them! Mah says I'm a Hah-vahd chick," she said in her best Boston accent.

Stark shook his head and laughed. "Don't you think it's a bit warm for that get-up?"

Maggie batted her sparkling cobalt eyes at her big brother. "Not for me! Now, where's my pink pea coat?" Maggie set off back down the hallway in search of the hot pink Burberry coat he'd bought her for her birthday. Stark rolled his eyes and watched her prance back down the hall. He knew his parents were going to flip when they found out about the puppy. He and Maggie had conspired in a plan to win them over.

"What are you smiling so slyly about?" his mother asked as she glided into the kitchen. Caroline Stark was effortlessly graceful. Her soft voice flowed through the kitchen, warming him.

Owen looked up. "Hey, Mom. Nothing—just glad you girls came to see me. I missed you guys."

"Yeah, yeah. I know you gave up some things with your friends this week to entertain us. I appreciate that, Owen. Maggie does too," she finished, smiling . . . that smile.

120

Suddenly they were at the airport, walking quickly, hustling down to the checkpoint for security. As they rushed, Stark turned to help his sister with her bag and ran into a man approaching the same checkpoint. The man staggered back slightly and almost dropped his bag. The dark-haired man in the blue shirt exchanged glances with his younger companion.

"I'm sorry," Stark said as the man steadied himself. The man nodded in his direction but did not speak. Stark stared into his eyes. Cold death burned in those soulless eyes. The hair on the back of Stark's neck stood up. Cold sweat on his palms, heart racing, he lunged after the man with all his rage and a decade of painful regret. But as always, the evil coward dissipated, leaving Stark alone in his apartment, watching the horror unfold on his television. His mother and sister were gone. He watched them go, watched them walking away with that man. Those men who would take everything and vanish like cowards.

Stark awoke sitting bolt upright in bed, his heart racing still. His fists were clenched tightly and a sheen of sweat covered his still naked body. He willed himself to calm down. Slowly, he got his bearings. He hadn't had that dream for a while. Talking about it tonight had brought back so many sleeping demons. What he wouldn't have given to have stopped it. He had been so close and he'd just let them walk away.

He remembered Kira's words. All was dark except the silvery light streaming in from the moon, Kira's sleeping face illuminated by the soft glow. He sat holding her, watching her sleep. Her soft features seemed so small and delicate as he traced his hand across her cheek and lips. Her warmth stirred him. He hadn't felt this alive for ten years. He moved his fingers down her arm and laid his hand over her tiny one. Something about her had captivated him from the moment he had first seen her. Now, here she was, sleeping so soundly in his arms. She was his completely. The darkness of his past, all the pain, seemed further away somehow. Silently, he vowed to be there for her, and to wait as long as it took for her to feel the same way. He knew that when the weekend was over, he would have to let her go. They would go back to their lives, but he would never really let her go—just give her room and wait.

Chapter 7

Crash!

Stark was jolted awake by a clattering explosion in the kitchen. He instantly realized Kira was nowhere to be seen. Heart pounding, he jumped out of bed and ran down the steps two at time in the direction of the commotion. When he burst into the kitchen he was met with the appearance of a startled and open-mouthed Kira. She stood there in his T-shirt, surrounded by a sea of pots and pans that had just fallen from the rack overhead. She was unable to speak, standing there jaw hanging quite near the floor and her cheeks turning a deep crimson.

Holy fuck! Kira thought as she basked in the glory of the completely naked Sergeant Sex God himself. In his haste, Stark hadn't bothered to put on any clothes. All his magnificence was standing alert and at attention. "I surrender, I surrender," Kira teased. "Don't point that thing at me!" She threw up her hands in mock surrender.

Stark laughed. "Looks like you're having enough trouble on your own. What happened in here?" he asked, looking at his expensive pots and pans scattered across the kitchen floor. "Are you hurt? Did any of them hit you?"

"I'm sorry, Owen. I wanted to make you breakfast and I was trying to reach that pan," she said, indicating the single frying pan still hanging on the disheveled rack. An overturned chair lay as evidence to her acrobatic intention. Stark laughed as he reached up and easily retrieved it. As he leaned past Kira, his hard, naked flesh pressed against her. She watched his exposed muscles flex as he moved. Kira shivered and exhaled a slow, heady breath. She was no longer thinking of breakfast. "Thank you," she breathed. She couldn't take her eyes off him. He was standing there fully naked: his tight body was incredibly sculpted, and his dark, tousled hair suited him well. The perfect V of his abdomen drew her attention down toward the enormous hard-on between his legs. Kira gasped lightly and blushed deeper still.

"At your service," he said with a wicked smile as he handed her the pan, his fingers brushing hers. "Now, is there anything else I can do for you, or should I head back upstairs to get dressed?" His eyes were locked on hers. The searing intensity of his stare sent a surge of arousal through her.

124

Kira's eyes lit up. "Hmm . . . service . . ." she said slowly. Kira reached out and took him firmly in her hand. She was surprised by how hard he was. She looked up at him, smiling. Before he realized what was happening, she dropped to her knees before him. A long, slow moan escaped his lips as she took him into her mouth.

***

"Fuck woman!" He loved when she took control. The soft, warm sensation of her mouth, those glorious lips surrounding his cock, were electrifying, causing him to lean forward and brace himself on the counter.

He grasped the back of her hair with his hand, as she sucked gently on the tip of his massive cock, toying with him. With a wicked look in her eyes, she swirled her tongue around the tip and took him in again. The slow, tortuous waltz caused him to moan and push eagerly on the back of her head. "Patience," she whispered softly, pouting up at him. She was enjoying playing with him. She took him in again, deeper this time, sucking harder as she withdrew.

He began to move in rhythm with her, his moans becoming lower, more intense. "Yeah, baby," Stark growled. "Suck that cock." He couldn't take his eyes off hers. Soft flowing curls of chestnut hair framed her face and fell around him. Unable to resist, he tightened his grip on her silky locks, pulling her deeper on to his cock as he spoke.

His words seemed to . She took him as deeply as his thick cock would go. His hands tightened in her hair as he fervently fucked her mouth. Suddenly he stopped. He picked her up and kissed her hard on the mouth. Holding her to him tightly, with one swipe he cleared the counter with the other hand. A large sack of flour unfortunate enough to be in his way fell to the floor and exploded in a cloud of white. He grabbed the front of her T-shirt and pulled it up over her head, pinning her arms and exposing her breasts. He stared at her with a wild smirk.

"My turn," Stark sneered, as he picked her up and set her down firmly on the counter.

Kira squealed as the cold granite hit her naked ass. He pulled her legs apart and held them firmly in place. Without breaking eye contact, he knelt in front of her and blew gently on her sex, setting her on fire. She squirmed, but he tightened his grip. He looked up at her, his mischievous eyes dancing. Opening his mouth again, he slowly trailed his tongue up from her slit to her now yearning clit. She squealed again as he bit gently, panting with anticipation. He growled into her, making enticing sounds as he sucked gently. She moaned and grabbed his hair with her hands. He took one final tantalizing lick and stopped, standing up. He was so close, she could feel the pressure of his powerful erection. He paused to gently savor each breast before kissing her wildly. She tasted herself on his lips, and the intimacy of this was so erotic she became lost in his kiss. Suddenly his cock invaded her. With a forceful thrust, he entered her completely.

"Oh God, Owen!" Kira screamed. Hearing her scream his name only intensified the fury building in him. She was warm and tight. Stark grabbed her ass violently as he entered her again and again. In this moment there was nothing on earth but her; all else faded away. He became lost in the sounds of her moans and cries. The incredible softness of her skin felt otherworldly against his rough, weathered hands. The image of her restrained like this in his shirt and his arms was all his wild thoughts and desires brought to life. Stark closed his eyes, picturing her as he has imagined her since the day they'd met.

Kira's hands were still pinned to her sides by the shirt, Stark holding her up in his strong arms. As he moved in and out of her, the incredible friction of his rhythm electrified her erogenous flesh. She wriggled to move away a bit, but she was pinned beneath him on the counter. Kira threw her head back in ecstasy, just in time to see a pair of red Louboutin boots tapping on the wooden step leading into the kitchen. *What the fuck?*

"Well, well. Owen, isn't this *quite* the cooking catastrophe! Looks like you got a little whore in your pancakes." The smooth voice dripped with sarcasm. The bright red boots were attached to a pair of long shapely legs in Monique pants.

Kira's eyes rose, along with her nausea, up those legs to a sparkling gray sweater and a mink Gorsuch coat (which Kira knew cost more than her car). Atop of all this couture was a strikingly beautiful, pouty face surrounded by flowing blond hair. Kira lay frozen in the mess of flour and pans, for a moment too paralyzed to move. Stark was still *in* her.

"What the fuck are you doing here, Simone?" Stark yelled, as he helped Kira straighten up and put her shirt on right. "Get out of my house. You have no business being here. Get the fuck out!" Stark stood so that the kitchen island shielded his lower half from full view.

"Oh, Owen," Simone started softly, as she carefully made her way into the kitchen. The honeyed tone in her voice was betrayed by the look of disgust on her face. "Darling, I know you have needs. Wild oats and all, but seriously, when you're done playing G.I. Joe and slumming with the help, you need to come back to the real world and start considering your future. Your father wants to talk with you."

"Stop!" he shouted, just as she started toward the island. Stark's voice had changed, his tone dark and angry. "Go into the living room, Simone, and wait there."

Simone froze, a wry smile crossed her lips like a cat that knew just how far it could go. As she walked away, she said, "Darling, the G.I. Joe thing has been good for you. You keep looking that glorious, and I'll forgive you for leaving me at the altar."

"Come on," Stark said to the still shell-shocked Kira. They climbed the back staircase in silence. Kira's mind was racing. *Who the fuck is that* Vogue *bitch? Left her at the altar? They were engaged? God, she looks like a perfect fucking Barbie doll in a ten thousand dollar outfit. FUCK!* Kira went into the bathroom and slammed the door behind her. As she caught a glimpse in the mirror of the ragged, flour-covered girl with stringy unkempt hair, she began to cry.

"Kira, please." Stark stood for a moment outside the door. She could hear him breathing but he didn't say anything. After a moment, she heard him throw on some jeans and a shirt and head back downstairs.

Simone's words played over in Kira's mind. Her embarrassment boiled inside her. *What a way to meet his fucking flawless ex-girlfriend!* How could she ever compete with someone like that? Aside from the fact that she was a real bitch, Princess Barbie looked like every man's dream girl. *Someone he had been engaged to!* Kira realized she didn't fit in Stark's life. *Who is he anyway?* Kira slumped against the wall of the shower. She felt like she was going to throw up. How could she have been so stupid? What did she even know about him? She turned on the shower. Her hands trembled as she washed the remnants of flour and their interrupted morning down the drain.

***

Stark ran his fingers through his hair in frustration as he descended the stairs. He found Simone sitting casually in the great room. As he walked through the hall by the kitchen he caught a glimpse of the catastrophic mess. A slight smile crossed his lips. *Breakfast, it's the best meal of the day!*

"What are you doing here, Simone? And what does this have to do with my father?" His tone was flat, keeping his fury contained.

"I missed you, too," she said in mock offense. "Honestly, Owen, I don't even know what you see in this one. When are you going to outgrow this angry GI thing and come home? We aren't getting any younger."

"Simone, I'm serious. You had better have a good reason for barging in here like this." His tone held a fierce warning. "What are you doing here?"

"Your dad is sick, Owen. He sent me to talk to you. You never return his calls. He's so sorry for the way things turned out. I tried the base and they said you were gone on leave. I know you, Owen—this is the one place you would come."

Stark's anger began to dissipate. "You could have knocked or rang the bell. Hell, you could have picked up the phone."

"I'm sorry. Please don't be mad. On the way up I started remembering how we used to meet up here. I don't know . . . I saw your truck and it brought back memories. Remember all those weekends we snuck up here? I wanted to slip in and surprise you. Well, surprise! I never expected to find you like that with some slut." Nostalgia trailed off into sadness.

"She's not a slut! She's my girlfriend. Damn it, Simone! I . . . I really care about her. You and I have been over for a very long time. I'm perfectly capable of calling my dad on my own. I don't need you or anyone else to help me. If that's all you came for, then it's time for you to go." He stood to show her out.

"Your enlistment is up in six months. Please reconsider coming home," she purred as she followed him to the door. "Your dad needs you. I need you. I'm sorry I wasn't more supportive when your mom and Maggie died. I loved them, too. I made some bad choices but so did you. How long are you going to hold that over my head?"

"Just go, Simone, and tell Dad I'll call him when I'm ready. This doesn't change anything. The army is my life. You know that." Stark held the door open for her to go.

Simone leaned in, grazing his cheek with her fingers. "Owen darling, you know I'll always love you. Finish up with all this nonsense and come home." She finished by kissing him softly on the lips and spun around with a gleeful smile, knowing Kira had been standing at the top of the stairs taking in the whole devastating scene.

***

Simone's cell rang just as her Audi's engine sprang to life. "Hello," she barked. "Yes, I've been to see him. No. No, I'm afraid it's worse than we thought. Not just another fling. I think this one's going to be trouble." She hung up her cell and tossed it into the passenger seat. As she raced away, her pouty lips set into a determined line. Trouble was her specialty.

Chapter 8

Stark heard movement at the top of the stairs. He looked up to find a wide-eyed Kira staring down at him. The horrified look on her face spoke volumes. "Kira, wait!" he pleaded as she turned and walked away from view. Stark bounded up the stairs. "Please Kira, don't walk away," he pleaded. He crested the stairs in time to see the door shut. Panic set in. He raced across the landing and threw open the door. Kira was stuffing her clothes in her bag. "What are you doing?" His voice was raspy and tight showing his desperation. He crossed the room, taking her by the shoulders and turning her to face him. "What are you doing? Are you leaving? Why, Kira? Talk to me, damn it!"

Kira looked up. He could see she had been crying. She had showered and her wet hair clung to her tear-stained face. "Stark . . . Owen. I don't even know who you are. You were engaged to her? When? You have this whole life I know nothing about. I can't compete with that . . . devil in Prada. I'm not like that, Owen. I never will be."

Stark stifled a laugh. "I don't want that plastic bitch. I want you," he said. "I don't know why you can't see how incredibly beautiful you are. I've been waiting my whole life to meet you and I'm not about to let you go now." Stark pulled her tightly against him. He couldn't bear the thought of letting her go.

The warmth of his embrace flowed over her, enveloping her. Here in his arms she struggled to remember why she was mad. "You were engaged to her. You loved her." As she spoke the words, searing jealousy cut her deeply. She realized that this hurt the most—he had been in love with someone else.

Stark tipped her face up to look him in the eyes. "Kira, that was a long time ago. We were never formally engaged. Everyone expected us to get married, I guess. We were still kids. I'm not that person anymore."

"Did you love her? Do you love her still?" Kira's voice trembled.

"I thought I did. I was nineteen, for Christ sake. What did I know about life or love? That was a lifetime ago. I've been to war, seen more people die than I care to discuss. I'm not that boy anymore. I don't want to be." His voice softened, as he leaned into her.

"And now?" She had to know.

"I want you. Only you," he whispered as he kissed her hair.

Kira tilted her face up to his. *How can I ever resist this man?* "So where were we before we were so rudely interrupted by bitch Barbie?"

"I believe I was about to have some very dirty pancakes," he answered, grinning as he reached down to pick her up. Kira shrieked as he reached through her legs and picked her up by her butt and thighs. His brute strength was breathtaking. With ease he lifted her up so that her sex rested right in front of his mouth. "Mmm, yeah, that's what I'm hungry for," Stark rumbled into the crotch of her jeans. She squealed with delight at the sensation of his hot breath through the fabric.

"Ooh. You're going to make my pants wet on the inside and the outside," she said in mock disapproval.

"We can remedy that," he said laughing, and carried her over to the bed, tossing her lightly. He pounced on the bed beside her.

"Who said you get pancakes?" she teased. "It's way past time for breakfast." She began to crawl away.

"Ok, then we'll have brunch," he countered, just in time to catch her by the ankle and pull her back to him. "You're not getting away from me that easily." And then more seriously, "I will never let you go." He stared at her for a moment before taking her face in his hands and kissing her deeply. He rolled on top of her, kissing her as if he would eat her up. Kira giggled and returned his kiss, opening her mouth and allowing him full reign.

Never let me go! All the pain and embarrassment of the morning disappeared as his words suffused her. All her life she'd been so damn independent, yet when he took control and she surrendered, she felt more alive than anything she'd ever known. The heat of his body warmed her to her core. Kira's breath came heavy and short as he kissed down her neck and began to unbutton her blouse. *He still has flour in his hair!* A wicked thought filled Kira. *The whole time he was talking to bitch Barbie she had to be staring at that flour. That's right, bitch. He's mine!* She kissed him back, hard, running her fingers through his thick dark hair. *Mine!* He had her blouse undone, and an appreciative smile grew on his lips as he exposed her lace bra. He traced his finger down her breast and over the nipple. The sensation sent electrical shocks deep into her, and she felt the now-familiar ache between her legs begging for attention.

"Owen, please," she begged, her voice thick with desire.

"What do you want, baby? Tell me what you need." His voice was wanton and heavy.

"I want you," she said between breaths, "inside me."

He groaned loudly at the words and pressed his hardened cock against her silky thigh. Kira was so anxious for his touch it hurt. He raked his fingers deliciously down her abdomen to her sex, rubbing through the fabric, setting her throbbing clit ablaze. The smell of his cologne permeated the air as she breathed him in. She panted helplessly and he smiled, knowing he was in complete control. Expertly, he peeled her jeans away. Again, his lips pressed into the soft satin of her panties. His hot breath was torture. She whimpered, impatient for gratification. He grinned wickedly up at her and discarded the panties.

"Wrap your legs around my neck," he ordered.

Eagerly she obeyed, envisioning the pleasure that awaited. But he did not kiss or lick or touch her aching sex. Instead, he picked her up and stood. She squealed, surprised and impressed at his strength. At first she was a touch uneasy being held six feet off the ground. He stood upright, holding her up by her ass, and she held on to the back of his head, her fingers tightly laced into his hair.

"Relax," he ordered. "I have you."

His words trailed off as he buried his face into her waiting slit, and she screamed at the intensity of the pleasure. His strong arms held her firmly. Involuntarily Kira's thighs tightened around him. His tongue between her legs was warm and wet as he paid lavish attention to her aching sex, her body becoming a growing inferno. The sweet anguish of pleasure and pain took over every muscle, every nerve ending. As if far away, she heard herself moaning between ragged breaths, and she surrendered as the explosion racked her shattered body. Kira fell limp into his waiting arms, still shuddering from the aftershocks of the intense orgasm. Gently he laid her back onto the bed.

"There, baby, does that feel better?" he soothed. A big satisfied smile spread across his face. "You are mine," he whispered quietly. "I'm never going to be able to let you go."

"Hmm," Kira sighed, as she lay contented on the bed. "That's . . . nice." She barely registered what he was saying.

Stark climbed up in the bed beside her. He lay there, gently stroking his hand back and forth over her abdomen. Kira smiled up at him, looking at the incredible strong, sexy man lying beside her. She knew without a doubt that he cared for her and that she wanted to be with him. She didn't care what phone-sex queens or plastic bitches he had in his past. She would stay and fight if necessary. He was worth it, so very worth it.

Kira rolled on top of him. "My turn," she said, smiling. "Now, let's get rid of some of these clothes."

As they cleaned up the disastrous kitchen and made lunch, Stark explained his history with Simone. They had dated through high school. She was from a very affluent family in San Francisco, as was he, which had put them in all the same social circles. When they started college, he moved to Boston but she had gone to Berkeley.

"What school did you go to in Boston?" Kira asked, surprised.

Stark laughed. "Don't sound so surprised. For your information I went to Havahd," he said in his best Boston accent. "We were still dating seriously when my mom and Maggie died." Stark was quiet for a moment.

"You don't have to. Owen, it's ok." Kira didn't want to send him back to that dark place.

"My whole world had changed but Simone's hadn't. She was still the spoiled socialite who was so self-absorbed she didn't even notice my world spiraled out of control and fell away. The things in my life that had once seemed so important were pointless. In the weeks following their deaths I lost my grip on that life. I was so racked with guilt and pain that I stopped participating in my own existence. I was drinking heavily. Instead of being there for me, Simone was busy planning sorority events and fundraisers. I was expelled from school. Instead of going home, I came here." Stark looked up at Kira. She put her hand on his arm.

"I reached out to Simone, who told me to get my shit together. 'We still have a future to consider,' she said, and hung up. I sat in this very house, alone. So very alone. Days stretched

139

into a week. I found a pistol of my grandfather's and sat at the table, wondering how long it would be before they found me. I had reached my breaking point. Life seemed empty, void of any real measure of worth." Stark was very quiet. Kira's heart ached, realizing just how close he had come to ending it all. She reached out to hold him while he talked.

"It was then in my darkest moment that the phone rang and a crusty old voice asked for Owen Stark. It was the breeder calling about Maggie's dog. What was I supposed to do with a damn dog? He insisted I come to pick the dog up. I contemplated hanging up on the old bastard and finishing what I had planned to do, but something stopped me." He paused, looking at the falling snow out the large window.

After a few minutes, he said, "I think it was Maggie. I think she and Mom were reaching out to me." Stark told her how he'd driven his truck from Aspen to the breeder's in northern California. The breeder was an old retired Army Master Sergeant. The experienced sergeant could see at once that Stark was broken.

"Come on in, son." His gravelly voice had reverberated with years of smoking. He offered the young man a beer and told him to have a seat. Decades of dealing with traumatized young men gave the sergeant the ability to reach Stark. For the first time since the tragedy that had

*claimed his family, he was able to talk to someone who
really understood.*

"I don't know why, but I could talk to him. He knew
what I was going through. He'd been there so many times
before. And he reminded me of my grandfather. My mom's dad
was a great man," Stark continued, remembering his time with
the old breeder.

*"I have someone I want you to meet," the older
man said to the younger. He led Stark out back to a large
kennel. Reaching in, he scooped up a wriggling puffball of
speckled white fur and handed it to Stark. "I put a tag on
her just to mark her for your sister," he said. "You can
name her whatever you like." A small tag hanging from her
collar was barely visible through the billow of white fur.
"Maggie" was written crudely on the tag. Stark's heart
leapt inside his chest. He held the little fuzzball up and
looked into her frosted cobalt eyes. They reminded him of
Maggie. "She would love you," he said to the fuzzball. The
little pup cocked her head to the side and wrinkled her little
pink and black nose. At once she wagged her stubby tail
and licked his face. Stark's heart was won. He had never
been able to say no to his sister, and as he held the little
pup he felt his sister's spirit and love.*

141

"I knew there was nothing left for me in California or Boston. I spent a week with the old sergeant before deciding to come back to Colorado. Over the course of that week the sergeant told me stories of his days in the army: the family, the band of brothers, and their inseparable bond. I recalled the stories of my grandfather and his days with the Marine Raiders in World War II. That's when I realized what I wanted to do with my life. The sergeant made a call and set up an appointment for me to meet a recruiter at Fort Carson. I left with little Mags to start a new life."

Kira drank a glass of much needed wine and listened thoughtfully as he talked and cooked their lunch. "So little Mags and the sergeant saved you?" she asked tenderly.

"I guess so," he said softly. "And my team. Kira, I had so much anger. I poured myself into revenge, worked night and day to be the best soldier and teammate that I could. I will not stop until the terrorists are gone, all of them. I won't give up. I can't. I have to keep fighting."

"Relentless," she said, smiling sadly. Kira knew this goal defined him, but still, she wondered if he could ever be happy and really live again.

"I'm sorry. I don't know how to explain what it does to you to lose your family, your parent. To have the whole world change in an instant."

"You don't have to explain." *I know all too well.* Kira reached out and touched his hand, reassuring him. Her sweet confident smile hid the all the doubts and fears looming just beneath the surface.

"Let's suit up. I want to take you on a ride. This is our last day before we have to head back to the real world. I want to make it good," Stark said after they had eaten. He and Kira went to the ski room and donned their heaviest gear. "It's going to get really cold before we get back so bundle up."

Kira was excited; she loved snowmobiles but hadn't been on one in years. Stark led her into one of the three garages. "Whoa," she said in a low voice, looking around the large space. All manner of outdoor gear was contained here. It was like an REI warehouse. The far wall was lined with kayaks, oars, and life jackets. Large floor-to-ceiling wooden shelves contained totes labeled by activity. She saw what looked like a mini mountain bike shop in one corner. On another side of the room was a yellow and black Ski-Doo XM Summit X 154 snowmobile. Stark opened the garage and moved the big sled out onto the snow. After checking to make sure everything was ready, he turned to Kira. "You ready?"

"Oh, yes!" she exclaimed as she climbed on behind him. Stark started the engine and raced up the mountain. They followed trails through the trees in the deep snow, the boughs of the pines heavy with snow, almost making a tunnel. Other than

143

the engine, the world seemed silent. The wind was cold but invigorating. Kira held on tightly as Stark raced through fields and passes, climbing higher and higher, above the rest of the world. Here with him it was easy to imagine they were the only two people on earth. Kira looked up. The high sunlit clouds drifted aimlessly across the clear blue sky. The troubles that were so overwhelming down in the regular world were nonexistent here. The snow covered all flaws and made everything appear new and perfect. Kira smiled and held him tighter. They reached a clearing that overlooked the entire world below. Kira gasped at the incredible beauty and knew in that moment there was hope. If they could hold on to each other no matter what they had to face when they went back, they would be all right.

Stark must have felt it too because he stopped the snowmobile and got off to stand beside her. He wrapped her in his arms, the smile on his face genuine and finally happy. "I'll stand by you with all that I am. Promise me you won't leave, and I know we'll be ok." They stood there together, holding each other and watched the sun slip away.

Chapter 9

Kira awoke to the hateful buzzing of her alarm. Ugh, how was it already time for work? She thought back to her lovely weekend with Stark. It was like a dream: perfect, except maybe for the plastic bitch Barbie, but she wouldn't think of her now. So much had happened—it seemed more like a lifetime than just a weekend. Kira was a little sad to be heading back to work. Then she thought of Abbey, who would no doubt be waiting for details. Kira was getting ready when her doorbell rang. *Could it be him?* she wondered, suddenly excited. She answered the door. A deliveryman was there, shoving a clipboard in her face and asking her to sign here, please. Surprised and bewildered by the early morning intrusion, Kira fumbled with the clipboard.

"Well, here you go. Have a good day," the curt deliveryman grumbled and thrust a long box into her arms.

"Uh . . . thanks, I think," Kira answered as she watched him hurry back down the walk. Kira took the oblong box back into her apartment. *Now what is this? Who is it from?* She unfastened the bright red ribbon and opened the white box. Inside were two-dozen roses, all white except for two deep red ones. The stark contrast of crimson on white was spectacular. Kira opened the note and her heart melted.

Sometimes in the white noise that is our everyday lives

Fate hands us a surprise

A spark of passion

In the midst of the mundane

Thank you for a lovely weekend

Owen

Smiling like a schoolgirl, Kira held the note up to her lips. She closed her eyes for a moment and pictured him on top of the mountain. The red roses surrounded by all the white made her think of the two of them sitting at the top of the mountain as if there was no one else in the world. She took a long, lingering breath, inhaling the fragrant aroma of the beautiful flowers. She was sure it was her imagination, but they smelled like the honey-jasmine body wash and sensuous showers. She could still taste him on her lips.

Realizing that the morning was passing her by, Kira quickly put the roses in water and ran out the door. She would have to hurry across base to get to the clinic on time. She cursed herself for not taking Stark up on his offer to let her use his Jeep until she got a new car. *Damn Kira, way to be stubborn*, she thought as she raced down the sidewalk. Kira jumped as a car horn blared behind her. Turning suddenly, she saw Holt's red

BMW slow down. It pulled up beside her. *Oh, great.* Kira had hoped to avoid him today.

"Kira, you're running late. Would you like a ride?" Holt asked hopefully.

Lacking any believable excuse, Kira accepted his invitation and hopped in. "Thanks for the ride, Captain Holt. I was running a little behind this morning." Kira thought of the roses and smiled.

"You're welcome. You're lucky I came along. It's really unacceptable to be late for clinic," Holt said in a self-satisfied tone.

***

The clinic was already busy when Kira got there. She quickly settled in and started with her patients. *At least with a busy clinic I can get my mind off Stark.* She was just finishing a physical when her phone vibrated to life in her pocket with a text. Once out of the room she checked the message.

Did you get the delivery?

Her racing heart made her realize how anxious she had been to hear from him.

Yes, thank you.

They are absolutely beautiful.

Kira cursed herself for not thinking of something more original to say. His note had been as lovely as the flowers. Her phone buzzed again.

Not as beautiful as you.
How is your morning?

She knew he would be upset if he knew she had to get a ride from Holt and didn't want him to push the car issue. She vowed to look for a new car that weekend.

My morning's ok.
You really didn't have to send me anything.
You catered to me all weekend
I should have sent something to thank you.

Immediately her phone buzzed back. Kira scoffed at the elation she felt each time he responded. *You are hopeless!* She thought to herself.

I wanted to send you something to say thank you.

Kira starred at her phone, confused. He had rescued her. He had taken her to a wonderful cabin and taken excellent care of her all weekend. She couldn't think what exactly he should be thanking her for.

For what?

He quickly responded and Kira's heart melted all over again.

That used to be my place but the last several years it has been so lonely. This weekend with you . . . it was all new again.

Kira sat holding her phone. There were so many things she wanted to say, but how? And that was definitely not the type of conversation she wanted to have over text.

Thank you, Owen
I really had an amazing time.
You are a lot more fun than I imagined.
How's your morning so far?
His response was quick.

My morning's ok, I guess.
Pancakes are a little bland though . . .
They're missing something . . .
I just can't put my finger on it.

Kira could almost see his mischievous grin. She thought of the way he cleared the counter, throwing flour everywhere. He'd been so crazy for her at that moment. She had never felt so wanted. So sexy.

Well, now, that is a shame. We may have to remedy that.

Kira giggled as she typed. She knew that she had to keep a professional demeanor at work but she felt giddy and wanted to sext with Soldier Sex God. But she knew better.

***

As for Stark, he was on a break and could afford to pine for her for a few precious minutes. *This day's looking better already*! Stark shifted his growing bulge. He sat back in the barrack break room. He pictured Kira all covered in flour on the kitchen counter, wanton and ready for him. He cleared his throat and shifted in his seat. He knew he would be thinking about her all day.

Surely sitting around sexting all
day isn't part of your itinerary today.

Well, there went the fun, Stark thought, but he couldn't resist jabbing back just a little.

Sexting?
You are dirty! Here I was talking
about wholesome breakfast foods.
Don't you have some lives to save
or diseases to stamp out Captain?

Stark laughed out loud as he sent the message.

"What the hell are you laughing about?" Sergeant Colin griped as he walked in. "You look like you had a good weekend."

"And you look like shit. What the hell happened?" Stark asked, staring at the battered and scuffed-up Colin.

"Long story," Colin said, wincing as he iced a bruised and very swollen right hand. His left eye resembled an overly ripe plum. Multiple abrasions decorated his face and neck. He continued, "One that started with a little tequila and a friendly game of pool and ended with a vagina on my face." He finished by pointing dramatically at his battered eye.

"Man, when are you going to learn to quit starting shit? How many were there? 'Cause I'm picturing one little old lady with an umbrella."

"Fuck you, man. If my backup hadn't been off chasing tail in the mountains, it would have turned out better."

"You need to control your liquor and your mouth. You're going to end up getting shot."

"Yeah, yeah . . . that's what Paige said."

"You were with Paige this weekend?" Stark was a little surprised. He knew that Colin and Paige knew each other, but they didn't exactly run with the same crowd.

"You got a problem with that, bro? I know you two were hot and heavy at one time. If you still like her, man, just say so."

"Paige and I are just friends. She's a wildcat, man. If you're brave enough to go down that road, be my guest. But be good to her or you'll have me and her girlfriend Zoe to deal with. And trust me, if that happens, you'll have more than a vagina on your face," Stark said, flicking Colin in his swollen eye.

"Ah, fuck!" Colin winced in pain and punched Stark in the arm. "Fuck. Duly noted . . . Shit!"

Stark couldn't help but laugh. He knew his redneck friend would be blown away by Paige and wondered how he would handle her unique abilities. If Colin thought the eye was bad, he was in for a whole new world of hurt with Paige. She was a professional. When it came to relationships, her only steady was Zoe. They had been partners for years. Stark had found that exciting at one time. Paige, he knew, would just be having fun. She enjoyed alternating as a dominant and submissive, and had introduced him to both. For poor Colin this would be quite an education.

Paige was an incredibly beautiful woman and he had no doubt she would have Colin under her complete control. He wasn't sure what her real name had been but she had been Paige for as long as he had known her. Stark assumed the name and her looks came from her obsession with Bettie Page. She had been born in Korea but had lived in the United States most of her life. Her long hair was jet black, always cut and styled in perfect Bettie Page fashion. She was an incredibly talented tattoo artist, and thus the majority of her torso and legs, and part of her arms, beautifully displayed her art.

That's how she and Stark had first met. Stark had come back after his first deployment and had found out all the shit that Simone had been up to. It was the final straw. He needed to blow off some steam and had gone out drinking. He ended up with a couple of buddies, wasted, in a tattoo parlor. In had walked Paige.

The three drunken soldiers had stared open-mouthed as Paige entered the room with her jet-black hair perfectly rolled and as shiny as her five-inch patent leather heels.

"Well, well, what do we have here? Fresh little NUGs come to see Paige. You man enough for tattoos, soldier boys? What you want, a little unicorn or some flowers?" Her Vietnamese accent was thick, but Stark thought perhaps it was a little forced. Though young and relatively inexperienced, he had picked up that she was toying with them.

He was instantly turned on by her, as were most men—he imagined—if not a little intimidated by her pin-up girl makeup and the artful tattoos that covered a large portion of her body. She stood tapping a sexy black heel, sizing them up. The soft skin of her pale leg was covered (barely) with thin fishnet stockings that disappeared beneath her fire engine red halter dress. The backless dress allowed the full view of her extensive artwork. "You," she said, pointing at him. "Come here, little soldier boy. I want to see what you are made of. You want tattoo?"

Stark stood in the center of the room. His heart rate had picked up. He did his best to control his breathing. He had never been in the presence of this kind of woman before. She produced a small riding crop from one of the tattoo stations. Stark's eyes lit up. He suddenly didn't care what she was about to do. The confident young man was excited and needed to blow off a lot of pent up energy and frustration. She walked around him slowly, her stilettos clicking on the tile floor. She tapped the crop gently against her other hand. Slowly, she circled, like a shark. Tap . . . tap . . . tap. Then suddenly—whap! She smacked him hard on the chest with the crop. "This goes," she said, indicating his shirt. "Hmm," she murmured appreciatively, once the obstructive fabric had been discarded. "This we can work with," she said, slowly dragging the crop against his skin. Stark's face remained calm and in control, his breathing evened out, but his eyes remained deadlocked on her. The growing bulge in his jeans, however, betrayed his true feelings. Paige laughed. "This one has promise," she said, slapping him again. "Ok, you go have a seat over there. You two," she said, turning to his friends, "Mark

155

and Lena will take care of you." She started toward the back with Stark, and turning, she said, "This is no massage parlor, boys, so don't get any ideas. No happy ending here."

"That was pretty intense," Stark said, staring up at her as he settled into the tattoo chair.

"You have no idea." The wicked gleam in her eyes as she answered, smiling, should have raised a red flag for trouble. But at twenty years old, trouble was exactly what he was looking for.

Stark snapped back to reality. Memory lane with Paige was not somewhere he needed or wanted to be. It was an interesting and adventurous part of his past, and he and Paige were still very good friends, but that was all. Now his life was going in a new direction. He smiled, thinking of Kira again. Then he instantly shuddered at the thought of Kira meeting Paige. It was bound to happen at some point. He remembered how well the encounter with Simone had gone. Stark sighed heavily. That was not something he would like to repeat. And with Paige he feared it would be worse. Simone was a catty bitch but Paige represented a whole different chapter of his life, one that had become a big part of him. It was a part he feared Kira would never be able to understand.

***

Kira was in her office finishing her morning notes when Abbey came in with fresh coffee. "To what do I owe this?" Kira asked suspiciously.

Abbey shut the door behind her and handed Kira the coffee. "Ok, spill it," she said anxiously. "I've been waiting for some kind of details all morning. When you left here Friday you were piping mad, and then Stark called, all frantic, looking for you, and Holt came by—"

"Wait, Holt came by?" Kira asked, worried. "What did he want?"

"I'm sure he wanted to spend the weekend with you. By the way, you were off visiting your family this weekend if he asks," she said quickly.

Kira laughed. "Ok, ok." She wondered why Holt hadn't asked about her family this morning when she rode to work with him. Either he knew that hadn't been where she went or he was too self-absorbed to care about her family. For now she would have to hope it was the latter. If Holt knew about her and Stark, it could make things very difficult.

Abbey sat staring at her, waiting for her to elaborate on the weekend. Kira knew she would have to tell her some details, and to be honest, she really wanted to be able to talk to someone about everything that was going on. Kira felt she could trust Abbey. After all, she had already covered for her once. "Abbey," she began, "I can't stress enough how top secret this has to be."

"Are you kidding?" Abbey said, sounding a little hurt. "You don't get to be the wife of a Sergeant Major for twenty-plus years if you don't know when to keep your mouth shut. So spill it. Did he find you? He sounded hot and heavy when he called here looking for you. He was so damn worried about you and that death trap of a car."

Kira recounted the events of her car crash and walking to the bar in the snow. Abbey had a look of horror on her face as Kira described the awful scene. She told her about the bar and Stark bursting in and the kiss.

"Oh," Abbey said, leaning back in her chair. "That is so stinking romantic! Did you guys go on to the mountains? Did you get to ski?"

Kira told her about Stark's house and the fun they had skiing. She left out the sordid sex details.

"Wow, a big house in Aspen, that's pricey. That's way too pricey for an Army sergeant," Abbey said, alarm bells going off. She looked concerned.

Kira explained with minimum details about Stark's family and the death of his mom and sister.

"Oh, bless his poor sweet heart," Abbey said purring like a mamma cat. "So, what do you think of him? How do you feel about him?"

"I'm not sure. I never wanted anything like this to happen, especially not with an enlisted man. Oh, Abbey, this really complicates things. Spending time with Holt is bad enough. But Owen Stark . . ." She paused, sighing as she said his name. "Owen is different altogether. I'm afraid I feel more for him than is healthy." She finished just as Holt came knocking at her office door.

"You ready for lunch?" he asked impatiently. Kira could see he was in a hurry as usual.

"I might just stay in today. I have a lot of work to get done. Can we take a rain check?" she asked politely.

"Nice try, this is a rain check for Friday." He laughed softly and held out her coat. "You're going to turn into a hermit if you don't get out some. It's not healthy to work so much. You have to get out and live a little."

Kira felt a twinge of guilt. *Oh if you only knew*, she thought. *Poor Holt.* She could see that despite his self-absorbed nature, Holt was trying. "Ok, lunch it is," she said, allowing him to help her with her coat. As she followed him out of the clinic, Abbey shot her a *what the hell are you thinking?* look. Kira was wondering the same thing and how she would manage to work it all out.

On the drive to the restaurant Holt talked endlessly, almost nervously, about random events on base and his weekend. Kira was only partly paying attention. She nodded and commented in the right places but her mind was hundreds of miles away in Aspen. Oh, how she longed to be sitting by the fire nestled in Stark's arms. She loved the smell of him when she placed her nose at the crux of his neck and shoulder. *Mmm.* Kira snapped back to the present as they stopped abruptly at a stop sign.

"Fucking idiots," Holt snapped as two guys on motorcycles crossed in front of them at the intersection. "Clearly we had the right of way. What kinds of assholes drive around Colorado in the fucking cold on motorcycles anyway?"

Kira looked up as they passed. To her it seemed like slow motion. On the blacked out motorcycle, the rider in black leathers and a full-face helmet turned and saluted Kira as he passed. *Oh God, it's him!* Suddenly her heart raced like a motor and Kira realized she was holding her breath. On the other side of the car Holt was still ranting, but he sounded a million miles away. Kira knew Stark had seen her. What she wouldn't give to jump on the back of that motorcycle and go with him.

Her mind was competing for speed with her heart as they pulled into the diner. Kira wondered what Stark must be thinking. She knew that she and Holt were just friends, but she wasn't sure that Stark and Holt understood that. Holt jumped out quickly and ran around to open her door. His gesture, while genuine, seemed a little out of place for lunch with a friend. Kira got the sinking feeling that Holt was hoping for something more. As they made their way to the door Holt placed a gentle but possessive hand on the small of her back. She stiffened slightly and the hairs on the back of her neck bristled. While Holt was growing on her as a friend, she was not interested in this type of affection from him.

They sat in a corner booth. Holt didn't seem to mind sitting with his back to the door. This bothered Kira but she couldn't place exactly why. She understood that perhaps he had never really faced any danger, that he had never existed in a real theater of war and thus the survival instincts that her father had so notably possessed were lost on him. Maybe it was a fine point in the distinction between him and Stark. She was beginning to realize that Stark was more like her father than she cared to admit, the very thing she had set out to avoid. Yet how could she avoid falling for a man who resembled the man she grew up idolizing her whole life? She was buried in these thoughts while Holt was still talking until she heard the roar of motorcycle engines pulling up outside.

Once again Kira's heart quickened as the diner door opened. She maintained a calm exterior except for a fine sheen of sweat that appeared on her palms and neck. From her vantage point she could clearly see Stark and his team enter the restaurant. Thankfully, Holt was oblivious. He was too busy talking about his advantages in their upcoming survival training and how she should stick with him during the exercise.

"Clearly my experience and attention to detail will get us through," Holt said confidently as Stark passed within three feet behind him. Stark walked past calmly with no outward sign of recognition save to meet Kira's gaze. The twinkle in his eyes excited her. She could feel her breathing pick up. His proximity stirred her in ways Holt could never hope to. She shifted her gaze back to Holt who finally seemed to sense the change in her demeanor.

"Don't be nervous, Kira. With my help you'll make it through survival training just fine. Stay close to me. We don't want any repeat of the disaster at the confidence course." His patronizing tone pulled Kira harshly out of her fantasy about Stark.

What the hell? Disaster at the confidence course?
Fuck that! White-hot anger coursed through her. She saw with
painful clarity what Holt really thought of her. A lifetime of
determination, her strong drive to succeed, and a history of doing
exactly that—succeeding— fueled Kira's resentment. She knew
Holt just saw her as a pretty face, an incapable fragile flower
who was hopelessly out of place in the United States military.
She knew that she wasn't Rambo or as strong or fast as some of
her counterparts, but she was damned good at her job. She would
train and serve with all that she had in her.

A clatter of plates caught her attention. She looked up
and her eyes grew wide. She fought hard to resist laughing out
loud. Not eight feet away sat a team of Special Forces operatives
sharing a huge platter of pancakes. Their interactions were that
of brothers who have lived, served, and bled together. They
laughed fully and freely, tormenting and playing with one
another. The large platter was passed around family style, with
each operative piling on as many toppings as possible. They
talked over each other about their favorite toppings and how
plain pancakes just weren't the same.

Stark was seated so that he directly faced Kira. When his
turn came around, Sergeant Colin asked how he liked his
pancakes. Stark looked up and his eyes locked with Kira's. She
could feel her temperature rising. He smiled and said, "I like
mine sweet and dirty, all covered in powder," and with a swift

move, he took the syrup and the canister of powdered sugar. He clinked them together with such force that a small cloud of powdered sugar billowed over his pancakes and onto the table. The team erupted in a cheer.

"Sounds like one hot mess," Colin laughed.

"My favorite kind," Stark said, and almost no one noticed as he nonchalantly licked his lips before taking a bite. No one but Kira, who instantly grew wet, wishing those lips were on her.

The cheer from the men was finally enough to register Holt's attention. He turned around to see the team of laughing men enjoying their very late breakfast. He turned around in obvious disapproval. "This is why I like to eat off base, Kira," he said. He didn't seem to recognize Stark. If he did, he was hiding it well. Perhaps the recognition that this was a Special Forces team prevented him from making further comment.

Kira worked diligently on her California salad. She loved the taste of cranberries and blue cheese. Holt had gone back to talking and Stark seemed to be absorbed in the conversation of his crew. Watching him interact with his brothers was enlightening. She saw that he was truly in his element. They were his team, his family, his life.

She could feel him watching her. Slowly Kira looked up from her salad. As she looked up their eyes met and a wicked smile passed across his lips. The hunger in his eyes was not for pancakes. Kira felt her cheeks growing warm. She lay down her fork and placed her napkin delicately on the table. "Liam, I need to go to the bathroom. I'll be right back, ok?" she interjected into his self-praising monologue.

"Hurry back, we need to be back in clinic in thirty," he said matter-of-factly. "They may just disapprove of us dating if we start taking long lunches. Holt sat, back, a very self-satisfied smile on his face.

Kira shuddered and hurried out of the room. She made her way down the dark hallway toward the bathroom. She had almost reached the door when a firm hand grabbed her arm. He spun her around and she was standing face-to-face with Sergeant Owen Stark. He was standing so close, his body pinning hers against the wall, his lips only inches away. "Hey there, beautiful," he murmured, almost whispering into her mouth. His lips grazed hers as he spoke. *So warm!* She felt herself quickly melting into him. Any thoughts of self-preservation were futile with him so close. Kira closed her eyes and breathed him in.

"What are you doing with Dipshit?" Stark's voice was calm and self-possessed.

"Having lunch. What are *you* doing here?" Kira asked, slightly annoyed, though it was incredibly hard to stay annoyed with Stark so close she could taste him.

"Improvising." He smiled but offered no other explanation. The wicked expression said everything. He gently trailed his free hand down the side of her face and across her lips. Kira kissed the tip of his finger as he paused over her mouth. She could taste the sweetness of the pancakes. He gently pressed his finger on her lower lip, and she opened her mouth slightly taking his finger in and sucking syrup gently off the tip. Stark groaned deeply and pressed her up against the wall. She leaned into him and kissed him intensely before pulling away and disappearing into the bathroom.

Stark was left alone in the hall, staring at the back of the door.

Chapter 10

Kira noted a chill as she opened the door to her apartment. That was odd. She had expected the apartment to be warm and toasty after her long walk home from work. She noted a slight rustle in the curtains by the French door to her balcony. Upon inspection she found it slightly ajar. She opened the door fully and went out onto the small space. Nothing was amiss except a broken flowerpot. The flowers inside had long since died, as Kira did not have an especially green thumb. *The wind maybe? I might have forgotten to shut the door fully,* she thought as she set the pot upright. She went back inside, locking the door behind her. After taking a thorough survey of her apartment and finding nothing out of place, Kira decided it must have been her own carelessness. Still, she couldn't shake the feeling that something was wrong, that someone had been there. The feeling stirred some dark memories and old fears. They threatened to return to her. *You are being childish. That was years ago and thousands of miles away. Stop this!*

Kira's phone buzzed. She snatched it up, desperate for a distraction from her present craziness. Looking down, a smile crossed her lips. It was Stark.

I've been thinking

Of those lips all day

I ought to spank that little ass

For leaving me hanging.

***

Kira laughed as she read his text. She remembered the look on his face when she left him in the hallway. She had wanted to pay him back for crashing her lunch. But now she ached to see him again.

You wouldn't dare!

Christmas is only a month away.

You don't want to end up

On the naughty list.

***

You have no idea what I would like to do to you, Stark thought, smiling, but that would have to wait. His thoughts shifted to the afternoon's obstruction. Captain Holt was beginning to get in the way. He hated the little shit for being able to spend so much time with her. He had worked very hard to control his jealousy when he saw them together. He was used to having things under his control. Everything in his life was set, regimented. Kira threw all of that into a whirl. She was the one unpredictable variable in his life and he was beginning to crave it like a drug. He quickly responded.

Honey I live on the naughty list.

***.

This one sentence stirred memories of their weekend. The excitement, heat, and desire poured over her.

You make that sound like

A fun place to be.

***

Quickly he typed back.

You have no idea.

Maybe one day I'll show you.

***

His invitation both excited and frightened her. She loved the idea of spending more intimate time with him. But something, something dark between the lines, terrified her.

You better behave.

Santa won't come see you.

***

Stark looked at her response and smiled. He sent one last message before heading out the door.

He already has.

See you in a few.

Kira was embarrassed to realize she was giggling like a schoolgirl. Thankfully there was no one there to hear her. She placed her phone on the counter and went to have a shower and change. She let hot water envelop her. With her mind on Stark and the distraction of the shower, she never heard the French door open and the intruder letting himself out.

***

One thing Kira was thankful for in her small apartment was the water pressure. She had a seemingly endless supply of glorious hot water at her disposal. Taking a moment to fully enjoy the sensuous heat, Kira's mind took her back to the weekend's showers with Stark. The sight of that man's body naked! She slowly rubbed the soapy sponge over her breasts and down her abdomen, exhaling softly and imagining it was him. His need possessed her. Something in the tone of his text and the intensity of his eyes when they were together hinted at a darker yearning. This frightened Kira but she was becoming too obsessed with him to turn back.

The apartment was chilly as she stepped out of the shower. She quickly dressed and dried her hair. She was just finishing when she heard the knock at the door. She took one last glance at her wayward chestnut mop, quickly ran a brush through it, and ran to the door. As she entered the living room she stopped dead in her tracks. The icy blast through the slightly open French door sent her into a panic. *I locked this! Or at least I think I locked it.* She peeked out onto the balcony but there was no one in sight. Pulling the door shut, Kira was careful to lock it this time. Then she hastily ran to answer the door. Stark stood there waiting. He was all smiles from their earlier conversation. Silently she debated whether she should tell him about the door. *No, I'd sound crazy. I am seriously overreacting.* Kira dismissed it.

"Are you ok?" Stark asked, concerned. He could see the anxiety she was trying to hide.

"Yeah, I'm fine," she lied. "I just thought I heard something. But it's nothing." Kira noted the rustle at his feet. She looked down to see Mags pacing impatiently.

"Kira, this is my Maggie. Maggie, this is Kira," Stark said warmly, introducing his two girls for the first time.

Kira knelt down and nuzzled the dog. "Hey there, Maggie, it's nice to meet you." She laughed as Maggie got excited and licked her face. Kira loved dogs. "Owen, she's beautiful!" Kira exclaimed, still petting Mags's soft fur.

Stark smiled. "I thought we could take Maggie for a walk," he invited. "If you want to bundle up, we can drive to the head of an impressive trail not too far from here."

"That sounds great," Kira said as she grabbed her coat. She was thankful to get out of the apartment. Taking one last look around she was careful to lock the front door and secure it tightly. She glanced around the building and scanned the alley as they got into the truck. There was no sign of anything unusual. She knew that she was just being paranoid.

They drove into the mountains with Maggie between them. Stark petted Mags, then stretched his arm out over Kira's shoulder. *Slick move*, she thought and shot him a playful glance.

"What?" he asked, laughing. He strummed his fingers over her shoulder. "I missed you today," he said finally.

"I saw you at lunch," she replied, realizing she had missed him too.

"That didn't count," he said in mock desperation. "Captain Dipshit was there. Watching you have lunch with the Ken doll does not count as my idea of a good time."

"Oh, poor thing. Well, if it's any consolation, I was too distracted by the dirty pancakes to have much of a conversation with him," she finished, smiling sweetly.

They got out of the truck and started up the trail together. Far away from the prying eyes at base, they could be themselves. Stark reached out and took her hand as they walked. Mags ran around them, happily barking and leading the way up the trail. The late November wind was bitter but they didn't notice.

After a few minutes of walking and just enjoying each other, Kira spoke. "Today, watching you guys in the diner, I could see what you mean about the team being your family."

"They are my family. We're brothers. We've been through hell together. We have each other's backs in all things," Stark answered pensively.

Suddenly she missed her father more than ever. She didn't know why the thought bothered her so. She even realized that her reaction was irrational, but seeing Stark like that with his team had made her appreciate that her father had had a whole other life, one he couldn't walk away from. She wondered if Stark ever would. "I guess they always will be the biggest part of you. It was like that for my dad, too." She didn't even realize she said it out loud until it was too late.

"Your dad? What does my team have to do with your dad?" Stark asked, confused. Kira had avoided any questioning about her family up to this point. He needed to know what she meant. He had obviously seen her sadness when they ran the first time. They crested a small hill and Stark stopped abruptly. He pulled her to him and kissed her softly, then deeply. After a moment he stepped back and took her face in his hands. "Tell me about your father." Stark stood very still. His voice was soft but intense.

"Owen, I don't think this is the best time," Kira replied. She tried to turn away but Stark held her to him.

"It's better than in the middle of a five star restaurant," he said curtly. This struck Kira like a blow to the gut. She painfully remembered pressuring him to talk about his sister's death and his subsequent breakdown at the finest restaurant in Aspen.

"Ouch!" she said, admitting defeat. "Ok, let's walk and I'll tell you. But Owen, you may not like how this story ends."

A look of fear came over Stark's face. "I can face anything except losing you, Kira" He paused for a moment but continued. "There is no turning back for me. I want you, all of you. We'll be ok. Tell me," he said, trying to sound confident. They continued on the trail up through the woods.

"I idolized my father," Kira began. "He was everything a man should be. He was strong and fierce, yet incredibly gentle and tender. He loved my mother and she loved him. I didn't grow up with a lot of money or have ski houses or anything like that. But I had a wonderful childhood. It was everything a little girl could dream of. We lived on base in Georgia."

"Your dad was in the army?" Stark asked, starting to piece it together.

"Yeah, Special Forces like you. He was a Ranger. I believed he hung the moon," Kira said, her voice nostalgic. She told Stark stories from her childhood, silly games she and her father would play. How he taught her to love running.

"You were really close." He observed. His voice lowered as if he was afraid to ask, "Then what happened?"

"I was ten when the MPs came to our house," she continued shakily. She paused for a moment, looking away. When she looked back at him tears were brimming in her eyes. She recounted the horrifying moment when her mother had opened the door. "They told us he had been killed in action. Just like that, he was gone. It was as if all the air had been sucked out of the room. I could not breathe. I remember my mother's stunned silence that turned into screams, screams and wailing that lasted for days. She stopped bathing or eating. She was so absorbed in her own mourning and loss to realize we were still there. I remember the wives of the men from my father's team coming to help us. They were wonderful, cooking for us and helping us until we had to leave base. We weren't in the army anymore and couldn't stay there. My mother slipped into a hopeless state." Kira stopped talking, choking back a sob.

Stark put his arm protectively around her. "At least I was an adult. I can't imagine facing that loss and insecurity as a small child. God, I remember Maggie at ten. The thought of you all alone, trying to keep your family together, makes me sick." He pulled her close to him as they walked. "What did you do?" he asked tenderly.

"My mother had family back in West Virginia. She was from a small town called Davis. She still had an aunt and uncle there. They were older but it was somewhere for us to go. One of the women from the group helped me pack. She told me I would have to take care of my brothers and my mom. We boarded a train with what we could carry, and just like that, left the only life we had ever known behind." As Kira finished, she let Stark see the depths of her raw vulnerability. But as she began to speak again she became rigid once more.

"You are strong Kira, stronger than you give yourself credit for." He squeezed her reassuringly as he spoke.

"I knew we had to stay together. I wouldn't let my little brothers be taken to some group home. Sitting around feeling sorry for myself was not an option," she explained. As they walked on, Kira told him of growing up in the hills of West Virginia with a shell of a parent and two small brothers to look after. With a sense of humor and true love of each other, her family survived all the pain, hunger, and hopeless times.

He chuckled. "Your tenacity kept you guys alive and together. You are a fighter, there is no doubt about it."

They had reached the top of the overlook and the end of the trail. Stark stopped and looked into her eyes. He gently tucked a wayward strand of hair behind her ear. "When I said I couldn't explain what it was like to lose a part of your family and have your whole life change, you said I didn't have to. It wasn't just because you were kind and understanding. It was because you had been there." He pulled her tightly to him and held her as if somehow wrapping her up in his arms would make up for all those lonely, scary days.

"You see," she said, at last pulling away from him, "this is why we can't be together. It's crazy. Seriously Owen, what the hell have we been thinking? It's not just fraternization, it's everything I've ever wanted to avoid. Damn it, this wasn't supposed to happen! I was going to finish my four years and get as far away from the military as possible. I wasn't supposed to feel so tied to the service. And I sure as hell wasn't going to fall for a guy with the exact same fucking job that killed my father!" Her words were sharp. She turned to go back the way they had come but Stark still had hold of her. As she pulled away, his hand caught in her dog tags. The chain gave way and the tags fell into the fresh snow. A hush fell over them. As they stood staring at the broken symbol of her identity, Stark gently took her hand.

"God help me, Kira, but I can't let you go. I know if I was a better man I would walk away but I can't. You're right about the fraternization. I hold the honor of the military above all else in my life. At least I did until I met you. Everything in my life was set until I ran into you. Even though there is so much stacked against us, unless you tell me to leave, I'll never be able to let you go." Stark's voice was tense and breathless. "I need you, Kira."

His words hit Kira like a lightning bolt. *I don't want him to let me go. Ever.* Her lips found his. Before she realized it, she was kissing him with such fervor it was almost as if she was trying to devour him. Her hands found his hair. Holding tightly, she braced as he returned the kiss.

"I don't want you to let me go." Kira's soft voice filled the darkness.

Stark reached down and retrieved the tags. With new purpose he handed her the broken chain. With a steady hand he took off his own tags. Kira wondered what in the world he was doing. "There will be times," he began softly, "that we are separated—by rules, by miles, by war—but this way you will know that you are always with me. I will be thinking of you every day." He then took two of the tags—one of his and one of hers—and placed them on his chain. With the gentle precision of a plastic surgeon he fastened the chain around her neck.

"Kira, I've been waiting my whole life to meet you. Now that you're here, now that you're mine . . ." he said, his voice trailing off. He slowly rubbed his fingers over the tags that hung between her soft breasts. They had wandered slightly off the trail and were surrounded by darkness. Kira leaned back against the trunk of a tree. Stark began softly kissing her forehead, her face, her neck. As his hands slipped under her jacket, Mags began to bark.

Her bark was fierce and aggressive. Both Kira and Stark looked up, startled by Mags's response. She wasn't looking at them; she was barking at something in the darkness. Fur bristled and teeth bared, Mags made ready, positioning herself between the couple and the perceived threat. "Hey there girl, what do you see? What's out there?" Stark asked in a cool voice, suddenly alert. His demeanor changed. The tender man was gone, a battle ready soldier in his place. Surveying the area, he navigated their best route out of the woods.

Kira followed every command as they left the woods. She didn't want to overreact. After all, it was probably just an animal or a jogger. Mags's demeanor said otherwise. She had just met Mags, but she suspected the dog didn't spook easily. Gauging by Stark's very serious response and careful retreat, Kira feared it was something more than an animal or hiker. Her mind shifted to the open balcony door. Old fears and anxiety threatened to surface. *Get a grip!* she told herself silently. *You are a captain in the United States Army. You are going to have to be tougher than this or Holt will be right about you. What happened in med school was ages ago. He is nowhere near here.* Kira repeated this to herself silently until they reached the truck.

Once there, Stark shook his head. "That was really odd," he said. "Mags isn't skittish. Something had her really upset back there." He made sure Kira and Mags were safely in, then went around to his side. Kira looked out into the darkness.

When Stark asked her to come home with him she readily accepted. Not only did she want to be alone and very naked with him, the thought of going back to her apartment now made her sick. Once in the truck Mags visibly relaxed and they settled into the drive. Something about being with Stark and

Mags felt complete. Kira smiled and looked up at him. Her fingers traced over the tags around her neck. He would be with her always, no matter what. Stark turned and saw her hands on the tags. "When we get back, I want you naked . . . except for those," he said sternly and reached over, gently rubbing his hand across hers and the tags.

***

Stark looked at her with heated anticipation. The thought of her wearing nothing but his dog tags made him ache. He knew it was an image he was going to take with him when he left. He had planned to tell her on their walk that he would be leaving for a short deployment in a week, but after she had told him about her dad, he couldn't bear to. He decided it would be best to wait until morning. At least they would have this night first. He planned to make enough memories tonight to last until he got back.

He lived several miles farther from base than she did. He hoped she liked his contemporary two-story. At least he was sure she would like the view of Pikes Peak. The clean lines and modern design blended with the landscape. "It's a very green design," Stark said, his boyish excitement showing as he described the combined system of solar panels and wind energy.

"This house is quite the contrast to your family's ski home. This is all you isn't it?" She beamed up at him.

"They paused at the doorstep and he took her in his arms and kissed her vehemently. Once inside, he scanned the area to be sure it was completely devoid of clutter.

Kira winced " Wow this place is immaculate! Remind me not to let you in my small apartment until I have a chance to organize all the boxes!"

As they walked through the house He was suddenly aware of voices . . . or moans? Was there a movie playing? Stark got a frustrated look on his face.

"Did you leave the TV on?" Kira asked.

"No, but Paige may have," he said, aggravated. Stark shook his head. Paige usually took good care of things but occasionally she left the TV on or her magazines scattered about. Stark was very meticulous in the care of his things. This was his biggest pet peeve with Paige. She was a free spirit and sometimes ignored his neurotic tendencies. As they walked into the great room, Stark stopped suddenly and tried to put his arm up to stop Kira. But it was too late. She was already beside him and staring in horror at the images on the giant screen.

Chapter 11

Stark's usually tan face had turned ghostly pale, his calm demeanor replaced with panic and then rage. Kira stood horrified. Her mouth could not have hung open any farther. She forgot to breathe. The only thing louder than the moans reverberating in full surround sound was the pounding of her own heart echoing in her ears. There, before her in all his glory on the screen, was Stark, his rippled muscles highlighted by a directional light in what must have been a dim room. *What the hell is he holding? A riding crop?* Before she could wonder what it was for, he began an onslaught, with the precision and grace of a master swordsman, on a bound and leather-clad woman. Kira was vaguely aware of the actual Stark frantically searching for the remote in order to stop the shocking display. The camera angle changed and Kira could fully see the woman. Her striking features were unforgettable: the jet-black hair, the tattoos, those beautiful almond eyes looking adoringly up at the camera. From this angle, Kira could see the woman was fully restrained. Her bust, heaving in a mix of pain and pleasure, threatened to spill out of the tightly laced leather corset. As the scene unfolded before her, strangely graceful and poetic, like a dark and twisted ballet, Kira was filled with anger, disgust, and .

. . curiosity. The woman's mouth opened in ecstasy as Stark grabbed her with both hands and . . .

The screen went dark. Stark had finally found the remote and ended the sordid exhibition. Kira looked from him to the now blank screen. The pink had drained from her cheeks and was replaced by a greenish hue. She fought the urge to vomit. Before Stark could say anything, the other star of the film came waltzing into the room, wearing nothing but black lace boy-short panties. She froze. Her gaze shifted from Stark to Kira and back again. Her silky black tresses caressed her face and neck and lay gently around her breasts. Her silence lasted only a moment and then, like an actress hearing the call to action, she came to life with a wicked gleam in her eyes. "Hello, you must be *Captain* Riley," Paige said with coy amusement, extending her hand dramatically to Kira.

"Paige, what the hell is going on here?" Stark yelled, stepping between the two women. Simultaneously, they sidestepped him, sizing up each other.

"I just came by to do some laundry and check on Mags. You guys were gone and I have several loads since my machine is broken, so I looked for a movie to watch. I forgot you had all of these movies! This one's a *real* classic! But my personal favorite is Zoe's first time in the suspension cuffs. Man, did she look . . ."

"Enough, Paige!" Stark's voice had taken on a deadly tone, stopping Paige mid-sentence. She looked up at him, knowing instantly that she had gone too far.

"Kitty!" A soft melodious voice called out. "I got take-out. Where are you?" Into the room drifted a very graceful redhead. Her eyes were pale green and her flowing scarlet locks were cut in long layers that bounced with each step. "Whoa! Is this a party? If so, I'm in!" She squealed delightfully when she saw Kira. "Is this the surprise?" She grinned widely, patting Kira on the ass as she crossed the room to Paige. Kira jumped, startled by Zoe's comment . . . and the ass grab.

Paige couldn't help but laugh. "No, Vanilla here is Stark's girlfriend. I was going to surprise you with some videos we haven't watched in a long time, our videos with Stark. But these two walked in just as I was getting to the good part," Paige said with no attempt to hide her disappointment.

"Well, it *is* his house. You can't get mad at a guy for coming home," Zoe reminded her.

Stark started to usher Paige and Zoe into the kitchen. "Where are your clothes?" he questioned Paige sharply.

"They're in the washer. I threw them in with this load," she said contritely.

Kira picked up her purse, which had fallen to the floor. Without saying a word she turned to leave. Stark caught her as she reached the door. "Where are you going?" he asked, pleadingly.

"Owen, I have had just about all I can stand of your crazy train of Victoria Secret nympho bitches!" Kira was truly mad now. "They come in and out of your houses like they still live there. They watch us have sex. They walk around your house half naked. This is madness. Clearly you have problems getting rid of exes or else you're some kind of fucked-up sexual deviant."

"Don't be mad, Vanilla," Paige called from the kitchen. "You can't blame Stark. When you've had all thirty-one flavors, it's hard to settle for plain vanilla."

"Damn it, Paige!" Stark yelled back. Then turning to Kira, he asked quietly, "Please don't go. This has been a very fucked-up misunderstanding. That was all in the past. Don't leave. Please."

"Misunderstanding? Are you freaking kidding me?" Kira turned, facing him. She was flaming mad. "You have your hands full with California Bitch Barbie, Tall Dark and Slutty, and The Little Mermaid over there. I'm not going to compete with your Neapolitan-array of groupies. After all, I'm just *vanilla*."

"I see you've met Simone," Paige called out. "She's a real piece of work!"

"Paige, go get dressed. You and Zoe need to go. Now!" Stark's voice was intense. He and Kira had so much to overcome and Paige's antics were not helping in any way. "Kira, please don't go."

But she was already heading down the walk and into the darkness. "Kira, stop! Let me take you home!" he called after her desperately.

"I am a captain in the army," she reminded him sternly. "I have legs, I can walk, and if I want, I have a cell phone and can call for a cab."

***

He started to go after her, suddenly terrified he would never see her again. But she waved good-bye over her shoulder firmly with a single finger salute. Stark stopped and went back inside to deal with Paige. "Paige, what the hell are you trying to do to me?" he asked, walking into the kitchen. His voice lacked the cool control she was used to. In the bright light of the kitchen she could see the magnitude of the pain in his face. He crossed to the cabinet and poured a double shot of Maker's Mark. Swigging it down, he started to pour another.

Paige and Zoe exchanged glances. "Paige, I'm going to go and let you two talk this out," Zoe said. She crossed over to Stark and hugged him. "I'm sorry, sweetie," she said. "I was just having a little fun. I didn't mean to upset her or you. She really does seem like a nice girl." She hugged and kissed Paige. "I'll see you later, Kitty. Love you." She cast them both a sympathetic glance as she walked out.

"Owen, I . . ." Paige started, struggling to find the right words. "You know I love you. Zoe and I both do. We just don't want you to get hurt. The movie was just something I came across. I really didn't think you would be home. I was going to surprise Zoe but then you walked in with that woman. I really am sorry." She had covered up with a silk robe. Moving across the kitchen with the familiarity of someone who had always lived there, she grabbed a shot glass and pulled up a stool beside Stark. "I don't want to see you throw away everything important to you for some piece of tail."

"She's not just a piece of tail," Stark said firmly. He was numb. Fifteen minutes ago Kira had been in his arms, kissing him wildly as he opened the door. Now she was gone. "Paige, I really care about her. I need her."

"You need her like a hole in the head," Paige insisted. "In case all this hormonal frenzy has completely clouded your judgment, she is a *captain* and fraternization is a serious offense. This isn't like you. You don't take unnecessary risks

188

like this. These kind of careless mistakes are going to get you killed. Let her go and be done with this bullshit." Paige's heart ached. This was more than petty jealousy. Stark had been her best friend for several years. It wasn't just the alternative lifestyle they had shared. She loved him dearly. The thought of him getting himself killed was more than she could take. He had always seemed so invincible: a concrete hero, unscathed by mere humans. But seeing him like this, so hurt and broken over this girl, made her realize just how vulnerable he really was.

"You're right. She's a distraction," Stark admitted slowly. "But I'm somewhere else when I'm with her. All the pain and the bullshit are gone when I'm with her. In those moments, everything is perfect. I can't let her go, Paige. I need her." Stark stared into the now empty glass.

"You're already married to the army and your team. This little distraction, while fun, may just get you killed," Paige said. As she spoke, Paige realized that Kira was much more than a distraction. He might not realize it yet, but Stark was falling in love. Paige poured them each another drink. They were going to need it.

***

Kira shrugged her coat up around her shoulders. She hadn't realized it was this cold outside. The biting wind picked up, sending a shiver through her. *What is going on with you? Why did you even get involved with him? You knew this was a mistake!* Kira's thoughts raced as she walked through the bitter cold. Hot tears stung her eyes. *Vanilla?* The thought of Paige's word hurt her as much as seeing the awful video. Seeing Stark with another woman was painful enough, but the carnal look on his face was at the same time riveting and heartbreaking. She had seen hints of that look when he was with her—but never like that. Hot jealousy burned inside her. She hated Paige for being that intimate with him and she hated that Paige was still very much in the picture.

She didn't care what Stark said. You don't walk around a platonic male friend's house in your panties. Every time she closed her eyes she could see Paige, bound, dressed in that leather corset, and Stark's eyes. His eyes had blazed as he worked her over with the crop and then took her. Then anger and jealousy was clouded by the intense eroticism. She couldn't help but picture herself in Paige's place. Would he do that to her? Would he want to? *Get over it! He is some kind of sex freak. This is* not *what you need right now, or ever.*

Kira's thoughts were interrupted by the high beams of a car approaching behind her. She continued down the sidewalk, waiting for the car to pass but it didn't. It seemed to have slowed

190

to her pace and was following her with the high beams on. Kira's heart beat faster. *Is it really following me?* At first she thought it might be Stark. She turned around but the high beams were too bright to see the car well. She could tell, though, that it wasn't Stark's big Dodge. She picked up her pace. The car sped up behind her. Panic began to set in. Kira's heart was racing full-force now and she could feel her breath coming faster. The car revved its engine just behind her. Kira tried to stay focused and keep her strides fast until she reached a more public area. She wondered if Paige or Zoe were toying with her. She hoped it was them, then she could just be mad. But this seemed more sinister.

Whoever it was stayed just far enough back so that she couldn't see them, but close enough to intimidate her. Fear gripped her as she realized that if they tried to take her, her only defense would be her own skills and strength. *Way to go there, Nancy Drew. Leave your firearm at home. That's just perfect!* She had not had enough combat training to fight off an attacker yet. She was in a very dimly lit part of town. It was still a nice area, just not quite on the scale of Stark's. The houses were closer together here but the street was dim. Would anyone even hear her scream? Suddenly the headlights went out. She turned but the car had faded into the darkness. *Was it still there?* she wondered in a panic. *Did they stop? Did they get out?* She tried to reason with herself that maybe, just maybe, they weren't following her at all. Maybe they were just looking for a house and now had found it. *I am just being irrational. I can't let this happen. I am in control and I am fine!* Kira repeated the mantra to herself. But she knew it wasn't true. It wasn't all in her head. Painful memories flooded back to her. She closed her eyes, unconsciously gripping the dog tags for comfort. Despite her best efforts to stay calm, she gave in to panic and started to run as fast as her legs would carry her. She ran for her life. Instantaneously the high beams came back on, flooding the street with light and filling her with panic. *He's still here! It's not in my head! He's here!* Kira struggled to breathe. She saw a gas station a block ahead. She ran to it as fast as she could. When she reached the light of the parking lot, relief filled her. She turned to the road but there was no one there.

Kira paused, looking up and down the road. The car had been right behind her. At least she thought it had been. *It's been a long night. I'm not going crazy. I'm just stressed.* She willed herself to put it out of her mind and went into the gas station. She decided the comfort of gas station coffee and some Swiss Cake Rolls were much needed. *Anything but Ho Ho's,* she thought. *I've had quite enough of those for one night.* She would call a cab from here. Crazy or not, she was too tired to test the theory tonight. As she looked over the plastic-wrapped selection of pastries, she noticed a very familiar BMW pull up slowly to the pump. Sure enough, Holt stepped out of the car and started pumping gas. *Fuck! What's he doing here? Surely that wasn't him? Now I* am *being crazy,* she thought before dismissing the idea. *How am I going to explain being here?* Before she had a chance to come up with a suitable excuse, Holt walked in.

"Kira, hey, how are you?" he asked with a puzzled look on his face. "What are you doing out here?"

"I, oh . . . well, I went for a jog," she stammered, remembering she was in exercise clothes and had gone for a hike earlier, so this wasn't entirely untrue.

"Wow," he said, looking impressed. "You're more dedicated than I thought. Ten miles at night in this cold. That's pretty intense."

"Ma'am, your cab's here," the man behind the counter said gruffly.

"Cab?" Holt asked, looking surprised.

"Well, it's like you said. I ran much farther than I intended and the cold was starting to get to me, so I thought I'd get a ride back. Well, it was good to see you," she said as she paid for her armful of pre-packaged goodness. "I'll see you in clinic."

"Kira, wait. I can give you a ride home. Come with me." He moved between her and the door. His voice was soft, but there was an underlying urgency.

"Thanks, but the cab is already here and I don't want to keep you from what you're doing," she answered hastily.

"I was just heading home. I live in this neighborhood. You should come over and see the place," he said, obviously very proud of his residence.

"That's lovely. But I'd better pass tonight. It's late and I have clinic early. There's some reading I need to do before bed." Kira made an effort to sidestep him and go out the door. She was almost past when Holt grabbed her arm. She winced, surprised by the strength of his grip. "Let go!"

"Kira, come on, at least let me give you a ride home." His voice had a darker tone now, still quiet but more commanding.

"Holt, let me go. I told you I'm not going anywhere with you." She was angry now. She pulled her arm but his grip was tight.

"It sounded to me like she said she didn't want to go with you," an assertive female voice said from behind Holt.

Behind Holt stood a very angry Zoe. Her scarlet hair looked like fire. "You can just back the fuck up and let her go." Zoe's voice was so commanding it took Holt by surprise. The soft melodious voice from Stark's house was gone, replaced by a very dominating tone. Holt's grip lessened. He seemed captivated and disarmed by Zoe's stunning beauty and presence.

Seeing her opportunity for freedom, Kira wriggled away from Holt and toward the door. Zoe followed her out, leaving an openmouthed Holt to wonder what the hell just happened.

"Mouth-breather," Zoe muttered at Holt as she walked away.

"Kira, can I give you a ride?" Zoe asked sweetly, her soft voice back. "I think we should talk. I would really like to explain some things."

For a moment Kira wondered where Zoe had come from. How had she found her there? But curiosity won out over skepticism. She needed to know more about Stark and this other life he had.

"Wow!" she exclaimed as she climbed in to Zoe's 1955 Chevy Bel-Air. "Holy shit, this is one amazing car!" Every detail of the fire-engine red-and-white car was perfectly restored. Even in the dim lights of the gas station, the chrome shone like the top of the Chrysler Building. She slid into the spotless white seat. "Where did you get this?" Kira was momentarily distracted from Stark and the sordid details of the night.

"It's Kitty's car," Zoe said, smiling brightly. "Well, I guess it's mine, too. But Betty here is Kitty's dream."

"Kitty?" Kira said, looking confused.

"—Paige. I call her Kitty," she said, smiling fondly. "Stark helped her completely restore Betty here from the ground up. It took them five years. Paige is very handy with a wrench," she said coyly.

Kira shuddered. "They've really shared a lot," she murmured, painfully realizing how big a part of his life Paige was.

"I know it's hard for you to understand. It was for me at first, too. But they are family. Like best friends, I guess. It's hard to explain. He's not in love with her and she's not with him. But they do love each other." Kira looked at Zoe with distrust. "They were really into the rockabilly scene, especially the cars. They were just starting to remodel this one and went to a lot of car shows. That's how I met them. I was a model at one of the shows. I was drawn to Paige right away. There I was, posing in my rockabilly get-up with shoes and lipstick as bright as my hair when I saw her. She looked like a perfect Asian Bettie Page, and my heart stopped. I wanted to talk to her so badly. Then I saw her fine hunk of a boyfriend. Needless to say, by the time they came over to talk with me, my legs were like Jell-O."

"Ok, I'm not sure if this is supposed to help, but picturing you all hot for the both of them is not helping me forget what he has done with both of you!" Kira blurted out.

"Sorry, I'm not trying to make you more upset; I just want you to understand. They introduced me to a lot of things, and somewhere along the line, Paige and I fell in love. What you saw—that is part of his life. It's who he is," Zoe finished, trying to gauge Kira's reaction.

"Why didn't he just tell me from the beginning that's what he is into?" Kira asked, still fuming.

"Yeah, how was *that* conversation supposed to go?" Zoe asked sarcastically. Imitating Stark, she said, " 'Thanks for going to dinner with me. You look ravishing. I barely know you, but I want to take you back to my place, tie you up, spank you with a riding crop, and torment you till you scream and cry and come at the same time.' He might as well have thrown in a non-disclosure agreement for good measure," she said, laughing at the ludicrous idea. "He respects you and cares about you. Deeply, it seems. I'm sure that when the time was right he would have told you. Are *you* really proud of everything you've ever done? Surely there are things in your past you've neglected to mention," she finished, raising her eyebrows knowingly at Kira.

Shit, does she know about my past? Kira shook the idea from her head. Zoe was just speaking figuratively. "I guess you're right," she said slowly. "This is a lot to take in. I don't know if I can handle all of this." She looked up as they approached her apartment. "It's this one right up here."

Zoe pulled the immaculate piece of American history up to the curb. "Thanks for the ride home," Kira said as she climbed out.

"So you'll talk to him?" Zoe asked hopefully.

"I don't know. I've got a lot of thinking to do." Kira turned and walked into her apartment. She was tired. Bone-achingly tired. She was too emotionally worn out to worry about stalkers, or boyfriends, or rockabilly tattoo artists. She wanted— no, *needed*, sleep. She settled in for a much needed rest but as she drifted off, her dreams were haunted by shadowy images of dark places, forbidden pleasures, and past fears.

Chapter 12

Kira woke as tired as she'd been when she went to bed. A night spent tossing and turning had left her sore and confused. She couldn't deny how she felt about Stark. He was intoxicating, but watching him have that kind of sex with someone else was too much to take. Her stomach churned at the thought. *Vanilla!* She could still hear Paige taunting her. *Is that how he sees me? Vanilla?* Hot tears stung her eyes and threatened to break free. *I can't compete with those women. They're like kinky supermodels and I'm . . . I'm plain old vanilla.* The tears made their escape. Kira hated herself for crying over this. It was stupid and she knew it. But she already cared about him so much. The thought of saying good-bye and walking away from him now broke her heart.

Kira was thankful to be up early. She needed a really long run to shake off her crazy night. She laced up her shoes and got bundled up for the cold. She set off to the mountain to run. The air was sharp, but the biting wind soothed the ache that gripped her. Kira ran hard, trying to drive all the hurt and anger away with each step. As she fought her way up the hill, her mind replayed the evening with Stark. When he took her in his arms and told her he couldn't bear to let her go, she had melted. She closed her eyes for a moment, remembering how he took one of her dog tags and gave her one of his. That simple act was the most tender and beautiful thing anyone had ever done for her. She knew that was not something given lightly. In their present situation, it was the strongest commitment they would be able to make. She had felt so connected to him. She had felt that somehow it would work out all right.

Feeling shattered as she ran on she remembered walking into Stark's house and seeing Paige. *Seriously, who wouldn't be furious to find your new boyfriend's ex running around his house in her panties, watching sex tapes of the two of them!* Kira's anger boiled all over again. She didn't care what Zoe or anyone else said. She was not ok with this situation. There had to be some boundaries and she was starting to realize that, given their lifestyle, that wasn't something they understood. Kira struggled with her composite of emotions. She was angry and heartbroken, but a very small part of her was curious. What is it that captivated him so about tying women up? She was surprised that despite her anger, she had been turned on to see him that way. The rippling of his muscles as he had moved in the dim light, the fire that had burned in his eyes as he tortured and pleased the leather-bound Paige. Kira couldn't help but picture herself in Paige's place. *How would it feel to be bound up?* Kira quickly dismissed the idea. This was not a place she was willing to go.

She hustled back to her apartment and in for a lightning fast shower. Her morning of sordid reflection left very little time to get ready for clinic. In her haste she failed to notice the slight breeze coming through the balcony door. She rushed through her small apartment, stripping off clothes as she went. The sweet painful pleasure of the steaming water took her breath away. She relaxed and let the stream wash all the tension away.

A leather-gloved hand grasped the edge of the slightly open bathroom door. Edging it open farther, the intruder was given full view of Kira's moment of shower bliss. The hand trailed down the door edge and disappeared around the edge. The intruder silently moved through the sparsely furnished apartment and into her study. Papers were evaluated and found wanting, her computer having been previously examined. The intruder paused momentarily on his way out to watch her wash herself and then exit the shower. Water sparkled as it dripped from her flawless body. *One day she will see!* And with the same silence used during the invasion of Kira's home, the gloved hand took a single rose from the vase and laid it gently on the table. *One day you will know it was always me. Only me.*

Kira stepped from the shower and finished drying off. She exited the bathroom clad in her fluffy towel. Instantly the chill hit her. As she approached the living room, the stinging cold told her something was very wrong. She followed the frigid draft to the slightly billowing curtain of the balcony door and her blood ran cold. *Oh God!* she thought, instantly nauseous. *He's here. I know it. I am not crazy! Oh God!* Her legs felt weak. With Jell-O legs, she made her way to the phone. Kira called the only person she could bear to talk to at the moment. As her shaky hand dialed the number Kira saw the single rose on the table.

Abbey's car came screeching to a halt in front of the apartment. Kira was ready to go the second Abbey arrived. "Thanks for coming. I can't tell you how much I appreciate this," Kira said breathlessly as she climbed into Abbey's car. On the drive to clinic, Kira began to spill her guts to the closest and dearest friend she had. Silently, she prayed that Abbey would not find her crazy.

Abbey listened intently as Kira told her about the craziness of the previous day: the woods with Stark, the dog tags, and the horrific movie. Abbey quietly took it all in. "So the Sexy Tattoo Girl and her lover still live with him?" she asked, understandably confused.

"No," Kira said, completely dejected. "They come by to check on Mags. I guess they're all still friends. At least that's what they say." The confusion in Kira's voice spoke volumes to Abbey.

"So they are still close?" she said in a suspicious tone. "Twenty-plus years as a military wife has taught me to examine all aspects of a story. I don't believe in coincidence. If something happened, nine times out of ten there was a reason for it. This Zoe character says they are just friends now? Do you believe that?"

"I don't know what to believe," Kira admitted. Her heart hurt too much to make a rational decision at this point.

"So what about Paige? What does she say?"

"I haven't talked to her," Kira said, realizing she didn't want to face Paige. Paige represented a part of Stark's life she couldn't begin to understand. It also seemed that Paige was his closest friend, except maybe for that big guy, Sergeant Heisel. Kira struggled to understand how she could possibly be ok with this. She chastised herself for being too chicken to disclose to Abbey the recent craziness at her apartment and the mystery car. She couldn't help but wonder if it was all in her head. Memories of the scrutiny of the university trials and her own embarrassment remained fresh in her mind. They were wounds that would never be healed. *I'm a captain in the United States Army!* she told herself, vowing to let the past go.

***

For three days Kira maintained a professional exterior despite her inner turmoil. She managed to focus solely on her work, hiding her heartbreak. Stark did not call. Now, she was as angry at his absence as she was about his past. As day four rolled around, Kira's frustration hit a peak. And she had to admit that despite being mad as hell over the video, she couldn't help her curiosity. She had been having increasingly insatiable fantasies after viewing it. If she was forced to be honest, the idea of him controlling her body was obsessing her. The act of trusting someone enough to surrender to them was completely overtaking her imagination. She made her way through her work. Yet when she closed her eyes, she could smell him. Kira was jolted from her salacious thoughts by a ruckus in the hallway.

"You absolutely cannot go in there!" Abbey's sharp tone rang out.

"I need to see Captain Riley right now." Paige's voice was equally fierce.

Knowing the two women were more likely to tear into each other rather than back down, Kira hustled out to prevent the office from turning into a MMA exhibition. "Hey, what's going on out here?" Despite her shock at seeing Paige in her office, Kira maintained a cool and professional tone.

"This tag chaser insists on being let in to see you, Captain," Abbey replied. Disapproval dripped from her every word and her scowl matched her tone. Abbey stood with her arms crossed, ready to hold her position. The stoutness of her determination reminded Kira of a bulldog preparing to attack.

Paige looked equally determined. Her long black hair was done up tightly in some kind of bun. The combination of eyeliner and her glowering expression made her almond eyes appear menacing. Kira stifled a giggle.

"It's ok, it's ok. Look, this is not a good place for us to talk. It's lunchtime anyway. Let's go for a walk."

"I'm no tag chaser but I'm no grunt either," Paige said. "Marching around all over this base in the blistering cold is not going to happen in these shoes. We'll take my car." Paige turned on her Jimmy Choo heels without looking back to see if Kira was following her. "Let's go, Vanilla," she called over her shoulder.

Abbey started to take a step toward Paige, her hand in a tightly drawn fist. "Whoa there, Abbey," Kira said, quickly stopping her friend. "While I may not like her, I have to know what she wants. I haven't talked to Stark in four days and it's killing me. I need to know."

Kira grabbed her coat and followed Paige to her car. Kira was secretly glad to get to ride in that car again. In the bright daylight it was even more stunning. The sun reflected brightly off the candy-apple red and stark white paint. The chrome was flawless. Kira could see just how much work they had put into the car. Then it hit her that it was the product of hours and hours of work shared by Paige and Stark. She slumped into the perfect pearl white leather seat. Before her mind could wander, imagining Stark and Paige together, she blurted, "What do you want, Paige? Why are you here?"

"You know very well why I'm here, you catty vanilla bitch!" Paige retorted as she sped out of the parking lot.

"Excuse me? You don't get to talk to me like this. I'm not one of the submissive cocks you boss around. Either tell me what you came to say, or stop the car and let me out." Kira's voice was heated.

"Let me start over." Paige tried again in a calmer tone. "I don't know what you think you are doing with Owen, but whatever it is, you need to get it figured out before he leaves. He can't go out on deployment with his head all wrapped up in this shit or he's going to get killed. He needs to know one way or the other what you want."

Deployed? What the hell is she talking about? Panic set in. "What do you mean, deployed? When is he leaving?" Kira asked, suddenly feeling as if all the air had been sucked out of the car.

"Didn't he tell you? He's leaving in less than a week! He was probably going to tell you the other night after he found out, but you went all bat-shit crazy and left." Paige's voice was sharp and angry. "So you really didn't know he was leaving?"

He's leaving . . . Oh God, he's really leaving. She felt sick.

"Did he send you here to talk to me?" Kira asked, suddenly disgusted.

"Hell no! If he knew I was here he would shit a brick! I love Owen, just not in the same way you do. We've shared a lot of things, experienced a lot together, but now we're just friends. But I do love him and I don't want to see him hurt or killed because you've got him so messed up in the head that he can't focus. You're an officer, for God's sake. Aren't you supposed to know better?" Paige's voice went up an octave as her frustration grew.

"I don't want him to be hurt either," Kira countered. "And I can see that you love him. But I don't for an instant understand what it is you two had or have. Seeing the two of you like that . . ." Her voice trailed off. Kira's emotions were a stormy mix of hurt and anger as she struggled to finish her sentence. "He's not who I thought he was. If that's what he wants, I don't know that I can give that to him. And you, you're there in his house in your freaking underwear. I'm not ok with that. I will never be ok with that."

"So that's it, then. You're done with him. You'll just let him go? Grow the fuck up. I don't know what he sees in you but there must be something. The way he looks at you, the way he looks when he talks about you . . . he hasn't cared for a girl like this in . . . well, ever. He's falling in love with you and you know it. Don't toy with him. I know you're mad, but don't do this to him. He is devastated. Talk to him. You owe him that much. Get this resolved one way or the other before he leaves." Paige's voice was stern, but her compassion for Stark rang through.

Kira was shocked. She still hated Paige, but it was clear that she needed to talk to Stark. She couldn't let him go, not like this. "I'll talk to him. I really miss him. But Paige, I'm not making any promises. I don't know that I can be what he wants."

"Suits me. I'm not asking you to make any promises. And no, Vanilla, you'll never be able to fill my Jimmy Choo's. But he hasn't asked you to do anything—you're the one assuming what he wants. He seemed pretty happy with the way things were between you. Why don't you talk with him and find out what he wants?" A slight cattiness had returned to Paige's tone.

"I just don't see why he kept it from me. Why he didn't tell me about that part of his life?" Kira asked, still hurt.

"Zoe told me you said that. Seriously, when was that supposed to have come up? He's not some kind of freak. He wants to be with you, for *you*. Not to have you as his sub. You have no idea what that is about, so before you pass judgment you should back off and give him a chance. When and if he ever wants to go there with you, it will be something you explore together. It's about trust and pleasure, not punishment," she said matter-of-factly.

They circled back to the parking lot of her clinic. Kira was thankful they hadn't gone for food. Her appetite was a little ragged after their confrontation. As the car stopped Kira reached for the door handle.

"Kira, just remember beneath his tough exterior he's very vulnerable. Other girls have come and gone and he barely seemed bothered by it. But you seem to mean more to him."

"I'll talk to him. I'll go by tonight—unless you're planning on being there," Kira said in an exasperated tone.

"No, I'm keeping my distance. Besides he's still hopping mad about the other night," Paige answered with a chuckle.

"Ok, then tonight. And Paige," Kira said as she stepped out of the car, "the best thing about vanilla is you can dress it up any way you want. I don't need to fill your shoes. I've got my own." Kira walked into the clinic and didn't look back.

"Well played, Vanilla," Paige said, smiling, "Maybe you're not so bad after all."

***

Kira stepped out of the cab. *Ok, at what point did I think this was a good idea?* she thought as she wobbled slightly in the strappy black heels. She had been thinking about this moment all day. What exactly had possessed her to come dressed in this outfit, she wasn't sure. She paid the taxi driver and straightened her dress. Pulling her coat tightly around her shoulders, she made her way up to the door. Kira nervously bit her lip as she rang the bell. She knew he would be home. She had texted him right after work and asked if he wanted to talk. He had asked if she wanted to go to dinner but she'd said she would rather meet him here. Kira decided that if they split, a public place would be a bad idea. And if things went as well as she hoped . . . well, the restaurant would be a bit awkward. She could feel her heart fluttering to life as footsteps approached the door.

***

Stark gasped as the door opened and light spilled out of the house, illuminating the sexy vision on his door step. "Holy hell!" he breathed, taking her in. Stepping back, he held the door for her to come in. "You look . . . um. Wow. Amazing! Are we going out? I thought you wanted to stay in and talk about the other night?" He couldn't take his eyes off her. His growing desire was going to make it very difficult to talk about anything objectively.

Kira smiled up at him. "We're staying in," she said simply, allowing him to take her black wool coat. His fingers traced gently over her shoulders as he took the coat, revealing a short, strappy black dress. His tags still hung around her neck. "Are you ok?" she asked coyly. He was just standing there, staring at her, his expression a mix of disbelief and wanton need.

"I'm not sure," he said quietly. "I thought you were gone. About the other night, I'm so sorry it happened that way. Those movies were shot years ago. I forgot they even existed. It wasn't something I keep around to watch."

"So do you still do that stuff? Do you like tying women up and punishing them?" Her voice was flat, unreadable.

"I want to be with you," he replied. "I've told you before that I would never ask you to do anything you didn't already want to do. I could never risking losing you." His voice was deeper, huskier. Discussing bondage with her dressed like this was too much.

"Is that what you meant by living on the naughty list? Do you fantasize about tying me up and dominating me? Spanking my ass with your riding crop?"

Her sultry voice nearly unglued him.

Is she testing me? Fuck me . . . Thoughts of ripping her out of that dress and turning that pale ass bright pink with the sting of his hand raced through his head. "What are you trying to do to me?" he asked. The colossal bulge in his dark jeans revealed just how aroused he was. He leaned forward, putting his hand in her hair and pulling her close to him. He closed his eyes for a minute, breathing her in. "Kira, stop this," he said, backing up abruptly. "This isn't you. I'm not going there with you. I won't risk losing you."

"But you've had Paige and Zoe and God knows who else in here. Why not me? Am I not sexy enough for your games?" Kira looked at him innocently. His eyes were locked on her fingers gently playing with the dog tags that hung down between her perfect breasts, which he noted were mostly exposed in that dress.

"You're killing me! That was different. Those were flings, just sex. *You* are different. You mean more to me. You mean everything to me." His voice was torn.

"Show me," she said, smiling, biting her lower lip and twirling her hair innocently. "It's supposed to be about trust and pleasure, right? So show me."

Stark could hold back no longer. The combination of the way her dress gently outlined the curve of her ass, her perfectly toned legs in those incredible heels, and finally, her invitation, put him right over the edge.

***

"Come with me." His voice had changed. It was darker, and the fire was burning in his eyes like she had seen on the film. Her heart raced with excitement and fear as he led her upstairs. He paused on the landing and pressed her against the wall for a deep, encompassing kiss. One strong hand grabbed her ass and pulled her thigh up around him.

His kiss was forceful and needy. Her breath came heavy. It had been four days but it felt like a thousand years since she'd felt his hands on her. His tongue gracefully rolled across hers. His lips were warm and tasting of whiskey. His kiss deepened. Kira smelled the mix of his cologne and whatever he had been cooking. Her only appetite now was for him. His hand held her leg firmly around him, holding her open to him. His massive cock pressed through his jeans and her lace panties. His hips grinding into her made her so very wet. A soft moan escaped her lips. She wanted him terribly. His other hand took her wrist and pinned it over her head. She gasped, wincing slightly. The sharpness of the sensation was electrifying.

"So you want me to tie you up?" he growled into her mouth. He seemed to be fighting a war with himself like a beast in a self made prison. "You have to trust me. Do you trust me, Kira?" His hot breath and the gravity of his words ignited her.

"Yes," she whimpered, because she was too breathless to fully speak. Her heart raced a million miles a minute. *Am I really going to do this?*

Chapter 13

As soon as the consent escaped her, he was alive and wild. Still holding her wrist, he led Kira up the remaining stairs. Her heart beat faster with each step. She was excited and terrified to find out what awaited her. *I do trust him*, she thought as she followed him down an immaculate hallway with three heavy oak doors evenly spaced on each side. They were all closed. Her curiosity burned to see inside each one. Her anticipation was suffocating and her breath came short and shallow. He moved quickly down the hall then paused abruptly at the door, one hand on the knob and the other held her wrist. He turned and pulled her tightly to him, and kissed her hard, as if he was getting one last kiss just in case. She closed her eyes and surrendered to his mouth, but he stopped. His lips barely touching hers, he spoke.

"Kira, I . . . I want you to know you mean more to me than anything. I will never ask you to do anything you don't want to do. For this to work you must do exactly as I say." Each word vibrated on her lips. A mix of terror and unbridled excitement coursed through her flesh. Before she could speak, he continued. "Let me have complete control. Surrender and lose yourself in me. You have to trust me completely. And I will trust that, when you need to, you will tell me to stop." He paused for what seemed like an eternity, then finally said, "*You* are ultimately in control." His voice was low and stern.

She could feel the vibration of his words on her lips. Fear and delicious anticipation surged through her. "Like a safe word?" she asked and almost giggled at the ludicrousness of this moment. *Am I seriously going to go into this room and let him exact whatever sexual torture he wants on me? Oh, yes . . .*

"Something like that," he said with a smirk. "All you have to do is tell me to release you and you are free."

"Release me," she said softly, trying the words out. So simple and yet the implication was immense.

"Good girl." Stark's deep tone sounded more authoritative.

Kira realized she was holding her breath as he turned the knob slowly and the door swung open wide. Her breath caught and she gasped at the magnificence of what must be his bedroom. The lights were out, but the room was illuminated fully by a soft blue light coming from the moon reflecting off Pikes Peak. The phosphorescence of the moonlight transformed the room into an otherworldly stage. Opposite the walls of glass lay a very large, modern bed. Its massive wooden frame was dark and the soft sheets and comforter appeared to be a silver-gray.

The walls, a deep slate, seemed to fade into the shadows. The far wall was made of rock or slate and held a see-through fireplace, through which she could see the bathroom on the other side. With the touch of a button he turned on a roaring fire. The magical ambience of the room was transformed by the flames into something more sinister.

A moment of doubt filled her as he led her to the bed and instructed her to sit. *Calm down, Kira! He doesn't want to hurt you. Just relax.* Kira struggled to keep calm despite her aching anticipation. Stark walked over and pressed on a panel in the wall. A door slid open, revealing multiple drawers. He pulled a thin drawer open and took out a simple black silk scarf. His face was stern, but the fire in his eyes revealed his inner pleasure and his need for what was about to happen.

"Stand up," he commanded, walking with deliberate steps toward her. "Turn around."

Apprehensively Kira rose and did as she was told. With eyes downcast, she rose and turned. Her breath caught slightly as she felt his hands clasp her zipper and begin to pull it slowly down her back. Silently the silky fabric drifted to the floor. He gently placed the scarf over her eyes and tied it tightly so that she could not see anything he was about to do. She was in total darkness. *What the hell? Do not panic! This will be fine.* The darkness was alarming. Kira struggled to hear what was going on around her. She could feel her bra being unfastened, exposing her to the night. Her breasts and nipples ached with the exposure to the cold air. Silently repeating her mantra to remain calm, Kira slowed her breathing.

***

A slow smile spread across Stark's face as he beheld the dream before him. She stood there in the middle of the room, clad in only stockings, heels, and the silk blindfold. He saw the uneasiness on her face and the way she bravely tried to hide it. "Be still!" he commanded and knelt before her. *Oh God, this woman!* For a moment, Stark rested his head against her. With each breath he inhaled the scent of her growing excitement. Kira breathed in sharply, feeling the warmth of him against her sex. Each hot breath warmed her entire body. Then suddenly he pulled away. Despite the overwhelming desire to throw her onto the bed, Stark maintained his control and slowly removed the delicious heels and peeled the stockings away from one glorious leg at a time.

He grasped her elbows, binding them behind her. This arrangement immobilized her upper arms, opening her chest and thrusting her breasts forward, exposed to his view. Though the tightness of the binding bit slightly, it caused Kira to grow wet with anticipation. The loss of sight was frightening at first but now heightened her other senses. She was acutely aware of the sharp coldness of the room but this was offset by the warmth of the fire. When he came closer, she could smell the scent of his cologne mixed with the smell of her arousal. The room was silent except for the sound of his breathing and . . . was that the sound of instruments moving? Metal maybe, clinking together— and the pounding of her own heart.

"Breathe, Kira," he instructed. His voice pulsated through her.

***

He is behind me, she thought, trying to get her bearings for what was happening. Though he said nothing, she felt his presence. With deft fingers he grasped her panties and pulled them slowly downward. Kira fought to maintain normal breathing. In one swift move her panties fell to the floor. She gasped for air as cold metal slid gracefully down her back. *What is that?* Panic gripped her as the frigid instrument trailed downward, pausing for a moment at her ass, then moving on down to her ankles. Kira felt a tightening around her ankles as metal and then a leather strap was fastened. Her other foot was pushed wide and then fastened as well. A rod was between her ankles, holding them into position, bound tightly with the straps. Stark said nothing but she heard him breathing. He was so close. She felt him staring at her, bound and naked in the middle of this room.

"I have dreamed of this moment since I first laid eyes on you," he growled like a starved animal about to devour his prey.

Despite her racing heart and impending fear, she was elated to be wanted in this way. The eagerness of his voice excited a long-ignored need in her.

***

Stark stood staring at the exquisite vision before him. A clash of moonlight and firelight danced across her heaving breasts in a dark waltz. Stark felt his already hard cock strain painfully in need. *Patience*, he ordered himself. He had waited too long for this moment to rush it now. It was all about self-restraint. He would pleasure and torture her to her breaking point, then make her come until she could not breathe. He desperately wanted her to understand this part of his life. He had been so surprised when she had called today. He knew he wanted only her, needed only her.

***

The heat from his body warmed her, yet he did not touch her. Kira wanted to beg for him, but was afraid to speak. Suddenly she was hoisted by the bond at her elbows, sending her slightly forward. Her weight shifted to her toes, causing her to arch her back to maintain her balance, forcing her ass back and out. With her ankles fixed in place she was helplessly exposed, positioned for his pleasure. Becoming painfully aware of her current predicament, she contemplated asking him to release her. Yet the promise of things to come stifled her resistance. Rugged hands drifted over the sides of her face, down her neck, across her shoulders, and came to rest over her dog tags.

"I see you are still wearing my tags," he said flatly. "That's a good girl. I want you to keep me close to you always. I am always here with you," he finished, his lips almost touching the tags and her breasts.

The sensation of his hot breath on her chest made her throb for him. Without warning she felt the wet warmth of his mouth clamp down on her nipple. He sucked and bit gently, sending electrical impulses surging directly to her clit. She squirmed, but as trussed up as she was left her powerless to move.

"Be still, baby. We're just getting started. You wanted to see what this is all about, remember? Here you are mine, only mine." His voice was dark and low. And then he was gone.

The absence of his presence was more painful than the restraints. She listened intently for a clue to his next move but all was silent until a melancholy song filled the air. The music was dark and powerful. Her anticipation built with the crescendo of the music, the tortured melody saturating every inch of her. Suddenly he was all around her, rough hands groping her breasts, a vibrating pressure finding her clit, followed by his tongue. The sensation was intense and powerful. She cried out as the vibrating pressure filled her and the soft lapping of his tongue became a forceful sucking on her overly sensitive clit. Heat encompassed her. She fought the need to come but became lost in the music and the intense sensations between her legs. A sudden sharp sting erupted across her ass. She couldn't help the cry that escaped her lips. The intense sting was followed by another. Kira could not explain why the burning sensation excited her so. She struggled slightly in her restraints. Then nothing. He again was absent. She waited, trussed up like a twisted Christmas present, unable to move. The music dwindled into a slow serenade softly calling, haunting her.

***

Stark stood back, just in the shadows, watching. He could see she was nervous but was impressed by how in control she remained. He wondered how long she would be able to withstand the deprivation. How long would *he* be able to last? He wanted her now, wanted to taste and feel her soft skin. With her elbows pulled back like that, her breasts were so open to him, perfect mounds just waiting to be tasted and licked. He longed painfully to take her, but he remained very still, waiting.

***

After what seemed like an eternity, slow, dark music began to build. The momentum heightened her anticipation. She listened fervently for some clue as to what would happen next. There was nothing. Then softly, something brushed over her foot and up her right leg slowly, softly, like fifty leather fingers trailing over her skin. She struggled to think whether she'd ever encountered an object like this before. Suddenly the soft sensation was gone, then the object reconnected sharply on the skin of her upper thigh. *Holy fuck! What is that?* It is surprising but not quite painful, and she gasped.

He was in complete control. With gentle fingers, he swept the long dark hair off her back and let it spill over her chest and onto her breasts. Every movement caused the hair to dance, exciting her very receptive nipples. Kira was suddenly distracted by the sensation of warm, almost hot, oil dripping onto the nape of her neck and upper shoulders, turning into a slow, sultry cascade farther down the curve of her back. Slowly the hot liquid found its way over her skin and into her most sensitive crevices. *Oh my!* The heat, while almost painful at first, was immensely pleasurable. The fear drifted away as she began to enjoy the many sensations that enveloped her.

The oil flowed faster now and was joined by strong hands massaging her back and shoulders. The powerful hands worked their way slowly down her back to her ass. The tempo of the music built, as did her desire. Kira felt herself giving over completely, overwhelmed by the intensity of sensations and emotions. Though bound she began to feel alive and strong. Her fears and anxieties faded to a distant memory as ardent desires took complete control of her body and spirit. The coarse hands now rubbed and excited her upper thighs, gently tracing over the opening to her pleasure. Kira became so aroused that she shuddered with each pass. Each tiny nerve ending was brought to life by the warm oil, each nerve now screaming for attention. Desperate with need, Kira struggled against her restraints. Owen's fully naked body pressed against her arched back. His rock-solid cock pressed firmly against her ass as he ground against her, grabbing her supple breasts with both hands. The hot oil glided between them. With this much lubrication his massive cock could easily slide wherever he chose to put it. In her present bondage she would be powerless to stop him. Suddenly Kira was desperate to be fucked. All reservation was gone—she wanted his cock, needed it now.

"Stark . . . please," she begged, desperation dripping from her voice.

"What, baby, tell me what you want." His voice was firm, still in control, commanding.

"Fuck me!" she pleaded. "I need you inside me!" Kira was aware her voice had gone up an octave. The ache for him was almost unbearable.

"Not yet, baby. You're almost there." The quiet reserve of his voice was unsettling. She realized now the full helplessness of her situation. He alone held the key to her release.

Despite her attempts to rock back into him, he only glided back and forth across her opening but would not enter her. Desperately she tried to twist and grind but was unable to find relief.

"You promised to trust me . . . remember?" His voice was calm, authoritative, but not condescending. "Trust me in all things. Do you trust me, Kira?"

"Yes!" she whimpered. "Yes, Owen, I trust you." Kira struggled with the words as they spilled from her mouth. *I don't put faith in people. They will eventually let you down. But he is different!*

Strong hands encompassed her upper thighs, holding her firmly against him. The broad tip of his cock pressed hard into her. She was wild, like an animal now, needing him. *Fuck me now!* The large tip of his cock was poised just over her slit. *Now, please!*

"I trust you," Kira cried out. Just as the words escaped her lips, the massive cock slipped into her with such force she was sent lurching forward. The stretching was exquisite and painful.

"Oh God, Owen!" she cried out, unable to maintain any composure at this moment. He held still for a moment, allowing her to steady herself. Then slowly at first, he began to move. Her desire had built to such a frenzied state that every nerve ending was alive and on fire. She trusted him to hold her up, and let her full weight rest into his arms and the restraints. She thought of nothing but the immense pleasure coursing through her with each thrust.

The darkness of the blindfold heightened all of Kira's other senses and set her free. A new sound joined her ecstatic chorus. The low deep moans escaping from Stark were crude and guttural. His feral excitement sent her over the edge and every piece of her exploded into the most vicious orgasm Kira had ever experienced. As if on cue, Stark met her violent exultation with his own. He tensed, held her tightly to him, then finally released her.

Spent and quivering, Kira collapsed into his arms as he undid the restraint at her elbows. He carried her gently over to the bed and laid her down. Kira, only semi-conscious after the powerful orgasm, was vaguely aware of the restraints being removed from her tiny ankles. Stark crawled onto the bed beside her and wrapped her up gently in the silver cover. She quietly fell asleep, spent, in his arms.

***

Stark held her for what seemed like hours, watching the moonlight and flickering fire reflected on her pristine skin. He couldn't explain why this had felt like his first time. The release and power of this form of sex had been such a big part of his life at one time. He and Paige had explored and tested every limit. In some ways, it had set him free. Yet in the last year, it had begun to feel empty in some way. He couldn't explain it. But tonight with Kira it had been different. Stark was suddenly aware of just how much he needed her. She made everything new. Even though the goal had been to teach her what this was about, he realized that he was the one learning. Maybe, just maybe, he could learn to love again. He fought to stay awake, to stay in this moment and soak it up as long as possible, but sleep at last claimed him too.

Chapter 14

Breathe! Just relax and breathe! You have to get out of this! Kira struggled to remove the gag from her mouth. If only she could breathe! Panic set in when she realized she couldn't move her hands. She began to thrash and fight to break free. Her heart was racing like a jet engine roaring in her ears and pounding in her chest. She could not see. There was total darkness, filled with a mix of sounds and images, the horror of her past and the pleasure of that evening. The intense smell of leather in his back seat still filled her nose. The pain and helplessness of being bound threatened her every breath. She could see the black gloves in flashes as if they were everywhere. She struggled to calm herself and fight off the haunting images. Scenes that were long oppressed threatened to claim her as she fought to grasp what was real now and what was memory. Memories, feelings evolved into a swarm of emotion that overtook her. She began screaming but her voice sounded so far away. Then she could hear him laughing wildly. That sick depraved laugh had haunted her for years. Now it echoed all around her. She felt strong hands on her arms. Kira lashed out wildly, her arms suddenly free.

"Kira! Kira!" A familiar voice yelled. The voice seemed to cut through the laughter. "Kira it's me, Owen! Wake Up! Kira stop. You are going to hurt yourself. What's wrong?" Stark's voice sounded nervous and far away. Then it changed. Through the darkness and terror he reached her. His voice had grown calm. "Kira, stop this. You are fine. You are safe."

A sweat-soaked and very disheveled Kira opened her eyes. The laughter was gone. She looked up at Owen and burst into tears. *Oh God! It was only a dream! I really am going crazy!* Though he didn't understand what had happened, he wrapped her in his strong arms and held her close. The warmth of his presence was calming. Slowly he untangled her from the web of blankets, holding her softly against him the whole time. Finally free, she collapsed into his arms as he laid her onto the soft, silvery bed. Kira could feel his warmth all around her as she lay there shuddering and crying silently. After a few minutes, her distress turned to humiliation. She was so embarrassed for him to see her this way. *I was supposed to be sexy and wild yet here I am a sniveling mess.* She tried to turn away but his hand held her cheek.

Kira's chest heaved with big sobs. She appeared confused and still very frightened. "It's ok. Hey it was just a dream. It's ok." Stark rocked back and forth holding her and trying to soothe the broken girl in his arms. "Kira I'm so very sorry. If I had known for one minute that tonight would affect

228

you this way . . ." His voice trailed off. "I should have known better. Damn it Kira, I don't want to loose you."

As Kira awoke more fully, her eyes began to focus on the havoc she had caused during her nightmare. Pillows and blankets were tossed onto the floor. Poor Stark had a bleeding scratch on his face. She reached up and placed trembling fingers over the cut. "Owen, you're bleeding!" Gently she wiped away the blood. "I'm sorry. I didn't mean to . . ." She didn't get to finish. Stark put a finger on her lips.

"Don't apologize. I should have known better. This was a really bad idea. I got carried away earlier. Why didn't you ask me to release you?" His voice was strained.

How do I tell him what really happened? How do I tell him I enjoyed his touch immensely but being tied up like that brings back horrid memories? I don't want him to know about that part of me. I can't bear it. How do I explain something when I don't even know what was real and what was imagined? She was crying harder. Realizing he was trying so desperately to comfort her, she buried her face in his bare chest. His arms enveloped her like a familiar blanket. She felt safe there. In the mixed light of the moon and the fire dancing on his skin. *How do I tell him about the ghosts of my past without him thinking I am crazy?* As the thoughts raced through her rattled mind she struggled to answer. "I didn't want you to release me. I got as caught up in it as you did. Every moment was incredible. This is different. I just had a bad dream that's all. Maybe I should go." Kira tried in vain to sound relaxed and in control.

"Hell, no! You're not in any shape to go out. Stay with me. Stay with me till I have to leave."

"You mean for your deployment? That's three days from now. How exactly will I get away with that?" she asked with a chuckle.

"There's that beautiful smile. You could come each day after work then and stay with me. I'll make you breakfast," he proposed hopefully.

"Mmmm, breakfast! A really hot guy once told me that's the best meal of the day! Especially when there are pancakes involved," she taunted playfully.

***

"That could definitely be arranged," Stark said smiling, starting to feel more at ease. He wanted to believe her about the dream but he knew better. He had been around enough soldiers with PTSD to recognize nightmares created by some past trauma. Hell, he had his own demons that followed him into his sleep, haunting him and robbing him of much needed rest. But Kira hadn't ever been to war. This was something else.

Something dark that frightened and terrorized her. The thought that their activities tonight may have triggered the dream made him sick. He couldn't bear to think of anyone hurting her . . . ever.

***

The realization that he was completely naked except for his tags brought Kira out of the horrible past and back to the delicious present. *I came here to be with this man, to feel him, to have him.* She shifted so her thigh grazed his length. He tensed and moaned in response to her touch. Light as a feather, she placed soft kisses on his chest and the side of his neck. At first he tried to resist, "Kira wait, I don't think." She cut him off by rolling her hips into his. He moaned again, his grip on her tightening. He kissed her face gently and then found her mouth. She could taste the saltiness of her tears on his lips. He was awakened like a hungry animal once more. When his lips found hers he came alive, kissing her fervently. In a swift motion he rolled her up on top of him.

"There now, my darling. You are in control," he said through thready breath.

"I am in control and right now I want you inside me." The sultry words poured out of her mouth. She dragged her nails down his chest and smiled down at him biting her lip. "Now let's see. If I were to stay, how do you suppose we would pass the time?" Kira's attempt to distract Stark from her nightmare, though transparent, was effective.

***

Despite his best efforts he could not resist a naked Kira straddling him. He took a deep breath as he looked up at her. Disheveled chestnut hair cascaded in every direction off her shoulders and onto her bare breasts. The wild look in her eyes revealed her true state of torment that lay just beneath the surface. He could see her desperation to put it behind her. His heart ached and he wondered if the source of her nightmare was what they had done or something else. He could feel her need to be with him at this moment and separate herself from the darkness that tortured her dreams. She began to move her hips back and forth, gliding over top of him. He could feel her warm juices along the length of his growing desire.

"Mmmm like this?" Stark lifted her gently by her hips as he spoke and lowered her onto his already thick cock. Kira exhaled a slow deep moan.

***

The sensation was exquisite. The simultaneous stretching and filling took her breath away. He held her still on him for a moment to let her acclimate to his full length. Then, slowly at first, Kira began to move, raising and lowering herself onto him. Stark groaned loudly as her wet heat encompassed

232

him. Kira's pace began to pick up and Stark grabbed her hips and pulled her to him thrusting to meet her movements.

In this position, the grinding pleasure of his thick cock electrified her clit with each thrust, driving her to the frenzy she so desperately needed. She felt his hips tilt as he held hers, and began to work her back and forth as she rode him hard. Kira arched her back. Her hands went up into her hair and held tightly as the rhythm became devilishly forceful.

***

"You feel amazing, Kira," he moaned. He relished the soft light of the fire dancing across her flawless skin. The sight of her delicate arms above her head, the soft tresses of hair cascading around her fingers, the hypnotic movements of her body as she glided back and forth, filled by him, were enchanting. He could feel her body tightening around him as her growing frenzy brought her very close to release. Her moans became louder more intense.

"Kira!" He breathed, "You are so breathtaking. I wish I could tell you how it feels to be inside you, but there just aren't enough words." His words struggled to escape between breaths.

***

The rugged abandon of his voiced reverberated through Kira like shock waves from an earthquake. A tsunami of orgasmic pleasure engulfed her, releasing all the tension and pain she had felt earlier. In this moment of complete release she had no worries, no cares in the world but the ecstasy of this man.

Stark groaned loudly as the tight spasms of her orgasm gripped him like a vice. He buried himself in her, coming hard for the second time that night. She collapsed onto his chest. Stark wrapped her in his strong arms and held tightly to the one thing he couldn't bear to lose.

They lie entwined like two perfect circles on the silvery sheets. Two lovers wrapped in a moment, they both wished would never end. Kira squeezed his arm and tucked her face into his chest. The realization that he would be leaving in just a few short days was tearing at them both. Neither of them could sleep but no words could express the heaviness that hung in the room. So they lay there just holding each other, afraid to let go and fall asleep. He hit play on her iPod. As they lay there listening to music she whispered, "This is one of my favorite songs." The soft melancholy melody of Death Cab for Cutie wrapped them up and sang of the end of a beautiful life together and going off together into the dark.

I'll follow you into the dark.

***

The blaring alarm startled Kira. She jumped up panicked, realizing Stark had gone. She had spent every spare moment over the last three days with him. She could smell him all around her on the sheets, on her skin. She knew this day had been coming, but now that it was here the ache was so much more than she had imagined it would be. They had said good-bye last night, as he had to be at the Isolation facility (ISOFAC) by 0430 and she wouldn't be able to say good-bye. Kira felt tears on her cheeks and laughed, recalling lying in his arms the night before trying so desperately to stay awake and savor every last moment. And now he was gone. *Quit crying, you baby! You knew this was part of the deal! No surprises here.* Kira's vain attempt at bravery was fleeting. She jumped out of the bed and dressed with lightning speed. Throwing on her BDU jacket she raced out the door and jumped into the jeep he had insisted she use while he was gone. *You are an idiot! A complete, blubbering idiot!* She cursed herself as she drove to the airstrip. As she approached the outer fence her silent prayers were answered. They hadn't left yet.

She knew that she couldn't approach him. No one could ever know they were together. She pulled the jeep onto the rough gravel beside the road. She stepped out in time to watch Stark and his team exit their vehicle and walk across the tarmac to the plane. She fought the urge to call to him. It would have made little difference if she had, as the plane's engine roared to life. Tears choked in her throat as she watched Stark and his teammates walk in what seemed like slow motion. They were men on a mission, a team of brothers. She pictured how they'd

235

been in the restaurant. They were strong, passionate, goofy, and damn fierce. As they climbed the ramp onto the plane, Stark stopped. *Does he sense that I am here?* He turned toward her and ever so slightly nodded and touched the tip of his hat. A smiled crept across his lips and he disappeared into the plane.

Chapter 15

The first week with Stark away was almost unbearable. The nature of Stark's work made it impossible for him to contact her for weeks at a time. He had told her it would be this way. Still, it hadn't prepared her for the worry and emptiness that accompanied the waiting. She poured herself into work and running. She had eagerly accepted Stark's offer to stay at his house while he was away. Somehow being around Mags was a little like still having him there. Also, if she were taking care of Mags, there would be fewer reasons for Paige to skulk about. Kira still struggled with the idea of Paige being so involved in his life. The other reason she'd accepted his offer was her growing fear of her own apartment. She believed that her worries were unfounded and that the idea of an intruder was crazy, but she couldn't shake an uneasy feeling that came over her whenever she was there.

Kira looked up from the paperwork on her desk as Holt walked stiffly into her office.

"Captain Riley," Holt's voice sounded out, cold and clinical, "if you're going to pursue training as a flight surgeon, you'll need to report for Dunker training. Mine is scheduled in a few weeks. Do you think you'll be ready for that?" Holt had been acting quite strangely the last few weeks. Kira wondered if he knew about her and Stark or if he was irritated that she had put in for an assignment as a flight surgeon. He hadn't said anything outright but he seemed irritated with her most of the time.

"Yes. Well, I think so." Kira did her best to sound casual. The truth was she was terrified at the idea of a helicopter she was riding in crashing into the water. She knew that to be a flight surgeon she would have to be certified in emergency water egress. Given the alternative of figuring it out during an emergency situation, she would rather be prepared. Panic was the enemy. Panic led to fatal mistakes that could be avoided. Kira knew that to be successful she would have to be calm, relaxed, put her own fears aside, and focus on the best way to achieve the task at hand. In this case, the task would be escaping a twisted metal cage and swimming to the surface without drowning. She attempted a smile. Holt relaxed somewhat.

"It's going to be fine," he said. "You're a strong swimmer. You can do this. If you want you can sign up for the same training that I am scheduled for. There are several other doctors going this time." His tone had softened. He gave her a reassuring smile as he sat in the chair opposite her desk.

"Thanks for the reassurance. But how do you know I am a strong swimmer? For all you know, I may need a life jacket in the kiddie pool," Kira teased as she gathered the rest of her paperwork. She had been joking but she couldn't help noticing Holt stiffen slightly at her remark.

His voice remained calm and cool, though he answered abruptly: "I've seen you at the gym in the morning. I saw you swimming laps while I was there working out." Then much more casually he added, "You really are a strong swimmer. Pretty impressive, given your size."

And there it was. She was instantly annoyed. Holt would never see her as anything more than a frail little girl. As much as that pissed her off, she really was scared to face the Dunker training. "I don't know, Liam. Being strapped inside a metal cage and dumped upside down in water in the pitch dark sounds like a setup for a Houdini act." Kira laughed nervously. Despite her fear she couldn't help wondering why she hadn't noticed him at the gym in the mornings.

Holt's smile widened and he laughed out loud. "Talk, you, or you'll get the Dunker, see. Yeah, the Dunker. Yeah, see," Holt said in his best James Cagney impression.

Kira giggled and feigned surrender, putting up her hands playfully. "Oh no! Not the Dunker! Anything but that!" She laughed and swatted him with a file as she passed. "You're a shit!"

"Maybe, but you're laughing, and that's a hell of a lot better than being nervous. Are you leaving? Do you need a ride home?" His voice had become hopeful. He stepped around quickly to hold the door open for her.

"No, thanks. I drove." Kira hoped he wouldn't ask about the jeep. She grabbed her jacket and started toward the front of the office.

The sharp chill of the wind surprised Kira as she stepped outside. *Seriously! It's December in Colorado. A little cold is to be expected!* She pulled her jacket tighter around her and started across the parking lot toward the jeep.

"Nice ride." Holt said suspiciously, coming up quickly behind her.

"Oh, thanks. It's used but it will definitely do the job," she said casually. *Ok, you didn't lie. You may have omitted a few details but technically you didn't lie.*

"Well, it will get you from point A to point B anyway," he said with a hint of disdain. He tapped the key fob and his bright red BMW beeped cheerfully. "Do you want me to pick you up in the morning? We can ride together."

Kira froze, remembering she hadn't been staying at her apartment. "No, that's ok. I would rather drive. I've got a couple of things to get done in the morning before training. I'll just see you there, ok?" she finished, smiling sweetly and reached for the door of the jeep.

Holt slid up against the door. "It's no problem. I can pick you up early at your apartment. It's on the way. You probably won't have time to get a run in before training anyway."

Alarm bells went off in Kira's mind. *How does he know where I live? Have I talked about my apartment?* "Thanks, Liam, but I can't. I know you're trying to help." She reached past him, opened the door to the jeep, and climbed in quickly. "So, I'll see you tomorrow, ok?" she called as she started the engine. A defeated Holt got in his car and started it up. Kira waved nicely as she pulled out of the parking lot. *Has he been following me? How does he know where I live?* Kira did her best to get a hold of herself. *This is crazy! He isn't following me. There has to be a reasonable explanation.* Just to be sure, though, she drove around for a while before heading to Stark's house.

Kira noticed the bright red Chevy Bel Air as soon as she pulled in the driveway. *Damn that's a fine car!* Her joy was followed immediately by the sinking realization that the car meant Paige was there. Kira parked and got out slowly. She dreaded spending any time with Paige. She contemplated driving around for another hour or so but decided gas was too expensive to waste. As she approached the house, the front door flung open.

"Ok, ok, girl calm down. What's wrong?" Paige's voice was tender and soft as she tried to calm Mags. Paige looked up and saw Kira coming up the drive. "Oh, I see. Vanilla, I don't suppose you would go away if I said we are full up on bitch at the moment." Her voice grew darker for that last part.

"Nice try, Paige. I'm sure Owen told you that I'm staying here to look after Maggie while he's gone," Kira answered flatly as she knelt down beside Mags. "Hey there, girl. How was your day?" She ruffled Mags fur and hugged her.

"Yeah, he said you would be around. Though, it looks more like you moved in. Little soon, don't you think?" Paige smugly held the door open for Kira and followed her into the house. Kira saw Paige's characteristic magazine and half glass of wine. Over the last few weeks that had become the telling sign that Paige had been there. Kira knew she should be angry or jealous at Paige's presence but she realized she wasn't. It was nice knowing someone was around, even if that someone was Paige. Kira laid her laptop case and purse down on the sleek bench in the hall.

"So you want to tell me why you're really staying here?" Paige's voice, while catty, had an air of concern and skepticism. She poured Kira a glass of the merlot she had been drinking. "Well . . .?" she asked to Kira's silence, handing her a glass.

Kira stood there dumbfounded by the audacity of this bitch. *Who the hell does she think she is?* She took the glass and a long drink before answering. "Paige, Stark and I are none of your business. He asked me to stay and I agreed and that's all you need to know."

"I'm going to let that snarky little comment slide. That was your one free pass," Paige countered. "I've got to tell you I'd really like to hate you but I don't. You are good for Owen. I wasn't sure at first but I see how he is when he talks about you." Paige's tone softened. She refilled her own glass, finishing the bottle. "Looks like we're going to need another one of these," she said as she put the bottle in the recycling bin.

"Another bottle? Are you staying long?" Kira made no attempt to hide the aggravation in her voice. She longed to take a hot shower and change into her sweats. She wanted to get to bed early to be well rested for training in the morning.

"As long as it takes for you to open up and talk to me about what's really going on with you." Paige was more direct this time.

"What are you talking about, Paige?" Kira was really irritated now. "You just said yourself how happy Owen is. So what's your problem?"

"Ugh! So much for being tactful. I don't have the patience for it," Paige said, exasperated now. "Look, I'm not here just because I'm worried about Owen. I'm here because you need someone to talk to. You're going to drive yourself crazy keeping it all inside. I know. I've been there." Paige was very serious now. She tapped her deep purple nails impatiently on the butcher-block bar.

"I miss him. I'm worried sick. But you are hardly the person I want to talk to about that," Kira blurted. Her emotions were rising to the surface all at once.

"Oh Jeez, for a doctor you sure are an idiot sometimes," said Paige. "I'm talking about being attacked. You were raped weren't you? How long ago? Was it that little shit from the gas station? Zoe told me about him." Paige blurted out the words callously, having lost all patience.

All the color drained from Kira's face. The half full glass of wine slipped from her numb fingers, hit the counter and then crashed on the floor. Deep red wine splattered like blood from a massacre over the wall and the floor. She struggled to speak but couldn't find the words. *How does she know? How the hell does she know?* Kira was suddenly nauseous. Her palms began to sweat and the room seemed to spin. She wanted to jump and correct the wine disaster but was unable to move.

Paige eased Kira into the chair at the bar and began to clean the wine and broken glass from Stark's impeccable kitchen. "When he first told me you agreed to stay I was confused," she explained. "You don't seem like the rush-into-things type. And I don't think you're like Simone. Owen can see right through that gold digging whore. There was something that just didn't add up until he told me about your nightmare." She put the broken glass gently in the trash can. Her careful actions contrasted with her direct approach to Kira.

"What?" Kira's eyes shot daggers. "He told you about that night?" she hissed. Kira was furious and hurt. *Why? Why the hell did he talk to her about that?* "What else did he have to say?"

"Hold on. Damn, did you have an extra scoop of bitch in your Cheerios this morning? He was really upset. He was afraid that introducing you to bondage (although very mildly if you ask me) caused you to have nightmares. He told me how violently you thrashed in your sleep, like you were fighting for your life. He was worried that maybe it reminded you of something else. He said you clammed up and wouldn't talk to him about it. He is really worried about you. He was hoping I could help."

"When did you talk to him? I haven't heard from him in weeks. How the hell could you help? How could you possibly understand?" Kira's voice was barely audible.

"Before he left he asked me to talk to you because I've been there. About a year before I met Owen, I was raped by a guy I met in a bar. I thought he was so cute that I went willingly with him. That's the part that haunts me the most. I should have said no. I could have stayed at the bar with my friends. I didn't know this guy from Adam but I went with him anyway. How could I have been so stupid?" Paige took a long sip of her wine. "Maybe I should have poured whiskey instead," she said, finishing the glass and opening the second bottle. The look on Paige's face was genuine. Her exotic features looked tired and worn. Kira noted for the first time that she looked vulnerable.

"That's an easy mistake to make," Kira said softly. "Until you meet a predator you don't suspect anything. By the time you realize who they really are, it's too late."

"Exactly, but that's a mistake I won't ever make again," Paige went on. "I was beaten, Kira, and raped repeatedly. I thought the sick bastard was going to kill me. He just left me there in that flea bitten hotel room like a discarded pizza box. I was so ashamed and embarrassed I didn't tell anyone for a very long time. I just kept it inside." Paige stopped talking and looked at Kira, giving her a sad smile. "That's what nearly killed me. Hiding it, I mean. Trying so hard to pretend everything was ok when it had all fallen apart and turned to shit. I started toying with all kinds of self-destructive behavior. It's crazy, I know, but somehow BDSM was the only way I found release."

Kira's eyes widened. "But you were raped. How could you possibly stand to be bound? Didn't it make you sick?" She felt her own panic rising just thinking about it.

Paige laughed. "I know what you're thinking. But I didn't start out being dominated. I entered into this with dominance, not submission. One of my previous girlfriends introduced me to the idea. I found that when I was in complete control I could relax and really enjoy myself. It was about that time that I met Owen." She paused, a wicked smile spreading across her face as she remembered meeting him for the first time. "He came in shit faced drunk with some of his buddies after his very first deployment to get a tattoo. He got a tattoo all right. And so much more." She let out a long slow sigh and bit her lip as she savored the memory.

"Hello, I'm still right here. That's my boyfriend you're talking about," Kira said, shaking her head, disgusted. She suddenly thought of the sexy-as-hell tattoo across his back. *Relentless.* Kira had always thought that described him in life and in battle but now she wondered if it was something else entirely.

"Ok, sorry. I'm just trying to help you understand. We dealt with our demons together. He had all that grief and rage built up and needed an outlet. Me, well, I guess over time I needed to learn to trust again. I was finally able to let go." Paige finished and took another sip of her wine.

"That's great and all," said Kira. "I'm glad you and my boyfriend had such an awesome sex life when you were together. But I'm not sure how that helps me at all. You do realize that the

247

fact that we are even having this conversation is pure craziness?" Kira ran her fingers through her hair exasperated. She filled a new wine glass hoping the scarlet liquid would help soften the madness.

"I just want you to know that whatever happened, you can talk to me about it. I wanted to tell you everything so that you would know that I would never judge you. And I would never tell anything you didn't want me to, even to Owen." Paige finished giving her a reassuring look.

"Why? Why would you do that for me? Why do you even care?" Kira implored. She couldn't help but be skeptical. She didn't trust anyone except maybe Owen. She was trying so hard to open up to him.

" I love Owen, not the way you do. But I know the poison that is eating at you will kill you if you keep it in. It will come between you two. You have to work through it, talk about it. Talk to me, Kira," Paige urged. Her voice was almost commanding.

Kira sat at the bar in Owen's immaculate kitchen staring at the wine glass in her trembling hands. She had kept it all bottled up for so long. She struggled with the impulse to just leave but the ache and the fear and the shame that she had lived with so long gripped her and held her fast to the seat. She realized in that moment that more than anything she wanted to be free from all the pain and craziness. Tears started slowly at first then faster as she began to speak. Secrets and emotions that had been locked away broke free like a dam and erupted in Class V rapids flowing and crashing freely. "It was the beginning of my senior year of undergrad. I was finishing up my bachelor's in chemistry. I had been so busy trying to get perfect grades and get as many classes into each semester as possible, I hadn't wasted much time on boys." Kira closed her eyes and paused as if perhaps she could blink and erase it from ever having happened. "Robert was in several of my classes that semester. Since we were both premed we had had classes together every semester since my freshman year. We were never close friends but I had seen him around a lot. He seemed like a nice guy: quiet, cute, but a little shy. A group of us went out to celebrate midterms being over. He came over and started talking to me about an experiment we had been working on. We had a few drinks and he asked me to dance. At first I was thinking, this is amazing. He is so nice and cute. I was excited. As we made our way onto the dance floor everything was spinning like the earth had fallen off its axis." Kira's voice waivered as she spoke. Beads of sweat began to glisten on her forehead. She struggled to find the words as she began to relive the most terrifying night of her life. "The music was thumping in my ears, pulsing. It seemed surreal. I -I stumbled and fell into his arms. I remember his voice saying don't fight it baby just relax and then everything went black."

Kira closed her eyes again, her head hung slightly as the shame that she had been holding so deeply inside began creeping out.

"He drugged you?" Paige gasped. "Why? You liked him."

"That's what makes it so bad, I mean I would have gone out with him," Kira said sadly. She struggled with a mix of shame and anger. Kira shook her head and looked at the floor. "God, I was such a fool! The rest of that night was a blur of semiconscious voices, shadows, pain and that awful laugh." Kira shuddered, remembering him laughing wildly. She put her hands over her face as if somehow she could block it out. But the memories were flooding back now. Moments that she had tried so hard to forget flooded her conscious. She choked on the words as she continued. "The thing is it was all a haze, I only remember bits and pieces." Kira gulped hard. She hadn't talked to anyone about this in years. No one at all other than the school psychologist whom she wasn't sure even believed her. Hell, she wasn't sure she believed herself. Now here she was about to utter words she had been afraid to say, even to herself, to a perfect stranger. Yet somehow she couldn't stop. With a trembling hand she reached out and braced herself against the bar as if the words were strong enough to knock her down. "I-I know that he raped me." Her voice waivered. So much pain, each word felt like it was ripping out of her. "I remember being tied up. I couldn't move my arms or legs. I was too groggy to put up much of a fight." Kira shifted in her seat. The genuine concern and vulnerable acceptance in Paige's eye encouraged her to go on. "When I would start to gain strength he would pour liquid down my throat and the whole world would start spinning. When I finally awoke, I was in my apartment and it was two days later. I lost two whole days." Kira was crying hard now.

"So, wait. Two days went by? Did he have you that whole time?" Paige asked stunned. "Did you tell anyone? Did you go to the doctor?"

"Not at first. I was too embarrassed and confused. When I finally did try to get help he denied it. He said that I had had too much to drink and he'd simply given me a ride home and that we'd had consensual sex. He was questioned by the school board, and said that I had made the whole thing up because he didn't want to date me. Everyone who saw us leaving together saw him helping me walk. They all assumed I was trashed. Suddenly I was the pathetic bad guy." Kira choked out the words between sobs. She paused, then decided to go for broke. She had kept the rest from everyone. "If it had ended there, it would have been bad enough."

"But it didn't." Paige interrupted, angry and almost afraid to ask what happened next.

"No, it didn't. For the rest of that year he stalked me. I thought I was going crazy. Who knows? Maybe it was all in my head. At times I would come home and know someone had been there. Things would be moved around in my apartment. More than once air was let out of my tires. I began to run into him wherever I went." Kira wiped clumsily at her tears. Paige handed her a tissue. "I could never prove anything. To be honest, I know it sounds crazy. Even the school psychologist felt I was suffering from some kind of delusional disorder secondary to the pain of rejection by this boy." Kira balled her small hand into a tight fist. The memories of the humiliation and self-doubt were too painful to relive.

"What did you do?" Paige asked quietly. She reached out to touch Kira's arm. Kira jerked away instinctively. "I'm sorry, Kira."

"I realized no one would believe me. After the sessions with the doctor I wasn't sure if I believed me. So I buried it. I told myself it was just a horrible, horrible dream. I finished school and went to med school on the other side of the country. I wanted to be as far away from all of that as I could. As for your self-destructive behavior, well," Kira half-laughed, "I signed up for the military." Hearing herself say it out loud for the first time made her realize just how ludicrous it was.

"So that was it, then. You were fine after that? He left you alone?" Paige's voice was suspicious. She could tell there was something Kira wasn't telling her. She knew there was more. "Is he still bothering you, Kira? Is that why you don't want to go back to your apartment?"

"I haven't seen him in years. Not once in all the time I was in med school. I don't know why, maybe because I am getting closer to Owen, but I have started imagining that he is back. It is literally just my imagination but it scares me. I don't want to be crazy, Paige, but I feel like I'm losing my mind." She paused looking up at Paige. "You think I'm mad, don't you?"

"No, Kira. I don't think you're crazy. I think you have been through a horrible ordeal and that makes you a little paranoid. If you feel more comfortable here than your apartment, that's fine. I'm sure Owen feels better knowing you are here, anyway. Are you going to tell him?"

"What? No! I don't want him to look at me like some kind of crazy freak," Kira blubbered wringing her hands. "No, absolutely not. And you can't either. You gave me your word."

"Hold on there, Sandra Dee. I'm not going to say anything, but you two are over before you start if you can't be honest with him. He deserves more than this. Until you trust him enough to tell him the truth, you'll never be able to be really close. Intimacy takes trust. That's what I was able to find with him through the BDSM. I'm not saying that's your cup of tea, princess, but you have to find a way to trust him and yourself."

253

Paige got up and ruffled Maggie's fur as she started toward the door. She paused as she put on her jacket and said, "He deserves better than that and so do you. You both deserve the chance to be truly happy. You have to trust him enough to be honest with him and know that he will love you just the same." Paige turned and headed out the door before Kira had a chance to respond. On the front stoop Kira could hear Paige lock the door behind her.

Exhausted, a tearful Kira made her way to the living room and cuddled up on the couch with Mags. Just as she began to relax she heard her phone vibrate with a text. *Who could that be?* She reached over and looked at her phone. At once all her senses came alive. It was Stark!

Hey baby! Are you up for some video chat?

Kira couldn't believe it. She was so excited she could barely catch her breath as she texted back with shaky fingers.

Hell Yes!! When?

He's all right! He's all right! Three weeks of hearing nothing had been killing her. Each night she went to bed and prayed desperately for him to be ok. Once asleep, her dreams took over. Sometimes they were wonderful steamy memories of his skin on hers. *Oh God, the smell of him.* But then each night her dreams turned into nightmares with Stark being ripped away. He was gone and there she was in that awful room tied up, unable to move, with that laughter all around her, suffocating her.

Now. Do you remember how to set up the link on the laptop?

You bet I do! Kira ripped the laptop out of the case and began logging on at lightning speed.

Yup, got it. I can't wait to see you.

Kira waited for what seemed like an eternity as a connection was established. A path would be blazed through cyberspace from her laptop there on the plush sofa clear to a dusty laptop in a ramshackle barrack in the mountains of Afghanistan, the other side of the world. A moment of static flashed and there he was. Tears filled Kira's eyes and she struggled to speak. Staring back at her was the most stunning man on the planet. He was perhaps slightly thinner than when he left. His dark stubble was longer and a bit more unruly. Despite his rough appearance his eyes sparkled wildly.

"There's my girl. Hot damn, I didn't think it was possible but you are even more beautiful than I remembered." He smiled and spoke softly. Kira felt her breath escape her at the sound of his voice. She couldn't believe he was actually there right before her.

"Hey, you," Kira started, struggling for what to say. "Nice suntan."

"Well, you know, that happens when you're bumming in the desert. How are things there? Are you getting the hang of clinic?" Instantly his conversation was casual and comfortable as if they were nestled on the couch after a long day.

"Ah, you know, saving lives and stamping out disease." Kira giggled.

"I've missed your laugh. Actually I've missed everything about you. Seriously, though, what have you been doing?"

"I put in for flight surgeon. I am training all month. I go for Dunker training in February." Kira did her best to sound relaxed.

"You sound nervous. It won't be as bad as you think. Just stay focused and relax. I know you. You're stronger than you give yourself credit for. You've been my strength every day." His words poured over her.

"I really miss you. Do you know how much longer you'll be there?" Kira suddenly realized just how much she missed him. It was like a giant ache encompassing her entire body.

"I'm afraid that's classified ma'am. Way above your pay grade," he said grinning.

"You shit! Just for that I'm gonna drink all your whiskey while you're gone," she said, giggling again.

"You do and when I get back I'm going to spank that little ass till you can't sit down!" he growled, smiling at her. He took a moment and a deep breath.

"What? What are you staring at?" she asked, suddenly more serious.

"You. I want to soak you in," he said dreamily.

"Quit fooling around," she corrected playfully.

"I can't help it. I love the view from here. We may only have tonight but in this moment you're mine. I've got to make it last."

"Ok, silly. I'm yours. What ever will you do with me?" Her voice became sultry and inviting.

"Mmmm, I can tell you what I'd like to do to you." His need for her was evident in the gravity of his words. Kira could feel herself getting wet for him. The weeks had been so very lonely.

"Keep that up and I'll have to take a cold shower when we're done." She gazed at him in the monitor.

"What a coincidence. That's the only kind we have here," he said, chuckling. "It's ok, though, because I'm going to need one after seeing you. I want to bury my face in the curve of your neck and kiss down to those breasts. God, I can't wait to see you. I want to taste you." His voice became husky with need. Kira could feel her own need growing, becoming almost painful.

A distant siren sounded in the background. Stark looked over his shoulder as the picture blurred for a moment. The quiet backdrop became a bustling base in an instant with soldiers moving about at lightning speed and more sirens sounding.

"What's that?" Kira asked, panicked.

"Duty calls," he said casually. "Guess we'll have to cut this short."

"Oh, Owen, no. Be safe! Oh my God!" The picture blurred again for a moment.

"I'm still here, Kira. I just wanted to say . . ." His sweet voice was cut off by static and then her laptop fell silent.

"Owen . . . Owen . . . Can you still hear me?" Kira tried frantically to get the connection back for a few minutes but it was gone. He was gone.

Chapter 16

Walking across the tarmac in the bitter cold, Kira was reminded of watching Stark board his plane nearly two months ago. How could the time have passed so quickly? She had been working hard in clinic and in her training. Preparing to be a flight surgeon had taken center stage in her life. While she missed Stark tremendously, his absence allowed her to focus solely on her goals. She climbed into the commercial passenger plane and made her way to an empty seat. It was more economical to fill empty slots on a commercial flight than it was to dedicate an entire Army plane for the transport of eight soldiers to Fort Campbell, Kentucky and the Allison Aquatics Training Facility located there. This is one of the best facilities in the country. She reminded herself. It's going to be fine. I just have to relax and focus. Kira knew that these three days of training could mean the difference between life and death if she was in a real HELO crash. But the thought of being strapped into a sinking metal vault with a human Cuisinart on the top and back was a little overwhelming.

Drowning had always been one of her worst fears. She recalled the first time she had gone whitewater rafting as a teenager and the horrifying "safety talk" about "undercut rocks" and the danger of being sucked down under one by the current, trapped in a dark tomb until the last painful breath of air was replaced by water filling one's lungs. By the time they had arrived at the river, her friends had to drag her onto the raft. Once they drifted downstream and she had relaxed, it turned into one of the best experiences of her life. But the idea of, being trapped under water, whether under a rock or strapped in a metal cage, made her heart race and her blood pressure rise. She sat back in her seat and closed her eyes, determined to relax for the flight

"Kira!" Holt's enthusiastic greeting startled Kira causing her to jump. "Little nervous?" he asked playfully.

"No, Captain Obvious, but thanks for that," Kira chided back almost giggling at the poor stewardess who was too busy gazing dreamily into Holt's blue eyes to look where she was going. *Thwap*! The stewardess walked smack into another passenger. She stumbled, flushed crimson, and quickly made her way up the plane. Holt flashed the retreating stewardess his million-dollar smile, causing her blush to deepen. He helped himself to the seat next to Kira.

Kira shook her head. "Do women always act like that around you?" she asked rolling her eyes. She had to admit he was easy to look at.

"Yeah," he said, smiling that smug self-confident grin that was such a turnoff to Kira. He turned back toward her and caught her disapproving look. His smile faded. "Well, most of them anyway," he grumbled.

"Perhaps I just know you too well," she offered in mock consolation.

"Thanks a lot," he said sarcastically. "You can try to hide it all you want. I know how you really feel."

Kira rolled her eyes again and rubbed her fingers over a small leather bracelet on her wrist. There was only one soldier who caught her eye. Her fingers traced over the single word on the metal plate of the bracelet: Relentless. A smile crept over her lips. The box had been waiting for her on the front porch when she got home last night. From some dusty outcrop on the other side of the world, Stark had ordered it for her. The delicate red and white gift-wrapping was from a company called Endorphin Warrior. Carefully she had opened the small box to find the leather band bearing a sterling silver plate. Relentless. She knew instantly who sent it. The message on the enclosed card was simple. "Into the dark." The Death Cab for Cutie song had become their song. She would never be alone with his strength she would make it through the training fine.

The irony that he was sending her encouragement for a controlled training exercise from a chaotic corner of the world where people were actively trying to kill him was not lost on Kira. She relaxed back into the seat, staring out the window imagining those deep blue eyes. She imagined running her fingers through his thick dark hair and tracing her lips along his sculpted jaw. The idea of being with him was still as crazy as the day she first gave in to her own desire up at his house in Aspen. If Holt or anyone else found out, their careers would be over. She glanced at Holt who was droning on about some perceived events. As usual with his self-promoting tirades, Kira lost interest and turned back to the window and her own thoughts. She thought of Stark, and wished him home safely.

***

Damn that woman! Holt stared at Kira as she looked out the window. He could tell she had long ago tuned him out. How could she not see that they were perfect for each other? They would complement each other's careers. Of course there was the matter of her lower class background, but he felt with a little work she would make a fine wife. It has to be that she's intimidated by me. Why else would she act so oblivious to me? He grimaced silently acknowledging that she had a thing for that idiot enlisted guy. He had seen them together a couple of times. He refrained from making a scene of it, though, as it simply would not do for his wife to have fraternization on her record. He watched her pouty lips as she stared out the window. Her dark hair glistened despite being hastily pulled into a ponytail.

262

He stirred in his seat. She continued to stare out the window. His frustration mounted. I will have her. It's only a matter of time. For now, though, he would have to find a suitable surrogate for his needs. The plane reached maximum altitude and began to coast. Holt turned his attention to the strawberry blond stewardess. She smiled brightly at him as she brought sodas and snacks through the cabin. Hmmm, yes. She will do just fine.

Holt pushed the eager stewardess up against the counter. Forcefully he kissed her, probing her mouth and throat with his tongue. The limited space of the lavatory provided little room for conventional sex. He pushed her down onto the seat and took out his rigid cock. He had been straining against his slacks back in his seat watching Kira twirl the loose strands of her damn hair. Now he would have release. This little strawberry tart was more than eager to fill her place. Kira doesn't know what she's missing. He groaned as the little vixen swallowed him whole. He gripped her hair with both hands and began to fuck her mouth. Holt felt no guilt treating her like the dirty little whore she was. Suddenly he stopped. "Get up and turn around," he commanded. She readily obliged and Holt pulled up her skirt. Moving her panties aside he slipped his fingers into her waiting cunt. Sopping like the little whore she is. He ripped off her panties and let them fall to the floor. He put his hand around the back of her neck and bent her forward. Then in one powerful thrust he entered her. He pictured Kira bent over, ass in the air taking all that he had to give her. He was tired of being ignored. Damn

Kira! His knuckles went white as they gripped the back of her neck barely containing the weeks of anger and jealousy. He unleashed all his pent up frustration on this girl. Holt barely noticed how beautiful she was and how she tried so hard to please him. He couldn't only look at her with contempt because she wasn't Kira.

***

Kira broke from her daydream and realized Holt had gone. Thankful for the moment's reprieve, she scanned the cabin but didn't see him. Well, he's gone to the bathroom. She thought and secretly hoped whatever he ate last night would keep him in there for the duration of the flight. Kira took the opportunity to pull the small card out of her bag. The simple phrase on the card made her heart jump. Into the dark. So simple but the implication of its origin was powerful to her. It was from her favorite Death Cab for Cutie song, "I Will Follow You into the Dark." They had listened to it the night before he left for his deployment. Though it seemed a little morbid, it gave her comfort. She knew he would be there with her in spirit as she would be with him. No matter what they faced, they would face it together. She slipped the card back into her bag.

**

Kira stood nervously with the seven other officers as she waited for the bus to pick them up outside the hotel. This was it: Dunker Training, also known as HUET, or Helicopter Underwater Egress Training. She had heard multiple people tell her about it, had practiced in the pool back at base, and had watched about two hundred YouTube videos on the subject. She was as prepared for this training as she could be but the nerves were still there. Strangely, she found herself thankful they had to train in full fatigues. Swimming around in a pool with all that crap on would be difficult, but she would be able to keep her tags on. The bracelet, too, would be concealed inside her shirt.

The bus ride to the Allison Aquatics Training Facility was mercifully short. Kira had not slept well and wanted to get her first day of training under her belt. Upon arriving at the facility, they filed into a training room. A brisk, stout officer barked out roll, then pressed play on a series of rousing videos of everything that could possibly go wrong in a helicopter each followed by vivid and devastating crash footage. The purpose of the audiovisuals was to emphasize the importance of Dunker Training, but it really gave Kira the warm fuzzies knowing she would actually be strapped to the metal contraption and plunged into water. Next came a riveting speech instructing proper egress from a destroyed HELO. Chief Instructor Park walked them through what to expect. Kira was impressed to learn that the famed 160th Night Stalkers had received Dunker Training at this very facility. At least they were in very good hands. Park went

265

on, explaining that it would be a crawl—walk—run scenario. No being strapped into a submerged helicopter until they learned the progression. *At least they're not going to let me drown.*

"It's all about muscle memory," AFT Park explained in a confident baritone. "We want you to have this down so that if you are in a crash, instinct and muscle memory take over and fear won't have time to kill you."

Day One wasn't as bad as Kira had expected. She learned to use a HEEDS bottle. Why does EVERYTHING in the military have a ridiculous acronym? she wondered. The HEEDS, or Helicopter Emergency Egress Device System, was a small SCUBA tank about the size of a can of hair spray with a regulator attached to it. First she practiced using the device at the bottom of the pool by blowing to clear it and then breathing like you would with a regular SCUBA. Next, Kira and her fellow trainees had to do this upside down. She was disoriented at first, but that quickly passed and she cleared her device. The next step, however, was upside down and strapped to a chair. That stage was a little more challenging, for the chair was in a metal cage.

They fastened her in with the same five-point harness found in helicopters. She held her breath and the cage was flipped upside down, slamming her into the surface of the water on its way. Kira focused hard on methodically undoing the harness buckles, kicking to the cage door, and unlatching it before making her way to the surface to give the proverbial thumbs up. The challenge was staying calm. She practiced this several times with and without the HEEDS bottle, growing more comfortable with her temporary underwater entrapment each time. She noted that this wasn't too terrible save the fact that with all the face slamming and inversion, chlorinated pool water found its way into every square centimeter of her sinuses. She acquainted this to near drowning. However with all her time spent rafting in the New River this wasn't an entirely foreign feeling.

Six hours later, Kira changed quickly in the locker room and made her way back to the bus. Day One left her feeling almost confident, though quite a bit water logged. She paused and bent down to tie her shoe. From somewhere inside the hidden crevices of her head about a gallon of pool water spilled out her nose and mouth onto the pavement.

"Sexy," a male voice said behind her.

Kira turned to see Holt and another captain. "We're going to get some dinner when we get back. You want to come along?" Holt asked, smiling at the dripping Kira.

"I don't know, I'm really tired. I want to get some rest before tomorrow," Kira replied, hoping to avoid spending the evening with Holt.

"Come on, Captain," the other soldier chided. "As savory as that pool water was, you have to be hungry. Come with

267

us. We passed a place called the Black Horse on the way here. It will be fun, I promise. We'll have you back in plenty of time to rest." The twinkle in his blue eyes was playful and friendly. He grinned widely and held out his hand to help her up. "My name's Cody. Er . . . uh . . . Captain Bryson, sorry," he stammered as he helped her to her feet.

Kira smiled. "Thanks, Cody. My name's Kira." She giggled back at him. Holt shot them a fiercely disapproving look that went completely unnoticed.

"Oh, I know who you are," Cody said, chuckling fully now. "I've heard all about you." He grinned slyly and slapped Holt on the back. Holt shot him a menacing look and shook his head.

Kira nodded. She was starving and the idea of spending time with someone who could playfully torment Holt would be entertaining. Throughout dinner she learned that Cody had gone to med school with Holt. He was very charming and a bit more down to earth than his med school buddy. His comical nature provided much needed distraction from the challenge they would face in the morning. As Cody joked, Holt seemed a little quieter than usual and increasingly distracted. She was starting to notice that he was not used to having someone around who would talk to him and make fun of him like a regular person. Her phone buzzed to alert her of a text message. It was Stark!

So how does it feel to have a few gallons of pool water in your head?

She smiled. She knew he meant it when he said he would always be thinking of her. She ached to see him again.

About as much fun as drowning could be.

How did it go? Did you get your bracelet?

Kira giggled and responded.

That was you? I wasn't sure who sent that.

Kira pictured his face forming a playful frown, when he read that. She knew she was drawing a playful line in the sand and was hoping he was up for the challenge.

Testing the water a little are you? Sure you want to do that?

Kira laughed. She knew what she was doing.

LOL. I'm wet in places I don't even want to talk about.

She couldn't stop herself.

Oh now that's just not fair. Good thing I'm coming home.

Kira sat bolt upright in her chair, startling her two dinner companions. Her heart began to race. She couldn't believe what she was reading.

"Excuse me," she fumbled and rushed to get up. "I need to go to the bathroom. I'll be back in a few." Kira raced to the safety of the restroom and responded to Stark.

You're coming home? When?

She was so excited to see him, feel him. Now her panties really were getting wet. It seemed like an eternity before he responded, although it was only a few minutes.

Soon. Very soon. I have to go now. Good luck tomorrow.

Kira was ecstatic, her head buzzed with excitement, as she returned to the table.

"Damn that must have been some dump!" Cody exclaimed as she returned to the table feeling giddy. "That or the women's bathroom is really full service!"

Kira laughed out loud. She knew she had to be careful what she said but she was so excited. "A little of both," she said with a wink.

Their waiter appeared tableside hefting steaming plates of burgers and fries. Kira was thankful for the distraction. The rest of dinner seemed to sail by. She laughed at their jokes and enjoyed the friendship of her two fellow captains. Even the next day's training didn't seem as scary knowing that soon, very soon, he would be home. She smiled again for no reason. She could barely contain her excitement.

That night in the shower she was thankful for the exquisitely hot water that melted her soreness from the day. Alone at last, she was able to fully focus on the one thing she couldn't stop thinking about. He was coming home! Sergeant Owen Stark is coming home to me! She leaned back against the cool tile of the shower and listened to Colbie Caillat sing of simple things that mean the most. Kira closed her eyes and let her hands drift down over her taut abdomen. As she found her clit, she imagined it was Stark touching her. She pictured his tongue flicking her, his coarse sun baked lips clasping her. She let out a soft moan and let the fantasy take her away.

~

Kira opened her eyes and felt a shudder run through her body. This was it: the final day of training. Today she would face the actual HELO dunker. As she walked into the training center the smell of chlorine engulfed her. In the locker room she donned her gear and double-checked her HEEDS bottle. Then outside, lined up poolside, she and her fellow trainees were informed that they would need to escape a submerged helicopter six times: three times with the HEEDS bottle, and three without it before they would endure a set of Final Mock situations that would mimic a real combat zone. Kira's heart raced at the thought of the final drills, which would be unpredictable. *Slow down. Take one thing at a time*, she reminded herself as she prepared to get wet. Kira was in the first group of nervous trainees. She strapped into her harness. Found her point of reference and took a couple of deep breaths. She felt the HELO start to spin and took one last deep breath just before the wall of water engulfed her. Kira's heart raced but she kept her movements calm. She cleared her HEEDS bottle and when the motion had stopped she unbuckled her harness. She jettisoned out of her window. Some light above the water helped her to see which way to go. She followed the bubbles up to the surface, broke through, and gave the thumbs up. *I did it! I did it!* Shivering, Kira made her way to the platform to do it again, this time without the HEEDS bottle.

Crash survival would be simpler if helicopters had the good manners to crash in the daytime in calm seas. However, helicopters also fly at night, meaning they could crash at night. So the next step was to be done in the dark. Scuba clad instructors would be hovering outside the ready to help if there was an emergency. They were also there to make sure escape was performed correctly. If trainees panicked and egressed too soon, back up the platform they'd go to do it all over again. Early escape in the real world meant risk of getting chopped into bits by spinning chopper blades.

The first blacked-out ride was from the pilot's seat, which wasn't so very bad. Except that crashing into the water and rolling over was fairly disorienting in daylight, and incredibly so when you couldn't see. Even worse, the trainees didn't know which way the dunker was going to roll.

For the blacked-out scenarios, they had been taught to find a tactile reference point. Kira had chosen the edge of her seat and the window to help her find her way out of the HELO in pitch-blackness. She grabbed a hold of the seat back and gulped a big breath as the chopper spun and plowed into the water. She remained seated with her seatbelt attached until all violent motion had stopped. She calmed herself and reminded herself that early egress risked death by Cuisinart, getting chopped into bits by flinging rotor blades.

Once motionless and upside down, Kira kept one hand on her reference point and removed her seat belt. Then she jettisoned the window and crawled her way out holding her breath the entire time. Once free from the wreckage, she guessed which way was up and started swimming in that direction. Thankfully, she guessed right, and broke the surface of the water as her lungs were beginning to burn.

Shaking from nerves and the frigid cold, she made her way back to the platform for the final test, putting together everything that they practiced and doing it with the group and in storm conditions. The wave machine started. This was the big

273

one. The waves and storm crashing all around Kira and her fellow training crew as once again she was strapped in her seat. She was in the back left now in an engineer seat. Her task was to go out the emergency exit on the right. She looked at Holt just before they turned out the lights. Their eyes met and Holt's were fixed in a gaze that reminded her of panic. He seems terrified, she thought, stunned for a moment. She would have to pass through the area he was now occupying in order to exit as instructed. She knew that the only thing that could possibly be worse than being blindfolded in a tube with seven other soldiers, slammed into the water, and rolled upside down is that same scenario, but next to a person who finds it even more terrifying than you do. The only thing Kira could picture was the image of getting tangled up with a freaked out Holt who was trying to kick free.

It took a little bit before the dunker rolled over, so she didn't want to start holding her breath too soon. She didn't want to find herself out of air just when her need was greatest. As the HELO descended on that short but terrifying drop into the water Kira said a little prayer and thought of Stark. Since she didn't know which way the HELO was going to roll, the timing of that last breath would be critical. Suddenly she felt the water coming up her legs before it got to her face, meaning it was rolling toward the side she was on and she was able snatch that last breath. Holt wasn't so lucky.

Kira held fast to her reference point. Cold water permeated her nose and every last crevice of her sinuses. She held her breath, took a second to calm herself, praying that Holt was clearing the exit. She tried to hold still upside down in the dark but finally had to move. She hastily unbuckled and keeping hand over hand on the seat back then Holt's seat edge as she made her way across Holt's seat. She was preparing to exit when she felt a firm grasp on her arm. It reminded her of the day he had helped her on the confidence course, only it grasped her more firmly, panicked even. He had helped her that day in the frigid water, and Kira knew immediately that she wouldn't leave him behind. Keeping one hand on her reference point, she grabbed his arm with the other hand and guided it toward the edge of the HELO. He exited and swam toward the surface. She couldn't see him but she was thankful she didn't get kicked in the face as she quickly exited and swam like hell. Her last breath burned in her aching lungs. She broke the stormy surface and gasped for air just as a huge wave crashed over her head and pushed her back down. She fought her way back up again and began swimming through the waves and the rain toward the lights of the life raft. Through the darkness she could hear her teammates who were already reaching the raft. When she felt its rubbery side, Holt was already in. He reached over the edge and hoisted her up in one swift pull. They began bailing water out of the craft, swamped from the prolific fake storm and awaited word that they were all clear. *We did it!* she thought, relieved to have "survived."

After changing into dry clothes, Holt came up from behind her as she walked toward the training center exit. "Thank you, Kira," he said. "You saved my ass in there." His voice was sincere and his smile slightly humbled.

Kira had never seen this side of Holt before. "What happened in there?" she asked, concerned.

"I didn't get the timing of my breath right. The water hit and I didn't get the last breath I needed. I panicked and lost my reference point." Holt sounded defeated. "If you hadn't helped me I would have failed the session and would have had to do it again. Or I'd have drowned."

"Well, you did fine. We made it out and that's all that matters." Kira smiled at him reassuringly.

"Let me take you out to dinner," he said, stopping suddenly as they reached the doors.

"Holt, I don't know if that's a good idea," she said, stopping beside him.

Holt put his arm gently on hers. "I've had enough humiliation for one day. Since you practically saved my life, please, dinner is the least I can do."

Kira's face softened. She really had never seen Holt like this before. "Ok, but just dinner," she said smiling, linking her arm in his.

***

Captain Bryson and AFT Park stood packing things up and preparing to leave for the day. "Thanks for your help," Park said to Bryson as they finished up. "Say, what happened to your boy Holt in that last evolution? When he was here last time he did excellent. He has that sequence timed down to a science. Why did he pause down there?"

Captain Bryson laughed and motioned with his head toward Holt and Kira as they exited the building together arm in arm. "Why do you think?" he asked smugly.

Chapter 17

"Three more physicals and we are done for the day," Abbey reported as she put the last patient in a room. "Then I want to hear more about your training and how it all went."

Kira was so thankful for Abbey. Having someone like her to confide in made everything more bearable. After the last patient had gone Kira slumped into her chair. The wait was killing her. He had said soon, very soon. However, two more weeks had gone by and still no word from Stark or his unit. Abbey came sauntering into her office with coffee. "We've been so busy since you got back and Captain Holt has been around so much I haven't heard more than bits and pieces of how it went." Abbey did little to hide the disdain in her voice.

Kira sipped her coffee and started telling Abbey about the ins and outs of Dunker training. She was just getting to the last day of training when they were interrupted.

"Kira. Hey Kira are you still here?" Holt's voice drifted down the hallway.

"Nobody's home," Abbey said sarcastically.

"There you are," Holt said bursting into her office. "It's Friday come out with me tonight," he said to Kira, ignoring Abbey as usual.

"No thanks. It's been a long week. I've got a lot of things to do at home. Maybe another time." Kira tried in vain to put Holt off.

"You can't possibly have that much laundry," Holt rebuked sounding mildly irritated. "You've had things to do every evening for the last two weeks."

"That's got to tell you something," Abbey said flatly shooting Holt a look and starting toward the door.

Smugly Holt held the door for her to leave. "The best things come to those who wait," he replied with a sly smile and watched Abbey leave. "Now, Kira, seriously, come out with us. You remember Cody from Dunker training he will be going too. Maybe you have a friend you want to bring. Just friends going out for a beer, it's not like I'm asking you to marry me."

You're being silly, she thought. *He's trying to be your friend and you're acting like a bitch.* But she really was tired. She had been so very excited when Stark said he was coming home. For two weeks she had barely been able to sleep. "Ok maybe just a drink. I really do need to unwind." Kira patted him on the shoulder as she walked out to head home.

"So do you want me to pick you up?" he asked unable to mask his excitement as he followed her to the parking lot.

"No I can meet you there. Where do you want to go?" she asked nonchalantly.

"Let's meet at Jack Quinn. Say eight thirty? But really I don't mind to pick you up at your apartment or if you're not staying there." The words slipped out before he could stop himself.

Kira froze for a split second a chill running down her spine. Then she continued walking as if nothing had happened. "Oh no there's not that much room in your car and I want to bring a couple of friends." Her voice remained calm and relaxed though inside she was trembling like an earthquake. *Shit! How does he know I'm not staying there? Is he following me? Does he know about Stark?* Fear and panic coursed through Kira's veins. She couldn't back out now but she knew this was trouble. "Ok, then see you tonight," she said as she climbed in the Jeep. Once the door was shut she let out a long deep sigh. *What the hell am I going to do?* She turned the ignition. As the jeep roared to life Kira knew what she had to do. Though it would be painful and she was going to have to swallow any shred of dignity she had left she reached for her cell and made the call. *Fuck Me!*

***

It was 8:45 p.m. Holt was growing restless. She was late! He would not be able to tolerate her constant tardiness.

Jesus! Does she not have a watch? Holt sat fuming and looking back and forth from his iPhone to his watch. He was starting to tap his foot in the most annoying and persistent way.

"Will you chill the fuck out?" Cody said laughing. "Its only eight forty-five. That's practically early girl time. They won't be here for at least another forty minutes." He motioned for the sexy blond bartender to get them another pitcher. "I'm not sure why you're so hung up on this girl. She's not that into you." Then he really laughed hard. "Oh wait now I see. She doesn't like you. That's why you're so obsessed." Cody continued chiding his friend as he flirted with the bartender. She had long blond hair streaked with brown. She smiled knowingly as she brought the pitcher.

"Is there anything else I can get you?" she asked with a half grin.

"I'll have to get back to you on that," he answered playfully. Then turning sharply he kicked his friend under the bar. "Will you quit tap tap tapping that damn foot. You're starting to make me nervous."

Holt stopped but he wasn't listening. His eyes were glued on the door of the bar. In walked Kira and her two friends. Kira's dark hair fell in loose waves around her shoulders and down her back. Her dress was a simple black sheath dress with spaghetti straps. The way the fabric clung to her small frame and curvy hips was anything but understated. He couldn't talk.

"Now what's wrong . . ." Cody started to ask but trailed off as he followed Holt's gaze to the door and saw the three women walking towards them. *Holy Hell!* He leaned over to Holt and whispered, "Is it too early to do a wing man victory dance? Shit I thought I was going to get stuck with some hobbit in a skirt. This rocks!" Cody's whispered voice was laced with excitement and trepidation. The redhead was exquisitely beautiful. Her bright green eyes were spellbinding. She seemed to be gliding as she walked toward him. Equally as exotic the last girl had raven-black hair and almond eyes. Here Asian features were flawless like she was a doll. A 50s rockabilly doll with more tattoos, he noticed, than he had seen on a woman up close before. Her eyes took mischievous to a whole new level and instantly made him uneasy but very excited.

"Hey guys," Kira said casually. "Captain Holt, Captain Bryson, this is Paige and Zoe."

Holt nodded in their direction. He sat a little dumbfounded. He had engineered this little date to further his chances with Kira but the other two women were very distracting. Cody nearly knocked him off his bar stool to greet the girls. He grinned ear-to-ear and patted Kira on the shoulder. "Nice to see you again," he said genuinely. He remembered that she was not a hugger from the training trip.

"Good to see you too. Do you guys want to grab a table?" Kira's smile was bright but apprehension lurked just beneath the surface. They found a table that could hold all five of them. It killed Kira to have to call Paige for help but she didn't know what else to do. Holt was potentially a very serious problem for her and Stark. Cody and Zoe sat on one side and Kira and Paige sat on either side of Holt. They set about getting to know each other and making initial small talk while looking at the menu. Zoe was already getting quite comfortable with Cody, sitting very close, she crossed her legs so that the left leg came across rubbing his thigh as she gently tapped her foot. Paige on the other hand was sitting very close to Holt. Every gentle glide and accidental touch of her hand was very distracting.

Kira looked up to ask Paige if she wanted to share some sushi but when she caught her eye Paige looked like she had seen a ghost. Her eyes were wide with panic but only for a second. Kira turned quickly to follow her gaze but she didn't see anything out of the ordinary. Just then her cell phone buzzed in her purse.

Having fun tonight? I miss you.

It was Stark! Why now she thought? She discretely wrote back.

Not much. I miss you to. When are you coming home?

283

She was a little aggravated first he said he was coming home then no word at all for two weeks.

You look like you're having fun. In fact you look damn gorgeous.

Kira's heart stood still. She could have died in that moment. *He's here!* Pure elation and joy was followed by panic. *Oh God he's here and I'm here with Holt!* While she had absolutely no intention of dating Holt she had to figure out what was going on. She wanted desperately to run into Stark's arms.

Where are you?

She typed knowing damn well he was in the restaurant somewhere. Paige had to have seen him. That would explain Paige's fleeting moment of panic.

Close enough to smell honey and jasmine.

Her heart leapt. She could feel the rippling effect of his words deep inside. Kira looked around frantically. She had to see him, touch him. She couldn't wait another second. Before she could do anything she got another text.

Tell them you have to go to the bathroom.

Eagerly, she obeyed. "I am so very sorry but I need to go to the restroom. Something I ate today is suddenly not agreeing with me." Kira politely excused herself as Paige gave her a knowing look. Holt started to get up. Paige by proximity was able to block him from getting up very quickly.

"Are you ok? Do you want me to drive you home?" he asked concerned.

"No no no. I'll just be a minute or two," she said over her shoulder scampering off before anyone else could stop her. Kira made her way back toward the bathrooms. As she made her way down the dimly lit hall a firm hand grabbed her by the arm and pulled her into the entrance to the wine cellar. Kira was spun around and was face to face with Owen Stark!

"You crazy, wonderful, sexy shit of a man, I was so worried! You said you would be home and then—" He cut her off with a deep kiss. As his tongue gently took control of her mouth he wrapped her so tightly in his arms. Kira felt her body melt in his embrace. It had been so very long since she had seen him. All the nights spent dreaming of this moment. His beard and hair were as unruly as the first day she had met him. She closed her eyes and drank him in. She could taste the sweetness of his favorite whiskey. The intoxicating scent of his cologne danced and swayed with the aroma of the many bottles of wine that surrounded them.

He paused for a moment and looked at her keeping her wrapped tightly in his arms. His lips brushed across her cheek and down her neck. Then he stopped and looked deeply in her eyes.

"Where have you been?" she asked almost tearfully.

"I've been to hell and back, but I've always been here," he said placing his hand gently over her heart. The warmth of his hand resting on her breast stole her breath away. "You are mine you belong with me always." His voice had become heated and needy.

"About Holt it's not—" she started but he kissed her passionately again. Her head was reeling the room was very, very warm.

"Kira," he breathed, "I'm not worried about Captain Candy Ass. I know you; you are a part of me. I trust you enough to know better."

This time as his lips found hers Kira surrendered completely. No longer was she worried about the table of people waiting fifty feet away in the restaurant. She didn't care about anything but being in this moment with this man. She had waited for what seemed like an eternity for him to return to her. His kiss enveloped her pulling her into him as his hand clasped around her thigh and slid upward pulling her dress with it. He reached her ass and held her tightly pulling her to him. The pressure of his immense cock thrilled her longing clit. She gasped and her breath caught as he pulled her close again. Suddenly he picked her up and she wrapped her legs around his waist. Still kissing her fervently now, he easily carried her over to the wine tasting table and sat her on the edge. The cold hard wood on her backside was startling. Her dress was hiked up around her waist at this point from being carried. He slid his hands up and down her thighs in a slow hypnotic motion each time getting closer to the lace hem of her panties. His finger reached her skimming back and forth over the silky fabric sending exquisite sensations through her overly sensitive flesh.

"Kira I have to have you now. Right now," he growled slipping his fingers past the delicate fabric and finding the sweet slick opening. "Oh God, Kira you are so wet. I want to make you come so hard you will never forget that you belong to me . . . only me." He slid two fingers deep inside her and found her now swollen clit with his thumb. When his expert fingers found their mark he began working and grinding her clit and G-spot between his fingers and his thumb in a tantalizing swirling dance that unraveled her completely. Her breaths began to come in short excited pants. He supported her with his other arm as she became so enthralled with his touch she could not hold herself up right.

She surrendered fully allowing him to manipulate and caress her body the way only he could. The fury between her legs built like an inferno awakening and exciting every nerve ending. "That's it my love," he commanded. "I want to feel you come." His words were her undoing and Kira cried out softly as she came digging her nails into his shoulders. He gently laid her back on the table. He put his put his fingers in his mouth and tasted the juices of her explosion. "Mmmm," he growled. "You taste amazing. Now I want to taste you for real. For months I have been dreaming of the way you taste." He leaned into her, gingerly removed her panties and placed them in his pocket. He kissed softly up her thigh. Kira was still spinning from her orgasm. Her tender flesh was so sensitive she struggled to stay still on the table. His tongue found her, lapping at first licking the juices of her climax before finding her clit. He nibbled and sucked in and expert ballet holding her thighs firm to the table so that in her ecstasy she would not fall off. The warm sensation grew again building, sending spasms of pleasure clenching through her.

"Lets go home," he said sternly.

"What about everyone out there?" she asked through the muddled post orgasmic haze.

"Let them enjoy their dinner. I want to enjoy you. I want to take you home and fuck you and make love to you and make up for lost time."

"I have to go tell them we I mean I am leaving," she said more alert and with genuine concern.

"Ok, go tell them," he said smiling shrewdly.

"Can I have my panties back please?" she asked as she stood up and straightened her skirt.

"Oh no," he said, his smile widening. "These are mine."

"You have to be joking. I'm not going out there without my panties." She was horrified.

"So come with me." His voice implored her to give in. But Kira was not going to give in that easily.

"Fine. Commando it is," she said defiantly and walked out the door. She walked into the dining room of the restaurant and approached her table. As she stood there with all eyes on her feeling the juices of her little escapade trickling slowly down her panty-less leg, she suddenly wished she had gone with Stark.

"Kira, are you ok?" Holt asked alarmed at her disheveled appearance. If Kira could have seen herself in a mirror her panties would be the least of her worries. Her hair bore the resemblance of having been in a windstorm. One of her spaghetti straps hung loosely on her right shoulder. And her lipstick had found its way to places it had no business being.

Trying to keep her composure despite the horrified and bemused looks of those at her table Kira said, "I'm sorry guys I had lunch at Frank's Franks and frankly I don't think they like me very much. I'm going to have to go." Her flushed cheeks helped to sell the story.

"Let me take you home" Holt insisted.

"No, no you guys stay and have fun. I'm gonna run. I'll see you later ok?" With that Kira turned on her heels and went out the door before any one could say anything.

Kira knew she should go back. She knew Holt would be furious. She knew there were a hundred reasons she shouldn't be doing this. But none of that mattered now. She wanted only him. She followed Stark's truck in the jeep and they took off into the night.

Kira shrieked out loud when she caught a look at herself in the rearview mirror. *Holy Hell! I went out there like this!* Kira's already red cheeks ignited when she saw her deranged appearance. *God knows what they are thinking right now! Well I know what Paige is thinking,* she thought and laughed out loud at her self as she drove, her heart racing to follow Stark home. He had said, "Let me take you home." *Home!* She knew he was just referring to his house but the way he said it implied so much more. *He's back! Safe and mine!* Kira's heart was bursting so with joy and anticipation she didn't notice the car

290

following her. Her eyes were focused on Stark's taillight. All she could think of was jumping into his arms when they got *home!* She stopped almost suddenly at the red light. She had been so lost in her thoughts she had almost ran it. The car behind her slammed on their brakes and skidded barely missing her rear bumper. Kira looked apologetically in the rearview mirror but couldn't see the drivers face. "Sorry!" she said out loud as if they could hear her. She took a minute to straighten her hair and put on lip gloss just before the light turned green. Kira's heart leapt. Just a few more blocks and she would be *home.*

Kira pulled into the drive and turned off the jeep. Stark was at once beside the door opening it and lifting her out. He spun her around and kissed her hard in the night air.

He kissed her as if making up for all the lonely nights he spent dreaming of this moment. "Mmmm honey and jasmine." He growled into her mouth. Lost in his massive arms her tiny feet dangled off the ground. She could taste herself on his lips. The thought excited her as she remembered where those lips had just been. Stark carried her to the door.

"I can walk," she said laughing.

"Not tonight," he said sternly. "I've been waiting four months for this. I don't want to let go of you for a second. I can't begin to tell you about the ache and deep sadness of where I've been. All I know is that I have been dreaming of this moment for

291

what felt like an eternity in hell. Right now I don't want to think about any of that. Right now all I want is to hold you and feel you for real. You are the most beautiful distraction in my life."

She could tell by the intensity in his bright eyes that he meant every word. He opened the door with one hand and they were nearly knocked down by the frantic and very excited Mags. "Looks like I'm not the only one who missed you!" she said giggling.

Stark set her down and began hugging and petting Mags. She was wagging her tail so hard her entire back half was wagging with it. Four months was a long time for all of them. Stark sat on the porch for a moment petting Mags and staring up at Kira. Tenderly she smiled back at him and couldn't help but feel things were complete.

As they disappeared into the house they were so absorbed in each other they didn't notice they had an audience. The stranger smirked at the touching scene and almost felt sorry for what would happen. Almost but not quite enough to stop from yanking the false bottom out from under her happy little life. In the darkness a car started and drove off without alarming anyone.

Once inside Stark took time to feed and water Mags then turned his attention back to Kira. "You are mine," he said sweetly. "I want to take you upstairs and remind you why you missed me." His sweet voice became darker now oozing sex.

"Who says I missed you?" she asked innocently. "Were you really gone that long? What was it like a week?" She smirked and looked up at him licking her lower lip and grinning.

"Are you testing me?" His eyes danced wildly. "You think taunting a desperate man is a wise move there, princess?"

"I'll take my chances," she said coyly, stepping closer to him and tracing her finger down the buttons on his shirt. She stopped just at the edge of his jeans and looked up again staring into his eyes.

"I don't know whether to kiss you or spank your stubborn sexy ass!" He huffed bemused and frustrated.

"Well?" she asked. "Whatever are you going to do?"

"Both!" He said tossing her over his shoulder like a sack of potatoes and carrying her up the stairs getting in a few good smacks as he went."

"Stop!" Kira shrieked between giggles as she wriggled around in his strong arms. "Aaahh." She gasped as his hand made contact with her bare ass. The wriggling had served to displace the skirt of her short dress exposing her still very bare backside. His hand lingered on the soft fleshy cheek before he struck again. Kira half gasped half moaned. She couldn't explain how incredibly wet this was making her. The only thing she could think of was how much she ached to have him inside her.

They were down the hall and into his bedroom in seconds. Stark paused to turn on the fire and then tilted her chin up to his lips and kissed her with all the months of built up desire. He let her feet down gently and slipped her dress up and over her head. She heard him gasp when he saw her standing wearing nothing but a lace bra. He immediately picked her up again pressing her to him and then sat her down on the bed. She edged backward up the bed and he followed crawling after her all the while still entwined in deep long kisses. He gently laid her head back on to the satin pillow. As he slid his hand under the pillow to support her head he hit something. He stopped kissing her and had a puzzled look on his face. Kira instantly froze and realized what he had discovered. Before she could stop him He pulled the satin pouch out from under her pillow.

"What's this?" he asked with a puzzled grin on his face.

Kira flushed scarlet. "Its nothing . . . Let me have that!" She sputtered trying to get it out of his hands. Stark was straddling her and had the obvious advantage. He held the pouch up and out of her reach.

"Let's see. What do we have here?" he teased as he opened the pouch and started to look through it. "So I'm off risking life and limb and you move your battery operated boyfriend in?"

"Owen, four months is a long time. BOB was just keeping me company till you got back," she pleaded giggling in embarrassment.

"I guess it didn't seem that long, you had company!" he said in mock disgust. "So you think BOB is up for a threesome?" he asked laughing.

"Shut up. BOB doesn't play that way. Give me that bag!" she pleaded.

"Oh no! Not till I see what else is in here." Stark emptied the contents of the bag on the bed and flipped on the light. Kira squinted as the unexpected brightness temporarily blinded her.

"Very nice!" he exclaimed picking up a bottle of Pjur lube. He smiled knowingly. "Pjur, one of my favorites. Good choice! What else do you have here?"

Kira wanted to melt into the bed. Her cheeks burned with embarrassment. "Owen . . ." she pleaded. "I was lonely and I missed you! Please put that away!"

The self-satisfied smile on Stark's face told her he wouldn't be giving this up any time soon. She reached for a pillow to bury her face in.

"You aren't even going to introduce us?" he asked playfully clearly enjoying the torture of her humiliation.

"What?" she shrieked covering her face. "You are truly terrible!"

Stark laughed loudly and proceeded to pick up and inspect the purple and white vibrator. "Show me." His voice suddenly darker.

"Oh hell no!" she yelled from under the pillow. Kira pulled the pillow tighter but she felt strong hands pulling it away. She giggled and squealed as the soft fabric slipped from her fingers.

"Show me," he said again. His baritone voice lowered to a soft rumble that oozed sex. Kira felt her skin tingle at his request. "I want to see how you pleasure yourself when I'm not here. Give me something to dream about when I'm outside the wire."

Kira hesitated, her cheeks burned with embarrassment. She opened her mouth to protest but he put his finger over her lips gently. "Show me," he said again and handed her the purple silicone device. She held it in her hands and closed her eyes. "Show me," he whispered, his voice barely audible now. Kira lay back on to the bed. She knew she would do whatever he asked her to do. She could feel him watching as she trailed the phallic object down her chest pausing at the fastener of her bra.

She paused for a moment and pressed a button turning it on. The low hum of the vibrator filled the silence. Suddenly intense soulful music filled the room. She felt Stark's hands unfastening her bra. She moved the vibrator in a gentle circular motion over her left nipple. The vibrations sent little jolts of electricity through her breast. She could feel herself getting wetter. She heard Stark settle back in the chair by the bed. Her inhibitions and embarrassment began to fade. She wanted to give him a show. She trailed the pulsing object slowly down her abdomen and paused just above her freshly waxed pussy. She heard Stark gasp quietly. She knew he was watching her intently. She rolled it around her clit ever so slightly building pressure in her throbbing nub. She paused and grabbed the bottle of Pjur lube and drizzled it over the purple silicone tip and spread it around with her fingers. She worked the lube up and down the phallic object holding it tightly for Stark to see. She looked up to see that he had taken out his thick cock and was stroking it slowly but firmly. A sly smile crept across her lips as she leaned forward and drizzled the silky liquid on the massive head of his cock. He moaned louder. "I want to watch you," he said again his voice now raspy and tight.

***

He watched her lay back on the bed. He couldn't get over the beauty of her chestnut hair as it spilled in soft loose curls all around her. Her firm breasts were fully exposed soft pink nipples erect standing at attention. Her delicate hands searched the satin sheets until they found the purple and white vibrator. He was happy to see it was considerably smaller than his cock. She took the well-oiled machine and worked it against her nub and then slid it into her waiting slit. He heard her moan softy as she hit just the right spot. The Lelo Ina was shaped so that one part went deep into her vagina and pressed against her G-spot, while the other pressed against her clit firmly vibrating everything in between. He watched her back arch and her muscles tense. She was writhing with the pulsations of the machine now. One hand fiercely worked the silicone instrument back and forth the other gripping her breast and pinching her nipple tightly. Stark pumped harder. His large hands grasped firmly working the thick shaft to rigid fury. He felt the pressure building. Her leg drew up and her hips tightened as she grew closer and closer to her climax.

"My turn." He growled and stood taking the purple beast from her delicate hands and casting it onto the floor. In one swift motion he pummeled his well primed fully lubed cock deep into her. Her eyes flew open with panic and surprise then softened with pleasure as he began to move back and forth. He heard hear breathing become raspy and erratic as her legs tightened around him. The months of ache and throbbing pain missing her boiled up and threatened to escape but he held firm . . . complete control. Sweat beaded across his brow. The intensity gripped him as her soft cries fell into rhythm with his movement. The combination of lube and her juices allowed him to move more freely despite her small size. He could feel her tender flesh stretch to allow him in. He could not stop the onslaught, he had needed this . . . needed her. He fought his own release until he heard her screaming his name. Her nails were digging into his arms as she came. He could feel her spasm around his cock. The tightening sensations sent him far beyond what he could control and he blasted deep into her releasing months of desperation.

Chapter 18

"Pack your bags!" Stark said, gently shaking a very sleepy Kira. "Come on, wake up. I am on R & R and you have a long weekend off. I want to take you on a little trip."

Kira groaned and rolled over, pulling the pillow tighter around her head. She had been on trauma call the last four nights and had only been home a couple of hours. "Sleep," she mumbled almost incoherently. "I need sleep."

"You can rest in the Jeep. Seriously, wake up. This is the army, not the holiday hotel. Wake up, or I'll pack for you and you'll just have to wear whatever I pick out." Stark laughed as he pulled at the blankets. Kira was wrapped up like a mummy in his sheets and gray duvet. How she had managed to wind up so tight in there he would never understand. With a quick jerk of the blanket he unraveled her cocoon.

"Hey!" Kira squealed as she bounced onto the bed finally waking up. "What are you so excited about? Where are we going?" she grumbled as she struggled to pull bits of blanket back around her. Rolling over she pouted as she looked up at him.

"Hmmm, we may have to be a little late. There's a gorgeous young woman lying in my bed wearing only cotton boy

shorts. Someone should have warned her how dangerous that is."
Stark's eyes sparkled wildly as he pulled her gently by the ankles
toward the end of the bed. A grin spread across his face. "I know
what I want for breakfast," he said as he knelt by the bed and
began kissing just above her knee and working his way slowly
upward.

Kira giggled and tried to squirm away. "That tickles,"
she said between shrieks as Stark tightened his grip on her thighs
and continued kissing, inching closer to the edge of her boy
shorts. "You win! You win! I'm awake!" she continued.

"Too late for that, I've got you right where I want you
now," came his muffled reply as he nuzzled against the soft
fabric separating him from her now very eager clit. "I want to
taste every inch of you," he growled, sending delicious
vibrations through the flimsy material, electrifying her sensitive
flesh.

Kira shivered. She forgot all about being sleepy or her
long week at work. All she could think of now was this half-
dressed sex god kneeling between her legs. Kira let her head fall
back on the bed. She put her fingers in his hair and held on as he
reached his prize, slipping her panties out of his way. She let out
a surprised moan in the exquisite moment his tongue made
contact. She arched her back as the pleasure of his feasting took
her over. Stark worked his magic, licking and sucking her
throbbing clit and darting his tongue deep inside her. Now Kira

301

squealed with delight as immense pressure began building, driving her to the edge of orgasm. Her breath came faster, her sex tightening as she held tightly to his thick dark hair. She was transfixed by the contrast of the soft curls that spilled through her fingers against the sheer intensity of the muscles of his massive back and arms.

Her legs begin to quiver and her thighs spasmed involuntarily around him. He knew she was getting close. He worked his hand up to her exposed breast and found her delicate nipple. He began rolling and tugging sending waves of pleasure through her. Kira cried out her body giving in fully to her frenzy as she came. "That's it baby," he purred, blowing gently on her still searing flesh. "I love when you come for me. Only me." His voice was soft and possessive. Slipping out of his sweats he crawled up on the bed and on top of the still quivering Kira. "I want all of you," he whispered, wrapping her exposed body in his powerful arms. "Kira I wish there was a way to tell you just how much you mean to me." He held her tighter and stared out the window as if his thought physically pained him. "My enlistment is coming to an end and I would never have considered leaving until I met you, but the team is my family, my life." Owen pulled her closer, as if somehow he could hold on tight enough to keep her forever.

They lay there for the longest time. Kira had no idea how to answer him. When she came down from her orgasm and finally caught her breath, and changed the subject. "Well, good morning!" she said, playfully looking up at him with dreamy eyes. She could scarcely believe this was real. How she had managed to be waking up in the bed and the arms of this chiseled god she would never know. The heat from his body was all around her. She could smell his shower gel. He must have just come back from working out and gotten in a shower. "You have me," she said, answering his earlier request. "I'm all yours. If you want me, show me." She teased softy biting her lower lip and tracing her finger gently over his chest.

"Is that a challenge?" he asked, grinning once again. Stark shifted, positioning the head of his massive cock at her now slick entrance. A fire once again sparked in his eyes. "I never back down from a challenge. You are the only thing I want. I'm going to spend the rest of my life showing you just how much." As he spoke he slid into her fully, aided by the juices of her previous orgasm. Kira gasped at the sudden fullness. She held tightly to his thick arms. She could not explain the intense feeling of being surrounded by those arms. The rest of the world faded away. She nuzzled her face into his chest, breathing in deeply the intoxicating aroma. Stark continued moving in a slow deliberate rhythm. He was not hurried or forced. He took time as if to savor each exquisite stroke stretching over her throbbing clit and then filling her completely. Kira arched her back, her long hair spilling down onto the silky sheets. Her fingers clenched the soft fabric tightly as the slow burn of his entrancing rhythm grew to encompass her entire body.

***

Still he remained slow and steady, enjoying her reaction, letting her build, pulling her tightly to him. He wrapped his big arm around her small back and cradled her head in his hand. He supported her there in the perfect position to feel every movement of his bounding cock. He watched smiling as her eyes closed and she lost herself in the moment. He truly loved having this effect on her. He bent forward and began gently kissing the soft skin of her delicate neck. Kira let out a deep moan at the added pleasure. His motion never faltered. Kira wrapped her legs around him, holding on. Feeling her body tighten, Owen began to increase his speed in concert with her growing need. Just when it seemed she could take no more, he positioned his other hand behind her hips and tilted her upward ever so slightly, causing the head of his cock to collide fully with her G-spot. Kira cried out loudly, "Oh . . . God . . . Owen!" She struggled to speak. With each movement now, she jerked as if explosions of pleasure were taking over all of her senses. He felt her release into him fully, coming harder than she ever had. Owen held her quivering body; a smile settling on his lips as he gently kissed her glistening forehead. Though he couldn't put it into words, he had felt it. For a brief moment, like the vibrant rain that showers the forest, touching each leaf, her sensuality had washed over him, permeating every inch as if they were one. He had never felt that before. He knew in that moment he would never really be able to let her go. Yet, like a dark storm looming in the distance, the day would come and he would have to choose. He hoped that she would remember this moment forever.

***

"Hey in there," Kira said, playfully bringing him back to the present. Having regained her composure she was ready to see what this adventure was all about. "So, where are we off to?"

"You'll see. Can you be ready to leave in twenty minutes?" he asked, not giving anything away. "I'll go make you some coffee while you shower." His bright eyes twinkled with excitement. He hustled out of the room. She could hear him taking the steps two at a time down to the kitchen.

His anticipation was contagious and Kira jumped up and into the hot shower. Standing there, letting the delightfully hot water run over her, she said good-bye to all the stresses of her week and immersed herself in the steam. She was so grateful for this man. Never before had she wanted to be with anyone like she did with him. He was a bright ray of warm sunshine into her (at times) dismal and dreary life. A dark voice inside her warned that this bliss wouldn't last, but the aroma of fresh brewing coffee rescued her from her self-doubt. She quickly finished showering. She stepped out, finding a new Northface pack on the bed for her. Her fingers traced along the blue and black fabric. She grinned, seeing he had managed to find her favorite blue. He was getting really good at that. Not knowing where they would be going, she hastily packed for a variety of activities. She decided to wear hiking pants that would roll up into capris if it got hot. As an afterthought, Kira put on her new soft Quinn Prana top and matching hoodie that Owen had gotten her. Grabbing her Merrells, she ran down the steps with five minutes to spare.

"Nice," Owen commented, noting the time. "Very nice!" he said, looking her up and down. "Your coffee, madam." He handed her a stainless steel thermos cup. The aroma of the freshly brewed nectar was intoxicating. Kira sipped, noting just the right amount of cream and agave.

She looked up at him and smiled appreciatively. "Mmmm. Thank you. So where are we headed exactly?"

Before he could answer, they were interrupted by Mags walking in with her leash. "You ready for a trip, girl?" he asked, ruffling her fur. He took the leash gently and grabbed Kira's bag. Mags followed him eagerly out the door. Kira took her coffee and the woolen blanket laid out on the counter and followed them. She gasped and stopped suddenly as she stepped out the door and saw the shiny new bright blue kayak strapped to the top of his jeep next to his yellow one. She couldn't hide the excitement and joy on her face. She had been looking at kayaks in magazines all winter while he was away, dreaming of an outing just like the one they were about to begin. She raced over to inspect the vivid blue and white Perception Prodigy kayak. She traced her finger along the edge.

"How did you know?" she exclaimed, clapping her hands and climbing up on the Jeep to get a closer look. Stark grabbed her thermos as she almost spilled her coffee in her excitement. It had every feature she could have wished for. She stood in the Jeep between the two kayaks and clasped her hands.

"Hold on there, let me get your picture," he said. "It wasn't too hard to figure out. Someone left magazines and cut out pictures all over the house." He laughed. She climbed down and wrapped her arms around his neck, almost spilling the coffee again.

"Thank you! Oh my God, Owen! It's perfect!" She hugged him again.

"Lets go try them out shall we?" he asked coaxing her back into the Jeep.

Kira settled into her seat and sipped the delicious coffee. Mags, nestled in behind her, and poked her head through the seats. Kira turned to her warmly and gave her a hug. "Were you in on this, girl?" she asked softly.

Stark smiled and pulled out of the driveway. "I have so much to show you. This is going to be epic."

The sun shone down brightly overhead as they drove higher up the mountain. Aspen and Hemlock cast great shadows over the winding road. They came to a clearing and the trees fell away, revealing a bluebird sky dotted with white clouds. The great valley below was visible stretching to the next towering peak. She drew in a deep breath and felt so free and alive. She reached her left hand up toward the sky between the kayaks and felt the wind on her fingers. Stark reached his hand up also. For a moment they rode along with the wind and sun dancing around their extended fingers. It was surreal. Kira closed her eyes and felt like she was flying. Stark took her hand and kissed her fingers. "We are almost there. We just need to make a little stop and get some provisions."

He pulled into a small gas station with a store aptly called The Store. Kira giggled. She guessed if you were the only game in town you could call it whatever you wanted. The old white building had clearly seen better days. The walls, covered in peeling paint, held signs in various stages of disrepair advertising Shell gasoline and Coca-cola. She got out, following Stark past an old sleeping hound that didn't bother to get up and bark to alert his master of their presence. The rickety door stuck slightly and creaked loudly as Stark pulled it open, jingling the rusty bells. Kira stifled a giggle and smiled politely at the owner who was as ancient and dust covered as the store itself. She wondered how long the old man had been there and who had come first, the man or the store. He brightened when he saw Stark. She was surprised to see Stark round the counter and hug the old man. She couldn't be sure, but she thought she saw a tear in the old man's eye.

"Ralph, this is my girlfriend Kira," Stark said turning to introduce Kira. The man extended a weathered hand and took Kira's.

"So nice to meet you," Kira said sweetly, a bit taken back by the fond exchange.

"My pleasure," the old and slightly toothless man replied. "Cookie's got sandwiches and cold beer packed for you. You two be safe out there. The waters a little up from all the rain, may be a bit of a bumpy ride today." Turning to Stark he said, "You look more like your mama every time I see you, boy. She sure was a beautiful girl." As Ralph spoke, the creases on his face portrayed a lifetime of joy and sadness. His eyes twinkled but Kira could detect a longing sorrow as he remembered those who were long gone.

"Ralph was my grandpa's childhood friend. They grew up not too far from here." He patted the old man on the shoulder as he spoke. "He and Cookie used to look after my mother in the summers." Then pausing, "Where is Cookie?"

309

"Cookie!" the old man bellowed. "Owen is here!"

"No need to yell, you old fool," Cookie cackled back in a slight German accent. The short silver-haired woman stood no more than five feet tall, Kira guessed, and walked with a mild limp. She crossed the floor to Stark and hugged him firmly. "How are you my boy?" she asked lovingly. She turned to Kira and looked her over. "A little thin," she said. "But we can fix that."

Cookie hustled promptly off to the kitchen and returned with a dry sack packed thoughtfully with sandwiches and beer. "If you put these down in the dry storage of your kayak the beer will keep cold," she said authoritatively.

"He knows that, woman!" the old man retorted, giving her a playful look.

"Oh, how would you know? You can't remember where you left your teeth!" she spat back and grinned.

Kira let a giggle slip at the exchange and couldn't help but think that could be Owen and her one day. Through the mock battle their deep love was heavy and apparent. They were bonded together for life. They had seen a lifetime weathering every storm, celebrating each joy together.

"All right, woman, let them go," Ralph said as Cookie gave them each one more hug good-bye and they climbed back into the Jeep to continue on their journey. "We'll see you at the take out, boy."

Heading on down the road, Stark reached over and took her hand as they drove. The sun was fully in the sky now. The light danced through the trees and across their faces. He let go of her hand as they pulled onto a bumpy path that led down to the river. He masterfully drove the jeep down the rutted dirt road to the put-in. He pulled to a stop, kicking up a cloud of dust on the dirt and gravel parking area.

Kira could barley contain her excitement as she helped him unload the kayaks. They packed their gear carefully in the dry storage being sure to seal them in tight. Kira struggled to tighten her PFD. Stark laughed and came over to help.

"Here let me help with that. Arms out," he said, commandingly. He fastened the straps and pulled them tight.

"That's tight!" Kira squeaked. She couldn't help but be reminded of the straps she had seen on Zoe in the video. Bound and tethered. Kira shook the thought from her head. Still, there was something about the restricted feeling in the vest.

"Perfect," he said with a knowing smile and finished with his own. He fastened their helmets and prepared to launch into the river.

"Are you ok?" he asked, turning to be sure she was ready.

"Oh, I'm great. Let's go!" Kira was filled with nervous enthusiasm. She realized that was becoming a trend with Mr. Owen Stark, always pushing her beyond her comfort zone to her very limits. The rational part of her brain blared a red siren warning. But her heart and every excited nerve ending squealed with delight and said go for it!

Stark helped launch her into the water and then climbed in his own kayak and set out in front. Maggie rode in the front of his boat wearing a life jacket of her own. Kira was surprised at how still and calm Mags was riding in the kayak with Stark. The water was cold coming out of the bottom of the dam. The current was enough to take them with minimal paddling except to steer.

Kira followed him to the right as they approached the first rapid. She could feel her heart pounding despite his promise that these were Class I-II rapids. She gasped, as small waves broke over her boat and ice cold water spilled into her lap. The river was taking them swiftly on. The power of the rushing water was abundant. She did her best to steer and follow the line Stark appeared to be taking. She realized she was holding her breath as she followed him through the next set of rapids. Would it always be like this? A mix of fear and excitement? Kira couldn't remember feeling so alive before meeting Owen Stark. *What's happening to me?*

312

A group of geese had settled in to an eddy off to their left. The geese honked loudly at the passing boats. Kira laughed when Stark acted like a goose putting his elbows out like wings and honked back at the geese. These little glimpses of a carefree humor reminded her that somewhere inside this guarded man was the boy he used to be. They followed the winding river on through the beautiful canyon and eventually came to a large eddy where the water was as clear and flat as glass. The river here was wide and had risen above plants with millions of tiny yellow flowers. Some were tall enough to break the surface of the water. The rest of the golden treasures lay just beneath the surface. The kayaks floated effortlessly over the submerged field of flowers as if they were flying. Kira trailed her fingers gently in the cool water brushing along the delicate petals. She had never seen anything so beautiful. The warm sun caressed her and all the world was quiet except the chorus of birds in the trees and the gentle breeze. She inhaled deeply, enjoying the fragrant honeysuckle growing along the banks. They paused in the flat water for a picture. Kira wondered if they could tuck this moment away forever.

They made their way through several more rapids and Stark began to paddle toward a grassy meadow on the bank. Kira paddled hard against the current and followed him. He hopped out and pulled his kayak up onto the bank, then helped Kira out of hers. Once both boats were secure, he pulled out the picnic lunch and cold beer. They sat side by side on the bank of the river and enjoyed turkey sandwiches on sour dough bread smothered with peach preserves and crispy onions. Kira thought the flavor combination just might be genius! She shared nibbles of her sandwich with Maggie, who was nestled at her feet. She leaned against Owen's shoulder. At this moment, the world was perfect. Kira looked up at Stark and caught him staring out over the water. His expression wasn't happy and dreamy like hers. He looked intense and concerned. She could tell something was really bothering him.

"Are you ok?" she asked tentatively. Warning bells went off in her mind.

His look faded and was quickly replaced by a slightly forced smile as he looked down at her. "Yeah, I'm great. This day is perfect. I'm just wishing I could keep it."

"Who says you can't?" Kira reached up and put her hand on his arm.

"Let's get moving, ok?" He helped her up.

After lunch they paddled on for several more miles. The rapids in this section of the river were slightly faster and a little rougher, but still manageable with their touring boats. Kira was starting to get the hang of maneuvering her new kayak. Her confidence rose slightly. Small channels and little islands allowed them to separate for a moment then rejoin each other further downstream. They made their way playfully splashing each other with their paddles. Kira shrieked as the icy water trickled inside her PFD. Up ahead she saw Ralph and Cookie standing beside the bank next to the Jeep. They had brought it down to the take out to pick them up.

Pulling the boats out of the water, Kira turned to Owen. "Thank you for this," she said. "It was a wonderful day!"

"The day's not over yet," he said. "We still have a few more hours of sunlight."

They hugged Ralph and Cookie good-bye and thanked them for bringing the Jeep down to the take out point.

"Ok, so now what?" she asked, shedding her river gear and climbing into the Jeep.

Stark finished strapping the kayaks on the top and started the engine. "Feel like taking a little hike?" he asked mysteriously. He pulled the Jeep onto a rough and steep winding passageway that felt more like a 4x4 course than an actual road. A gentle mist and fog had risen out of the gorge. It gave the area a mystical feel. Kira, still wet from paddling, pulled her jacket tighter around her as they climbed the makeshift road. Finally they reached the top and a small clearing. Stark pulled the Jeep to a halt on the dirt lot and helped her out. An old sign marked a forgotten trailhead. Stark got their packs and gave her a headlamp.

"What's this for?" she asked, puzzled since it was still daylight.

"The way back," he said, smiling. They began their ascent through the slightly overgrown trail. Kira stayed close behind him. The forest was so dense she was surprised that they almost needed the headlamps in the day. They scrambled up rocks and over fallen trees. The terrain became rockier. She could tell they were nearing cliffs. They made it to a clearing and climbed out onto a rock ledge. Kira's palms grew sweaty when she saw just how high up they were. They had managed to climb out onto a boulder that overlooked all of Colorado. Kira's breath caught in her throat. The entire world lay before them. Mountains in the distant horizon cradled a great valley.

Evening was setting in and the sky was a display of color. Distant pinks and blues swayed out from a blazing setting sun. The golden remnants of light illuminated wispy clouds below them. They sat side by side watching the sun disappear, saying good night to a perfect day. Stark reached out and set the rugged Pentax on the rock to capture their silhouette against the vanishing light. As the sun slipped beyond the horizon, Stark turned toward her pulling her close. He kissed her deeply. "Do you remember the first sunset we saw together? God I wanted to kiss you so fucking bad. But I knew better. Hell I should know better now, but I never wanted to miss the opportunity again."

Kira sat in the warmth of that moment. She didn't want it to ever end. Sitting at the edge of the world, she felt inevitably safe in his strong arms. The joy and completeness of the moment was overwhelming. She had never imagined that she would ever be able to feel this completely happy. She turned to him as the darkness settled in around them and murmured, "I could stay here with you forever." She nuzzled against his chest as she spoke. They held each other as the last rays of light slipped away.

"As much as I would like that, I have a surprise for you. Off we go," Stark said, turning on her headlamp and carefully picking her up and guiding her back to the trail.

The way down was a bit trickier. Using their headlamps they moved slowly back down the trail and over the rocks. Even though he knew she was capable, he paused to help her through the steepest rocks. Eventually they arrived back at the lot where the Jeep and Maggie sat waiting for them. After taking a minute to walk and water Maggie, they loaded back up and set out again. To Kira's surprise they did not turn back toward Fort Carson when they reached the main road. Instead Stark turned the Jeep toward Estes Park. Kira leaned her head over onto his shoulder and watched the stars. She drifted off to sleep.

"Wake up, Sleeping Beauty. We're here." The softness of Stark's voice woke Kira from her slumber. It was only 9:30 in the evening but she was exhausted after kayaking and hiking for the better part of eight hours. She stretched and looked around. One look at her surroundings and she was wide-awake. "Where are we?" Her mouth was gaping as she took in the magnificent white exterior of the charming old hotel. Large stone steps led up to a grand entrance. Kira shook her head, thinking it must date back to the early 1900s. She climbed down from the Jeep as Stark grabbed their bags and tipped the valet. "What about Mags?" Kira said, suddenly worried as Maggie jumped down beside her.

"This is the Stanley Hotel," he said, smiling at her concerned face. "Mags is welcome. They allow dogs here. Midge the innkeeper loves dogs, especially Mags. She even bakes her special peanut butter banana dog biscuits." As if on cue, Mags ran ahead of them and up the old steps, her tail wagging. Clearly she knew this place well. Stark grabbed their bags and wrapped his arm through Kira's. They walked together up the steps and into the grand lobby. They crossed the dark wood floor. The Elizabethan architecture and rich dark wood everywhere gave the hotel a warm, but slightly eerie, feel. Mags ran to Midge as she entered the lobby from an office just off the lobby.

"Hey girl! You missed my biscuits, didn't you?" Midge addressed Maggie and smiled genuinely. Her oval glasses and short reddish brown hair framed her face well. She bent and took a biscuit from her apron pocket and gave it to Mags. Kira noted that she was quite pretty for her age. Gauging by her hugs, she was a true dog lover. When she was finished with Mags, Midge stood and turned to Stark and Kira. "Owen, it's so good to see you. It's been a while. How have you been and who is this lovely lady?"

"Thanks, Midge. This is my girlfriend, Kira. We've been playing in the river today," Stark said, beaming. Kira couldn't get over how all the people they met just loved him. It was more than his incredible good looks and piercing eyes. They all seemed to regard him as their long lost son. She also couldn't escape the feeling of pride when he had called her his girlfriend for the second time that day. She grinned up at him and then looked back to Midge.

"It's so nice to meet you," she said to the older woman. The woman squinted as she studied her. Kira felt like a bug under a microscope. She could feel herself shrinking under the scrutinizing gaze. Midge's ample eyebrows furrowed deeper.

"This one's got a troubled soul," she said quietly, and then paused for what seemed like an eternity, taking both of Kira's hands in her weathered ones. "But a good heart. She's a lot like you, Owen." She seemed satisfied with this and went to the front desk. She came back holding room key cards. "Got you a lovely king suite all set up with amenities for Mags. We were so excited when you called. It's been a long time." She smiled and patted Stark on the arm and Mags on the head before turning and heading back to her work.

Kira looked up at Stark with a puzzled expression. *What the hell was that?* "What's with all the cloak and dagger?" she whispered as soon as they were out of range.

Stark leaned in and said, in a low voice as they climbed the grand staircase, "Midge is a self-proclaimed psychic of sorts. Just go with it. It kind of adds to the charm of the hotel. It is supposed to be haunted after all," he said laughing, and kept going up the stairs.

Kira stopped in her tracks. "Um, what? Wait did you actually just say this hotel is supposed to be haunted? Are you shitting me?" Kira hurried to keep up with him. *This has to be some sort of joke.*

Stark was still grinning when she caught up. "Nope. Stephen King wrote The Shining in Room two-seventeen. If that doesn't make it spooky, I don't know what does. The hotel was built in the early 1900s and there has been a death or two, which naturally leads to ghost stories." He pulled her close, kidding her as they went down the hall to their room.

"Great." Kira's sarcasm dripped off each word. "A haunted hotel where a master of horror fiction was inspired to write probably the scariest book about a hotel ever, now that's romantic!" Although she definitely did not believe in ghosts, Kira felt herself shudder and scoot a little closer to Stark. When she heard him chuckle, she elbowed him in the ribs.

"Hey, what was that for? " he asked playfully. The grin on his face revealed he knew exactly what it was for. They made their way down the long hall to their room. Kira couldn't help but notice how, with a little imagination, she could picture the scary little twins at the other end and that poor kid on the tricycle. *Well, it's a good thing I got a nap in the Jeep. Probably won't be sleeping much tonight.*

Stark paused and checked the keys. "This is us. Don't worry, the rooms are beautiful," he said. "This is an amazing old hotel. It just has an interesting history." He handed Kira the key and she opened the door.

Stepping in, Kira was amazed at how spacious yet cozy the room felt. Warm colors and big dark wood furniture gave a nice contrast to the fluffy bright white bedding and pillows. To Kira's aching muscles it looked like a heavenly cloud. She resisted the urge to flop onto the glorious bed. She could smell the river on herself. "God, we stink!"

"To the showers then," Start commanded. "Come on, dirty girl, let's get you in the shower and see what we can do with you." Stark led the way into the granite and wood trimmed bathroom. She noted they had stayed with a rustic mix of old world charm. He flipped a switch to warm the slate floor and turned, pulling Kira close. He stared at her with his deep blue eyes. She imagined herself sitting on that island in the sea. His voiced brought her back. "You make every minute of my life worth it," he revealed.

Kira felt her knees buckle. "What?"

"Every painful minute of my life until I met you, every broken road I traveled, every desert hole I've crawled through are all worth it when I look at you." He bent and pulled her up to him. Wet, needy kisses enveloped her mouth and she gave into him freely. She suddenly forgot she smelled like the river and miles of hiking. He pulled her shirt off over her head and began to unfasten her bra. Kira caught sight of the horror in the mirror. Her hair was a tangled mess that used to be a ponytail. The removal of her shirt and bra had exposed creases of dirt and river water all over her skin. She felt her Prana shorts being unbuttoned. For a moment she closed her eyes. The warmth of him so close made her tingle all over. The anticipation of his touch made her quiver. Her panties hit the floor as she opened her eyes. Her distaste for her own appearance was overshadowed as Stark began to undress. She hated that he had this kind of power over her. The world slowed. Mesmerized, she watched his fingers undoing each button of his shirt. The wet T-shirt underneath clung to each rippling muscle. He pulled the T-shirt off over his head, exposing his tanned, sculpted perfection. Kira heard herself sigh out loud. *Oh dear, sweet Lord, that should be illegal.* He reached down and pulled of his Kuhl shorts. *Holy hell! He's been commando all day!* Kira drew in a sharp breath as his already erect cock sprang to freedom. He turned to start the water and get the shower room ready. Kira watched his perfectly taught ass and massively strong thighs as he stepped into the shower. She couldn't help but giggle at the little river weeds that were stuck to his butt cheek. She stepped in after him and knocked them off with a playful smack.

"You wanna play rough, little girl?" he asked, pulling her into the water.

"Aaaahhhh! Son of a— Oooh ooh, God! Owen that's c-c-cold!" Kira shrieked and flailed, trying to escape. He held her in, laughing, and turned up the heat. "Oooh that's better," she cooed as the warm water engulfed her. Kira liked showers hot. Hot enough to just about seer her flesh.

Still laughing, Stark took some of her favorite shampoo and began to make a lather. "Did you pack that?" she asked, puzzled since she hadn't seen him get it out.

"No I arranged for them to have it for you. I have all of your favorite things. Now just relax and I'll wash your hair." The deep rasp of his voice could be so tender at times. Kira closed her eyes and leaned into his chest. She let him work his magic on her long hair and scalp. He massaged her neck and worked to loosen each muscle group, then turned her around to rinse. He gently helped rinse all the soap away. Kira was feeling happy and dizzy. She could smell the honey and jasmine of her body wash and knew he was soaping up a soft loofah. She felt like she was drifting off to heaven as he worked slow circles all over her shoulders and back with the loofah in one hand and massaged with the other. She felt the loofah dip lower and lower. Her legs stiffened with anticipation. Each pass of the loofah was followed by his hand massaging, groping as he reached her ass. Kira reflexively stepped apart to allow him easier access to her waiting and eager flesh. But he passed right over and sat on the floor of the shower and began to work on her legs and feet. As good as the continued massage felt to her tired and aching muscles Kira struggled to hide her disappointment. He worked his way back up her legs and stopped just short.

"We better rinse this off. Better yet, maybe I'll just use my hands for this part." The deep sexy rasp was back in his voice. Kira new it was game on. She felt her heart and breathing quicken as he opened the bottle and poured the honey jasmine body wash into his bare hand. A sinister smile crossed his lips. "Hold on to the shelf," he instructed and proceeded to very gently massage tiny circles into each fold of skin of her most delicate region. The light touch was almost too much to bear but he didn't stop. He found her clit and began gently circling being ever so careful not to apply too much friction. With his other hand he shared the soapy lather and worked her cheeks and then slid between and made small circling motions teasing her ass. Kira jumped in surprise. "Hold still," he told her. "I'm just getting you clean. We'll save that for another day, when you're not already so sore," he said laughing.

He took the shower nozzle and began to rinse her from her neck down to her feet. Then he returned the nozzle and sat back on the shower floor. "What are you doing?" she asked a little puzzled. "You already got me all clean." She looked down at his smiling face and knew exactly what he was about to do. She bit her lip and breathed deeply.

"Hold onto the shelf," he said again. He grabbed her thighs and pulled her to him so that she was standing with one leg on either side of his as he sat in the floor. He picked her up slightly by her ass and buried his face deep in her waiting slit. She squealed with delight at the contact. The licking and sucking on her sensitive and now throbbing clit caused her to throw her head back. She was panting and clawing at the shelf with one hand and holding tightly to his hair with the other.

"Oh . . . dear . . . God!" she shrieked as the onslaught continued. The intense suction of his mouth on her clit was making her legs weak. Suddenly one then two fingers were working their way in and out of her sopping pussy. The rhythmic gyrations of his fingers sliding in and out, pressing on her G-spot while he sucked her clit sharply in his mouth, was building into the most insane orgasm. "Fuck me," she begged. Her words seemed to awaken him like an animal that had been lying in wait.

***

He stood and positioned himself behind her. He held her hips firmly, lifting her slightly and entering her from behind. Her tightness was incredible around his cock. The sudden intrusion hadn't given her time to adjust. Kira let out a sudden gasp and then a moan as he entered her. Her noises fueled his aggression. His need to have her, possess her, his primal need to bond with this beautiful creature overpowered all else. He thrust into her again and again. He was not making love this time. No, this was Fucking. Intense, carnal fucking. Kira's moans and squeals of ecstasy told him she was enjoying this as much as he was. He saw her knuckles whiten as her fingers tightened around the shelf. He lifted her further off the ground so the curve of his penis could strike her g-spot perfectly with each thrust. Her squeals became screams at a fevered pitch as she reached the peak of...

CRACK! There was a loud noise and then crash. They flew forward into the wall as the shelf Kira had been bracing on with all of their weight disintegrated. Kira's head hit the shower wall. Her blow was softened somewhat by his arms around her. Shock was replaced immediately by concern as Stark assessed the situation. "Oh Shit, Kira are you ok?" he asked, panic hitting him like a brick. *Oh god if she is hurt! Fuck!* "Kira are you ok? Can you talk? Sweet Jesus, say something."

Kira looked up, a little dazed, and smiled. "I think I'm going to live. But for the record you don't have to knock me out to get my attention. I'm starting to see you as a caveman with a club," she laughed with a sly smile on her face.

"God, I am so sorry! Let's get out of here. Wait, let me look at your head." Stark's eyes got as big as saucers when he looked at the growing lump on her forehead. "Shit, Kira! That looks like it hurts!"

Kira stepped out of the shower and looked in the mirror. "Oh, hell!" she said looking at the purple goose egg on her forehead. She giggled and then said, "Ok, at least I have a med kit. Seriously, if I end up in the ER what story are you going to come up with?"

Stark's face wrinkled in panic. "Oh fuck, do you think you need the ER?"

"Oh, holy hell. For a ranger you sure are panicky when it comes to girls." Kira laughed. She couldn't believe this strong, brave man was reduced to rubble when looking at a bruise. "Surely in all of your training you've seen a bruise before."

"I've seen a lot of things before. But it's different where you're concerned." Stark stepped closer, still examining the wound. "With anyone else I would tell them to laugh that shit off. I would die if I hurt you."

"You're just silly. I'm an officer like any other. I'm sure you've taken care of injured officers and services men with worse," she mocked as she stroked his hair.

Stark spoke before thinking, "Yeah but I wasn't in love with them." His words filled the air like a thick fog. They both forgot about the bruise as their eyes met in an intense gaze through the mirror into their lives.

They stood there like that for a few moments, both afraid to speak. The admission was heavy, like a sand bag *hanging* desperately onto a balloon, keeping it from floating away. Neither one of them was able to speak or react to what had happened. After what seemed like an eternity, Kira looked away. He couldn't mean it.

"Orgasms will do crazy things to a man," she said, nervously laughing. She knew this was just an excited admission and quickly changed the subject. It didn't change anything between them. She knew that there was no way after their short time together that he could mean what he had said.

Following her cue, Stark pulled away and began to get dressed. He could feel her resistance and iciness. He pulled on his boxers, joking as he said, "Sorry, I guess you are the first officer I nearly killed while fucking." He smiled and added, "You are right, I've seen much worse, just usually under different circumstances." Stark hustled to dress and then turned before leaving the room. "Let me order us something to eat. We can get room service. What are you hungry for?"

"Everything!" Kira called from the bathroom. *Nothing!* Her stomach was in knots and she felt as if she was going over the tip of a roller coaster. The free fall had taken her breath away. Kira took her time getting dried off. She wrapped up in a thick white towel and looked at the mess of a girl in the mirror. Dark strands of wet curly hair stuck to her face and shoulders. She could hear Stark on the phone ordering God knows what. The purple goose egg on her forehead stuck out vividly, reminding her of their tryst in the shower. He couldn't have meant what he said, could he? Still, the warmth of his words played over and over in her head.

Kira made her way out of the bathroom to see Stark lying back on the bed. He was still wearing only his boxer shorts. His perfect, relaxed muscles sprawled out over the crisp, white sheets. Kira marveled over the stunning sight. Despite the earlier tension, Stark looked calm, as if he hadn't said anything out of the ordinary. His expression changed when he saw the scarlet bruise on her forehead. Kira smiled shyly and instinctively covered the swollen reminder. Stark reached out his hand for her to come closer. "I'm sorry, baby," he said, taking her hand as she crossed closer to him. He pulled her gently on the bed with him and wrapped her in his arms. "I never want to hurt you. I got carried away." He stroked her hair as he spoke.

"It was pretty hot," she said smiling up at him. "That is, until we broke the shower. I'm pretty sure they are going to charge extra for that." She laughed and nuzzled into his arm. She closed her eyes and breathed him in. The crispness of his body wash mixed sensually with his musk. She pressed her face closer to his skin. Stark's fingers traced gently up and down her arm. If she wasn't starving, she could have drifted off to sleep. Just then the buzzer rang and a voice called out, "Room service."

Stark got up, boxers and all, and walked to the door. Kira followed, eager to see what he had ordered. The door swung open and in strolled three bellmen with carts and trays. "Holy hell, what did you order?" Kira gasped and stepped back. The short, sandy haired bellman got a look at Kira wrapped in her white towel and his face lit up. It then turned to shock as he saw the bruise on her head.

Seeing his expression Kira quickly interjected, "I had an accident earlier. I slipped in the shower and bumped my head." She grinned her sideways quirky grin indicating there was definitely more to the story.

Beaming, he looked Kira up and down before catching Stark's deadly stare. "Uh-um, we have a little of everything just like you ordered," the man stammered nervously as Stark stepped between them defensively. Following suit, the other two looked everywhere except at Kira. They quickly removed the silver lids exposing every manner of delicacy. "We have smoked steak, medium rare, with baked potato and German coleslaw. In this tray we have ceviche, thinly sliced fresh seafood marinated in fresh lime juice, red onions and spices, topped with fried calamari. Here we have diced Spanish chorizo, sautéed onions, and red bell peppers, flambéed with Spanish Oloroso sherry and served with freshly toasted baguette.

The tall, thin waiter opened his tray and displayed hand cut potato chips in various flavors, onion rings, and, finally, braised maple leaf duck ragù in homemade ravioli, served with a creamy Cabernet Sauvignon reduction and a mélange of wild mushrooms topped with aged parmesan.

The final waiter had a bucket of chilled wine, glasses, and a dessert tray with delicate chocolate mousse and a crème topping. He smiled up sheepishly at Kira as he poured the wine. Kira smiled back and thanked him. Stark hovered close by. Kira could see his aggravation at having three strange men in the room with Kira in only a towel. He quickly tipped them and escorted them back out of the room.   He turned shutting the door a little too forcefully. Kira stifled a giggle as she looked up at him. She loved the flustered look on his face. His eyes were still flashing with anger, his hard jaw set firm. She couldn't help but laugh; she looked him straight in the eyes and dropped her towel. His eyes widened in surprise then a wild look spread over his face.

Stark pulled her close. He looked directly into her eyes and said, "You are dangerous."

"Me?" Kira asked puzzled. "How is that?" How could this rugged, war machine and sex god think she was dangerous? She looked in his smoldering eyes and thought she saw a hint of vulnerability.

"You are dangerous because you are everything a man could dream of or want," he explained. "You are the one thing I can't live without. You could make a man walk away from everything and you don't even know it." His voice was raspy almost strained as he spoke.

"What are you talking about? I don't want you to walk away from anything," Kira said and laughed nervously. "Let's just enjoy tonight and the time we have." She couldn't believe her own words. Kira knew they were playing with fire. They couldn't go on like this forever. Aside from the fact that they were putting both of their careers in jeopardy, he would eventually be shipped out again and she would be given a permanent assignment God knows where. She thought of his face on the river today and the contrast of the carefree boy and the worried intense man.

"Ok, you're right let's eat, then I'm going to have you for dessert." His voice was dark and wanton. The look in his eyes displayed his mischievous plan as his glance darted from the chocolate mousse to Kira's naked body. Kira smiled and didn't bother to put on any clothes as she went from tray to tray sampling all the delicacies he had ordered for her. She ate slowly, savoring each morsel and enjoying the way Stark watched her eat. The filet was cooked or, in this case, not cooked to perfection. Kira loved it, juicy, pink and just barely dead.

"Is your steak ok?" he asked, knowing it was. She could tell he had gone to great lengths to make everything perfect. "The way they flame and smoke it here is unlike any other steak I've ever had."

"Oh . . . it's . . . perfect." Kira managed between mouthfuls of the tender meat. It seemed to fall apart in her mouth, almost melting. "Owen, I have to say this is glorious. Thank you."

"I thought you might enjoy it. When you're done, I am going to cover you in chocolate and lick it off. I want to savor every perfect inch of your skin."

Kira giggled. "I that case, I'm stuffed and couldn't eat another bite." She set down her plate and slowly lifted the lid on the chocolate mousse. Kira dipped her finger in the mousse and rubbed it on her lips. She put her finger in her mouth and gingerly sucked it off.

Stark dropped his plate in a clatter on the floor and bounced across the bed to her. He licked her finger suckling it gently then his lips found hers soft and sensual. He kissed her softly, at first exploring and delicately savoring the mix of chocolate and her exquisite skin. Then his kiss deepened. His tongue found hers greedily. He pressed forward onto her and she lay back in the softest pillows known to man. She almost sunk in and he reached behind her catching the back of her head and neck. He pulled her into to him. His breath came hot and heavy. His need was unmistakable. Kira looked up into his smoldering eyes.

"I can't explain what you do to me," he breathed, his air hot and sweet and less than an inch from her skin. Kira felt her skin tingle as each word blew across her, creating goose bumps in his wake. He reached over and got more mousse, looking up with that wicked smile she knew all too well. With a large glob of the frothy dessert on his finger he made slow circles over each nipple. She laid back and closed her eyes, letting him take her to the place only he could. The sticky finger trailed a path down her abdomen and was replaced by hot, wet, very soft lips. Kira let herself be carried away by the swirling hypnotic dance as he suckled and caressed her electrified nipple. Kira could feel the sensations and ached deep in her pussy. When his sticky fingers found her slit she was already soaking wet. Stark growled approvingly. Without stopping his attention to her breast, he scooped more mousse and massaged it into each delicate fold. She heard him chuckle almost with excitement as he began to move down, kissing and sucking along the trail of mousse. He paused at her navel. The attention made her giggle.

"Hey that tickles!" Kira shrieked. She tried to push him up but he was not having it.

"If you think that tickles, just wait." The sparkle in his blues eyes when he looked up at her could have melted the moon. Soon all she could see was his thick dark hair as his face disappeared between her legs. Kira squealed at the first contact of his mouth on her clit. He began lapping and then drinking a mix of mousse and her juices. Kira disintegrated into the soft sheets. The sensations became extremely intense, like a thousand fireworks going off in her clit and spreading over her entire body.

"God you are amazing!" Kira panted as she sucked in a sharp breath. She couldn't help but squeal and wriggle beneath him.

"Be still, Kira," he commanded softly. Owen Stark had a calm way of commanding everything around him.

"I can't! Ahhhh, God that's so good I almost can't stand it!" Kira shrieked and tried to escape. Her panting and moans fueled Stark to keep it up and take her to the depths of her most intense orgasm and hold her there. "Oh . . . My . . . God . . . Fuck!" Kira screamed.

Her body clamped down around him as her legs and hips began to shake uncontrollably. She gripped his hair and arched her back screaming and wave after wave crashed through her. He didn't let up. Instead he alternated pressure from intense sucking on her clit to soft luxurious passes with his tongue, gently savoring every fold and teasing her overly sensitive clit. The combination kept Kira in a prolonged orgasm that wracked her body and sent intense pleasure into every fiber of her being.

Kira's heart was beating so fast, she felt like she was in another world. She could hear her own cries of ecstasy but they sounded far away. She clawed at Stark's head and back holding him tightly to her and yet wanting to push him away at the same time. Then when she thought it couldn't get any more intense, when her body threatened to give way, she felt the stretching of Stark's fingers entering her, bringing her to new heights. Finally, she crashed into a swirl of pulsing blasts and collapsed.

Stark looked up at her and smiled. "I'm not sure which was sweeter," he said, licking his lips.

Kira stammered and tried in vain to speak. She let her head fall back onto the pillow. He crawled up beside her and took her in his arms. Kira couldn't get over how warm and strong his body felt wrapping around her, holding her close. They lay together for a while, Kira in a happy post orgasmic coma, nearly forgetting Stark's earlier admission. The world seemed good and safe and whole.

***

He held her, twirling her hair rhythmically while she dozed in his arms. *How the hell could I have said that out loud?* he wondered. She obviously didn't feel the same. He didn't blame her. He knew that his life and his team would always be between them. He didn't blame her for not wanting to get attached. He knew that someday she would leave and he would have to let her go.

Chapter 19

The blasted phone was ringing again. It was on the third round of shrill repetition when Kira finally reached her limit. She scrambled out from under the covers. She crawled across the bed, cursing under her breath searching for his damn phone. *Ring! Ring!* The damn ringtone started again. *Who programs their phone with that damn 1950s rotary phone noise?!* "How can you not hear that?" Kira yelled toward the bathroom where she could hear him showering. As she finally reached his iPhone, the name blaring across the screen made her freeze. She almost dropped it as nausea swept her.

"Hello," she said coolly.

"Be a dear and tell Owen his fiancée is on the phone," Simone cooed in a silky voice as fake as her nails.

"Nice try, Simone," Kira said flatly. "I know who you are. Owen's not available right now." *Or ever.* "I'll tell him you called."

"Oh, darling, have we met? My Owen introduces me to so many people. Are you the new help?" Smugness dripped like syrup from each syllable. Suddenly Kira longed for the screeching of the phone. Nails on the chalkboard would have been better than another moment listening to Simone.

"No. We met in Aspen," Kira replied. She didn't even know why she was answering. She felt her blood pressure rising.

"Oh, the ski tramp! Forgive me for not recognizing your voice. I can't possibly keep up with all his little flings." Her voice was smooth but no longer warm. She sounded like the cold venomous bitch that she was.

Kira boiled on the inside but she did her best to sound calm. "Did you want to leave a message or were you just calling to be a bitch?"

"Oh, darling, don't be cross. Really, you're not even in his league. Better to wrap this up and save yourself the heartache later." The low icy tone of Simone's voice enraged Kira. She could feel her pulse pounding behind her left eye, threatening a major headache. Before Kira had a chance to think about what she was saying she was raising her voice at the snake.

"You don't know anything about me," Kira snapped back. In her anger the drawl of her West Virginian accent was strong.

"Aw, well, bless your little heart, darlin'," Simone teased, stretching each syllable. "I didn't mean to hurt your feelins none. Did you really think at the end of the day Owen would worry about some country fried soldier groupie?"

"I'm not some piece of trash, Simone. I'm a doctor, a captain in the Army for God's sake!" Kira was yelling before she realized it. Stark came running out of the bathroom to see what was wrong. Kira looked up at him in horror. All the color had drained out of her face. She dropped the phone onto the bed. *What the hell have I done?*

***

"Who is that?" Stark asked visibly alarmed. He ran over and picked up the phone. "Who the hell is this?"

A voice as smooth as silk and as deadly as poison greeted him. "Owen, sweetheart, I was just chatting with the captain…your …girlfriend…." She paused just long enough to let it sink in, "Seems you've done real well for a lowly enlisted man. I mean, a Captain! A doctor! Good work, darling. Practically the upper end of the service industry. Terribly scandalous though, I'm afraid. Don't you worry about a thing. I'll be on the next flight to help you sort all this out." She laughed loudly.

"Simone, I'm serious. You leave this alone. I'm warning you. Stay in California and stay the hell out of my life," Stark spoke, his voice dark. He knew what she was capable of. Simone was more than trouble. She was a time bomb filled with napalm.

"Oh and Owen," she said quickly before he could hang up, "While you've been off playing G. I. Joe with your little whore, you're father died. So when we get all this nonsense cleared up, we have business to take care of back here at home. I'll see you soon." And she hung up before he could say another word.

"Fuck." He couldn't believe her. What the hell was that conniving wench up to this time? Stark tried in vain to call his dad's cell. Nothing. His heart was starting to race. He started to leave a message. *What the hell would I even say?* He paced back and forth across the room trying to figure out what to do next. He looked over at Kira. She looked horrified. At this moment that was the least of his worries. He knew he should explain to her but he had to talk to his father. He tried his father's office, voice mail. *This is not good.* Finally he called the main house. He could feel the muscles in the back of his neck tighten. His father would never be there but maybe, just maybe, Rosalea would be. On the fourth ring her beautiful Spanish voice answered. Hearing her speak brought back the tenderness and joys of his childhood.

"*Hola*, Stark residence. May I help you?" Her thick accent was like a warm blanket comforting his soul. "*Hola*, May I help you?"

"*Hola*, Rosalea," Stark spoke softly.

341

"Oh mi dios en el cielo! Mi hermoso bebe!" She
began talking to him as if he were three years old again.

*"Por favor, dime que está bien. Simone llamó y . .
."* Stark's voice broke as he spoke.

"Oh, lo siento, Owen. *Su padre . . . murió . . . esta
mañana."* She was crying heavily as she spoke. The
confirmation felt like a sledgehammer blow squarely to his gut.
He relived the pain and loss of his mother and Maggie all over
again. The helplessness, the anger, the loss were too much to
bear.

"Rosalea . . . God . . . I'll be on the next flight, ok? I love
you." He shook his head and closed his eyes. He wanted to talk
to her, find out what happened. He wanted to turn back time and
have five more minutes with his father. In that moment he
wished a thousand things, but it was too late.

***

Kira watched Owen pacing, becoming increasingly
upset. *Man he is mad at me. Shit I have screwed everything
up.* She waited, not wanting to interrupt. Whatever Simone had
told him really had him upset. She watched him stare into space
and then dial the phone again. Out of the blue he began speaking
Spanish to someone. Although not intentionally eavesdropping,

342

the couple of years of Spanish she had in college allowed her to pick up a word her and there. When he hung up, he just stared at the wall for a moment as if he was trying to figure out what to do. Stark walked over and sat on the bed next to Kira. He stared straight ahead like an empty shell. After a deafening silence that seemed to go on forever, he finally spoke. "My dad is dead." Kira couldn't tell if he was informing her or trying to convince himself it was real.

"Oh God, Owen, I'm so sorry! Are you ok?" Kira wrapped her arms around him. Ten minutes ago the world was perfect. Now Stark's father was dead and she had just given that venomous snake all the ammo she needed to rip them apart. "Had he been sick? How did he die?"

"I don't know. I should know, but I don't," Stark said. He bent forward and put his head in his hands. "I feel numb. I mean, I know I should feel immense sadness but I don't feel anything. All the years of fighting with him are shit." He put his head back in his hands. Kira held him and rocked gently. She smoothed his dark hair trying to soothe the emptiness.

"I should have gone to see him sooner. So many things I should have said. Now it's too late. I'll never have the chance." He stood abruptly. "I have to go to California. I'm sorry, but we'll have to get you back to base. I've got to catch a flight home." He was up and packing with purpose. He didn't seem to even notice using the word home.

343

But Kira noticed. *Home*. She sat numbly realizing what that meant. He was flying home to *her*. She pictured Simone's smug smile and wanted to vomit. Kira knew there was so much more to Stark and Simone than she would ever understand. Hell, maybe she didn't want to know. Desperately wanting to support him but at a loss for words, she was in a fog as she packed her bag and helped load their gear to leave. Stark was unbelievably quiet. Was he mad or just grieving? Kira didn't know. She didn't want to upset him any further by asking.

From a distance Kira watched Stark as he spoke quietly to the owner of the hotel when they checked out. She saw the pity and sadness in the older woman's wrinkled face. She knew those looks all too well. Kira remembered the faces of the other base families as they spoke softly and helped her mother pack their things. She remembered the pain and nauseating pity. Panic and nausea hit her hard. Watching Stark, she wanted desperately to be there for him, but a part of her wanted to run away. She had spent a lifetime fleeing and avoiding that very look. She fought to be independent and self-sustaining. She never wanted to be vulnerable, to feel that ever again. Yet here she was, becoming desperately entwined with a man every bit as dangerous as her father. How could she be so foolish? Thoughts of his declaration in the bathroom, the knowledge that he would, without a doubt, leave her one day, and the pity of the old woman's face swirled around in her mind. It made her dizzy.

The Jeep ride home was spent in a quiet fog. Kira retreated further and further into her self-made prison, desperately trying to replace as many bricks in the wall Stark had torn down. She knew this had been a crazy idea from the start. He was leaving, going to California and Simone. He didn't even ask her to come with him, to be there for him. She realized that they had just been fooling themselves. He couldn't have meant that he really loved her. Even if he did for a brief moment, it wouldn't matter when they would inevitably have to go their separate ways.

***

Stark drove like a man on a mission. He cursed himself for not going home months ago when Simone had first asked. He had spent so many years being angry and resentful of his father and Simone that he let them down when he was needed most. He stole glances over at Kira on the way home. She looked lost and crushed. He knew this must be bringing back terrible memories for her. He felt sorry for her, and then aggravated. He felt for her, but his dad had just died. Right now he needed her to be there for him, not retreat into some hole. He turned his eyes back to the road. They could sort it all out when he got back. Right now he had to get to California. All he could focus on was taking care of things he should have faced a long time ago. His heart ached for his father, mother, and sister. He realized he was alone in the world.

***

When they first arrived back at Stark's house, he hastily packed while making flight arrangements and contacting his CO to let him know what had happened. She watched him moving around the house with military precision, executing each task. She wanted to help him pack, but she realized she didn't know where everything was. She decided it was easier on him if she just stayed out of the way. Paige would be better suited for this. She half wondered where Paige was. Surely he would call her. They shared so much of their lives. Kira suddenly felt like an outsider in this very personal time.

The truth was, she didn't want him to go. The idea of him going home to Simone made her sick to her very core. He was going to California to bury his father and deal with a life he had almost completely walked away from a decade ago. How would it be to step back into that world? Would he decide he liked it better? Would he fall back in love with Simone? Hell, they had been engaged. He had really loved her once. Not for a fleeting moment in a shower, but really loved her. What if he . . . She knew there was no way she could go with him. How do you explain to your CO that your boyfriend, an enlisted guy, had a death in the family so you need to drop your duties for a few days and go off to California? She was sure Simone would be there waiting for him with open arms.

Kira thought of her own father. How many times she had wished she had the chance to say good-bye. Her chest hurt. She thought of the pained look in Stark's tear-filled eyes and realized that regardless of your age, size, occupation or gender, when your parent dies, you are still their child. The immediate loss is followed by sharp memories of childhood. How they held you, played with you, how they knew you like no one in your life ever has or ever will.

"I took him for granted." Stark said quietly. "In a way I blamed him for Mom and Maggie. I blamed myself. But there was nothing either of us could have done. I was angry with him for such a long time. Now I don't even know what to feel."

Kira reached up and hugged him. She held him tightly before he had to leave. She struggled for words. "I'm so sorry Owen." She could feel the emptiness between them. He needed something she just couldn't give. He closed his eyes and wrapped her up in his arms. He held on for a moment as if holding on to a lifeline. Then without saying another word he set her down and let her go.

Kira watched him turn and head down the walk. Bags in hand, he made his way to the truck. Kira felt the hot tears burning her face before she realized she was crying. A lifetime of loss and fear came flooding back to her. Now alone, the tears streamed completely unrestrained as she watched Stark's truck disappear in the distance.

She walked slowly back into the house. Coming through the foyer, she saw it out of the corner of her eye. There, over the edge of the couch in the great room was the corner of his woobie. She smiled and felt warm all over remembering her dad telling her about how the ranger woobie served as a sleeping pack, pillow, or blanket. When in combat it was your one comfort. Kira walked over to it and wrapped up in the soft camo poncho liner. Immediately the smell of Stark was all around her. She knew he had carried this with him to hell and back. It had served as his bedroll, his warmth in bitter cold, one soft touch of home in times of desperation. Kira closed her eyes and snuggled in its embrace. Her thoughts drifted back through time over years of heartache she had blocked out for so long. She could see her mother now rocking silently in the chair by the window at their aunt's home in West Virginia. Those were long, cold days watching silent flakes fall outside. Her mother was always wrapped up in her dad's woobie. It had been in his effects when the service men brought them. Small dots of his blood had stained the fabric in a tattered corner. Her mother swore for years that it still smelled like him. Kira pulled Stark's woobie tightly around her and breathed him in.

That first winter in Davis had been a long, hard one. Her mother barely spoke, barely ate. Kira remembered feeling so helpless and scared. Her great aunt Melissa had given them a place to stay and helped care for her and her brothers. Kira knew without Melissa's love and hospitality she and her brothers wouldn't have made it. She thought of how when they were younger they would laugh at all the stray animals and children Aunt Melissa took in. Kira remembered helping her aunt set the table one cold winter evening, the smell of hot potato soup filling the house. Kira looked at her mother lost in her grief, wrapped up in the seat by the window, and her brothers playing on the floor by the wood stove. She realized then that they were the strays. With one parent dead, blown to pieces and forgotten by the army, and the other reduced to a shell, they were practically orphans. Strays. The weight of their situation, their homelessness crushed the breath out of her.

Her mother fell asleep and Kira saw the camo blanket slip from her fingers onto the floor and the soot from the wood stove. Kira ran over and picked it up and accidentally grabbed a small ember with it. The pain was sharp. But she didn't let it go. Instead, Kira held on tightly and ran for the door. In her aunt's large galoshes Kira ran outside into the deep snow. The world was white and quiet. She couldn't explain her need for hope and security that would not come. As she tried to trudge in the deep drifts, billows of powdery snow spilled over the tops of her boots with each step. She ignored their sting and fought on into the white wilderness. Her heart was exploding with pain and anger. It wasn't fair! She reached a clearing just beyond sight of the house. Kira remembered spinning around holding the last remnant of her father close to her and screaming into the silence.

She felt her aunt's warm arms wrap around her. "You're a strong girl, Kira," her Aunt Melissa said. Her voice had a roughness to it of someone who had made it in these mountains. She wasn't afraid of anything. Not that she showed, anyway. Her weathered hands had survived many storms in life and she always kept going. "You have to be strong for you mama and your brothers. That's your fate, baby girl. You can cry about it, try to hide from it like your mama is, or you can love it."

Kira looked up, tears still brimming in her eyes. "Love it?" she asked confused at how you could possibly love this.

The older woman's face wrinkled with lines of smiles through the years. "Life is always going to bring you hurdles, challenges that seem impassable. You can cower before them or you can love it and use that to fight onward. Love your fate baby girl and never be afraid."

She considered how Melissa offered comfort and love, found a way to provide for all these extra mouths on such a meager budget without a complaint, and knew this is what it meant to soldier on. Young Kira and her aunt had walked back to the house together. Kira wrapped the blanket around her shoulders. Once inside, she took it off and laid it over her mother. She knew that she would stand like her father did. She would find a way to protect and care for her mom and brothers and no matter what happened in her life, she would never give up. She would love her fate.

Mags jumped up on the couch beside her. Holding the blanket with one hand, Kira reached out with the other and rubbed Mags soft, speckled fur. She had a way of making the world ok again. "You would like my Aunt Melissa," Kira told Mags as she scratched her ears. "You would have liked my parents, too." Kira thought of her brothers. She hadn't spoken to either one for a little while. They had grown into such hard working young men. She reached for her phone and tried to call Jacob. No answer. He was probably at work. It would be nice to hear his voice today. She knew it was no use calling Nicholas. He would be far out of cell reach. As a sophomore in college, he was off on a research project. She didn't know much about it other that it had to do with fish. Kira thought of their parents and wondered if they would be proud. Suddenly Kira's mind drifted to a box her aunt had sent last year just after her mother had passed. Kira knew from her aunt's letter that it contained her mother's few things. Although at the time it had been too painful to open, she needed it now. Her aunt felt her mother's death was a result of all the drugs the doctors had her on for depression. Kira knew she had died inside a long time ago. She had to find that box. Kira jumped up and grabbed her keys. She got Maggie and raced for the Jeep. She was fairly certain that she brought it when she moved to base and that it would be in one of the closets at the apartment. She couldn't explain her overwhelming need to get it now.

Upon arriving at her apartment, Kira started tearing through every neatly stored box in her apartment. It just had to be here. After demolishing the three closets in her meager apartment she sat on the couch defeated. She was sure she had brought it with her. She racked her brain trying to remember whether it was in the things she shipped back to West Virginia between medical school and the Army. No, those things had been carefully packed and shipped and she had gotten rid of everything else she didn't need. Surely she hadn't accidently thrown it out. Kira's heart sunk. Then it dawned on her. The totes under her bed. She knew instantly it was in there. Kira ran to her bedroom and pulled the long, low tote out from under her bed. There it was, still wrapped in brown parchment. It was about the size of a boot box, addressed to her from Melissa Mathews, PO Box 23 Davis, WV 26260. Kira traced her fingers over the faded ink. She paused and took a deep breath before tearing it open. She couldn't help but laugh when she saw it was a boot box. Size 9 women's Justin work boots. Kira knew those were her aunt's. She untied the twine and carefully lifted the lid. Inside lay a lifetime of memories. She hesitated, unsure she was ready for this. *Love it. Love your fate. This is who you are. It's where you came from.* With trembling fingers, Kira began to remove and examine each item.

Everything was neatly packaged in Ziplocs and tied with ribbon. Kira removed the first packet and opened it. It was an envelope of pictures. Kira poured through photos of her mother and father as they were dating. She picked one up of her mother, so beautiful, young and carefree. Her eyes were bright and hopeful. Kira hadn't seen her like that for years. The grainy photographs were about thirty years old. Kira saw her father, so dashing in his battle dress uniform. He was the strongest and most beautiful man she had ever known. His dark hair was cut short and his eyes still held an innocence about them. This photo must be from before he had ever been deployed. Kira had never seen him so boyish. The man she'd known, while always kind and loving with her, had a hardness about him. His face was furrowed with deep lines from having been places and experiencing things he would never be able to talk about at home. The firm set jaw she remembered was smiling freely in the photo, undoubtedly saying something hilarious to her mother who was laughing and looking up at him with starstruck eyes. Kira watched their romance unfold through a series of aging photographs. It was a side of her parents she had never known. She could see so much of Stark and herself in this young couple. She wondered if they had any inkling of what they were in for. If they knew how things would end, would they still have embraced the path they were on? Her eyes brimmed with tears once more. The poor wide-eyed couple so very much in love had no clue what lay ahead. Kira wiped away stray tears as she put the photos back in the package. She wasn't sure she could stand to look at them anymore today.

The next packet contained a stack of bound letters. She untied them and examined the envelopes. They were letters from her parents to each other over the years. The worn envelopes displayed addresses of various posts from around the world. She tenderly opened a letter. The handwriting she immediately recognized as her mothers.

My Dearest Kendall,

I can still feel the warmth of your hand on my face. How I miss you so already. I know we have only known each other a few short weeks but I already feel I have known you for a lifetime. The moonlit walk we took on our last night together plays over and over in my mind and heart. When you took me in your arms and . . .

Kira abruptly put the letter down. She decided maybe she wasn't ready for all the intimate details of her parent's love life. She started putting the letters back when a tattered fragment of a damaged letter slipped from the pack. The paper was worn thin from years of being fondled by her grief stricken mother. Kira knew the fragile pages by heart. It was the letter her father had written from his last deployment just in case. His best friend Sergeant Bradley had delivered it after her father's death. Her mother had read it over and over. Though Kira hadn't looked at it in years, just seeing the envelope brought back every line.

Dear Ellen, Kira, Jacob and Nicholas,

I want to start by saying I am sorry. If you are reading this then I have failed to be fast enough, strong enough, lucky enough to return to you as I promised. I love you all dearly. This letter is so hard to write but there are things I need to say. Things I need you to know if I never have another chance to tell you. Ellen, I have loved you from the first moment that I saw you standing by the stadium steps with your friends. You were a vision. I knew from that moment that someday you would be my wife. You have given me more joy than one man could ever hope for or deserve. I am deeply sorry that I will not be there to do the same for you. You have given me a beautiful daughter and two wonderful little sons. I pray that you will find the strength to raise them up into men. Ellen, you are the light in the darkness. You are my best friend, my love, my life. I know that I cannot be forgiven for leaving you alone. You are always on my mind and heart. I don't know by what power in heaven you were brought to me but I am forever thankful. Know that if I do not return, when my last breath escapes my lips it will whisper your name.

My little Kira, my brave little spitfire, I trust you to always be strong and kind. Help your mother, help others. Serve God and your country as I have taught you. I rest knowing that you, my angel, are destined for great things. I cherish the touch of your little hand. My sweet child, grow into the woman I know that you can be. You make me proud every day. In my eyes no man will ever be good enough for you. You deserve more.

My sweet boys, you are so small. Your bright faces will grow into men of honor. There is so much I want to say to you, I am at a loss for words. I wanted to teach you to throw a ball, drive a car. I wanted to be the one to tell you about life and the world. I wanted to teach you how to treat a woman with love and respect. I wanted to watch you grow. Please listen to your mom and know that you can be anything, do anything you dedicate yourself to. I remember holding you, rocking you, and walking the floor with you while home from my last deployment. I dreamed I held you the other night. I was singing to calm you. I woke up to the sound of gunfire overhead and my arms were empty. Know that I have loved you from the first minute that I knew you existed. I loved you while you grew inside your mother. I will love you every day that I breathe and for everyday that you go on after.

My family, I will be with you all in mind and spirit. Your memories and the lives you build will keep me alive in you. I love you. I treasure you.

Love Always,
Kendall

Kira's hands were shaking. Her chest shuddered with deep broken breaths as she laid the letter down. Mags whimpered and tried to nuzzle in close. She laid her head in Kira's lap and knocked over the box. Kira started to scold her but stopped short. In the pile of priceless memories lay a gallon-sized Ziploc containing the stained and threadbare remnants of her father's woobie. Gingerly Kira opened the bag and took out the scrap of fabric, now so worn it was only about two foot square when unfolded. Kira held her breath as she gently traced her fingers over stains that told the story of her life. Reflexively she held it to her face, and though the scent of her parents had long since faded, the love was there.

Chapter 20

"Paige I really don't feel like going out tonight," Kira insisted. She knew her pleading was futile but she really didn't want to go anywhere. Paige and Zoe had shown up dressed to the nines ready to take her to some club.

"You have done nothing but go to work and hang out here like a spinster since Stark left. Besides, you owe us, Vanilla, remember? We took care of your boy Holt and his hot little friend Cody so you could escape with Stark. Time to pay up. You are going out with us." Paige's sculpted eyebrows and bright red lips were set in a determined scowl.

Kira rolled her eyes as Paige pushed past her into Stark's house and started up the stairs toward his bedroom. "What the hell?" she called out after her. "Owen didn't leave me. He is in California taking care of his father's estate. Stop this instant! Where are you going?"

Paige called down to soothe her. "Oh, we're not taking you out like that. I'm going to see what you have in that plain vanilla closet of yours. There has to be something we can put you in." Paige's voice trailed off as she ascended the stairs. She was in full dominatrix mode. She trudged up the stairs with Zoe following behind carrying two suitcases.

"What are those? You two are NOT moving in here!"
Kira didn't even try to hide the distain as her voice raised two
octaves. "I'm serious you two!"

Paige stopped at the top of the stairs and laughed out
loud. "These are for you," she countered. "Zoe has bet me we
won't find anything suitable for you up here so we brought
backup." With that, the two women disappeared from view in the
direction of Stark's room.

"You can't be serious. I'm not dressing up like some
1950s pole dancer. You can forget it," Kira continued. She
followed them up the stairs to make sure they didn't tear
anything up. She had been dying to know what happened with
Holt. He had barely spoken two words to her since she had
ditched him at dinner and left him in the hands of these two. "So
what exactly did happen with Holt and Cody?" She followed
them down the long hall to Stark's room.

Once inside, Zoe started dumping the suitcases, spilling
small pieces of sordid fabric that were possibly meant to be
clothes and piles of makeup all over Stark's immaculate king
size bed. Kira cringed as she watched Paige slip into her closet.
As uptight as Stark was about his things, Kira wondered how he
and Paige had ever lived together.

"Where are all your clothes? I thought you were moving
in?" Paige turned sharply looking a Kira.

"I don't officially live here, Paige. I have my own apartment. I just stay here some." Kira didn't want to admit that was most of her wardrobe: scrubs, BDUs, workout clothes, and a few civilian outfits.

"This is pathetic. You really don't have a life do you?" Paige said, then turned back to Zoe. "Ok you win. Nothing good in here."

"Yes!" Zoe was as chipper as a kid at Christmas. She started picking up tiny scraps of purple, red, and black fabric. She cocked her head as she held them up, eyeing Kira, looking for just the right ensemble. "It's like playing dress up with our very own Vanilla Barbie!" She squealed, choosing bits of material.

"Listen, I don't know what kind of crack you are smoking, but I'm not putting that on. It looks like a recipe for hepatitis!" Kira started to back away. They had finally lost it. She couldn't imagine that Owen was any more cool with this than she was. She hadn't heard from him in days. Upon arriving in California, he had called to let her know he was safe and would be there for a while taking care of things. He had sounded terrible but strong, too, in a way. There were so many things she had wanted to say, but the timing just wasn't right. Kira stifled the twinge of jealousy that she felt every time she thought about Simone being there, sharing this very personal time with him. She shuddered, thinking of the snake comforting Owen. She snapped back to reality in time to see Zoe coming at her with a hideously small excuse for an outfit.

"It's perfect!" Zoe practically purred. "Now if we can just get it on you. Tell you what, be a good girl and let us dress you up. Paige will tell you all about Cody and your boy Holt."

Damn! The curiosity was killing her. While she had no desire to go out in any kind of public space dressed like a hooker, she really wanted to know what happened. Based on Holt's evasive behavior it had to be good. "I'm a doctor, for crying out loud. I can't get all dressed up like a street walker and go out."

"Trust me, you won't know anyone where we're going," Zoe said. She and Paige exchanged looks, smiling slyly.

Against all better judgment Kira took the tiny outfit in one hand and looked it over. "This is clean, right? You have washed and sanitized it?" Kira wrinkled her nose as she looked up at Paige.

Paige just laughed. "Try to keep the doctor paranoia under wraps tonight, Vanilla. You need to let your hair down a little. Trust me, you're going to like this place as much as Holt did." Paige touched a panel in the wall exposing a mini bar that Kira never knew existed.

"Damn!" Kira said partially under her breath. Paige knew so much more about this house and Stark than perhaps she would ever know.

Paige smiled like a Cheshire cat. She took down a bottle of Jameson and confidently poured three glasses. "Here, Vanilla, this should take the edge off."

The combination of curiosity, jealousy, and frustration overtook Kira and she took the glass. She thought of Stark in California with Simone, the crazy relationship he had with Paige and Zoe and God knows who else. The intense liquid was smooth and warming. Kira felt it slide down, thawing her defenses. She finished the glass and held it up to Paige for another. Then Kira took the sultry excuse for an outfit defiantly and went to put it on. She caught the satisfied smile of Paige and Zoe's faces out of the corner of her eye. She decided she didn't care what anyone thought. Tonight she would have a good time.

While they fixed her hair and painted her up into a smoky-eyed temptress, Kira sipped Jameson and listened to Zoe and Paige take turns telling her how they had distracted and entertained Holt and Cody. Though Holt had been upset when she had left the restaurant that night, Paige had convinced him to stay put with a carefully placed hand on his thigh. Throughout dinner, Zoe and Paige had ensnared their evening toys. Finally Paige, sitting with her leg crossed slightly over Holt's, leaned in and whispered quietly, her soft lips brushing his cheek as she spoke. "Liam darling, I want you to take me someplace we can get to know each other better."

Zoe laughed and recalled how Holt's face had flushed when Paige stroked her black painted nail down his chest as she spoke. The four of them had piled into Paige's car and off they went with Zoe and Cody cuddled up in the back, wasting no time exploring each other. Holt was very serious and a bit more reserved, Paige remembered. She could tell that he was a control freak, her favorite kind to break. They took the boys to The Apex Club and started them off with dancing and shots. Paige described in graphic detail how she had danced seductively with Zoe, peaking the boys' interest and lowering their inhibitions.

"Where is that? I have never even heard of it. Then what happened?" Kira piped up. "What did you two do to them?" Kira looked past the two giggling harlots into the mirror. She barely recognized the Moulin rouge dancer starring back at her. "Oh, hell."

"Don't worry. You'll find out soon enough," Zoe said, smiling from ear to ear.

Before she could protest further, Paige and Zoe piled her into the Bel Air and they set off for The Apex Club.

"Don't forget the spare key," Zoe prodded."

"For what?" came Paige's coy reply.

"You know exactly what. I've been stranded there before. Just slip it behind the visor in case you get too tied up to go home." Zoe twirled a strand of Paige's hair as she spoke.

"Ok, but we both know you're not leaving without me." Paige winked at Zoe as she slid the key behind the visor and sped on down the road.

As they wound through the Colorado hills, Kira felt her nerves getting the better of her. *This is insane!* Before Kira could breathe another word of protest she heard the tires of the Bel Air pull off the main road and onto gravel. They started winding up a tight dirt and gravel road. *This is a crazy place for a club.* With no streetlights or markers to guide the way, they were surrounded by darkness. In a moment they came to a clearing. Rising out of the blackness illuminated by the moon was a mansion as old as the hills. Kira shuddered and looked at the tremendous beauty and eerie splendor before her. The car pulled to a stop and an enormous valet with a face as dark as the night took the keys and smiled at Paige.

"Good evening, Paige." The large man's voice boomed as he took Paige's delicate hand and helped her out of the car. Kira noticed him looking her up and down, an appreciative smile on his face. Zoe and Kira climbed out the other side.

"Thank you, James," Paige said. She warmly took Kira and Zoe on each arm and began walking up the massive stone staircase to the entrance.

Kira heard James let out a low whistle behind them as they walked away.

"You girls go get some drinks and find a table. I'll see you in a little bit," Paige said as soon as they walked into the grand marble entry. She kissed Zoe and then disappeared up a set of red-carpeted stairs as if she owned the place.

"Come on, Kira, let's get our drinks. We don't want to miss anything," Zoe urged. Kira had never seen Zoe so excited. Zoe led her into a sort of ballroom with a bar at the entrance that had several small tables rounded out with a dance floor and a stage at the other end. Kira tugged at the much-too-short black satin skirt, attempting to pull it just a little farther over the fishnet stockings. Her efforts were completely in vain, however, since the silver and black corset was severely limiting her movements. Zoe grabbed a couple of glasses of whiskey from the bar and directed her over to an empty table. "Wait there. I'll have the bartender mix us up something yummy!" Zoe disappeared in the growing crowd. Kira looked around the posh room and couldn't shake the feeling that something was off.

Just then, the lights dimmed and Paige took the stage. Kira watched her stride up to the mic commanding each step.

Kira found herself in awe of Paige's confidence. She really could do anything. Paige's jet-black hair glistened under the lights. Streaks of teal and purple placed earlier that day danced through her tresses, transforming her usual rockabilly style into a vaudevillian cavalcade. Her pale, inked body fit exquisitely in the black corset and kerchief skirt. Kira wasn't sure whether to be jealous or just plain impressed. How Stark was interested in her with Paige in his life she would never know. Looking down at her own thin frame she clearly lacked the curves and confidence that Paige so proudly displayed.

Kira was still wondering why Paige had brought her here in the first place when the lights lowered and the music began. A lone spot light illuminated Paige and the eclectic sounds of a violin, horns, and a wicked guitar filled the room. Kira wasn't sure she had ever heard music like this before. She took a long sip of the Jameson and let it absorb her. The energy in the room was transformed into another place in time, New Orleans maybe? The rich sounds made her want to move. Suddenly a low, sultry voice erupted into melancholy lyrics and the room began to sway in Paige's trance.

I digress in my self-loathing, collapse in my despair.

Sinking further from the light, buried in my complacent existence.

Do I let these hands choke around me or fight for a last breath of fresh air.

I wasted the days of my youth following the plan.

The perfect life, but the heart of a gypsy.

Always longing to be free.

Secret dreams to explore, the ever-lurking urge to roam.

Kira couldn't believe what she was hearing. It was like Paige was describing her. How could she know exactly how she felt? Paige was so open and free and in control. She never seemed to worry what anyone else thought. Kira found herself being pulled into the song along with the crowd.

As I sink into the ground I hear your winsome voice calling from the darkness.

A spark awakens.

I am entranced by the lure of your magic, the lust of your lies.

I know the danger that waits ahead, yet I am drawn in.

I feel the rhythm of your music sway me.

The illusion fanciful, smoke and mirrors, but through the haze I see your eyes.

Knowing better, I linger holding a last strand of light knowing

The darkness before me will swallow me whole.

You are mysterious and dangerous, everything and nothing.

You fill the room and suck out the air.

The asphyxiation of your presence makes me dizzy.

I want to cling to the strand and find I have let it go.

Captivated and inspired, I never felt it leave my fingers.

I am floating, swirling, alone but encompassed by you.

Flinging forward as if limits do not exist.

Inhibition now merely a word as foreign as my new surroundings.

Kira sat upright, startled when Zoe joined her at the table. Her long red hair bounced and swayed as she sat.

Carefully Zoe brushed the crimson locks aside. A group of well-dressed men with their carefully tailored suits and starched shirts strained to watch her sit. Kira stifled a giggle and rolled her eyes noting just how much Zoe resembled Jessica Rabbit.

"She's really lovely, isn't she . . ." Zoe's usually chipper voice was soft and smooth like melting butter. Her eyes twinkled with adoration as she watched Paige move with the music. "She's like a goddess up there!"

"I never knew she could sing. This is pretty incredible." Kira scanned the room noting the captivation of the audience. All eyes were on Paige. The sea of bodies flowing gently with each word reminded Kira of seaweed drifting with the current.

"She puts on quite a show when she wants to. It always leads to a lot of fun later," Zoe said, then turned and gave one of the expecting businessmen a wink, much to his delight. She turned back to Kira and said, "You haven't seen the best part yet." Zoe's smile spread across her face as she spoke. Her eyes danced wildly with anticipation.

I hear you calling to me . . .

At once a smooth dulcet male voice joined her and captured the room. He seemed to be calling out to Paige drawing her in. Kira felt herself being entranced as well.

In our past lives we were pirates and wanderers,

Lovers of the sea

Bound by no man,

Destined to be free.

Walk with me for a little while . . . let all your cares go by

Walk with me for a little while.

He moved slowly around the stage with hypnotic movements. Their voices blended beautifully. He was a captivating match for Paige, with his dark hair swept over in classic Cary Grant style. His dark shirt, black vest and pants were well-fitted over his thin, muscular frame. He could have stepped out of the 1920s and directly onto the stage. His haunting voice and movements flowed gracefully in an erotic duel back and forth with Paige until his hand met hers. He held her there, one hand touching hers, the other trailing slowly from her cheek down her neck and over her ample breasts. He took her around the waist and pulled her to him tightly. They stopped for just a moment and the lights faded.

The audience drew in a collective breath. Kira felt herself on the edge of her seat with anticipation. That couldn't be it. She turned to Zoe, whose Cheshire smile was about to take over her face.

When the lights came back up, the entire band was now visible and the tempo picked up encouraging the moderately intoxicated audience to leave their seats and dance. Kira swallowed down the sweet pink liquid that Zoe had brought her. "Mmmmm. What is this?" she asked slightly skeptical.

"Don't worry about what it is. Just finish it and let's dance!" Zoe grabbed her hand and pulled her onto the dance floor. The eclectic sounds of the gypsy funk band had something magical about it that Kira couldn't explain or understand. But at that moment she didn't care. She let herself go completely to the beat and danced. As she swayed and moved she could feel Zoe's hands on her. The violin picked up tempo into a heated mix. The band followed suit, pulling the patrons with it. Kira couldn't get over the lead singer's voice. It was so captivating. He sounded English but she wasn't sure. The horns, violin, and guitar swirled around her. Kira danced until the room seemed to spin. The dizzying trance took over her mind and body. In a moment of clarity, she looked around the room and realized she was not alone. The crowd was moving at a fevered pace in perfect time with the music. She felt herself being passed around from partner to partner. The room was whirling delightfully. Suddenly, she realized she was in the arms of the singer himself. Her breath caught still in her chest as the music played on. He twirled and spun her around the room. Kira couldn't explain the magic of his touch. She opened her mouth to speak but he twirled her away into the hands of Zoe and Paige as he once again took the stage.

"Who is that?" Kira asked, trying to catch her breath.

"My darling, that's Lysander. Trust me that's no place you want to go," Paige said smiling. Her eyes were shining like Kira had never seen before. She had never seen Paige like this. Not even Owen Stark made Paige look like that.

Zoe leaned over to Paige and pulled her lips to her own. Kira stood watching their soft sensual kiss. She knew she should look away but she was unable to move. Zoe's hands slid over Paige's curves, claiming them for her own. They moved together with the music as if no one else was in the room. But the room was filled with people dancing and finding partners of their own. Everyone was pairing off in groups of two or three. *What the hell kind of club is this?* Kira's foggy intoxicated brain barely registered a warning as she felt a set of masculine hands wrap around her small waist. He spun her and she was staring at an unfamiliar face. He pulled her close and leaned in toward her. Kira attempted to step back but was unsteady on her feet. "Hey, baby," he said his breath heavy and whiskey-laden. "I think this is what you're looking for." He took her small hand and moved it down, pressing it firmly onto his rigid cock. Kira gasped and stumbled back slightly. She felt small but firm hands on her shoulder.

"Back it up, asshole! She's with us," Paige said loudly and authoritatively. But he would not be discouraged so easily. He tightened his grip on Kira's waist and pulled her closer. Kira struggled absent-mindedly but Zoe and Paige were already moving in. Zoe stepped quickly between Kira and the intoxicated man and Paige pulled Kira away and close to her. Kira could feel Paige's hips behind her moving with her own, dancing her away from the drunken man on the floor. They spun and danced over to the edge of the room. Kira could feel herself surrounded by Zoe and Paige. She couldn't escape the erotic tension of being pressed between these two women.

The music of the band faded and house music started to play. The loud electric thumping was erotic but in sharp contrast to the band. Lysander appeared and stood watching them appreciatively. Kira stopped moving and stared back at him. She felt suddenly intimidated by his gaze.

Lysander reached out and took her hand. "My name is Lysander. But you can call me Ly. It's a pleasure to meet you." He gently pulled her hand up to his lips and kissed it. "Its very . . . *very* nice to meet you." The words slid effortlessly off his lips and caressed her in places she dared not admit.

Kira breathed out slowly and struggled to remember her name.

"Lysander this is Kira," Paige cut in and broke the spell. "Before you get too excited Ly, she's off limits."

Lysander stepped back slightly and looked down at Paige with an amused smile. "My dear, here nothing is off limits. I can take you places you didn't even know you wanted to go."

"This is Owen Stark's girlfriend," Paige said curtly. His smiled faded. He took another step backward.

Before he could say anything, an obviously intoxicated and very scantily clad woman stumbled over and draped an arm around Lysander. "Did you say Owen Stark? Is he here?" she slurred. Despite her inebriated state her eyes were bright with lust and excitement. "Where is that hunk of a man? Mmmm, I can't wait to sink my teeth into him again!" She licked her deep red lips as she spoke.

"Cool it, Lila." Paige rolled her eyes. "He's not here."

"I could have sworn I heard his name," Lila said.

"They were introducing me. I'm his girlfriend," Kira said, feeling her blood pressure rising.

"You, me, and everyone else, honey," Lila said, smiling smugly. She looked Kira up and down as she continued. "Baby girl there's not a woman in here that he hasn't nailed to the wall. That man can curl your hair and your toes and leave you unable to walk in the morning. But then, you know that, don't you?"

"Shut the fuck up, Lila," Paige said, stepping between Lila and Kira, pushing her back. "Why don't you go upstairs?

There's enough cock here to go around. Even for your gaping hole."

"Oh, don't take it so hard. You didn't really think you were the only one, did you? Come on, baby, come play with the big girls," Lila purred, and brushed a strand of hair out of Kira's face.

"Enough, Lila. Go upstairs," Lysander put in, his voice calm but firm. Kira recognized the tone. He spoke to her the way Stark had to Paige in the video. Kira shuddered. Lila immediately stopped. She winked at Kira, then turned and went in the direction of the stairs.

Kira's head was spinning. What was Lila talking about? Had she dated Stark? She looked from Paige to Lysander for an explanation.

"You brought her here, Paige. What did you expect?" Lysander was still talking but Kira could no longer hear him. Her heart was racing. She pushed past Paige and headed for the stairs. It couldn't be. Despite the alcohol and spiky heels she took the stairs two at a time. She had to see what Lila was talking about and there was no way Paige was going to stop her. Once on the landing, she crossed quickly to the first set of heavy wooden doors and opened them. The smell of sex hit her like a brick wall, thick and heavy before the moans even reached her ears. The dimly lit room was filled with nefarious groups of people all engaged in some stage of sexual act. The walls were a deep shade of red that reminded Kira of Lila's lipstick. The black marble floor had thick ornate rugs strategically placed with black leather furniture. Plush chaises, lounges, chairs and ottomans dotted the room, all covered with scantily clad or naked bodies. Kira struggled to grasp what she was seeing. She had stepped into a full-on orgy and no one seemed to think this was abnormal but her.

Kira felt like Alice in Fuckland. Despite her horror, she couldn't help but feel a familiar stirring beneath her fishnets. A loud moan immediately to her right caught her attention. A very muscular man was sitting in a large leather armchair. The woman on the ottoman in front of him, naked except for her stilettos, was lying on her back. Her long black hair pooled on the floor. Her well-shaped legs spread wide before him. The woman moaned again loudly as he worked her clitoris with his mouth and buried his massive fingers in her dripping slit. Kira felt her own breathing in time with the bare woman's heaving chest. She made eye contact with Kira and smiled before throwing her head back and coming hard. Kira felt a sweat break out on her brow. The woman was completely exposed and unashamed as she squirmed, her small breasts bouncing with each movement. The man kneeled forward. Kira watched breathlessly as his lips closed around her delicate nipple. She felt her own breast burn with the need to be touched. The man moved between her outstretched legs and positioned his thick

377

cock at the edge of her folds. He looked up noticing Kira watching. Her eyes met his and she bit her lip. His gaze dipped to the swell of flesh atop Kira's corset. He smiled and licked his lips as he entered the small woman. Kira felt her breath catch as the woman writhed and screamed, enjoying the sudden intrusion. She couldn't look away. The only sound louder than the moans in the room was the pounding in her ears. Kira couldn't tell if it was the intense bass of the music or her own heartbeat. The pulsing could be felt through the floor as if the room was alive. A loud crack from the other side of the room startled Kira and she looked up.

A stunning blond woman in a black latex corset that fully exposed her oversized breasts stood straddling a smaller brunette woman in a short lace dress. With one hand she held the back of the woman's head firmly. Her thigh-high Latex stiletto boot was planted on a man's chest who lay back on the chaise fully enjoying the blow job the brunette was being forcefully encouraged to give him. He moaned stridently as the woman's head moved up and down in a transfixing rhythm. In the other hand the blond woman held a small crop which she used at will on the brunette, striking her ass and turning it a bright pink. Kira gasped as the crop struck the woman loudly. She was appalled and aroused and frightened. She could feel her lace panties growing wet beneath her own fishnets. The man reached up suddenly, grasping the brunette with both hands as his body went rigid. He convulsed as he came, still embedded deeply in her mouth and throat. The blond woman jerked up on the other woman's hair exposing thick strands of cum dripping from his glistening cock and her ruby red lips.

Delicate fingers clasped around her arms. Kira looked down at jet-black fingernails and olive skin pressing into her flesh. "So you came up to play, baby." Lila's delighted voice echoed in her ears with the throbbing pulse of the house. Lila marched her forward. They stepped over the back of a redhead buried deep between the legs of a masked girl. Kira's eyes grew big as saucers as the onyx lips grinned at her from the cutout in the latex mask. Her heel grazed the woman's back as she crossed over her. Its vibration traveled straight up her leg and set her on fire. A beautifully tattooed hand reached up and caressed her leg, fingers trailing with the movement of her step. Kira's breathing shortened into excited movements as she allowed Lila to lead her deeper in to the web of this house.

They crossed into another room where bursts of blue light and total darkness danced in methodical strobes to the music. Images of taught bodies and latex flashed all around her, making her dizzy. She saw a man in black shorts and boots holding a black object toward a woman shackled in a medieval stock. Kira stopped walking and stood transfixed. Only a black mask and restraints on her wrists and ankles provided any cover for her pale skin. Despite being completely exposed she was not tense. She shuddered with excitement as the man came closer.

Kira watched and felt a shiver of her own, remembering how her other senses were heightened when Stark had her bound and blindfolded. When the man pressed on the black object, the woman began to writhe and moan in pleasure.

Kira was confused and aroused. She squeezed her legs tightly together. Then it came to her. He was holding a remote! The man and three masked women moved with animalistic prowess all over her exposed skin. The helpers wore metallic collars around their necks which were attached by a rhinestone-adorned chain to a silver ring just below their navels. Another chain encompassed their narrow waists. Yet another trailed down to their anklets. By their moans and reactions, Kira guessed the silver rings were attached to a vibrator of some kind inside each of them as well. They moaned and dripped as they moved with the music at the hand of their dominator. Kira couldn't help but picture herself bound, completely trusting her partner. The restraints took the place of your own inhibition, leaving you free to relish every sensation. Each girl held something with which to torture or please the bound girl who was merciless to their manipulations. Kira was afraid to even gasp out loud. She watched the woman thrash as she was encompassed in pleasure from her own vibrators and pain inflicted by the helpers. The flogger worked her over eagerly. Each strike left trails of pink excited skin. Kira subconsciously rubbed her own arms. Another helper had various clamps and added a new one each time it was her turn. Kira almost shrieked as she saw the clamp being applied to the woman's nipple. The woman cried out and then moaned deeply. Her head twisted back and forth but she was unable to move her arms and her legs. The third helper used only her mouth. Trailing her lips and tongue over the woman's flawless skin, she paused and lapped around the newly placed clamp. Kira held her breath. She couldn't look anywhere but at those lips surrounding the delicate and freshly violated skin of the bound woman. Kira felt parts of herself clench involuntarily. She knew that she shouldn't be enjoying any part of this.

A deeply chiseled man in ripped jeans and no shirt approached them. He looked Kira up and down. "You like to watch, princess?" He raised his sandy eyebrows and smiled at her. Kira stood frozen in her tracks. His dirty blond hair had a tousled I've just been rolling in the bed look. He probably had. Her eyes trailed from his piercing blue orbs down his tanned skin stretched over taught abs. Against her better judgment, her eyes and mind wandered further to his open fly. He stood there like a model at the end of the runway, one thumb tucked in the edge of his jeans, his hand obscuring her view. The other reached out to her. "Let's see how you like to play for real. I want to taste you when you scream."

Lila stepped forward and took his hand, practically pushing Kira aside. Kira stumbled slightly, mouth agape watching Lila slather herself all over the sexy creature. She could hear Lila cooing in his ear. Two other women walked up and joined them. They pulled him down onto a black, possibly latex, bench. Kira didn't even know such furniture existed. She watched the woman with raven hair and blue highlights fasten him down with attached cuffs. The sight of the metal cuffs tightening down around his thick wrists excited Kira. Her heart was pounding. The raven-haired woman was naked save black booties and a total tattoo sleeve on her left arm down to her fingertips. Her body was flawless. Kira watched in awe as she moved fluidly around the eager man. Lila wasted no time getting a hold of his jeans to free him. The jeans fell to the floor in a heap. For a moment Kira, saw his fully erect cock standing like a flagpole, waiting and ready for the color guard. She almost felt like she should stand at attention and salute. Before she could do anything, Lila descended on him. The entire shaft disappeared into Lila's mouth and throat on the first pass. Lila began working him up and down to the rhythm of the music. The strobe lighting made it feel more like an erotic dream than reality. His eyes closed and his head dropped back into the lap of a third woman with skin as dark as the night and exquisitely curly hair. She leaned forward and kissed him deeply.

"All right, Vanilla, keep moving. I've got special plans for you," Paige's voice came out of nowhere and seemed to surround her. Another glass of the pink liquid from downstairs was placed in her hand. "Drink baby," she said. "You'll like this." *Stop! While you still can,* Kira's conscious begged as she tipped up the glass and swallowed down the sweet liquid. It burned her throat and further warmed her nether regions. The thumping of the house was palpable like a bounding pulse swallowing her, pulling her into its center. Zoe appeared beside her and took her other arm. The music was mechanical, the bass pounding, commanding. Kira felt herself dancing as she followed them over and past bodies. Her head spun. The strobe lights were starting to give her vertigo. She held tightly to Zoe and Paige as she walked. They followed the maze of the house, going deeper into the labyrinth. In the next room, video screens played on every wall. Each screen held videos of different couples or groups of people. Something was strangely familiar about the setting in the videos. Around the room, women danced on tables or on floor-to-ceiling poles. Some danced only with each other, others danced around teasing, groping men with firm chests and black skin tight pants. In the dark edges of the room there were couches tucked in the shadows. A massive, black four-poster bed stood alone in the center of the room. The sheets were a crimson satin. The bed was untouched. Restraints hung from the rails atop the posts. Additional restraints were attached to the posts themselves. Kira knew she had seen this place before. But where? Paige and Zoe led Kira to a small table for one.

"This should be perfect, Vanilla," Paige said and kissed her on the cheek. "Now sit here and be a good girl." She laughed and started to walk toward the center of the room, then turned back to Kira and winked, mouthing, "Enjoy the show."

The liquid was kicking in fully. Kira could feel every pulsing beat of the music reverberating throughout her entire body. It was as if her every bodily function was being taken over. Either the lighting changed or the walls came alive with color and began to move with the sound. She sat unable to move, watching beautiful Technicolor renditions of Zoe and Paige approach each other on the dance floor. Their movements were slow, deliberate, and familiar. Kira was mesmerized, her breathing heavy. At once, the techno dubstep faded and a sultry, ethereal sound crept into the room. Like a fog, it spread until it encompassed every soul. It wrapped around her and seemed to pull her in. Kira stood, eyes on Zoe and Paige. Paige's fingers trailed slowly down Zoe's face to her pouty lips. Zoe closed her lips around the elusive tattooed finger. Their eyes were only on each other. Paige was clearly the dominate of the pair. She tilted Zoe's head to the side, lips grazing Zoe's neck. Her fingers clasped . . .

"I've been watching you." Lysander stepped out of the darkness. Kira looked up and met his gaze. Her mouth went dry. His eyes were piercing, electric. She fell into them. Her feet seemed to lift from the floor. Fear, anticipation, weightlessness, all swirled into the magic of his voice. "The way you move when you are afraid and excited is intoxicating. Tell me, darling Kira, how do you like my club?"

"I . . . No, this is all too . . ." Kira searched in vain for words. Her wanton body betrayed her, as she tried desperately to hide her desire. She could feel her chest heaving with short panting breaths. Kira closed her eyes for a moment and tried to regain her focus. Lysander moved closer. The heat from his body set her on fire.

"Kira." His smooth voice was more powerful than a tank rolling over her inhibitions. "Welcome to our wicked game, my love. Let go and walk with me. Step into the darkness."

Kira drew in a heady breath. She slowly raised her hand to meet Lysander's outstretched one. Suddenly the music stopped and the video screens all started playing the same video in sync. Kira's blood ran cold. It hit her like a ton of bricks. She knew why this all seemed so familiar. Her heart raced and she felt like she would throw up. There on every wall on six foot screens stood Owen Stark with Paige, Zoe, and Lila in a video like she had seen at his house. His voice boomed over the speakers as he commanded the women. She watched in horror as Zoe was bent over before him, her face buried in Paige. He drew back his hand and struck Zoe on the ass. Kira jumped. In the center of the room, Zoe and Paige looked horrified. Paige looked from Kira to Lysander, eyes wide.

Zoe yelled, "Who's in the control room? Turn that off now!"

Lysander reached out for Kira. "Kira, that was . . ." She jerked her arm away and stepped back, quickly bumping into very warm bare skin. She froze. She immediately spun around to face a chiseled masculine chest. His olive-skinned pecs were so taught, his nipples poked out like diamonds. "Holy fuck," Kira breathed out quietly. Almost timidly, she looked up into his dark eyes. Jet-black hair framed his firm features. He steadied her as she stepped back away from him. She was able to see him more fully now. For a moment she couldn't breath. He stood before her wearing much too tight boxer shorts that left nothing of his enormous package to the imagination, black combat boots, and nothing else. "I . . . um . . . oh," she stammered. He took her tiny hand in his own. For a moment she pictured Owen standing there, a beautiful sex god on display for all to see, open and willing. This is who Owen Stark was. This is what Paige wanted to show her. Kira's arousal turned to panic and white-hot anger. She pushed angrily past the sexy soldier and nearly ran over Paige as she fought to leave the room.

"Kira wait!" Paige called after her.

"What the hell?" She heard Lysander ask angrily.

"Don't look at me!" Paige was yelling back. "I had nothing to do with this. It's your house, who is in the control room? Kira, Please! Wait! I don't know how that got on there. I swear. Kira!"

But Kira was in a full sprint now. The pulsing walls suddenly felt suffocating. She had to get outside. Her head spun, her heart thumped, and she braced along a wall of the dimly lit hallway searching for an exit to this twisted wonderland. The corridor was distorted. The checkered patterns twisted on before her like a never-ending spiral nightmare. Kira cursed herself for drinking that damn mystery concoction. Her heart was thumping so loudly in her ears, she could barely make out Paige's words behind her. Finally she could see the large wooden staircase and hurled forward, trying to descend the landing as fast as she could. By the time her brain registered her toe catching the edge of the step, she was already falling. She reached out frantically, trying to grab the rail but it was too late. Out of nowhere someone grabbed her. Kira looked up in to the eyes of her savior. Something was horribly familiar about that face. Through the swirl of intoxication, Kira wrestled to make sense of what she was seeing. She knew she had to get out of there. As soon as she was back on her feet she made her way to the foyer. She didn't think she could take any more when she finally burst out of the front door. Kira inhaled, sucking a deep, cool breath of the night air into her burning lungs. Where was she going to go? How the fuck did she get into this mess? Kira ran into the night. She scanned the rows of exquisite cars. There it was, Paige's beautiful Bel Air. Kira knew she had to get out of there. Despite the heels and corset, and through the fog of the alcohol she managed to climb into the Bel Air. *Where the fuck was that key?* After a moment or two of fumbling, Kira remembered the visor. Paige's spare key. The engine roared to life and Kira took off like a bat out of hell.

***

He stood at the doorway and watched her drive away. He had seen panic, possibly even recognition, in her eyes when he caught her. Watching her maneuver through the house had been exhilarating. She was almost ready. She just didn't know it yet.

Chapter 21

Kira wiped angry tears from her face as the Bel Air
raced down the curvy gravel road. She peeled onto the black top,
her tires throwing a sea of gravel behind her. Fuck! She had been
so blind. Paige, Lysander, Stark . . . They were all part of this sex
club. The smug look on that bitch Lila's face was forever burned
into her mind. The edgy smoke-filled sound of her voice, "Oh,
honey aren't we all . . ." the fake pity, played over and over in
her head as she drove. Kira could see the lights of town
approaching and she barreled on. Street signs and lights meshed
in a blur of color. She wasn't even sure where she was going but
at that moment she didn't care. It all made sense now, the sex
tapes, the bondage. She wondered just how many of those
women he had been with. Lila's hadn't been the only head that
turned when his name was mentioned. Kira saw the eager look in
their eyes and the disappointment when he wasn't actually there.
Visions of the night played over in her mind. Seeing Stark up
there, larger than life, made him seem unreal like Superman in a
porno. And that face! Kira was sure she knew the last face she
saw as she broke free from that house. Something about it
unnerved her. She realized a moment too late that she was
passing the road she needed. She down shifted and slammed the
brakes to make the turn. Just as she started to shift again and
accelerate she saw the blue lights in the mirror. All at once her

buzz faded and panic ensued. *Oh, Holy Shit! This is bad.* It took a moment to sink in. She was being pulled over.

Kira pulled to a stop beside the curb. Her heart sank as she watched the officer get out and approach the car. She could hear his shoes on the wet pavement echoing in the night air. Each step brought the worst pop quiz of her life closer. She tried to control her breathing. With a trembling hand she rolled down the window and looked up at the officer towering over her head. The dark blue uniform stretched to fit his rotund form. "Evening, ma'am. You were swerving a bit back there. Have you been drinking tonight?" he asked leaning slightly into the car. His voice was stern and loud. It resonated in Kira's whiskey soaked brain.

Fuck me. "Just a glass of wine, sir. A few hours ago," she answered contritely. She could hear the unsteadiness in her own voice as she spoke. A fine sheen of sweat broke out on her forehead. *This is so fucking bad.*

"I'm going to need your license and registration." Every syllable hit Kira like a crushing blow. She fumbled to find Paige's paperwork in the glove box and pull her own license out of her purse. Her purse! *Shit . . . Shit, shit, shit!* Vomit threatened to escape as she realized her purse was back at the club. Her hand shook as she handed over Paige's documents. *Oh dear God, Please let there be a way for me to get out of this.*

390

"I just realized that I left my purse back at The Apex Club." She hated the words as she spoke them. They were like hot acid in her mouth.

The officer paused for just a moment and looked up at her. Then the sternness returned to his face. He stood for what seemed like an eternity looking over the documents. "I'm going to need you to step out of the car."

Fuck. Kira took a deep breath and stepped out of the car. For the first time since he pulled her over she remembered what she was wearing. *Oh Jesus, I look like a fucking prostitute.* Her black tulle skirt barely covered her ass. The tight-fitting silver and black corset held her breasts up and out for the world to see. The fishnet hose and stiletto boots sealed the deal. Kira's cheeks flushed red as she stood beside the road. She silently prayed that no one would see her. Her heart was pounding like a jackhammer in her ears. Though she tried to breathe calmly, it was no use.

"Stand with your feet together and look at me." His voice seemed very loud. Kira wasn't sure if he was really talking that loud or if her fear was amplifying everything around her. The rest of the world however seemed dead silent as if it were collectively holding its breath along with her.

"I need you to stand still and follow this light with your eyes," he commanded.

"Yes, sir," Kira squeaked. Her own voice sounded small and far away.

"Don't speak unless I ask you to," he corrected sternly.

"Yes, sir." *Shit!* Kira did her best to keep her mouth shut and follow the light. At the periphery of her line of sight, the world seemed to spin. *Fuck, I have nystagmus. I am so going to jail.*

"The next test is the walk and turn. I need you to hold this tape. I am going to stretch it out, then we are going to lower it to the ground together." He handed Kira one end of a measuring tape and backed away keeping his eyes on her. "Now we are going to lower this to the ground on three. One . . . Two . . . Three." Kira followed his lead and knelt down holding the tape slowly. Balancing in the stilettos was incredibly difficult. Kira exhaled a slow controlled breath as they lowered to the ground. Gently she placed the tape and awaited the officer's command to stand.

"Ok, stand up," he said. His voice was automated, devoid of feeling or sympathy. Kira rose and looked at him. "Now take nine steps heel-to-toe fashion in a straight line along the tape. After the ninth step, you must turn on one foot and return in the opposite direction heel-to-toe. Do not begin until I tell you to. Once you start, do not stop until you have finished.

Keep your arms at your sides, and count each step out loud as you walk. Do you understand?"

Fuck. "Yes, sir." Kira stood at one end of the line and awaited his command to start. *Nine steps . . . Just nine steps and back. I can do this.*

"Begin." One word, a single call to action. Kira lifted her left foot and started walking.

"One . . . Two . . . Three . . . Four . . ." She counted each carefully placed step as she walked. Nine steps that seemed like a thousand. "Five . . . Six . . . Seven . . ." She fought to calm her breathing and stay in control. She thought of Stark. What the hell was he going to say? "Eight . . . Nine . . ." She turned expertly on her left stiletto and placed the right foot directly in front of it on the line. *Whew that was close.* Kira could feel the sweat on her palms. "Nine . . . Eight . . . Seven . . ." She heard a car pulling to a stop behind her but didn't dare stop to see who it was. "Six . . . Five . . . Four." The engine turned off and she heard a door open. "Three . . . Two . . . One . . ." She reached the end of the line when she heard his voice.

"Stand back." The edge in the officer's voice gave clear warning. "You need to stay where you are. There is nothing to see here."

"This is my coworker." Holt's voice was unmistakable.

Kira closed her eyes. *Holy Fuck! What is he doing here? This cannot get worse. Fuck . . . fuck.*

"My name is Captain Holt. I can take her home, officer. If she needs a ride." Holt spoke with authority.

"You need stay right there, Captain. We are almost done here." His voice sounded uneasy. Then to Kira, "Turn around and stand on your left foot. Hold your right foot out eight inches off the ground. You must keep your leg straight and hold it up until I finish counting."

Kira turned and raised her right leg. As she did she raised her gaze as well and met Holt's eyes. The officer began counting slowly. As he counted Kira stared at Holt. He looked her up and down taking in her appearance, and then looked from her to Paige's car and back. He seemed to be piecing it all together. The look of disdain on his face softened. Kira knew that he knew exactly where she had been. She realized she had been holding her breath again and exhaled long and slow as the officer finished counting.

"Now I'm going to need you to blow into this Breathalyzer," the officer spoke with confidence.

She saw Holt mouth the word "Shit" and shake his head. *I am going to jail.* Every glimmer of hope faded. Methodically, Kira followed the officer's directions for the Breathalyzer.

394

"Stop trying to not take the test," he commanded impatiently as she tried desperately to blow hard enough to register the test.

"But I'm trying to," Kira explained.

"Stop talking. I didn't tell you to speak. You need to blow into the mouthpiece when I say. Stop trying to not take the test." He was getting loud as he cut Kira off and demanded that she start over. The test registered the second time. Almost as soon as it beeped he began to read her rights.

"Turn around," he commanded. "Place your hands behind your back." Kira felt the cold steel of the handcuffs closing around her wrists. The sound of them clicking into place would haunt her sleep. Tears started to escape her burning eyes. As he sat her in the back of his car she heard Holt's voice.

"Kira, this is going to be ok." She couldn't see his face but Holt's voice was strained with a forced confidence as he tried to reassure her.

She appreciated Holt's attempt, but she knew it wasn't ok and wasn't sure if it ever would be again. Kira watched Holt talking quietly with the officer through the window of the cruiser and wished she could hear what they were saying.

By the time they reached the station for booking, Kira was fully sober. The officer led her from the cruiser into the El

Paso County Jail. Kira fought the urge to vomit. She looked at the pavement, afraid to look up at the large front doors of the jail. The pressure of the officer's grip on her arm was somewhat comforting. Having never actually broken the law before, she felt closer to the officer than whatever lay waiting on the other side of those doors. The doors opened and the booking area strangely reminded her of the ER waiting room—the chaotic mess of people crying and yelling; the intense smells of vomit, urine, and body odor; people sleeping on the floor; and addicts of every shape and size. He led her to an intake desk where she gave her name and handed over her personal possessions, which since she didn't have her purse consisted of the relentless bracelet that Stark had given her, earrings that were her grandmother's, and a necklace she had borrowed from Paige. She closed her eyes as all that identified her was sealed in a plastic bag, tagged, and labeled. Holt had taken the keys so she didn't even have those. Not that Paige would ever let her drive the Bel Air again. *Fuck Paige. Why did she take me there anyway? Fuck her and Stark, too.*

She was placed with two other girls in a holding area before processing. Kira gulped hard as the officer left and she was alone with the two women. The taller girl had the pasty white skin and dark sunken eyes of a drug user. Her straggly blond hair had jet-black roots and appeared to not have been brushed in more than a few days. She wore an oversized shirt and vividly patterned leggings that seemed to be screaming for

396

mercy, since they were about a size too small. One black converse high top was untied but she didn't seem to notice. The girl eyed Kira as she entered the room.

"Heeeey girl. What you in for? My name's Neveah . . ." she began, with raised eyebrows and her head cocked to the side. Her words were slightly slurred and about two beats off tempo. Kira was too frightened to giggle.

"You got any pills on you?'' Neveah continued without waiting for Kira to answer. "You know they search you in here. If you got pills, you better pull them outta that snatchel and swallow them bitches. I already downed mine. You get an extra dime for possession, ya know. They pinched me for DUI for pot. Can you believe that shit? Since when is it illegal to smoke pot and drive?"

"Now, what?" Kira shook her head in disbelief. Surely she had heard some of that incorrectly.

"You know Drivin' . . . Underneath . . . Intoxicated. But I wasn't drinkin' or doing drugs. I was just smoking a little pot. They said when they pulled me outta the median that it is illegal to smoke pot and drive. They even took my pipe." Then louder, "And I better get that shit back! I'm not even sure that is a real thing, DUI for smokin' a little pot. Shit." Neveah twirled her finger around a greasy strand of blond straw as she spoke. Her nails were long and vibrantly painted with orange and green glitter.

"Yes, I think that is very illegal. Pretty sure that's a real thing," Kira told her. *Wow, just fucking wow.* Kira attempted a semi-understanding smile to cover up her sheer amazement.

"Really, fuck. Since when?" Neveah raised her eyebrows with suspicion, which almost made Kira pee her pants laughing, as they were already drawn on in a look of constant cockeyed surprise. It looked as if one eye was just a little more alarmed than the other.

"Um . . . since forever. Pretty sure . . . forever," Kira said, nodding to emphasize her confidence.

"On your feet, ladies." The officer's voice had the melodious ring of a seventy-year smoker. Kira's mind instantly flashed to the caseworker from *Beetlejuice.* Kira was still standing in the center of the filthy room, arms folded trying not to touch anything.

This has to be one of the seven levels of Hell.

They were marched to another room and instructed to strip for a full body search. Kira closed her eyes and said good-bye to the last shred of dignity that she possessed.

"So you think they'll put it in the little bag with my belongings and give it back when I leave?" Kira asked hopefully.

"What?" asked the gruff female officer.

"My dignity," Kira answered matter of factly. "I just wondered if it goes in the bag, too?"

The older woman chuckled. "Sure thing, kid. I'm sure it will be in there somewhere. What's left of it any way." The woman finished the search and handed her a little plastic cup and an orange jump suit. "Fill it to the line and get dressed," The woman instructed.

"What's this for?" Kira asked, horrified.

"Well, your dignity is in the bag so might as well fill the cup with urine. Got to check for drugs and pregnancy before we finish your booking."

Kira sighed and did as she was instructed.

Neveah piped up. Her loud nasally voice startled Kira. "Not me, I am one and done! No babies in this oven. Hell, no. My baby Jerome, his daddy so lazy. He don't pay me on time. He ain't neva got no job. This girl's one and done!"

One of the female officers rolled her eyes as she collected and labeled their specimens then left. The others stood guard while they dressed in snazzy orange jumpsuits and white imitation Keds sneakers. They were then moved down the block walled corridor to another room for mug shots. "This will make a lovely Christmas card," Kira mumbled quietly.

"Oh, girrrl you have to look good for this pic. My friend Alex met her last baby daddy cuz he saw her mug on Internet," she purred between missing teeth.

"You're joking, right?" Kira hoped to God she was joking.

"Oh, no, girl you can't make dis shit up!" Neveah swayed her head authoritatively.

"Apparently not." Kira shook her head in disbelief. How the hell had she ended up here? Kira moved forward in line. As mortified as she was and career ending as this would probably be, she couldn't help but smirk as the camera flashed. What did it matter now?

Kira was moved with her two cellmates down another long block hallway and through a set of heavy locked doors to their luxurious accommodations for the night. Once in the hall of cells, Kira noticed that each was filled with two to four people. She tried to look straight ahead but the cat calls from within terrified her. Kira peaked out of the corner of her eye at the creatures lurking behind the steel bars. Some were women but most cells were filled with men. The air was hot with the sour smell of urine and vomit. Kira fought the urge to throw up right there in the hall. Kira was immediately thankful for the coverage of the orange jumpsuit. They were placed in an 8-foot by 10-foot block cell with no window. The door, however, was only bars and provided little barrier from the masturbating tattoo and grease-covered man across the hall.

"Hey, baby, you like what you see?" His toothless grin and weathered skin made his actual age difficult to predict. "You know you want some of this! Don't wrinkle your nose at me, you little whore. You're in here too. You know you want this cock."

Kira gagged and looked away at the wall. Is that? Oh shit it is. Kira noticed a fine dried blood splatter on the wall and wondered how long it had been there. She reminded herself to touch nothing. Hepatitis, HIV. . . fuck, she was sure to end up with a disease before this was over. Three small dingy mattresses with no sheets or blankets lay on the concrete floor. Kira stared at them and wondered if at one time they had been white with blue stripes now were just a dismal shade of gray worn from years of sweat, vomit, and filth. Along one wall was a toilet that was covered in so many layers of grime, it made roadside gas stations look clean enough to eat off of. *Oh, holy shit. No Way!*

"Um, are we supposed to get sheets or pillows or something? Maybe a mattress cover?" Kira asked timidly.

The guard's throaty laugh echoed off the block walls as she shut the door behind her. "Whatever you wish, princess. Is there anything else we can do for you?" Her laughter could be heard fading all the way down the hall.

The other two women settled on the mattresses. Kira vowed to stand all the rest of the night if she had to. Bed bugs, scabies, pubic lice . . . her mind ran down the differential diagnosis of everything she was sure she would have by the time she made it out of here. Kira paced back and forth in the small cell. How will I ever get out of this? I don't even know who to call. Even if they did let her make a call without her cell she wouldn't know any numbers. They had mentioned she would face a magistrate in the morning. Fuck, what was in that pink drink? Kira began to panic about the hallucinations at the house. What was real, what did she imagine? What if she had been drugged? If she was and it showed up in her urine, she was screwed. Her medical career was over. FUCK! Fuck, fuck, fuck!!

Before Kira could continue her self-loathing, the gray haired female guard arrived back at the door.

"Congratulations, Mama, looks like you're pregnant." The older woman laughed as if this was happy or at least amusing.

"What the fuck?" Kira blurted out louder that she intended? "Oh, shit you have to be joking. Please say that you are joking." She felt faint. *This cannot be happening.* Nausea took hold and Kira turned toward the dingy excuse for a toilet.

"Reynolds . . . Neveah Reynolds, your pregnancy test is positive and based on your drug screen you better see a doctor right away. Lit up like a Christmas tree. Must have been some party." The wrinkly hag was enjoying torturing them.

Kira looked at Neveah, who sat wide-eyed on the flaccid mat. The surprise eyebrows stretched to her hairline. The confused and constipated expression on her face displayed the distress her neurons were experiencing, trying to process what had just been said.

"Now, say what?" Neveah finally in the game jumped up. The other woman had already passed out cold, apparently very cozy on the dingy mat.

"You sayin' I'm preg-nant? Shut up, you play-in!" She drew out the words.

"Trust me, I wish I was," the female officer replied dryly as if she was ordering a tuna sandwich and walked away.

"Well Shiiiiit! There ain't no way I could be knocked up. I know that shit's fucked up." Neveah's head was in full roll now when she spoke.

"Have you had your tubes tied?" Kira asked hopefully.

"Hell no!" Neveah attempted to frown. Her forehead wrinkled and her mouth scowled but her eyes said . . . unhappy surprise!

403

"Um ok, are you using contraceptives when you have sex?" Kira felt like she was trying to get through to a brick wall.

"Say, what? I'm not in to that S N M shit. Do you think I'm sum kinda hooker?" Disapproving surprise.

"No. No. Sorry, you know like the birth control pill?" *Please God don't let this person procreate.* Kira could see the burnt out wheels trying to turn. There was smoke, but no fire. Cue the crickets.

"No," Neveah answered. Vacant surprise.

"Patches, or an implant? Anything?"

"No, what would I do that for?"

"Do you use condoms for Christ's sake?" Kira asked exasperated.

"Uh, nooo. Tyrone, he always pull out." Neveah said confidently.

"Oh shit, you know that's not reliable, right?" Kira was starting to get really frustrated, but Neveah wasn't paying attention.

"Now Sketchy Steve, he said he been fixed . . ." She squinted and looked at the ceiling as if she was searching for something. "Darnell . . . Oooh he fine . . . and he got a job!" Her eyes lit up.

404

"Oh, dear God are you serious? What are you going to do?" Kira tapped the white Ked on the concrete as she spoke. "You really need to see a doctor, like, yesterday."

"Shit, what you know 'bout doctors?"

The cocky semi-toothless grin was almost more than Kira could bear. She started to really answer her but then thought better of it. "Nothing, really. I was just thinking with the drugs and all. I don't know."

"What-eva. You betta get some resssst girrrl." The handful of pills Neveah had downed earlier must have been getting the better of her. She curled up on the mattress as if she were tucked in at the Hilton. Sleepy surprise. Definitely not her first rodeo.

Kira looked around the spacious accommodations and tried to find a non-blood stained, non-parasite covered space to rest. The night was starting to wear on her and she was getting very sleepy. She moved to a corner that appeared less gross and sat down. She was careful to make sure only the jumpsuit and the Keds were touching the floor and the walls. Kira pulled her knees up to her chest and rested her head and arms on them. *Oh man, how am I ever going to get out of this? How did I let myself get into this? What is my commanding officer going to say? Surely Holt will tell him everything. Shit, the police will probably do that. What the hell was Holt doing there, anyway?* Alone in the dark with her thoughts, Kira let the tears fall. She had been in some shit in her life but this had to take the cake.

~

Kira sat up. The sweltering pain overtook her entire head. *Oh Shit.* She knew instantly that she was going to vomit. She opened her eyes and the fluorescent lights beaming overhead seared into her brain. *Oh, fuck.* She stumble-crawled her way across the concrete floor to the lone toilet and commenced praying to the porcelain gods. The vague foggy details of the night before slowly came back to her. *Oh, holy hell!*

Kira wasn't sure which was worse, the searing headache or the recollection that in the last twenty-four hours she had been to a sex club, stolen a car, and was arrested for drunk driving. Her stomach wretched again as she remembered seeing Stark on those screens. It was a blur of sex and debauchery. *Fuck, how could Owen Stark be a part of that?* Something else plagued her, too. But what? What could be worse than getting arrested and finding out your boyfriend is part of some deranged sex group? Kira couldn't help the uneasy feeling that something was very, very wrong. *Um, hello dumb ass. You are in jail, remember? Arrested for DUI.* But it was more than that. Something she couldn't quite put her finger on.

She got up slowly from the cool floor. The pain behind her eyes was immediately worse in an upright position. She held on to the block wall and began to make her way toward the bars. *Ooooh, fuck.* The masturbating man across the hall had fallen asleep with his shriveled meat in his hand. *Gross. Well, at least he didn't go to bed alone.* Kira chuckled quietly.

"You find jail funny?" The shorter quiet girl finally spoke. Her voice was rough and reminded Kira of one of the aunts from the Simpsons.

"I um . . . no . . . I mean . . . Sorry, did I wake you?" Kira turned slowly as if her throbbing head was a bottle of nitroglycerin just waiting to be set off.

"You've never been to jail before, have you?" the girl said, tilting her head at Kira almost sympathetically.

"No, is it that obvious?" Kira asked. She knew it was, though. Never in a million years had Kira imagined that she would be here. Locked in a block cubicle with a seriously burnt out baby mama and a . . . "What are you in here for, if I may ask?"

"Not exactly sure. Probably drunk and disorderly. I was pretty baked by the time they picked me up." She studied a bruised and swollen hand. "Maybe assault or domestic, too. Not sure. The old man and I were pretty into it last I remember. My name's Sam."

"Kira. It's nice to meet you. I got a DUI in my friend's car. At least I thought she was my friend," Kira said and winced. She put her hand to her aching temple. She had stolen Paige's car and then been pulled over! What a mess.

Neveah moaned and sat up. She had rolled around and drooled while sleeping so that one of her faux eyebrows had completely wiped off on the mattress. She sat up and looked at them, her expression still sleepy and unamused except for one still very surprised eyebrow. Simultaneously Kira and Sam busted out laughing. "What?" Neveah sounded less amused than she looked.

"Captain Riley." An authoritative voice called from the hallway. Kira cringed and turned around sharply. *Shit this is it.* "Captain Kira Riley?" The voice repeated.

"Yes, ma'am. That's me." Kira did her best to stand at respectful attention in her orange garb and straggly hair. A blond woman stood in a Class A uniform at the door. *Oh shit, I am in so much trouble.*

"Captain Riley. You need to come with me." The guard accompanying the officer opened the door and motioned for Kira to follow. Kira cast one glance back at Sam and Neveah as she left. The worried expression on their faces sent a chill down Kira's spine. She followed the blond officer to an interview room. "Captain Riley, I am Captain Brindell, United States

Army Military Police. Do you want to explain why I am down here at oh nine hundred on a Saturday?"

"Captain, I am terribly sorry," Kira started. She stopped and looked at the woman. Something about her was strikingly familiar. "I . . . was with friends . . . I got really upset and went to drive home. I shouldn't have driven. I know I am in a lot of trouble." Kira didn't even try to get out of it. She knew she was in for a world of penalties. She may even be court martialed.

"Captain, are you familiar with the Uniformed Code of Military Justice?" The woman's stern voice offered no consolation.

"Vaguely," Kira managed to say. *Shit. I am so screwed.*

"Captain Riley, you are being released by this court into our custody. Punishment for your crimes will be determined under Article 15 of the UCMJ. You will report back to base with me immediately. The officer will help you retrieve your things. After you change we will go directly back to base to meet with your commanding officer and Major Jennings.

Oh Fuck Me! "Um, may I stay in the jumpsuit ma'am?" Kira asked hopefully. The idea facing her commanding officer and the major dressed in that shred of whore fabric made Kira want to cry. The bitterness of rising vomit burned the back of her throat. "My, um, clothes are not exactly . . ." Kira stammered trying to think of a way to express what the officer was about to see.

"Not exactly fitting for an officer?" The woman snapped. "Perhaps you should have thought of that last night. Now get dressed. We are on a deadline and I don't have all day to sit around for your fashion show."

With a heavy heart, Kira took her clothes and went into the small restroom to change. She never dreamed she would be sorry to give up the orange jumpsuit. She slowly unrolled the fishnets onto her legs and donned the two-dollar stripper get up. Kira zipped up the stilettos and handed over the orange jumpsuit. After collecting the small bag of personal possessions, minus her dignity, which must have gotten lost in the shuffle, she followed the captain to the waiting car. As they stepped into the blinding daylight, Kira caught sight of her reflection in the tall glass windows of the jail. Staring back at her was the trash bin hooker, dead in the alley at the start of every episode of CSI Las Vegas. Kira slid into the back of the government sedan and buckled her seat belt. Captain Brindell came around the other side and slipped into the drivers seat. Without saying a word she fastened her belt and started the engine. Kira was too afraid to speak and decided to wait to be spoken to.

Kira looked out the window and watched the jail fade behind her. She thought about the night before. She thought of her arrest. Holt. Liam Holt had shown up out of nowhere. She still couldn't understand what he had been doing there. She thought about Stark. She hated to admit she was heartbroken. *All those women.* She struggled to remember the details of the club. The officer in the front seat was quietly humming some tune. Kira knew it but couldn't quiet place it. The tapping of the officer's fingers on the seat was distracting her from her thoughts. She struggled to remember more of the night. She thought of running up stairs, the couple on the first chair . . . then the blond lady in latex . . . then Lila and everything got fuzzy after that . . . then . . . Wait! Suddenly it came back to her like a slap in the face. Kira looked up and her eyes met the reflection of the officer's gaze in the rearview mirror. A smile crept across the blond woman's face. Kira had finally made the connection.

Chapter 22

"Owen Stark!" Simone's shrill voice filled his bedroom and aching head like a jackhammer.

"Don't you ever knock?" he growled as he buttoned his crisp white shirt. He stood facing the mirror in just a shirt and boxers as Simone entered the room.

"My, my you look absolutely yummy," Simone purred. She came up behind him and trailed her fingers across his collar. "Want me to fix your tie for you?"

"Not unless you want me to vomit on your shoes. Aren't you supposed to be in mourning?" he asked dryly. Looking up he saw her sultry expression turn into a venomous frown.

"You're a real piece of work, Owen. Do you not care about your family and your responsibilities at all? How can you be so cruel after all I have been through?" Simone lamented like a southern belle whose honor had been wounded.

"You're just bitter because you know you're not in the will. All that whoring with my idiot father for nothing. You are not my family, nor my responsibility. I don't owe you shit. Now get out so I can be alone with the few memories of my father and my family that don't involve you." His voice was like ice. They locked stares for a moment, neither one wanting to budge, but finally it was Simone who turned and strode from the room. She almost knocked over Rosalea as she brought coffee and toast.

Rosalea entered muttering a string of profanities in Spanish under her breath. "*Serpiente venenosa!*" she finished, shook her head, and spat.

Owen laughed loudly. "Oh, Rosalea, don't hold anything back. Please let it all out." He loved Rosalea. She had been his and Maggie's nanny but had stayed on to care for his father after the plane crash. Rosalea had mourned as deeply as Owen. She had always hated Simone and didn't bother to hide it.

"She would like to have rid of me. But your father, bless his soul." She made the sign of the cross. She was dressed in black and had her rosary around her neck. "He wouldn't let her. At least he stood up to her once in a while. She has been trying to take your grandfather's company for years. Ha, but the joke is on her, yes. Your father never even owned his *pantelones*. Your mama, she was a smart, smart girl. Or at least your *abuelo* was an incredible man. He made sure your mama's inheritance passed to you, not your father. Your father was simply the caretaker until you were ready. I guess no one expected you to find your way to the army."

"Life has a way of changing your direction," Stark said softly as he hugged Rosalea. "The company will be in good hands. I have a board meeting next week to announce the new

413

CEO and co-directors to take my father's place running the company. Well, we better get this over with. This funeral is going to feel more like a circus with all the sharks and clowns in their monkey suits clamoring for a piece of the money. Everybody wants to make a good impression. Insincere condolences, empty wishes. I remember them all from when Mom and Maggie passed." Stark was tired and his voiced trembled a little as he spoke. He was thankful Rosalea was there. It meant a lot to have one person sincerely in your corner.

"I'll go down and call for the car. You hang in there," Rosalea said before she turned and walked quickly from the room. Stark could hear her sniffling. He knew she would miss his father. He made a mental note to secure her future when he spoke to the lawyer after the reading of the will.

Stark reached into his bag and grabbed his phone. No missed calls. He picked it up and tried Kira. The sound of her voicemail again made him curse under his breath. He hadn't been able to reach her since the day before. What the hell? Where was she? He was mad, but he missed Kira and couldn't wait to get home to her. He couldn't stop worrying about her. He wanted to hold her. Today was going to be incredibly hard but her voice, her touch would make it bearable. More than anything, he wished she were there with him. He picked up the phone and tried her cell again. Hearing her voicemail, he tossed it on the bed not bothering to hang up. He sat down dejected, wondering how he was going to make it through the next few hours.

"Owen, darling, are you ready yet?" Simone's slick voice slithered into the room. "Wow, I do say I'm not sure which is better, with the pants or without."

"What do you want, Simone?" Stark's flat tone left nothing to the imagination.

"I was just thinking about your little fraternization problem and how your enlistment will be up very soon. Seems to me problem solved." Her soft seductive tone curled around his body like a python setting a trap.

"Dammit, Simone! I have told you, I am married to the military first. That is my life. I'm not leaving it for you or Kira or anyone else. What does it take to get you to understand that?" Stark jumped up and started out of the room shaking his head. *That woman has no boundaries.*

Simone caught him by the arm. "Oh now, what would your little captain say if she heard that? Think about it, darling, you could have your little tramp if you simply don't re-enlist. Stay out here awhile, run the company, take your birthright." She looked up at him eyes beaming.

"What's your angle, Simone? How does that even help you?"

"Help me? Why, darling, I'm not thinking of me. Oh, love, I'm thinking of you and that poor girl. What happens to her if her superiors find out she's been fucking around with an enlisted boy? And that tattooed creature you live with—where is she, by the way?"

"Shut up, Simone. I am dead serious, you will leave Kira alone. That's not a request."

"Hmmm . . . We'll see . . . All this jail business . . . My goodness."

"What are you talking about? You will not mess with her." Stark was yelling now. "Do you hear me? I am very serious. I will take everything you have. Nothing will protect you if you get her into trouble." He stood, fists clenched tightly, wishing it was ok to hit a girl. She was no girl.

"I think she's doing a good job of that all by herself," Simone triumphantly announced. She brushed imaginary dust from his shoulder and left the room laughing.

Stark stood shaking his head. What the hell was she talking about? Why couldn't Simone be a normal human for one day? This was going to be hard enough without having to worry about Simone or Kira. He picked his father's gold pocket watch up from the dresser and opened it. Inside were pictures of his mom and sister. The fact that he had kept this all these years, Owen knew some spark of goodness had remained until the end.

The limo came to a stop in front of a beautiful mausoleum. He wished Kira were there. He imagined her giving his hand a squeeze as he stepped out of the car. On the grounds perfect flowers and marble statues dotted the landscape. Walking toward the rows of white chairs, he wondered what her father's funeral had been like. The landscape less grand, likely, the patrons weary. He imagined a tired, thin woman with three children mourning the loss of all they knew.

Rows of beautifully dressed people stood waiting to pay their respects. Simone walked out to the crowd as if she were on the red carpet. Owen rolled his eyes. *And the academy award for most over dramatic goes to . . .* Despite Simone's showboat performance, the loss in the air was heavy. A beautiful, vibrant soul, taken far too soon. Stark heard the speaker begin, describing a hero, a friend, a husband, a father. He brought joy and honor to all he met. Stark heard them speak of the man he was and the life he lived. He loved his father but wanted to stand up and say that he was no hero. He had seen real heroes. He had watched the light fade from their eyes as they gave all. Stark looked at the plastic world around him and felt more alone than ever. Simone was sitting beside him and began tapping her foot impatiently. *She's fucking bored!* Owen resisted the urge to sweep kick her chair out from under her. The image of her mussed up dress covered in dirt and the scowl on her embarrassed face would perhaps make this day tolerable.

Stark stood listening to strangers talk about his father. He sadly knew that many of them knew him far better than he would ever have a chance to. The loss was too great for words. He felt the great emptiness of a house long since abandoned. Pieces of his heart and soul were like vacant rooms holding echoes of a life once lived. The service ended and everyone began to file slowly back to their vehicles. Stark remained, staring out across the cemetery. He knew that this was it. Once they walked away he would leave his father behind. *Where are you, Kira?*

***

The sound of breaking glass awoke Kira from a dead sleep. She sat bolt upright in the bed and looked around. The room was pitch black except for a sliver of moonlight coming through the window. She listened intently. Nothing. She knew it had been glass. It wasn't her imagination . . . was it? Kira had been having the nightmares again. Ever since her night at The Apex Club, she had been having dreams of her attacker. Though she knew it was crazy, she even thought she saw him twice around the base. Then when she would look closer it wasn't at all. She strained to listen harder. Nothing. All seemed quiet, but

418

Maggie was awake too. She sat curled up at the end of the bed by Kira's feet, ears perked up listening. The silence in the room felt like a weight pressing down on her, holding her to the bed. Suddenly Maggie's head snapped up and she jumped up to attention. She did not bark but was alert and ready. *She must hear something I can't.* Kira carefully and quietly retrieved her Beretta 9mm from the bedside table. Training took over. She disengaged the safety and pulled the slide back to load a bullet into the chamber. She grabbed her cell phone and carefully eased out of bed. Silently she slipped into the bathroom bringing Maggie with her. Maggie's muscles were taut and her head remained erect, listening. They positioned themselves behind a wall that allowed her to see the door but not be seen as she was in the shadows. Kira switched her cell phone to silent and listened for movement, for anything. She dialed 911 but did not hit send. Flashbacks of irritated policeman from multiple fruitless calls during her undergrad years prevented her from calling. She had to be sure. She couldn't bear the humiliation again.

Suddenly Maggie stiffened. Her hair bristled and she let out a low steady growl and moved a step in front of Kira. Kira's heart pounded. She held the gun in one hand and the cell phone in the other, her thumb hovering over the send button. An eternity passed. She thought perhaps she had imagined the whole thing and then the door to the bedroom began to open very slowly. Maggie's growl became louder. "Stop," Kira yelled in a

419

loud authoritative voice. "I have a gun and I will shoot." The door instantly stopped moving. Kira waited. Her line of sight was perfect. If the door opened a fraction of an inch more, she would shoot. She waited. She struggled to listen for movement over the rapid pounding of her heart. The silence and the darkness crowded in around her and threatened to squeeze the breath from her lungs. Suddenly from downstairs there was a crash and the TV came on blaring some infomercial. Kira jumped and called 911.

"Nine-one-one what's your emergency?" A much-too-calm voice asked over the phone.

"My name is Kira Riley. I'm house sitting for a friend and I believe someone may be in the house," Kira whispered sounding much calmer than she felt.

"What's your address?" the robotic woman asked. Her monotone response was completely unaffected by Kira's predicament.

"1708 Stanaford Drive, Colorado Springs," Kira managed to get out. She was very shaken and afraid who ever it was, may still be in the house.

As the monotone woman told her to stay put, that help was on its way, Kira's phone beeped in with another call. It was Paige. Paige wasn't exactly her bestie at the moment but she had managed to get Kira out of jail and out of trouble. Kira still couldn't believe that the MP officer was a member of the club. She wondered just how far reaching their little group was. Kira put the 911 operator on hold and answered the call. Maybe it was just Paige or Zoe in the house.

"Hello," she whispered into the phone.

"Kira is that you? You're so quiet are you ok?" Paige's voice strained over the booming techno music of The Apex Club. "The alarm was disabled at Owen's house. They called me. Is everything ok? I think they are sending a squad over." She sounded out of breath and worried.

"I think there may be someone in the house, I just called nine-one-one," Kira said, her voice slightly higher pitched. *If the alarm has been disabled someone is here!* "I've got my gun. If they come in I'll shoot."

"Hold on there, Rambo! Stay put. Zoe and I are on the way. Do what you have to do to protect yourself but the last thing you need is to have to explain why you shot and killed an intruder in a sergeant's house! One brush with the law is enough this week." Paige stopped talking to Kira for a moment and yelled to Zoe in the noisy club. Kira could hear the muffled sounds of them talking and then Paige returned to the phone. "We're on the way. Be there in fifteen minutes. Stark is already pissed as hell at me. If I let something happen to you, well . . ."

Kira switched back over to the 911 operator who surprisingly was still there. "Another friend was called by the alarm company and said the alarm system was disarmed," Kira blurted into the phone. Her anxiety was becoming harder to hide.

"We've already dispatched a unit and we have spoken with the alarm company. They called to dispatch a unit." The monotone woman was yet to be effected by the situation.

Kira was becoming increasingly irritated at the woman's complacency. *I wonder if this is how patients' families feel when we tell them we did our best and there is nothing more we can do?* "Can you tell the officers that I'm armed? I'm in the upstairs master bedroom. The door to the bedroom started to open but when I announced that I was armed the door stopped. Then I heard a TV downstairs come on. Now the only thing I can hear is that TV blaring." Kira was talking fast, blurting out every detail quickly into the phone as if somehow that would bring the police faster.

Minutes that seemed like hours passed and finally Kira heard a car pulling up in the driveway. She could see the red and blue lights flashing in the window. The 911 operator had remained on the phone with her. "The police are there. Stay put and let them come to you." Now the woman's calm monotone was reassuring.

Kira obeyed. Her phone began beeping repeatedly. It was Stark. Kira didn't answer. She wanted to be on the phone when the police came to the door so she would know when to put down her gun. She hit ignore. Almost immediately it began beeping again. Kira could hear the police downstairs clearing the house. "They are coming upstairs," the woman said. "Stay on the phone and stay put until they give you an all clear."

Maggie began barking loudly and snarling. She stood at attention, positioning herself between Kira and the door. Kira heard footsteps outside the door. She froze listening. Waiting.

"Ma'am, this is the Colorado Springs police department. Put your weapon on the floor and step away," a booming male voice said from the other side of the door.

"It's the police," the dispatcher said. "Follow his instructions. You are safe now."

Kira followed orders and put her weapon on the floor. She stepped back. "Ok," she said as low as she could muster. "It's on the floor." She stood and backed up.

The door flew all the way open and two armed officers entered and turned on the light. They searched the room and inspected Kira.

"Ma'am are you hurt?" the shorter officer asked. His curly, dark hair framed his round face. He was stocky but strong, like more of a CrossFit junkie than Dunkin' Donuts patron.

In the bright light Kira was suddenly aware that she was wearing only Stark's T-shirt and a pair of panties. She was immediately embarrassed and her cheeks flushed bright red. Just then there was a commotion of voices downstairs.

"Kira! Kira! Where are you?" Paige's voice could be heard increasingly louder as she mounted the stairs. "Are you ok?" She gasped, out of breath, with a red-faced, panting Zoe right behind her. Kira watched Paige's expression change as she entered the room and saw the two strapping officers. Her eyes twinkled and the grimace was replaced with a slow playful smile. "Well, well, if this is what you get when you call nine-one-one in the middle of the night, I may have to put it on speed dial," she mused. Then, turning to Kira, she became serious. "Are you ok? There is a broken window downstairs!"

"Who are you?" The taller officer asked. His brow furrowed in frustration. Kira could see that he was young and nervous. His hands gripped the 9mm a little too tightly. He glanced back and forth from Kira in her T-shirt to the two scantily dressed tattooed club hoppers. Kira almost giggled trying to imagine what he must be thinking.

"I'm Paige and this is Zoe. We were called by the security company. We are close personal friends of the owner and we're here to check things out," she said confidently. Her voice flowed like silk across her lips and grasped the young officer more effectively than if she had done it with one of her long acrylic nails.

Oh jeez! Kira rolled her eyes. "So about the house," she said, trying to bring everyone's attention to why they were here at two thirty in the morning. "Someone broke in," she prompted when no one responded.

"Oh y-yes ma'am," the shorter officer responded as if suddenly remembering he was on duty. "We'll need to get statements from all of you. We will need you to come downstairs and check to see if anything is missing. It does look as if someone broke in. The alarm system was cut which set off the silent alarms and the glass in the kitchen door was broken. The door was standing open when we arrived."

There had been someone there. Not ten feet from her. Someone had been in the house. At once Kira felt sick. The room spun and everyone sounded far away. *He was in here! Someone was in here!* Kira stumbled back and Paige grabbed a chair for her.

"Is she all right?" the officer asked, alarmed.

425

"Yeah, she's just a little shaken up, that's all. Zoe will you get her some sweats and a sweatshirt," Paige directed. They all jumped as Kira's phone started buzzing like crazy across the floor. As Kira pressed her head in her hands, she heard Zoe answer the phone.

"She's ok." By the tone of Zoe's voice, Kira could tell it was Stark and he wasn't happy. "Owen, she's ok, just a little shaken up, that's all. What do you mean all our fault? We weren't even here."

Paige strode in and took the phone from Zoe. "Calm yourself down. She's fine. The police are here. They've checked everything out. Looks like someone tried to break in but Zena the Warrior Princess here scared them off with her Beretta." She helped Kira stand up and gave her a glass of water from the sink. "Yes, you can talk to her give her just a minute."

Kira waved her away. She still hadn't brought herself to talk to Stark after the incident at the club, seeing him in that way with all those women. Kira had only stayed at his house due to fear. Fear of what she wasn't even sure anymore. The nightmares had to be her mind just playing tricks on her. And clearly this house wasn't any safer than her own apartment.

"Kira, you have to talk to him eventually. He's going to find out about everything. You two need to talk about it." Paige handed her the phone and turned to take the officers back downstairs.

Kira sat looking at the phone in her hand. She wasn't ready to face or hear anything he had to say. But here she was sitting in his bedroom, wearing his shirt. "Hello," Kira squeaked out trying to sound braver than she felt.

"God, Kira are you ok?" Stark's voice sounded panicked. "I've been trying and trying to call your cell for a week! Why the hell didn't you answer?"

"I was on the phone with the dispatcher. I didn't want to hang up with her until the police were in here. I'm ok." Kira steadied her voice. She knew he had enough on his plate dealing with his father's death and squaring things up in California. She couldn't put him or herself through this conversation now.

"For the last week? What have you been up to? I can't get a hold of you and I'm going crazy. I am trying to take care of things here and I am worried sick that you are dead by the road somewhere. Hell even Paige has gone MIA until tonight. Then I get this call from the alarm company. Tell me what the hell happened!" The helpless frustration was coming through clearly over the miles.

"I woke up and it sounded like someone was in the house. Maggie heard it, too. I took my Beretta and Maggie and I went into the bathroom and called nine-one-one. It may have all been a big mistake," Kira explained. She left out the details of seeing the door move and the broken door downstairs. She knew he would learn these things soon enough but she didn't want to stress him anymore with everything he had going on.

"I'm flying home," he said forcefully, as if he was making the decision right that second.

"You can't! What about your father's company? You have things to take care of in California. I'm fine. It will be fine," she answered quickly.

"The hell you will. You don't answer my calls. Now someone's trying to break in and kill you!" he yelled into the phone.

"First of all, no one tried to kill me. I handled myself just fine. If I'm lonely I guess I could always go hang out again at The Apex Club. And you can't be around every second to protect me. F.Y.I. next week when you're off fighting terrorists in the desert or the jungle I'll still be here, a Captain in the United States Army taking care of myself." She regretted the words as quickly as they escaped her mouth. The silence on the other end spoke volumes.

"The what?" he asked very quietly.

"I don't need you or anyone else to stay with me," she protested, angry at being treated like a little girl.

"What do you know about The Apex Club?" His voice was deadly cold.

Kira hesitated. "I don't want to get into this right now. We can talk later when you get back. You have enough on your plate right now."

"The hell I do. Tell me. Now." Kira recognized the dominant tone of voice. But it wasn't going to work this time.

"I know all about your fun little club. But don't you worry, I can handle myself," Kira spouted defiantly.

"I don't know what is going on there. I'm sending in my team to stay with you until we can revamp security on the house. Kira, promise me you will stay away from that club."

She had no intention of playing hostess to tattoo queens or a frat pack of soldiers. "I'm not your child. Hell, I don't even know if I'm your girlfriend," Kira blurted. "What I should do is just go back to my apartment where I actually live." What she wanted was to get a good night sleep. What was left of it, anyway. She had a long day of clinic tomorrow and then trauma call in the ER. Dealing with this emotional nightmare was not helping things any. She just needed to focus on salvaging her career at this point.

"You are staying right there. If I have to fly home and keep you safe then so be it. I love you, Kira. God damn it. You are staying there and they are coming to help you," Stark ordered. "End of discussion." He hung up before she could complain.

Kira sighed in aggravation and put on the sweats. *Damn it to hell!* She made her way downstairs to find the officers enjoying coffee and taking statements from Zoe and Paige. She rolled her eyes and went to join them. *Might as well have coffee. Doesn't look like I'll be going back to sleep any time soon.*

Kira was halfway through her statement with the younger officer when Stark's crew showed up. They were dressed in battle gear, each carrying enough munitions to take out a small country. She was surprised that the officers didn't react with alarm or even bravado at having the team intrude on their turf. Quite the opposite—it seemed as if the older, stocky police officer knew Stark's team well. She wondered if he had previously been a part of them or if he was just a big fan. She saw them nodding toward her and Paige and overheard Sergeant Colin tell the officer, "Oh no, not that one. She's off limits." Then winking at Paige. "And this one has no limits." He finished with a chuckle. Paige grinned approvingly. Kira rolled her eyes again. She could only imagine what the officer must be thinking with all these women in one house. She looked at Paige and Zoe. They had clearly been at the club, their usual rockabilly style amplified with a Lady Gaga twist this evening. Zoe walked around to each soldier serving coffee. She wore a small black satin hat with a large silk flower and a tiny fishnet veil. It contrasted drastically with her bright red hair. Her curled locks cascaded down her shoulders and bounced, along with some of her other parts, with each perky step. The black-and-white polka dot strapless top of her dress barely contained her more than ample chest. A tiny red bow on the top left hem had to be about where her nipple was stuffed into the dress. Kira almost giggled watching the men stare at it as they got their coffee. The large red bow at her waist accentuated her curves. Though she really did look like a pin up girl from the '50s, Kira wondered how those proportions were physically possible. She bent over balancing on a pair of Mary Jane-style stilettos. All the men bent in unison following her movements.

"Welcome to the dysfunctional family!" Paige said to Kira as she walked up behind her.

"How are you all so wide awake?" Kira asked still groggy and grumpy. Now that the adrenaline was wearing off she just wanted to go back to bed. "Are you all really planning to stay here?"

"You're part of the family now, kiddo. Whether you want to be or not. Owen picked you so you're in," she said, patting Kira on the shoulder. "Course that doesn't mean I'm going to be any easier on you, Vanilla." She smiled and started to go back into the kitchen. Kira watched her walk away. The tattooed beauty was barely covered in a halter top and sailor shorts. Her shapely legs and delicate ankles were covered with artwork. Despite the unnaturally tall shoes, she walked with grace. Kira realized that the police would have no interest in who she was. No desire to pry and find out she was a captain. She started to relax a little until she noticed the state of the living room.

"What the hell is all this?" Kira demanded as they set up a mock command post in the room. "Ok guys, this is a bit much. We're not exactly under siege here. You're taking this way too far."

"Stark gave strict orders. Secure the premises and upgrade the security system," Sergeant Colin answered mockingly. His smirk was telling and only infuriated Kira.

"You have got to be joking! He's not your commanding officer and I'm sure you don't have permission to take all this from the base."

"This is personal gear, ma'am. Just a friend helping a friend out," a soldier named Chip said, flashing an award-winning smile at Kira. She let out a long sigh. There was no getting around this crew. These guys stuck together like their very lives depended on it. Sometimes their lives did depend on sticking together, she realized, and cut him a little slack.

Kira finished her statement with the police. A thorough search of the house showed nothing missing. Nothing was out of place except for the broken window and the small wooden table beside the couch. It appeared that the intruder had tripped over it in his escape, knocking it over and falling on the remote, turning on the TV. She had to admit that was more unnerving than if they had stolen some of the valuables on the first level. They had completely ignored his office with papers and cash on his desk. Whomever it was had been looking for something. Kira had a sinking feeling that something was her. *This is crazy! I won't give in to paranoia. No one is after me. This was just a robbery interrupted.*

Sergeant Colin came up and put his hand on her shoulder after the police left. "Try to relax, ok? I know you've had a rough week. We're here. The security system is being revamped and when it's done, we'll be out of your hair. I think Paige and Zoe are sticking around, though, so you won't be by yourself."

"Thanks. I hate you guys having to go to all this trouble. It's a lot to do at three in the morning," Kira said, shaking her head and feeling like a baby. The truth was she was glad they were there. The idea that someone was looking for her brought back so many memories and fears. She was too afraid to voice them to anyone, even Paige.

"It's no problem. Stark would drop everything for us if we needed him. That's what brothers do. We would go to the ends of the earth to watch out for each other. We want to be sure you're ready. " He smiled reassuringly and got back to work.

The guys finished around five thirty. Pretty fast work considering they redid the entire system as well as installed cameras and infrared motion detectors in every part of the house. They put double and triple fail-safe mechanisms so that if someone did try to deactivate the system, it would immediately notify Stark, the police, the team, and Kira. They packed up their gear and told her to call if she had any trouble.

The house seemed quiet after they left. Zoe had settled on to the couch with Mags and was watching an old Lauren Bacall movie. Paige was cleaning up the kitchen and had changed into a velour lounge suit. Kira realized she hadn't even been in some of the downstairs guest rooms. For all she knew, Paige had a room and clothes here. The thought both aggravated and strangely comforted her. It was nice at times not to be alone, especially with Stark gone so much. However, there were so many things she had to accept to be with him: the plethora of beautiful exes, the Apex Club, and his lifelong dedication to the army.

"Well, I guess it's about time for me to get ready for work," she said sleepily. The hours of missed sleep were going to make trauma call tonight brutal. She started to head upstairs and Paige called after her.

"Kira," Paige said in a lower, confidential voice. Kira walked back into the kitchen. "Did you talk to Stark?"

"Sort of. I told him I know about the club. I just . . . I left out the rest. God, Paige why did you even take me there?" Kira wished she had wine instead of coffee.

"I wasn't trying to hurt you," Paige explained. "I wanted you to have fun. To let go a little. You are so damn uptight! You have to believe I never meant for him to be on those screens. Those films aren't even part of the ones we play there. They were from my private collection. Seriously, Kira I'm not sure what happened. I took you there because I wanted you to see the club. I wanted . . . I don't know . . . for you to know who we really are. I had this whole routine planned. I thought in the end you would like it."

"Like it? I find out my boyfriend is part of some deranged sex ring and I am supposed to like it?"

"We aren't deranged and for your information, Owen hasn't been there since he met you. You have changed him somehow. I guess . . ." Paige looked at the floor.

"You thought if I joined the club he would come back," Kira said, finally understanding.

"I never dreamed it would turn out like it did. Lysander has been questioning everyone to see who got into the control room. I am really sorry. It was probably Lila or one of her bitch friends." Paige sneered. She leaned over and put her hand on

Kira's shoulder. "I am really sorry. And I'm not even going to kick your ass for stealing my car."

"Gee, thanks. I'm sure spending the night in jail more than makes up for it. You sure have some friends in high places. When that MP officer picked me up at the jail I almost peed my pants," Kira admitted.

"Ha! I would have liked to have seen that! Man, she is one tough bitch! Love me some Adelisa. You're lucky she was really on duty or she wouldn't have just dropped you off here," Paige teased with a twinkle in her eye. "She might have had some fun with you first."

Kira shuddered and realized she had dodged a bullet. "I really thought we were going to meet the major and my commanding officer. Paige, I would have died!"

"We had to get you out of there. I felt so bad for you. Your little buddy Holt called us in a panic. He said he drove by and saw you getting arrested. He brought me the keys. He was as worried about you as Ly and I were. Ly knows everyone. He pulled a few strings and arranged for your release." Paige looked up and smiled confidently like a poker player who knows they hold all the cards.

"Who is Lysander anyway? He's very different. Almost, um, magical. How did you meet?"

"Hmmmm. Oh, my darling, that is a sordid story for another day," Paige said. She paused and looked out the window. A beautiful smile spread across lush lips. "The story of Lysander. Mmmmmm, oh dear, and the turning of Paige . . ."

Kira could see Paige was lost in her own thoughts. "That's a story I would make time for," Kira said eagerly.

"Another day, dear, I promise. We would need a whole night and several bottles of wine for that one. Aren't you supposed to be on base in about fifteen minutes?"

"Shit! I'd better get ready for work. Listen, I'm not going to bother Stark with this. He's got so much going on right now. I just can't. He's dealing with his dad's funeral and the business. It's killing me that I can't be there for him. Simone would just love to sink her teeth into this."

"Oooh, she is the devil in Prada!" Paige hissed at the mention of Simone. "I'd like to get my hands on that scheming tramp. I don't know what he ever saw in her." Paige huffed around the kitchen putting mugs away with more force than necessary. "She'll do anything to get him back to California. And don't for a second think it's because she loves him. Oh no! That one's all about the money."

Kira found Paige's dislike of Simone amusing. That's one thing they had in common. What was Simone up to? Kira knew that with his father's passing, the company would go to

437

him. He had made it very clear that he had no intentions of moving back and taking over the family business. While she couldn't bear the thought of him leaving and moving back to California, if he didn't reenlist at the end of his term then fraternization wouldn't be a problem. She hated herself for even thinking it. She could care less about the money, she wanted him. Selfishly, she wanted him with her, not in California and not in the army. But she saw how he was with his guys, how they would do anything for each other. She knew that if he left he would leave part of himself.

Kira was tired and overwhelmed. She left Paige in the kitchen and went up to shower and get dressed. Her heart ached for Owen. Once in the shower she could finally let all the fear and tension fly. She leaned against the cold tile and let go. Hot water streamed down and washed the tears away. She struggled with a mix of her own fear and frustration and deep sadness for Owen and what he must be going through. Despite being mad as hell, she wanted to be there for him. She hated that he was with Simone. The conniving minx would be all over him, using this time to sink her fake nails and perfect teeth into him. No matter how badly she wanted Owen to herself, no matter how much she loved him, she knew that very soon he would have to make a choice. As much as it hurt, she knew she wanted him to choose what was right for him. Suddenly she knew what she had to do.

Chapter 23

Kira's plane touched down a in a sea of fog. She shook her head. Wasn't California supposed to be sunny all the time? The sense of urgency to get to Owen was overwhelming as she waited for the captain's instructions to exit the plane. She still couldn't believe she had pulled it off. She had to forfeit most of her meager savings just for the round-trip ticket, but at least she was here. Getting permission for emergency leave had been tricky, but Abbey had proved a miracle worker as usual. She seemed to know everything about everything with the military. She just wanted to be there for him, give him comfort. Stand by his side while he faced this. She kicked herself for being so selfish before and missing the funeral. Three weeks had passed since Stark left for California. In the last week since her incarceration she had barely spoken to him. At first she had been furious about his involvement at the club and embarrassed by her night in jail. Ever since the break-in, Kira just wanted to see him. Hold him.

She silently cursed the airplane staff for being so slow. Finally the announcement came on. She stood and grabbed her small overnight bag from the overhead bin. Kira stood in the slowest moving line on the planet and made her way off the plane. Once in the airport she switched her phone on. Fifteen messages blinked at her. *Ugh.* Twelve From Stark, one from

Paige and two from Abbey. Kira imagined that Stark would be unleashing a posse to hunt her down if she didn't answer soon. She decided to listen to the messages later. For now she just needed to get there. She made her way out of the airport and hailed a cab. Climbing in, she looked at the information she had printed from the Internet. She had to decide if she should try to find the house in Hillsborough or if she should head straight to the office in San Francisco. She opted for the office.

"Where to ma'am?" the laid back driver asked.

"Could you take me to fifty Freemont Street? I'm trying to meet a friend. I'm afraid I'm going to be late," Kira said, rushed and anxious.

"No worries. I'll get you there. You sure that's the right place?" he asked, looking her up and down.

Kira realized she probably looked more like the help, but she was in too much of a hurry to let him get to her. "Yup, that's the place. Could we hurry?"

"Sure thing. Hold on." His voice was soft and relaxed.

As they drove, the magnitude of what she was doing began to weigh on her. Perhaps the driver was right. Stark didn't invite her. She was just assuming he wanted her support. But what if he didn't? As they drove from San Francisco International Airport into the ritziest part of downtown, it became painfully evident that she didn't belong here. She stared out at the towering skyscrapers and exquisitely dressed people. This was like no place she had ever been. Kira's stomach twisted into knots. Her palms were sweaty as she clutched her meager overnight bag. Maybe he hadn't asked her to come for a reason. Maybe he never wanted her here after all. She was a part of his other life, not this one. She kept hearing Simone's silky voice calling her trash and the help. *Holy Shit! What was I thinking? I spent all my savings on that stupid plane ticket. It probably isn't a fraction of what Simone will be wearing.* Kira suddenly had the thought that Stark might be embarrassed by her. Surely he wouldn't want to introduce her to these people. The taxi stopped all too soon.

"This is it," said the taxi driver. As he turned, Kira slid down in the back seat. She suddenly felt very small and out of place. "Are you getting out?" he asked after what seemed like a very long time with the meter still running. "I mean it's your dime, lady, we can sit here all day if you want."

"No, no. I, uh. ok. Thank you." Kira slowly paid the driver and slid out of her seat. The moment the taxi drove away, she wished she could call after him. *This has to be your worst idea ever!* She looked up at the massive forty-one-story skyscraper. This was no small family office. 50 Freemont Center was a vivacious and lively spot. Despite being located on a beautiful and busy street, the elegant building stood out. Its breathtaking art deco design made it a timeless classic. People dressed in luxurious business suits walked in and out of the large glass entryways. Kira felt suddenly very small and out of place. The fog gave way to a gentle rain. *So much for sunny California.*

She was about to turn and walk away when a group of limos rounded the corner. She stepped back out of the way and watched them pass. The rain was starting to soak Kira. She realized that she would have to call Stark to find out where to go. She reached for her phone and started to dial when the first limo slammed on its breaks and came to an abrupt stop. The screeching tires startled Kira and she looked up.

Stark half climbed, half stumbled out of the stretched vehicle in his haste. He stood in his crisp black suit, not moving for a moment, as if he couldn't believe what he was seeing. The light breeze played with his dark hair. Kira stood frozen, unsure if he would be happy to see her or not. Stark started walking toward her, then broke into a run, closing the distance between them in seconds. He scooped her up and held her to him spinning from the force.

"What the hell are you doing here? How did you–" His words broke off as he held her tightly. "I don't know how you knew I needed you so much today." He stood holding her off the ground rocking her back and forth. "I still can't believe you are really here."

"I didn't want you to have to face this alone. You said we could do anything together. I'm sorry it took me so long to remember that." Kira hugged him back. The smell of his cologne permeated her nose and sent tingles all over her.

"Well, it's a good thing he's not alone then," Simone hissed. It took her a bit longer to cross the concrete in her stilettos. Her black Alexander McQueen suit flowed elegantly despite the rain.

Kira suddenly felt like she was on a movie set. *How the hell do these people look so perfect?*

"Let's get in out of the rain, shall we?" Simone said as she walked right past them and under the awning of the building. "So nice to see you again, *Captain*." She started to enter the building as the doorman held the door wide for her, then stopped and turned back to Kira. "You should have called, dear, we could have picked you up. Oh, that reminds me. Owen, sweetheart, you left your phone in the bed this morning. I almost bruised myself rolling over on it. You really should be more careful." She smiled sweetly up at Stark and took the phone out of her purse, handing it over.

Kira's blood ran cold. She stiffened, every hair on her neck instantly bristling.

"Shit, Simone. Do you always have to be such a bitch? Can we please just get through this?" Stark's voice was dark and tense. He wrapped his arm through Kira's and started to lead her into the building.

Kira's legs were like Jell-O. She couldn't step or follow. Were they sleeping together? Or was Simone just yanking her chain? Fuck!

Stark stopped and looked her in the eyes. "Don't listen to her, Kira," he pleaded. "She is just being a bitch. I am so glad you are here. Please. Please come inside with me. I need you. You are my one shining light to get through this." The desperation in his voice penetrated all her anxiety and defenses. Kira squeezed tightly to his arm and followed him through the glass doors. He led her across a great marble lobby to a bank of immaculate elevators on the opposite wall.

Simone was right in front of them as they stepped in. "You made it in time for the reading of the will," she said icily. "That's convenient." Simone glared at her through the glass in the elevator mirror. She looked Kira over and wrinkled her nose.

Kira looked back at Simone's perfect blond hair parted on the side and pinned back into a braided bun. Her flawless skin glowed, even in the lights of the elevator. The dress suit she wore looked like it had come directly from a runway in Paris. Kira looked at her own reflection. Dark wet waves clung to her face. Her modest navy dress fit well but had faded since she bought it in med school. Her eyes dropped to the floor. *The will?*

Kira had no idea that was happening today. Stark hadn't said anything about it. She looked up at him puzzled. "I didn't know. I could wait in the lobby if you would like," Kira offered to Stark.

Stark squeezed her hand and tucked her arm in his own. "Are you kidding? What for?" he said. "You just got here and I need someone in there on my side. You are staying with me." He pulled her a little closer. Simone's nose wrinkled even further. She looked as if she had just tasted buttermilk for the first time.

The elevator was smooth and moved quickly to the 22nd floor. "It's convenient to have your lawyers in your own building," Stark said giving a wink as the doors opened. They stepped out into the lobby of the law office. Kira was instantly taken by the rich wood grain floors. She looked up at the white semi-circular reception desk. It was narrower at the bottom than the work surface and reminded Kira of the deck of the Star Ship Enterprise. The modern space looked like it was designed for function and class in equal measure. To the right of the desk was a group of plush gray chairs connected by small glass tables. Each table held a short chrome vase with white flowers. Panels of frosted glass made up the wall behind the reception desk. Many of the panels had been turned to perpendicular, creating doorways open to a large conference room on the other side. The stunning receptionist looked up and immediately flushed crimson when she saw Owen Stark.

"Mr. Stark," she said as she stood quickly, never taking her eyes off of him. "You're . . . um, the boardroom is ready for you, sir." She panted as if out of breath.

Kira looked at her amused. She was getting used to the effect he had on women. At first it made her nervous. Now it was more of a curiosity. After learning what she had about The Apex Club, she looked at all these women in a different light. She wondered about Simone. Did she know about the club?

They were escorted to slate leather chairs around the large conference table. "Would you like something to drink, sir, before Mr. Howard comes in?" the receptionist asked, batting her eyes at Stark.

"I'm fine. Kira would you like anything?" He turned toward her. Kira could feel his deep eyes burning into her. She certainly couldn't blame the woman. Kira felt a familiar stirring. Getting lost in those eyes must be similar to using heroine.

"No, thank you," Kira managed to say.

"I would like a glass of water with lemon," Simone interjected.

"Owen, my boy! It's very good to see you." The warm voice belonged to a handsome man in his early fifties. The touches of salt and pepper in his hair were distinguishing.

Owen shook the man's hand before turning towards Kira. "Greg Howard, this is my girlfriend, Kira Riley. She flew out from Colorado just this morning. Kira, this is our family lawyer, Greg Howard."

"How do you do, Kira?" Mr. Howard smiled warmly and shook her hand.

"Well, thank you, Mr. Howard," Kira responded politely.

"Just call me Greg."

"Isn't that nice she came all the way out for the will," Simone chimed in.

"Simone. Watch it," Stark warned.

"Is Rosalea here yet?" Greg asked looking around the room.

"What's that little taco eater doing here?" Simone's eyes flashed with anger. She looked like a cat being backed into a corner.

"She's in the will, Simone. She has to be here before we can begin," Greg said calmly. His smooth voice was reassuring.

The elevator doors opened and a small, middle-aged Hispanic woman exited into the lobby.

Stark jumped up and walked over to her. He hugged the woman and walked with her into the conference room. "Rosalea, this is Kira!" he announced proudly.

"Is this her? *Mi amour*! Oh Owen, she's lovely. When did you get in? My, you're thin. Have you eaten?" The Hispanic woman pulled her close and kissed each cheek. Stark smiled his half grin and took the seat beside Kira.

Owen beamed, proud and happy to have her by his side. "Kira, this is Rosalea. She has been caring for me all my life."

It was odd to see Owen Stark in the context of a little boy. But she could see to this woman he would always be her sweet baby.

Rosalea hugged Kira. As she took the seat beside her, she glared at Simone.

"I knew you would be a hit with the help," said Simone. "It's really best to stick with your own kind. Don't you think, dear?" Her tone was smug. The words spilled over Kira as if someone had cracked an egg on her head. Heat rose in Kira's cheeks in a mix of embarrassment and fury.

"You could always wait in the lobby," Stark said sternly to Simone. He grabbed Kira's hand.

Simone sat back in the seat mildly defeated for the moment. Kira looked back and forth from Owen to Simone.

They must have made a beautiful couple. Kira struggled to see where she fit in his world. Still Stark held firmly to her hand. He looked strained and tired. Her heart ached for him. She knew from experience that what he was going through was immeasurably hard. If nothing else, he needed her and she would be here for him.

The long conference table was empty save for their four seats at one end. Greg pushed a button and the frosted panels closed. Kira felt so sad for Owen. Simone and Rosalea were the only other family he had. The lawyer began reading the will. His father left the majority of his money to Simone. A house in Malibu and enough to keep her for some time went to Rosalea. He left instructions for his vehicles to Owen as well as the Aspen house. The will expressed some wishes for a few things that were Owen's mother's.

"That's it?" Simone shrieked. "What about the house in Hillsborough? What about the company? What about the rest of the money?"

"Those were never his to leave to anyone," the lawyer said calmly. Owen's father was merely the caretaker. The company, the money, the house in Hillsborough—all belonged to Owen's mother. When she passed, it went to Owen."

"What the fuck are you saying?" Simone was coming unglued. "I have helped build this company into the empire it is today. This is my company!"

"No, it's Owen's company. But you are right about one thing. You have been the face of the company for the last couple of years. Owen, they are going to need to see you as a strong player or you are going to need to establish a competent CEO immediately," Greg Howard directed. "Owen, you and Simone will have to work together to get this figured out. I realize it is a lot to step into, but it looks like you may need to be here for a while."

Simone's usually flawless face was wrinkled as if she was sucking on a lemon. Her eyes shot daggers at Stark. Kira turned to Owen and searched his face for some clue as to how he felt about all this. Was he surprised by what Mr. Howard was saying? What did he think about working with Simone and having to stay in California? The chiseled lines of his face gave nothing away. Simone fidgeted nervously but he remained completely calm.

They wrapped up the paperwork and Kira followed Owen to the elevators. Once they were alone he dropped his guard, he pressed the thumb and fingers of one hand against his temples and shook his head. Kira suspected he knew about the money already, but having to take control of the company was something he had actively avoided for years. She could also see he wasn't about to roll over for Simone either. She understood what he meant by someone being on his side. They rode back down without speaking. He squeezed her hand as the doors opened. Game on.

Simone's voice broke the silence like nails on a chalkboard. "Owen don't forget, we have a reception at the house tonight. Everyone is going to be there. Whether you are excited about this company or not, it's what provides your cushy lifestyle while you play G.I. Joe."

Stark cringed and turned. "What the hell are you talking about? I'm not going to some pretentious prom."

"Owen, darling, you're not going to go all sob story like you did with your mom, are you?" Simone continued. "Listen, you are now the owner of one of the biggest communications companies in the world. So put your big boy pants on and let's go. Your father held off for you as long as he could and now he's gone. We tried to get you to come home and protect what your family spent generations building." Her usually silky voice was firm and commanding. "Important clients, investors, and high level employees are gathering back at the house to pay their respects. They are looking to you to lead this company. You have avoided your responsibilities for long enough. Even if you have no intentions of running this company, you have to give the appearance of being in control until you appoint an appropriate surrogate." She turned her icy stare toward Kira. "Bring your little muse if you must. Although I'm sure she doesn't have anything appropriate in that little bag. Maybe she could wait in the kitchen."

Kira ignored the venom Simone spewed. She was content to stand with Owen as long as he needed. Stark stiffened and new resolve came over his face. She had seen that look before, of steel determination that soldiers have going into battle. His shoulders squared, his jaw set in a firm line; he turned and walked with Kira through the lobby to the waiting limo. He opened the door for Kira and escorted her in with Rosalea. He leaned in after her but didn't get in. "Rosalea, can you take Kira down to Herve Leger and get her anything she wants? Kira please don't take this the wrong way. You are beautiful in anything. These people don't know how to see that. But I do." He stood up and motioned the limo on.

"Wait, where are you going?" Kira called after him. But it was too late. As the limo pulled away she watched him take Simone's arm somewhat forcefully and walk back with her into the building. Kira felt sick. She couldn't help but notice the satisfied smile plastered on Simone's face.

"*Hijo de puta!*" Rosalea muttered under her breath and then in a soft voice, "I'm sorry, honey. She has always been that way. I know that doesn't make it any better." Rosalea reached out to comfort Kira.

452

"For a moment I really believed he didn't care about all this," Kira confided. "But I will never fit in here. I'm not a part of this world. Maybe it would be better if I wasn't here tonight. " Kira was not about to sob in a limo with a perfect stranger.

"Don't leave," Rosalea persuaded. "He needs you right now. Please come with me. Let's get you all Cinderella-like and show that fake bitch what a real lady looks like." Stark's oldest caretaker gave instructions to the driver and they veered onto the highway.

The next three hours were a whirlwind of dresses, hair, and makeup. First, Kira was whisked into Herve Leger, a gorgeous shop on Powell Street. Kira didn't even want to think about what things in this store cost. "There is no way I can afford anything in here," she protested as Rosalea ushered her in and spoke to the manager. Kira marveled at how strange this town was. Had she not been getting ready for a funeral reception, the whole pretty woman parade might have actually been fun. But this was ludicrous. She flew all the way to California to be with Owen, not be poked and prodded by designers and makeup artists. After an hour of trying on various dresses and gowns they decided on an elegant smoke-colored gown that framed her shape and made her eyes stand out like stars. Kira could hardly believe herself. She never gave much thought to her own figure, but the soft fabric accentuated her curves as it cascaded down her slender body. The scooped neckline and high waist enhanced her bust considerably and the satin fabric melted over her round ass. The length was such that her muscular calves and Gianvito Rossi black heels were showcased perfectly.

"*Aye de puta madre!*" Rosalea exclaimed a little too loud when she saw Kira. "*Oh sí!* Miss Simone is going to have a fit when she sees you!" The glee in Rosalea's voice matched the twinkle in her eyes. "Let's go, ok? We have one more stop."

They stopped outside J. Roland Salon and Rosalea ushered Kira out. "Lets go. *Vamanos.* They are waiting for you. The longer we spend away, the more time that minx has to work on my Owen!"

The salon, like the boutique, was chic and bright. Kira noted the subtle hues contrasted with rich wood tones. Every fixture was modern and sleek. An attractive olive-skinned man with dark hair approached her keenly. "So this is our little project? Hmmm, we have our work cut out for us, don't we?" he said, as he spun Kira around and looked her over. "Darling, my name is Eevan, I'm going to change your life." He marched a speechless Kira over to an immaculate chrome and black leather chair and whipped a drape around her with the pizzazz of a bullfighter.

Kira would have enjoyed the attention, but her mind was elsewhere. *Work on Owen?* What the hell did Rosalea mean? Kira worried and mulled the question over while she was washed and tousled, cut and styled. She wondered what had been going on here for the last three weeks. She knew Stark and Simone had considerable history but there was more to them than that. In some ways, they were like an old married couple that had drifted apart but stayed connected by their children. There were no kids that Kira knew of. Surely Simone's vanity wouldn't allow her to mar herself with childbirth. The company was like their child. If Stark owned the company, why not just fire her evil ass and be done with her? But Kira knew he would never do that. Maybe Simone still meant something to Owen after all this time. Maybe he didn't want to let her go. The thought made Kira sick. She thought of the college boy in his Ivy League school, the rugged military sergeant with his bisexual housemate, and now this business mogul with a platinum blonde by his side. Kira's head was spinning. Each facet of his life was more complex than the one before. The only common thread was that she didn't fit into any of them. Were she and Sergeant Stark just kidding themselves? Kira wondered why he was even attracted to her at all. He was literally surrounded by women far out of her league. Maybe Simone was right. Maybe she was just a fling or a phase. The words "plain vanilla" seemed painfully evident.

"*Magnifique!*" The flamboyant stylist proclaimed, whirling her around to stare at the beautiful stranger in the mirror.

"Ho-ly. Shit," Kira said slowly. She did not recognize the woman before her with subtle, exquisite makeup and long, boho waves of chocolate hair cascading effortlessly down her shoulders. "Wow. I'm not sure how you did this but you, sir, are a miracle worker. Thank you so, so much."

"That's it girl. You are my masterpiece," the stylist effused. "And I would do anything for that hunk of man. Now off you go." He shooed Kira in Rosalea's direction dramatically.

Kira was a mixture of intense emotions: extreme sadness for Owen and his loss, fear and trepidation of this environment and of Simone, and excitement to see Owen, to be with him. She struggled with conflicting thoughts as they drove, not paying attention to her surroundings until the limo slowed and paused on a brick street in front of a massive iron gate. Though the sun was just setting she could see tall rectangular pillars on either side that displayed impressive stonework. Each was topped with a stone statue of an eagle perched on a sphere. An ornate lantern attached to each pillar set off a golden glow. Just beyond the gate, Kira could see an octagonal guardhouse with the same stunning stone work and beautiful windows. "Wow," Kira breathed.

Rosalea laughed as the gates opened and they began pulling onto the long brick driveway. She looked at Kira with a smile and in her thick Spanish accent said, "Honey, this is just the entrance. Wait till you see the actual estate. We are going to park and I will take you in the back way so you can go up and change. I will set you up in a guest room upstairs."

Kira only half heard what the woman said. She was glued to the windows and the magnificent and beautiful world unfolding around her. It was like stepping back in time. The lush grounds were exquisitely manicured with shrubs and stone statues. The house, if you could call it that, was an English Tudor-style mansion. It was more like a castle, and it was large enough to stretch a couple of city blocks. It looked more like a museum or something you would see on a European hillside. Kira stared open-mouthed at the stories of stunning masonry, the delicate arches and turrets that offset magnificent chimneys at the roofline. Ivy grew up the walls and around the lovely two-story stone turret. Light shone brightly through the twelve windows circling the tower. It was the single most impressive thing Kira had ever seen. They didn't stop in front of the house but instead circled around to a large side parking area. It was in front of a series of stone and brick garages that were made to look like carriage houses. The limo stopped and the two women climbed out.

"We will go this way so you have time to change before he sees you," Rosalea said conspiratorially. Her smile was bright. Despite the sadness of the day Kira was excited to see Owen.

Kira could not believe her eyes. There was a racquetball court with gleaming wood floors. Next, they passed an indoor Olympic sized pool. Kira paused and stared for a moment, wishing she had time to swim. Archways spanned over the pool every five feet. A large stained glass window at the other end of the room cast a beautiful light over the water. "*Vamanos* girl! We don't have much time," Rosalea urged.

Rosalea led Kira through an impressive kitchen that reminded Kira of something from Iron Chef. She wondered why it wasn't warm and inviting like a family kitchen but then, she thought, if you live in a house like this you probably don't cook your own food. The space bustled with chefs and culinary staff working into a frenzy preparing food for the mass of people gathering in the main rooms of the mansion. She stayed close behind Rosalea through the stainless steel maze and into a service hallway and up a back stairway.

***

Owen stood next to Simone in a receiving line as major players in the communications industry and the global community made rounds and offered their condolences. Some he hadn't seen in years, some were perfect strangers. But they all knew his father. They all wanted a piece of the action, to be involved in some way with the company his grandfather had built. Stark knew his father had been a brilliant businessman, taking the company to new heights. But the pursuit of business,

458

power, and pleasure had taken over all Bryson Stark once was. The loving man he knew as a child had grown cold and greedy. His father's generous spirit had become self-indulging in his later years. Stark painfully remembered finally coming home after his first deployment to find his father in bed with . . .

A sudden movement on the stairs at the other side of the great room caught his eye. A hush seemed to fall over the room. All other thoughts ceased. Everyone, everything in the room dimmed and then faded away. The only movement that existed was her. She gracefully descended one step at a time. Stark stood frozen, mesmerized by her beauty. He had never seen her like this before. Despite her toughness and strength, she looked delicate. She flowed like a gentle brook down the stairs. The pale gray dress hugged her curves. Her thick chocolate tresses fell in silky waves and bounced with each step. She seemed to be scanning the large room searching for someone, and then her eyes found his. She paused. Time stood still. The only sound was the violent beating of his heart in his chest. When the air came back to his lungs he absent-mindedly pushed through the crowd around him and crossed the room in large strides. He reached the bottom of the steps and looked up, unable to move. The vision before him accumulated all his dreams and wishes, so real, so close. She met him at the bottom step and he took her hand and leaned in to kiss her.

"They are all staring at us," she whispered.

"Who is?" he asked, still looking only in her eyes.

"The room full of people you just pushed your way through," she said, a little bemused by his odd behavior.

"There is no one here but you and me. When you walk in the room, everything else disappears." He took her in his arms and kissed her and held her close for a moment. "Thank you for being here. Thank you for putting up with all of this. I don't know how I would get through this without you by my side." He took her by the hand and led her back across the room as the rest of the world came back into focus.

***

Kira was painfully aware of the stares and quiet whispers circling the room. Stark seemed completely unaware of it. Or maybe he just didn't care. He led Kira to the receiving line and held her hand tightly throughout the remainder of it. Kira could see Simone simmering beneath her cool exterior. Stark had placed Kira on the opposite side of where he stood, but she could see Simone looking around at her with a furrowed brow as she shook peoples' hands.

"So nice to see you," he said formally to a tall gray-haired gentleman as he firmly shook his hand with his free one. "Don, this is Dr. Kira Riley, my girlfriend. Kira, this is Don Crown. He has been one of my father's closest associates for years."

The older man was very distinguished and handsome. Smiling, he took Kira's free hand and kissed it. Kira blushed. "Very nice to meet you, Dr. Riley," he said in a voice that was smooth and enchanting. "Such a lovely girl, Owen. Your father would be very proud."

When Don Crown moved past them, Kira couldn't help but notice the look that he exchanged with Simone as they shook hands. The touch was familiar. Their eyes shared a deep understanding. Something about the exchange struck Kira as odd. Surely as an associate of Owen's father, he had known Simone a long time, too. Kira couldn't quite put her finger on it but something seemed off.

A tall waiter walked up and quietly spoke. "Mr. Stark, dinner is ready. Would you like us to announce for guests to make their way to the terrace?"

"That would be fine, thank you," he said casually as if servants and funeral galas were part of everyday life. He turned to Kira and held up her hand. "Would you join me for dinner Dr. Riley?"

"Yes, thank you." The formality was contagious. Kira almost giggled. She would have if they weren't at such a somber occasion.

"Owen, dear, I'm afraid we have a bit of a problem," Simone interjected as they made their way across the impressive marble floor. "You see, the seating at our table has already been arranged. So unfortunately there's not a place for your little unannounced guest. Perhaps she could sit at one of the open seating tables."

"What are you talking about, Simone?" He paused under the great mahogany archway. "Can't you just have them put an additional place setting beside me?" His brow furrowed in irritation.

"I would love to, dear, but it would throw off the whole table. There really isn't room. We have your father's closest friends as well as major investors all at our table."

"Fuck, Simone! Make room. That's the end of it," Owen directed. He started walking, towing Kira through the massive French doors onto the spacious stone terrace. Stark led her to a beautifully decorated table with cream linens, dainty floral centerpieces, and china place settings.

Urns of flowers were everywhere displaying explosions of color. The lush green grass of the lawn below was expertly cut in a chevron pattern. Kira could barely believe all this was real. Ornate stone statues of lions and maidens were strategically placed throughout the sprawling gardens. Sculpted shrubs and rose trees completed the landscape. The Elizabethan style of the home and grounds reminded her of something from Alice in

Wonderland. She fully expected the evil queen to show up at any moment and yell: "Off with her head!"

"See, Owen dear, there's not a bit of room to spare. She'll just have to sit somewhere else," Simone's shrill voice broke the peaceful silence.

Speak of the devil. Kira smiled genuinely and looked over at Owen. "I don't have to sit here. Really it's, ok. I'm just here to support you and if it makes it easier I can sit anywhere that works for you guys."

"Fine." Owen Stark had reached his limit. "So, there is really no room at this table?" he asked Simone.

"Exactly. I'm sorry, dear, it's just the way it is. Really, this is a family table," Simone said, her voice once again tinged with silk tones. She looked almost gleeful. Kira's heart sunk.

"You're right, Simone. Family only." He turned and motioned for the headwaiter, who rushed over. "I need you to make a place down at one of the garden tables, please, for Miss Simone. She will be moving down there since this table is really for family. Dr. Riley, my girlfriend, will be taking her place at this table. Thank you."

Simone looked horrified. All the color drained from her face. She stood frozen, her eyes shooting daggers at Owen and

Kira. "You wouldn't dare!" She shot back quietly as to not raise a scene.

"I would and I did. Now please go find your seat if you would like to eat at this dinner," Stark told her, his voice was cold and firm. The tone made Kira shiver. She watched as a smoldering Simone made her way down to the garden. Kira thought she could see steam radiating off her plastic veneer.

Dinner was served course by course by a host of waiters and waitresses. Kira waited at each course to see which utensils people used. She silently cursed herself for not paying attention during home-ec in middle school. *Who would have guessed I would ever need this?* She recalled thinking the class was very pretentious and a waste of time. Now she desperately tried to recall the rules of salad forks, pinkies here, and napkins there.

Owen spent time catching up with the various people at their table. They were eager to hear about his time in the service and his plans for the company. She noted that they talked to him as if the service was a thing in his past. Not his current life, not something he would be going back to. Stark didn't say or do anything to dissuade them one way or another. Kira couldn't imagine him leaving the military. Yet if he did, they could be together without consequence. Fraternization wouldn't apply if he were a civilian. They could live together without worry. Kira engaged in conversation with those around her. She learned about Stark as a little boy and a young man. A platinum woman in a stunning purple dress told her about the younger years she spent with Owen's parents. She and her husband had been friends with the Stark's for years. Kira could tell they all thought this army thing was an unfortunate phase. Boys will be boys, they seemed to think, and now he would be ready to step out of the military and into his father's shoes. Kira looked over at Owen. She noted the genuine way that he talked to each person at the table, sharing interests, bonding. She wondered if he was networking or really enjoying their company. Then it dawned on her. These people were all close friends and acquaintances of his father. The stories, laughs, and memories were all filling in missing pieces for Stark of who his father was. She realized he hadn't seen or spoken to him in a few years. In a way he was getting to know him all over again through these people and their remembrances.

Stark stole glances at Kira throughout dinner. He watched the gentle way she interacted with the table full of strangers. Despite their present surroundings the way he looked at her had her thinking he wanted to know what was under that dress. Each time she moved or leaned he tried to catch a peak. He started to imagine having her all to himself when everyone else was gone. He wondered how much longer this thing would last. Maybe the two of them could take off after dinner. Just disappear for a while. Though it seemed like dinner lasted forever, eventually they began to clear plates and they made their way to the entryway to say good bye.

Kira still couldn't get over the excess of Stark's family home. The entry hall gleamed with ornate panels of rich woodwork. Kira found herself mesmerized by the geometric patterns in the wooden panels. She couldn't decide if the carved cherub faces were beautiful or creepy, maybe a little of both. The goldenrod rug and matching tray ceiling gave the room a warm feel. She realized this one room was as big as her entire apartment. As Owen and Kira thanked everyone for coming, Simone resurfaced and squeezed her way between them. Kira grumbled inwardly. This platinum Barbie was just not going away.

As the last of the guests left, Simone turned and petted Stark's arm as she said, "Owen darling, this has been such a long and difficult day, I'm going up to get a bath. Join me in my sitting room in a little while, will you? We've got so much to discuss." Turning to Kira, she added, "if you're going to stay here, I'm sure Rosalea can fix up one of the guest rooms for you. Our room is pretty full." She kissed Stark on the cheek and went upstairs.

Kira stood speechless for a moment. "Wait. What the hell is she talking about?" she asked Stark. Once again Kira felt as if she was standing on the edge of a cliff, the whole world threatening to fall away. Her legs felt weak. "She lives here? You share a *room*?" She turned to Owen, tears brimming in her eyes. "What haven't you told me? What is going on here? I can

466

understand, barely, Paige walking around naked in your house. But Simone?" Kira realized she was pacing. Suddenly the entry hall felt very small. The walls were closing in on her. She felt her breath escape her.

Stark took her by the shoulders and shook her gently. "Kira. Listen to me," he said. "Simone has lived her for several years." He exhaled slowly and painfully. "She lived here with my dad." He dropped his head and shook it back and forth.

"So she took care of your dad?" Kira asked, trying to understand.

"Kira, when I came home from my first deployment, I came here," Stark explained. "I walked in to the life I used to know to find that my fiancée, was shacking up with my dad." His forehead wrinkled. His eyes shut in disgust. "Yes, she lives here, she has lived here in the master bedroom of this house for the last eight years. I have an apartment of my own in the house."

Kira was speechless. "Ok. So wait, Simone and your dad? Were they married? Is she, like, your wicked stepmother?" Kira hated herself for making light of such an awkward situation for Owen, but seriously.

"Fuck, Kira, not funny," Stark said rubbing his temples. "No, they weren't married."

"So just kick her ass out. End of story. Yellow brick road, the wicked witch is dead." Kira was giggling now. He had to see the humor in this. She wondered why Paige never said anything about this. Surely Paige knew.

"God, Kira. It's not that simple. Go ahead and laugh it up. You aren't all caught up in this shit."

"Well, since I just flew half way across the country to be with you, yeah, I kinda am," Kira said. She tried to reach out and touch his arm but he pulled away. "What is going on? Owen you have to tell me everything."

Before he could stop himself the words just slipped right out. "You mean like you told me everything?" His eyes squinted, his brows set for battle. "We all have skeletons in our closet, Kira. Things we wish weren't there, real or imagined."

"Wait. Now what?" *Has he been checking me out?* Years of humiliation after the case in college came rushing back with the contempt and pity in his eyes. "What are you talking about, Owen. Imagined? Is there something you want to say to me?"

"You should have told me about what happened with that guy in college, the court cases, the therapy. Hell, Kira, we never would have played like that if you had told me." His face softened with concern.

"You mean like you told me about your little sex club? Wonderful place there, Owen. It was so nice to see you on the big screens in the room with the bondage bed. You were part of some deranged orgy and you are judging me? You had no business digging into my past." Kira was seeing red. She suspected Simone was somehow a part of this.

"Not my business? Kira, I have a duty to protect all this. No, it's not my regular life but I have to take measures to ensure the longevity of what my family built. Simone is right. A lawsuit or a trumped up rape case could ruin everything my family worked for. We all make mistakes. I want to believe that you wouldn't do that on purpose. That you really believed it happened to you. But you should have talked to me about it. Trusted me enough to talk to me."

"So you had me checked out? What, you don't believe me, either? You. Don't. Believe. Me," Kira choked out between gasps. Kira's outstretched hand dropped limply to her side and she backed away. She turned and ran up to the guest room that Rosalea had fixed for her. She slammed the door, then locked it.

Kira leaned back against the door, panting and sobbing. Her whole world just crashed. She could hear Stark in the hall approaching at lightning speed. Then he stopped.

"Owen," Simone's voice interjected, smooth as silk. "Come on, darling, give her some time. Come into my sitting room. We've got so much to discuss before tomorrow."

Kira listened for him to approach her door. But he never came. She heard him walking away with her. Why was he so upset about Simone? What power did she have over him? Did he still love her? Kira made her way over to the massive four-poster bed. No amount of furnishings or tapestries could soften the loneliness of this moment. Kira collapsed on the bed in a heap of tears. That look on his face was one she had seen so many times before. The pity, the questioning. He was not really seeing her. Kira knew there was more to this story. If he really despised Simone as much as he let on, he could just get rid of her. But, no. No, she wasn't going anywhere. For Kira, it all started to make sense.

***

Simone and Stark made their way through the master suite into Simone's sitting area. "God damn it, Simone. What the fuck? What the hell have you done?" His voice was tense. His hands trembled with rage.

"Me, darling? You did that all by yourself. You are smart to just come out and talk to her about it. I mean can you imagine getting all caught up with a girl who made up a rape case in college to get back at her boyfriend? You've got enough to deal with without taking on all that baggage." Simone sat back on a chaise lounge in her black satin gown exposing long delicate legs and manicured toes.

"I don't know, Simone, she was pretty upset. I think she believes it really happened."

"Oh, great. So the little hill jack isn't just a gold digger, she's a psycho," Simone spat. She rolled her eyes and shook her head dramatically. "The last thing you need is to end up in court because the little bed wetter got her heart broken again."

Simone motioned for him to sit beside her. "You know the rules, Owen. Fraternization will end you both. What is she going to say if you guys get caught? Oh, he raped me. You've gone too far this time." Simone's slick voice was dripping with concern.

"I don't think she would do that, Simone. That was a long time ago. She really seems to believe it happened. Besides, we aren't going to get caught. We have been extremely careful."

"So no one knows your little secret, then?" The innocence in her eyes turned dark and calculating.

"Fuck, Simone, you wouldn't dare. Stop being a bitch," Stark said. He shook his head but he knew she was capable of anything.

"One call and I can end it for both of you. Is that what you want?" Simone sat back. A satisfied smile crept across her ruby red lips.

"I don't care anymore, Simone. Go for it." Stark was fuming.

"Really. You need to think about what you're doing. What do you think Kira's daddy dearest would say about his baby girl being dishonorably discharged? Well, I can say that will be a first. You will actually make a dishonorable woman out of her." Simone chuckled.

"What do you want, Simone?" Stark asked, his fist clenched. He had killed people for far less. Blackmail was so low, even for Simone. He actually thought she couldn't get any worse. He vowed silently to get her out of his life at all cost.

"You know what I want. Leave the army and marry me like you were always supposed to."

"Fuck no! You sort of derailed that when you fucked my dad."

"I wouldn't have had to resort to that if you hadn't gone all bat-shit G.I. Joe." Simone stood. She closed the gap between Stark and her. "Owen, while you ran away to the army, I followed our dreams. I stuck with school and got the degrees needed to run this company. I interned with your dad. All I ever wanted to do was stand side by side with you and lead this company into the next generation. Somewhere along the way you lost sight of our dreams, but I didn't. I have worked long and hard. Your dad and I fell in love. Do you think you were the only one who lost your mom and Maggie? Well, you weren't. We lost them too. And . . . and then we lost you." Tears brimmed in Simone's eyes. She turned away.

Despite how much he hated her sometimes, he knew what she was saying was true. He stepped forward and put his hand on her shoulder. Simone turned and looked up at him.

"Leave the army, Owen. Leave it and come back. Come back and be the leader you were always supposed to be. If not for me, then think of Kira." She looked up, her glistening eyes pleading. She leaned so close as she spoke. Their faces where almost touching.

***

Kira had started down the hallway in the direction of the heated voices. She was pissed. She wanted to confront Stark and that plastic bitch. How dare they look into her past. How dare they judge her. They weren't there. They had no idea what she went through. Being drugged, the rape, the shame and humiliation, all swirled back. Her heart raced and her chest heaved as she turned the corner to the sitting room. There was Owen and Simone in an embrace. *What the hell?*

473

Simone tilted her head and kissed Owen deeply. It seemed to linger forever. She stopped dead in her tracks and backed into the hall. *Oh my God! I need to get out of here!*

Stark pushed Simone away like one would a venomous snake. "Simone, I'm not leaving the army for you, or Kira, or anyone else. I've told you I am married to that first. That's not going to change!" His voice bellowed down the hall. "I don't know where Kira and I stand right now. But I am not leaving the military. Look, when my enlistment is up I am going to re-up. There is no question. No negotiation."

Kira froze in the hall. Stark's words cut her like a knife piercing deep into her soul. She felt a cold sweat break out all over. They continued to argue but Kira moved away numbly. She had heard all she needed to hear. Simone would always be in his life. He was never leaving the army, not for her or anyone else. He had a choice to make and he had already made it. Kira made her way back to her room and changed her clothes. She left the lovely smoky dress on the bed and left the room. She made it to the stairs before the tears overtook her. As she fled down the steps she heard Stark on the landing above her.

"Kira, wait! Where the hell are you going?" His voice was pitched higher in panic. He crossed the landing and descended the stairs in a run. "Stop. You can't leave."

"Why not Owen? Why not? You have made it clear I don't belong here in your platinum world. You inspected me for flaws. Congratulations. You found a whole closet full. I don't know why you even bother with Colorado. Clearly you're just as shallow and hollow as Simone and your dad ever were. I don't even know who you are. Yes, there is a part of me that wants to stand here and beg you. Love me. Be with me. Choose me. But the truth is, you already made a choice and it wasn't me." Kira turned and walked to the door. He started after her. "Don't follow me, Owen. I'm taking a cab back to the airport. You have a life here and you have a life back at base. The one thing they have in common is I don't fit in either one. I have been kidding myself. But not anymore." She opened the door and stepped out. Turning back she said, "Good-bye Owen," and shut the door.

Chapter 24

Stark sulked as he stood by the bar adding the empty shot glass to the upside down row. The smooth Irish whiskey did little to ease the bitter ache inside him. *How had this fucking happened?* He drummed his fingers on the empty glass. The question had plagued him for days. For the first time in ten years, his life had seemed so perfect. How had he let it all go to hell? Stark motioned for another glass across the noisy bar to the barkeep. The barkeep just shook his head and reached for a new bottle. Stark began to mull over the last few days. How could he have trusted Simone? He knew better than to listen to that conniving bitch! He thought of Kira's soft tear-streaked face as she left the house. He knew he would never see her again. It was really over. The thought was splitting his heart and mind into a million pieces. This was the right thing. He knew he was doing the right thing. He couldn't risk both their careers. He ran his fingers through his hair in an attempt to ease his aching head.

"You're going to drink them out of Jameson." Chip sighed, knowing it was useless to say anything. He had never seen his friend this wrecked over a girl. Sergeant Colin tried everything he could think of to cheer up his friend. They sat at the bar at Jack Quinn Pub. The Irish pub had always been one of their favorites. They came here for their hail and farewell parties.

He had hoped some good food and a pint of Guinness would help his friend, but Stark had gone straight for the whiskey. In the three hours they had been there Stark had disintegrated into the scouring drunk who sat beside him.

Chip ordered another pint. He realized this was going to be a very long night. The animated crowd moved with the lively music that filtered from the stage area. The tempo sped up, carrying with it the rising excitement of the patrons as the Commoners wailed out a round of "The Rattlin Bog." A tipsy blonde bumped into Stark as she made her way to sing along with the band. He was in no mood to even notice her. As the barkeep approached, Stark took the glass without saying a word. The bar lights shone down on him as he tipped the glass and engulfed the stringent liquid. He no longer felt a burn when it flowed down his throat. He couldn't feel anything. The crowd continued to row around him. The busty blonde was draped over the lead singer as they sang a soft melody. Chip seemed entranced with the swaying beauty but Stark had Kira on his mind. The music had changed to some Irish ballad that reminded him of her smile. He ached to see her again.

Just then the bar door opened and though for everyone else the world played on, for Stark it fell silent. It was her. He couldn't tear his eyes away. She walked in. The room began to spin. He watched her walk through the crowd in his direction. His heart began racing. Either she didn't see him through the sea of bodies or she ignored him completely. The white dress she wore hung perfectly over hips. It flowed with each graceful step. She walked to the other end of the bar and ordered a drink. She looked happy, beautiful. The little shit was with her as well as a few other officers. He watched helplessly as her delicate hand grasped the tonic and pulled it to her lush lips. Effortlessly she drank and laughed with her friends. The shit put his hand on her shoulder as they spoke. Stark could barely contain his fury and panic as he zeroed in on the little shit's fingers caressing the soft fabric of her dress. He knew he was staring but he didn't care. He couldn't look away. His tension was rising, causing a small sheen of sweat on his palms. A waiter approached them and began to guide her party to a booth.

He almost fell back into the large mahogany bar as they began walking toward him. She looked away as they passed but she was so close he could almost touch her. The scent of her perfume swirled around and transported him to another place. He could see her lying naked on his silver sheets. He was kissing her wildly. They were entwined together like two perfect circles. He'd dreamt that flawless moment would last forever. He could still taste the sweetness of her lips. He could feel the heat from her embrace. Memories flooded into his mind and he remembered that she was gone. He suddenly felt helpless and hopeless and desperate. The music rose to a high tempo and shook him back to the present. He frantically searched the bar for her. He caught a glimpse of her back at the door. *Holy hell, she's leaving!* She turned just for a moment and met his gaze. Their eyes locked. She stared directly into his soul before turning and disappearing through the door.

Stark stood motionless, his blood boiling, gripping the bar. Chip noticed his pale face and slapped him on the shoulder. "Hey, what's wrong?" he asked. "You look like you've seen a ghost."

But Stark barely heard him. The room was fully spinning now. All the music and people had faded into a muted haze. He bolted for the door, knocking over a stool in his drunken state, and ran out into the night. Panting with anger and fear, he ran into the parking lot. He had to see her. He just had to see her. He didn't care what anyone thought or said. He didn't care about fraternization, or the little shit, or Simone. At that moment for the first time in a decade he didn't care about the fucking army. He just had to see her, though he knew it would break him to.

***

Kira slumped into the seat of the car, still shaking. Holt got in slamming his door. "I don't know why Cody wanted to go there in the first place," he griped. He turned on the engine. "Are you ok? You look like you're going to be sick." Holt wrinkled his face as he spoke. She could tell he absolutely did not want her vomiting all over the interior of his BMW.

"I'm fine . . . really." Kira swallowed hard as she spoke. "I'm fine. I just drank too much at the last bar." Kira put her head in her hands to steady the spinning. She was anything but fine. *What the hell was he doing there?* Kira thought for sure he was still in California with Simone. She was so angry. She wanted to hate him. He was supposed to be thousands of miles away. But there he was. Tonight she passed by him so close she could have touched him.

"Look if you're going to throw up, say something, ok? Just give me time to pull over," Holt said. His words jolted her to the present. Kira wasn't making any promises. The mix of the alcohol and being so close to Stark had her near passing out or vomiting or both. She sat back in the leather seat, her heart racing a thousand miles faster than the speeding car. This was supposed to be an evening to cheer up. Get back into the real world. Holt and Cody had been begging her for days to go out and do something fun. This was in part due to her gloomy mood around the clinic for the last week. She had finally consented. She had been running insane distances and that didn't seem to be working. She'd agreed that maybe getting out and having some fun would help.

Kira had gone home after work and attempted to hide her despair with makeup and strappy heels. She chose a simple white sundress and went to check her reflection in the full-length mirror. *Ok, stress plus running equals unintended weight loss.* She frowned but decided it didn't look that bad for a casual night out. On the upside the shorter length showed off her calves, which didn't look too shabby in the three-inch heels. She rushed to grab her bag. As she did, she swept a pile of creepy notes into the garbage bin. She was too angry and tired of all this baloney to care about a stalker, real or imagined. After the events of the last week, she thought it was probably all Simone's doing, anyway. Just the thought of the plastic bitch Barbie made her furious. And Stark, the idiot, had gone with her. How he was naïve enough to believe the twisted snake she would never know.

"Hot damn, woman!" Cody exclaimed jolting her back to Holt's car in Jack Quinn's parking lot. "You look set to kill. I thought we were going out to have fun," he teased. She could see the look of pity on his face like one gets for a friend going through a hard time. She wondered what sort of story Holt had told him. "Come on, there are some really good places to let loose on Tejon Street."

Holt took his usual protective stance near Kira as they resumed bar hopping with a few other officers from the group. They stopped in a stuffy cigar bar, Holt's choice of course, and ordered a drink. After a while the stale atmosphere bored everyone but Holt to near tears and they decided to move on.

Kira was secretly thankful for the chance to calm down and get her nerves under control. Having seen Stark was driving her crazy.

Southside Johnny's was their next stop. Kira liked this place. She could hear the music pumping from the live band in back. Johnny's was a biker hangout but the bar was open to anyone and was a fun stop. Kira usually enjoyed people watching. The NUGs that went there and the preying cougars put on quite a show. But tonight Kira was barely keeping pace with the group. She couldn't shake the smug grin on Simone's face from her mind. Kira gripped her drink tightly and spilled a little on Holt. "Hey, watch it!" he scolded, looking at her disapprovingly.

Kira wondered if Holt ever relaxed and had fun or if somewhere in his self-righteous mind he was too good for that. She pictured him on the golf course wearing khaki pants and a polo sweater discussing the stock market and laughing at the little people. Her mind drifted back to Stark. He had been so close at Jack Quinn's she could still smell his cologne. She looked around the bar but he wasn't there. Cody was charming his way into the conversation of two very beautiful women. He glanced over at Kira and saw the forlorn look on her face. He left the two women gawking after him and strode over to Kira. Taking her hand, he pulled her off the bar stool toward the dance floor.

"Wait! Where are we going?" Kira asked as she stumbled along behind him.

He paused at the bar and ordered two shots. "Drink!" he ordered, handing one to her.

"Wait a minute." Holt appeared right behind them. "What the hell do you think you're doing?" He glared at Cody as he spoke.

"We brought her out here to have some fun," he replied before chugging his shot. "She looks like her puppy died. We need to liven things up."

"Kira, don't over do it with the alcohol. You and I both know . . ." Holt started, but Kira saw the patronizing look on his face and defiance took over. She swallowed the shot in one gulp and followed Cody to the dance floor. The liquid courage warmed her and Kira began to move to the music. She let the music flow through her. Arms and legs moving to the intoxicating beat, she let go. She released all the pain and hate and sadness she had been feeling over Stark. She felt herself flying free.

Cody picked her up and swirled her around. "Come on," he said laughing. "Let's move up the street to Rum Bay. You seem like a girl who needs to dance this night away." Cody grabbed her around the waist. After one more quick trip to the bar for a shot they were on their way up the road to Rum Bay.

Cody held her tight as they made their way up Tejon Street. The music drifted out from the various establishments they passed. Kira turned and saw Holt following closely behind, scowling as if Cody was overstepping his bounds. He quickly stepped out of the way when Cody twirled Kira to music flowing out of a lively bar they passed.

"This one looks fun," Kira said, laughing as he twirled her again and almost knocked Holt off the sidewalk.

"Oh no," said Cody. "Moves like that belong in a club. A dance club!" He clarified before she could say anything.

Kira could feel the thumping coming from Rum Bay as they got closer. The bouncer looked her up and down. He grinned and moved the ropes to let them in. As soon as they were through the door the beat was as intoxicating as the next shot Cody thrust into her hand.

She tipped it back, swallowing before Cody could even coax her. She grabbed his hand and made her way to the dance floor. She felt as if the pounding of the beat was moving through her veins, pumping life back into her dead soul. Eyes closed, arms above her head, she moved freely and with life. She let go of all else and danced. She dipped and moved in a sexy rhythm all her own as if no one was watching.

Stark burst through the door and staggered into the bar. Chip and Johnny followed closely behind. "This is gonna be bad," Chip said over his shoulder as Stark made his way like a steam roller through the sea of bodies to the dance floor. He froze when he saw her. There she was, sweat glistening from her body, wild chestnut hair clinging to her skin as she danced with total abandon. He knew that look. He painfully remembered the expression when she let go for him.

"Oh, hell no!" he shouted. Suddenly able to move again, he charged forward, moved Cody a few feet out of the way, and scooped up Kira in one swift motion. Johnny and Chip fanned out to contain Cody, Holt, and the other officers in their group.

"Whatsss the hell are you doing," Kira slurred, squealing over his shoulder. She struggled against him trying to push herself free but it was no use. He was so much bigger than her. It was useless anyway because she didn't want him to let her go. The intense heat and ferocity of his body electrified her. His dark curls felt soft against her face, the heady scent of whiskey mixed with his cologne smelled delicious. She instantly remembered the first night they spent together in the mountains. She fought to maintain some shred of dignity. "What the hell are you doing?" She repeated this time with more authority than she felt. "You wanted this remember? You made your choice and it wasn't me!" She was yelling now. She could give a fuck who heard her at this point.

Stark didn't answer. He just kept walking, carrying her through the kitchen area and into a back service hall that

485

connected the many clubs in the building. In the dark he set her down gently and then pinned her against the wall. He stood pressed up against her holding her arms above her head. In an instant his mouth came crashing down on hers. His kiss was needy and uncontrolled. It spoke volumes of the pain and wanton desperation he felt at losing her. "I was wrong," he began in a raspy voice before she could say anything. "I was wrong to let you go. You are my life, Kira, my soul, my everything. I was dead inside until I met you. You make me feel things I didn't know existed. You make me feel alive and it scares the hell out of me." He bent his forehead to hers. She could feel the dampness of his face on hers. In the darkness she couldn't tell if it was sweat or tears.

His mouth closed back around hers. The kiss was salty and laced with whiskey. Kira closed her eyes, drinking him in and returning his kiss. She longed to wrap her arms around him. No matter how mad she was she couldn't resist his touch. Powerful fingers held her and reverberated sex with each movement. She could feel the electricity between them pulling her from the darkness and back to life.

He let her hands go and slid one of his down to cup the back of her head pulling her up and closer to him. The other slid down her back. Stark inhaled sharply as if in pain as his fingers found the small of her back and the void in the soft fabric of her dress. The white sundress was open exposing most of her back.

"This dress is lethal!" He breathed heavily. "I'd like to wrap you up in my jacket and take you home! You are mine!"

Kira pulled away and looked up at him. She had to get a hold of herself. "You're not wearing a jacket. And you can't just go around like a dog marking your territory," she protested. She put her fingers up to Stark's lips before he could interrupt. "Before you say anything, peeing on my leg is out of the question," she added with a smirk. "Stark, I'm serious, nothing has changed. We can't be together any more today than we could a week ago. I love you. I do. It won't change but you know that's not enough. You said it yourself." As she heard the words coming out of her mouth, she felt her heart breaking all over again. She felt a knife ripping her soul in two but she held strong. She knew it was for the best. She hoped it was for the best.

***

Stark's eyes flew open wide. He felt as if ice water ran through his veins, draining every bit of life out of him. At first he struggled to speak, but after a moment he just pulled her to him tightly. "I can't let you go," he spoke, his voice small, a barely audible plea from a broken man. He knew she was right. The dim light in the hall from an aged bulb flickered and threatened to leave them in total darkness. He held her close to him for a tender moment. He thought about how you only miss the light when it's burning low. He realized how tragic it was that when he had finally come to love so deeply, he hadn't known just how much until he let her go. He dropped his arms to his sides, stepped back, and let her go.

Chapter 25

Stark sat on the bench in the team room of the Unit Building staring at a light blue box. It looked so tiny in his hands. He laughed, remembering how small Kira's hand looked in his the first time he held it. He closed his eyes and took a deep breath. He had just made the biggest decision of his life. Strangely he had no regrets. He thought that he would feel different, disappointed maybe, but he wasn't. He knew it was right and he felt free. For the first time in a very long time he would be free to be happy.

"What the hell, man?" Chip bellowed as he came into the room. His voice echoed off the metal lockers giving it a hollow tin sound. "I don't even know you anymore," he said, kidding his best friend and punching him in the shoulder. "So you've finally gone and done it. I know the Group Commander has been recommending you for the last two years but I thought you were stronger than that. Hell, buddy, I'm gonna miss you!"

"All right, knock it off. I'm not gone yet. I've still got to get in. I just sent all the paperwork with my application to the Selection Board. It will be a while before I know anything for sure," Stark said modestly. He kept it to himself that based on what the commander had said, he was fairly certain he would make it.

"Holy shit, don't act like that. If you can't make it, no one can. Hell, you are Achilles Dagger qualified, Level III qualified, you have six years experience with special forces, and you beat the shit out of the rest of us in freaking PT. There is no way they are turning you down." Chip's brow furrowed and his face became serious. "They are damn lucky to have you. You are going to make a great officer. If this is what you want, I wish you all the best, man." He patted Stark on the shoulder and turned to head to the showers. He stopped a few feet away and turned back. "When you marry this girl, I fully expect to be the best man so I can give you all the hell you deserve!" he said, laughing, and turned back to the showers.

Alone with his thoughts, Stark smiled. He hadn't given the officer commission a second thought before all this. For the last two years he had turned down the recommendation to apply. He had only wanted to stay with his guys. They were brothers, his family. He had thought that they were all he needed, but meeting Kira had changed all that. He realized now he could never let her go. Accepting the commission would mean they could be together without fear of the little shit or Simone exposing them. It would mean a life and a family. He carefully opened the Tiffany's box, removed the small black box inside, and gently opened it to reveal the stunning two-carat emerald cut sapphire. *Simple elegance*, he thought looking at the shimmering blue stone. The saleswoman had said the contrast of the exquisite stone in the understated platinum setting was breathtaking. He sure hoped so. He knew that most girls preferred diamonds but Kira was different. Everything about their relationship was different.

The sapphire was special to him. His mother had worn one and he remembered being a little boy holding her hand seeing it. It was also the stone of September, the month just one year ago when he had first met Kira. It had changed his whole life. He laughed at the irony of it. This month had been so hard for him after losing his mother and Maggie but today, September 5th, his life would begin a whole new chapter. He carefully took the delicate ring in his large fingers so very carefully and held it up. He pictured Kira sitting on the chair in the café.

Earlier Stark had sent Kira a note at her office by way of Abbey asking her to meet him at the Sunrise Terrace for dinner at Garden of the Gods Club. He laughed imagining her face at the pretentious location. But he wanted this to be special. He hoped he could count on Abbey to get her to at least come hear him out. He said he chose the location for secrecy so there wouldn't be a chance of running in to anyone they knew.

Stark went down through his mental checklist to make sure he hadn't left anything out. Great care and expense had been taken to make sure they would be the only people on the Terrace that evening. The planner had assured him flowers would be on the table and the lighting would be magical. He wasn't sure what exactly magical lighting entailed but he had requested something that was more like fireflies than Time Square. The silver-haired woman had assured him it would be perfect.

He closed his eyes and imagined Kira sitting there against the stunning backdrop of Pikes Peak. The evening light would play on the autumn hues and dance in her hair. He rehearsed, telling her how he could never live without her and about his plan to accept a commission as an officer so that nothing could stand in their way. He imagined a puzzled look on her face when he dropped to his knee and pulled the box out of his jacket. Then the change in her expression (hopefully happy) when he opened the box and asked her to be is wife. He felt a little nauseous. The precious ring felt precarious in his damp fingers and he put it back in the box. What if after all this she said no? *Oh, fucking hell!* She was still so mad.

***

Kira trudged her way through another long day of clinic. She processed multiple incoming and outgoing physicals. It had been two weeks since she last saw Stark during the crazy night

492

of bar hopping. *This should be getting easier! It's not.* She worked harder, desperately trying to ignore the bitter ache she felt. The horrid hangover she'd had the morning after Stark had picked her up and carried her off the dance floor had long since subsided. No amount of Motrin would ease the splitting pain left in his absence. She began to understand her mother's breakdown. She poured herself into her work and her mission to become a flight surgeon. Focusing on her career felt like all she had. She would cling to it and fight. She refused to let desperation pull her down as it did her mother. She spent her lunch finishing files over a day-old egg salad sandwich. She was just transferring one large stack of folders and grabbing another when the door to her office opened.

Abbey entered. She had a mischievous look in her eyes as she quickly shut the door behind her. Something was up. Abbey walked quickly and quietly over to her desk like a spy on a secret mission.

"What are you up to?" Kira asked, squinting at her friend's odd behavior.

"This came for you, captain," Abbey said in a low voice. She stood looking over Kira's shoulder, eager to read the contents of the letter.

"Seriously? You're just going to stand over my shoulder and watch me read this?" Kira asked, looking up at her with a raised eyebrow and her best look of disdain.

"Oh, hell yes! I mean yes, ma'am!" Abbey said wide-eyed with anticipation.

"Oh, good lord!" Kira said, shaking her head. She opened the envelope and her heart stopped. She knew instantly by the writing it was from him.

Kira,

I've been trying to reach you. The last time we saw each other, you said what you had to say. You are right. There are a thousand reasons we can't be together. But this is a fight I can't walk away from. My whole life changed when I met you. There are things I need to say in person. Please meet me tonight at 6:00 p.m. at the Sunrise Terrace at the Garden of The Gods Club. Ok stop smirking. It's the one place I can be sure we won't see anyone we know. Just hear me out. If you still feel the same way, I promise to let go.

Owen

Kira felt her hands trembling beneath the parchment. "I'm not going," she said abruptly and put the letter down. She pushed it away as if it were contaminated with the bubonic plague.

"You can't mean that," Abbey began softly. She had promised Stark she would do her best to get Kira to go. They both had known that would be an uphill battle. "He's just asking you to give him another chance to hear him out."

"For what, to torture ourselves some more? Who were we kidding?" Kira cupped her head in her hands to keep from crying. "He has more than enough women in his life. I'm done putting myself through all this pain. And for what? He had the opportunity to finish his enlistment and we could have been together. He chose to reenlist! He made his choice and it wasn't me." Kira struggled to regain her composure as rogue tears escaped around her fingers.

"Honey, some things are worth fighting for. It sounds like he believes that. I think you do, too. Give him a chance. Just hear him out." Abbey spoke with the authority of an army wife of twenty-three years.

Kira took a deep breath and steadied herself. She closed her eyes and wondered if she wouldn't be better off just to walk away and forget she ever got the letter. "I'll think about it. But

I'm not making any promises." As she said the words Kira wondered why she was even considering the idea.

The rest of the workday seemed to fly by as Kira spent most of it distracted and plagued by the decision she had to make. Her better judgment told her to go for a long run, then a shower and a pint of Ben and Jerry's and to forget all about meeting Stark. But the deep void in her soul that only he could fill called and begged for her to go and see what he had to say. She knew it would be emotional suicide. What answer could he possibly have? He had already reenlisted it was too late to change his mind. She felt selfish and bitter for wanting him to herself. She understood that his team was his family. She knew she couldn't ask him to give that up.

Before she knew it, the day was over and she was gathering her things. She smiled weakly at Abbey as she left the office. Abby's face had looked hopeful and a little sad. Kira started the car with trembling hands. *Go or don't go? Why am I even considering this?* Kira put the car in gear and punched the gas. She jolted forward, making a pact with herself to look for a new car as soon as she could afford it. Stark had insisted that she keep the Jeep. She pulled up to her box apartment and sat for a moment before getting out. She thought back over their time together. The intense look in his eyes, his smile, the heat of his kiss. She shook her head. Maybe a run instead.

***

Stark had finished his day of training. He was more nervous and excited about that evening than he had ever been before. In less than an hour he would be sitting across from Kira asking her to be his wife. He dressed and put on a light jacket to conceal the small black box. He held it out, looking it over. Before he could go over his plan again, a loud voice jolted him from his thoughts.

"Stark! Chip!" the captain bellowed. His tone was dark and stern. The deep creases in his forehead were unmistakable. "Notify the others we've been tasked. Report to the ISOFAC in forty-five minutes. Grab your A and B bags and your kit. The armory is open. Bring your personal and squad assist weapons." The captain turned and went to notify the others on the call roster.

Stark looked down at the little black box he was still clutching in his hand. His heart sank. Knowing his duty, he slowly put the box back in the pocket of his jacket and with it all thoughts and dreams of an evening that would never be. When called on a rapid deployment, there was no room for personal drama. Every man on the team counted on every other man for their very lives. Security mandated that they made no calls, just grabbed their prepacked gear and went. All focus now lay with the mission ahead. As he left the room with heavy bags on his shoulder, his mind fleeted to Kira and wondered if she would ever understand. He had hoped and prayed all day that she would show up. Now he might never know.

***

Kira raced to the Sunrise Terrace. She had taken time to shower and fix her hair, tucking most of her chestnut mane into a sweeping updo to contain it. Small trundles of hair spilled out and formed loose escaping curls. Final touches of makeup before she raced out the door ensured she would be late. *He can wait a little.* Her hands trembled as she drove. *Why am I doing this? I know I am just killing myself. What could he possibly have to say to fix this?* The twenty-mile drive felt like an hour though it took less than thirty minutes. *Why is it that every granny on the road is going the same way that I am?* She pulled into the lot but didn't see his truck. *Maybe he's late for a change.* She giggled at the thought of Mr. Punctual running late and having to scurry. She was immediately impressed and a little overwhelmed by the extravagance of the club. *Oh, I probably should have dressed up a little more.* Kira stood biting her lip and fidgeting with her purse while she waited for the hostess.

"Do you have a reservation?" The sliver-blue haired woman asked, her lip almost snarling as she looked Kira up and down disapprovingly. Kira could feel herself shrinking.

"My name's Kira Riley. I'm . . . I'm here to meet Owen Stark," Kira stammered nervously.

The woman's perfectly painted eyebrows shot up. Her collagen-infused smile stretched to its maximum as she cooed and gushed, "Oh, my dear, I'm so sorry. Right this way. You will be dining on the terrace with Mr. Stark." She grabbed two menus and led Kira to the lighted terrace.

Kira's breath caught as she walked into the stunning space. Small lights twinkled from every bush and tree. One lone table set exquisitely for two occupied the large terrace. A crystal vase in the center of the table held all white roses with two red ones nestled in the center. *What the hell is he up to?* Kira could feel tears in her eyes. The hostess encouraged her toward one of the wooden chairs and told her that Mr. Stark would be there shortly.

"Would you like a glass of wine?" She began to go down a list of expensive names and years that Kira had no clue about.

"I'll just have a chardonnay," Kira said numbly. The terrace opened up to an expansive green lawn that was bordered by lush shrubs and bushes. Beyond was the valley floor with massive rust colored rock formations. Pikes Peak lay in the distance towering and completing the spectacular view. Kira couldn't help but imagine what a wedding there would look like. Rows of white chairs looking out to the expanse of Pikes Peak would be adorned with blue flowers. A freckle-faced preschooler excited to be all dressed up would sprinkle delicate petals in shades of blue down the aisle.

Kira was shaken from her daydream by the waiter bringing her wine. He was tall, maybe six feet. *Not quite as tall as Owen. Where is he? It's not at all like him to be this late.* "Thank you," she said as he poured her glass. Kira glanced down at her watch. *Six forty-five.*

"Are you ready to order ma'am?" he asked hopefully.

"No, thank you," Kira replied. "I'm waiting for someone. He should be here shortly." Kira took her phone out of her purse as the waiter left. No messages. She checked her text and call log. Nothing. *He will be along shortly. There's no way he would go to all this trouble and then stand me up . . . Is there?*

***

Stark stepped onto the terrace. The sound of his shoes on the gravel caused Kira to look up. She looked confused and a little

500

angry. Her pouty lips were turned into a little frown and her forehead creased with puzzlement.

"Where have you been?" she asked. He could hear the disappointment in her voice. "You said six o'clock. I was just about to give up on you and go home."

A slight breeze had picked up and blew gently through her hair, carrying with it the fragrance of her perfume. He stopped for a moment to take in the exquisite sight before him. There next to the backdrop of the mountains was the angel who represented the rest of his life. He moved closer to her and took her hand in his. "Kira," he began, kneeling before her and looking up into her eyes, "I'm so sorry about the way things happened. You are right, though, we can't go on like this. It's not fair to either one of us. I can't give up the army. It's as much a part of my life as I want you to be. But I love you. With all my heart and soul, with all I am as a man, I love you. Imagining facing the rest of my life without you is more than I can bear."

"Owen, that doesn't change anything. You know that I love you, too, but the bottom line is you reenlisted in the army. You have already made your choice." Her voice wavered as she finished. Tears brimmed in her eyes. It was like a dagger to Stark. He groaned inwardly at her pain, recalling her saying the same thing when he saw her last.

Before she could say another word, he continued, "I'm taking a commission to be an officer." He paused while the sadness on her face was replaced by shock and then confusion.

"You . . . did . . . what?" Her voice was quiet.

"I accepted a recommendation for a commission. I have submitted everything and the commander tells me my chances are very good. I'll be 18 alpha, an officer, and we can be together."

"You'll still be in special forces. You'll still leave me and be in danger all over the world." Her voice was hesitant. He had expected that. He knew her fears based on what happened to her father and mother.

"Kira, I want to tell you that everything is going to be perfect and we'll never have any problems. But that would be lying. I could tell you everything you want to hear but I love you enough to tell you the truth and I have to trust that what we have is strong enough to take it. I believe you love me for me. This is who I am. The team is my life. It's something you live or die for. It's not a choice that you make. It's committing everything that you are. I thought that was enough for me until I met you. When I first looked into your eyes, my whole world changed. I realize now that I have found my home in your heart. I love you tremendously, completely, with everything that I am . . ." He paused and looked up into her eyes, which were now flowing with tears. He pulled out the small box. When he opened it, he heard her gasp. Her trembling fingers came up over her open mouth.

"Kira," he continued before he lost his nerve. "Will you . . ."

The jolt of the plane on the runway shook Stark from his daydream. He realized he was clutching the box tightly. He looked down at his combat uniform, reality crashing in like a tidal wave. *It would have been perfect. I wonder if she showed up.* Silently he tucked the box back into an inner compartment of his jacket. He would keep it with him. He reached up and touched his tags, one of his and one of hers.

***

It was getting dark. Curious waiters with worried expressions had made several trips offering wine and waiting to take her order. Three hours had passed. With each passing minute her hope faded. She looked out over the mountains and wondered if something had happened or if he had simply come to his senses and realized they had been kidding themselves all along. Her earlier excitement had given way to betrayal and anger. Now, those emotions faded to a complacent sadness. She stood and grabbed her purse. Opening it, her fingers brushed over her tags, one of hers and one of his. It had been a mistake. A wonderful, beautiful mistake, but it was over now. She took out a twenty and left it for the wine. The click of her heels echoed across the empty terrace as she made her way to the exit. As she reached the door, she turned and looked back at the lone table in the darkened space and wondered what might have been.

Epilogue

She almost missed a red light. Her tires screeched on the pavement as she stopped partially in the intersection. Large drops of rain started to fall from the sky. She drove more cautiously the rest of the way. She pulled up in front of her apartment and sat there for what seemed like an eternity. Finally, she got out and walked to the door. Smudged makeup lined her face. Tears mixed with raindrops as she raced to the porch. She opened the door and went into the dark apartment alone. *Alone.* As she disappeared inside, a beam of light could be seen shining out into the night. She hadn't closed the door all the way. *Well, then, that's practically an invitation.* He could hear sounds of a shower as he approached the door. After quietly slipping in, he pulled the door closed with a gloved hand and locked it.